ITCH CRAFT

www.**totallyrandombooks**.co.uk

ITCH CRAFT

SIMON MAYO

DOUBLEDAY

ITCHCRAFT
A DOUBLEDAY BOOK
978 0 857 53295 4

Published in Great Britain by Doubleday,
an imprint of Random House Children's Publishers UK
A Random House Group Company

This edition published 2014

3 5 7 9 10 8 6 4

The Random House Group Limited supports the Forest Stewardship Council®
(FSC®), the leading international forest-certification organisation. Our books
carrying the FSC label are printed on FSC®-certified paper. FSC is the only
forest-certification scheme supported by the leading environmental organisations,
including Greenpeace. Our paper procurement policy can be found at
www.randomhouse.co.uk/environment.

Set in 13/15 pt Bembo Schoolbook by Falcon Oast Graphic Art Ltd.

RANDOM HOUSE CHILDREN'S PUBLISHERS UK
61–63 Uxbridge Road, London W5 5SA

www.**randomhousechildrens**.co.uk
www.**totallyrandombooks**.co.uk
www.**randomhouse**.co.uk

Addresses for companies within The Random House Group Limited can be found
at: www.randomhouse.co.uk/offices.htm

THE RANDOM HOUSE GROUP Limited Reg. No. 954009

A CIP catalogue record for this book is available from the British Library.

Printed and bound in Great Britain by Clays Ltd, St Ives plc

For Hilary
83 in a world of 38

1

The Trans-Saharan Highway, Lagos, Nigeria
30 December

The armour-plated Mercedes swerved to avoid a pothole the size of a snooker table. The expensive suspension could smooth out the roughness of most roads, but the A1 from the Murtala Muhammed International Airport into Lagos was beyond repair. One wheel clipped the edge of the ruptured tarmac and the jolt shook its passengers. They grabbed the leather arms of the car's upholstery, and the loud cursing came in French and Dutch. Christophe Revere and Jan Van Den Hauwe, the co-chairs of oil multinational Greencorps, were not happy.

'Dammit – don't they know how to build roads here?'

'The answer to that, Christophe, is clearly no. The only way things get done here is through bribery and corruption. We know that much, surely?'

The Frenchman smiled and chanced another sip of his expensive brandy. 'We do, Jan – of course we do. We caused most of it, I believe.' He dabbed his lips with a handkerchief and checked his seat belt. The onboard satellite TV was tuned to a finance channel; both men watched the continuous scroll of information across the screen.

'More European madness, Christophe! They learn nothing . . .'

Another big swerve, and some of the spirit splashed onto the carpet. Revere closed his eyes as if in prayer. 'Give me strength . . .' he muttered.

Both men peered through their own tinted windows at the road outside, but the streetlights and neon advertising weren't bright enough to pierce the darkened glass. Ahead, the view through the windscreen was clearer, the powerful headlights illuminating a nightmarish, crazy night-time rush hour.

'It's gone midnight, for God's sake! Why so busy?' Van Den Hauwe aimed his question at the chauffeur, who spoke into his intercom, though his eyes never left the road.

'It is always like this, sir.' The driver glanced in his wing mirror as he pulled first into the outside lane, and then – to gasps from his passengers – into the other carriageway.

'What the . . . !' The oncoming traffic, now heading straight for them, swerved out of the way with barely a blast on the horn or flash of headlights. As though it was normal.

'Big hole in the road, sir,' said the driver. 'We call it "Mama's Dig". Everyone knows about it.'

The Dutchman shook his head. 'You actually have names for the potholes? This is one crazy country.'

The driver smiled. 'Yes, sir. You got that right!'

In front, their security team – in a polished four-by-four – seemed to be having an easier time, smoothly weaving between the holes in the tarmac, the dawdling, ancient saloons and the racing sports cars. It sounded as though the driver's hand must be glued to the horn, with yells and gestures aimed at any motorist who really annoyed him. On one occasion the barrel of a gun appeared from a passenger window, aimed at the driver of a soft-top BMW trying to overtake – who quickly dropped back behind the four-by-four and the Mercedes, leaving the Lagos road at the next exit.

The traffic thinned as most cars took the filter for downtown Lagos; the small Greencorps convoy continued south, following signs for Tin Can Island.

'I'm nervous about this meeting, Jan,' Revere said to his colleague. 'Who says this new Head of Police is trustworthy? And why do we have to meet so far out of town? I don't like it.'

Van Den Hauwe swivelled slightly to face him. 'I don't like it either, but after the spill, and Flowerdew's' – he searched for the right word – '*insanity*, we have to get control of this town again, Christophe. It used to be ours, but not any more. If we can buy ourselves the Head of Police – well, it's a start.

3

He sounded willing. Which is why we're both here.'

The car swung left, following a sign for the Apapa Oworonshoki Expressway, and a dark expanse of lagoon was briefly visible through the Mercedes' windscreen. It was the driver's sharp intake of breath that let his passengers know that all was not well. They looked up from their glowing phone screens.

'What? What's up?' asked Van Den Hauwe, but the empty road ahead gave him his answer.

'We've lost our security,' said Revere calmly.

They leaned forward to peer through the windscreen, but the twin headlights just picked out the dirt-covered tarmac, a few telegraph poles and an empty road.

'Where did they go?' shouted Van Den Hauwe. He pressed a button on his door; the window slid down and he put his head out into the sweltering night. The smell of the sea, along with oil and burning rubber, filled the car, and Revere pulled him back inside.

'Someone's paid them to disappear. I think we should go back,' he said. 'Back to the airport.'

The driver was looking worried now. The Mercedes might have all the safety features that money could buy, but he knew that Lagos was a lawless town, and if there was a price on your head . . . He swung the car round.

'Not much traffic for an "expressway",' said Van Den Hauwe quietly.

Revere nodded. 'None at all. I imagine we'll have company shortly.'

They were accelerating into a corner when the first of the pick-ups shot out in front of them. Three silver and grey Isuzu Rodeos spun on smoking tyres till they were facing the oncoming Mercedes. The Greencorps men were already braced and holding the leather straps that hung from the ceiling, but their seat belts snapped tightly around them as their driver stood on the brake. The car had an impressive stopping distance, but the pick-ups were too close, and there was the sickening metal-on-metal thud of a collision. While the air was still filled with sand and smoke, black-clad figures jumped out of the trucks.

'Back! Back! Back!' yelled Revere, and the driver threw the car into reverse. It pulled away from the tangle of bumpers and backed up to the edge of the road. As they spun away from the pick-ups, new headlights cut though the dark. Three more trucks hurtled round the corner and screeched to a halt, cutting off the Mercedes' escape.

'Looks like someone wants to talk,' said Van Den Hauwe.

'Let's hope that's all they want,' said Revere, and the Greencorps men sat and waited.

Palmeitkraal, Western Cape, South Africa

'Catch!' shouted Chloe.

'Why?' said Itch as the ball went sailing past his head, bouncing into the dusty scrubland.

'You could at least have tried,' said his sister.

'I could have, yes,' said Itch. He was on his hands and knees, scraping earth and stones towards him with both hands. Great clouds of dark sand and dust swirled around him, much of it settling in his wavy blond hair and sticking to his sweat-soaked T-shirt.

'Does Dad know what you're doing? I'm sure he said you're not allowed to do illegal experiments.' Chloe walked over to her brother, looking over his shoulder.

'No, you said that,' said Itch, packing soil around a glass jar.

'It is illegal, though, isn't it?' persisted Chloe.

'In England it is. But we aren't in England, are we?' He looked up and smiled at her. 'Come on, Chloe. I've always wanted to try this – give us a break.'

'If it's illegal at home, it's probably illegal in South Africa – have you checked?'

'OK, let me ask . . .' Itch looked theatrically around the hilly terrain: the low evergreen vegetation, the patches of bare sandstone and deserted old mine dwellings. 'No, no one around.' He smiled again. 'I'll just have to get on with it.'

Chloe sighed. 'Yeah, 'cos "just getting on with it" has been so great for you in the past. What did you say you were doing?'

'Stump removal,' said Itch.

'But I don't see any tree stumps.'

6

'Well, the key word is *reme*
anything, I think.' He measured ou
powder into the jar.

'Looks scary,' said Chloe.

'Really?' said Itch. 'It's only KNO$_3$.'

'Itch, I don't play your stupid games. In English please. I know K is potassium . . .'

'Potassium nitrate. Or saltpetre.'

'And the other powder?'

'Secret.'

'Let me guess. It goes bang?'

'Can do,' said Itch. 'If you mix them together and set fire to it.'

'That's what I was afraid of,' said Chloe, walking away to retrieve the ball. 'Sure you wouldn't prefer to play "catch"?'

Lagos, Nigeria

Whoever they were expecting to emerge from the six trucks, Van Den Hauwe and Revere stared open-mouthed at the figures who assembled in a semicircle in front of the Mercedes. Six women now stood in their headlights, dressed mainly in black denim and leather jackets, staring into the windscreen. Each of them wore a khaki cap pulled low over their eyes.

'Well, who are *you*?' exclaimed Van Den Hauwe, his eyes wide with surprise.

They looked young – twenties maybe – and a

mix of Nigerian, white European and Thai . . .
Malay, possibly. They stood motionless.

'Our move, Christophe, I think.'

'Agreed.'

Both men opened their doors and climbed out.

'Er, good evening, ladies,' tried Revere, standing
by the open door. 'You must want to see us very
much.'

'Kill the lights,' shouted a voice.

The driver, now with his window open, hit the
switch and the car went dark. Two powerful torches
came on and lit up the oilmen, who had started to
sweat profusely.

'Walk to the front of the car.' The voice was
heavily accented and authoritative – both men did
as they were told. 'Kneel down!'

Revere and Van Den Hauwe looked at each
other, then at the women. 'Who are you? Have we
upset you? I'm sure we can do business together,
but—'

'Kneel down!' This time the command came
with an added threat: the click of a gun's safety
catch being removed.

Both men knelt in the dust. The six walked a few
steps towards the car. The women at each end held
the torches; one in the middle held the gun. Tall,
with olive skin and jet-black hair, she looked at the
driver. 'Run away. Now. Take off.'

He didn't need to be told twice. He flung his door
open and sprinted away into the night.

The woman with the gun spoke again. 'My

8

name is Leila. These are my friends: Aisha, Sade, Tobi, Chika and Dada.' Heads nodded as names were mentioned, as though they were athletes being introduced to the spectators before a race. Each was now little more than a silhouette to the kneeling oilmen.

'How can we—?' began the Frenchman.

'We used to work for you,' interrupted Leila, 'but then you killed our friend.'

'I'm sure that's not true . . .' said Van Den Hauwe, squinting as the torch shone in his face.

Leila spoke again, her voice raised. 'We used to dive with Shivvi Tan Fook. Now she's dead and it's *your* fault.'

There were murmurs of assent from the others, and what sounded like curses spat in the direction of the kneeling men. Both Van Den Hauwe and Revere started to protest, but the diver with braided hair identified as Chika jumped forward, crouching just in front of them. Grit kicked up by her Converse hi-tops settled over their tasselled loafers. She put her finger in front of her lips.

'You don't have to say anything. We know you didn't actually kill her *yourself* – we know that was Flowerdew. But we haven't got him—'

'Yet!' called one of the others, and they all nodded.

Chika smiled, her teeth brilliant white. 'Right. Not yet. But we have got *you*: *you* abandoned her, so you have to pay.' She produced a knife from her Converse and both men recoiled, falling back against the radiator grille of the Mercedes.

'Chika, no!' called Leila. 'We agreed, remember?'

'Not yet, Chika,' called another voice.

Chika glanced back at Leila, then stared at the ground, carving grooves in the dust. Then she nodded and sheathed her knife again.

'I say shoot them now.' Five heads turned to look at the white woman with black hair tied back in a ponytail. 'Why wait? This is our moment. We owe Shivvi. Just do it.'

'But, Aisha, we agreed,' said Leila. 'We wait. Maybe sell them on. You know we'd get a good price.'

'I did think that,' said Aisha. 'But then I hadn't looked into their eyes. They're disgusting – their kind always win, always get away with it.' There were nods of agreement at that. 'But not this time . . .'

Leila looked at her friends again; they all returned her look, each one nodding in turn. 'Very well.' She stepped forward. 'Stand up and turn round.' She raised her gun.

Stumbling to his feet, Revere pleaded, 'We have money! How much do you need? Please—'

'*Turn round!*' shouted Leila. 'Who's first? Alphabetical order, maybe?' She walked round to where Jan Van Den Hauwe was gripping the bonnet of the Mercedes. He squeezed his eyes shut as she touched the gun barrel to his temple. 'Happy New Year, Jan,' she said, and pulled the trigger.

* ★ ★

'Happy New Year, Chloe,' said Itch, and a thunderous explosion tore through the hills. Brother and sister crouched in the dilapidated house and winced as the first clods of earth started raining down on them. A shower of stones followed. Ears ringing and eyes watering from the swirling clouds of dust particles, they peered through the open space that had once been a window.

'Wow,' said Itch in hushed tones. A small mushroom cloud had formed twenty metres above the explosion. As they watched, it moved and changed shape; sand and smoke were drawn in and upwards, then seemed to fold and rotate around the rim. After a few seconds it drifted and dissolved, the grit and earth falling like hail.

'But . . . that . . .' said Chloe, staring at the brown haze that still hung in the air.

'. . . wasn't a nuclear explosion, no,' finished Itch. 'Though it was amazing!'

'But it was a mushroom shape. I thought . . .'

'Just what happens when you have a large blast. Though I've never seen one before. I suggested it once to Colonel Fairnie, but he said no.'

'Can't think why,' said Chloe. 'Can you imagine the panic if a mushroom cloud like that appeared above our house? Fairnie got that one right.'

Jim Fairnie had led the MI5 team that had tried to protect Itch after his discovery of eight pieces of the fiercely radioactive element 126. He had

11

promised to stay in touch and was available if Itch ever needed him.

If it hadn't been for the ringing in their ears, Itch and Chloe would have heard the approaching Land Rover sooner.

'Dad's here,' said Chloe. 'This could be fun.'

Nicholas Lofte arrived in a cloud of dust, a brown haze hanging in the air behind the vehicle. Hurtling past the scene of the explosion, he headed towards the old mining cottage where his younger son and daughter stood. He jumped out of the driver's seat, the car still lurching from the abrupt stop.

'What happened? You both OK?' He ran over and took Itch by the shoulders. 'That was loud, Itch – explain!'

'Just stump removal, Dad. You should have seen it! We got a mushroom cloud and everything!'

'Er, *we*?' said Chloe.

'OK, yeah – just me, then. Dad, it was huge—'

'I know it was huge, son – I heard it down by the mine. I ran out of the office and saw the cloud forming. I was terrified, Itch – my heart is still racing. You're both OK, then?'

'Course we are, Dad. It was a bit louder than I expected,' said Itch, his eyes still wide with excitement, 'and we had dust and stuff raining down, but it was pretty cool.'

He couldn't stop grinning, and Nicholas's face twitched. Caught between anger and admiration, Nicholas Lofte stood looking at his son. At fifteen,

Itch was six foot and still growing, his twelve-year-old sister only nine inches behind. Itch's wavy blond hair was filled with earth and dirt; when he spoke or moved, it showered into his face.

'At least you kept some eyebrows this time,' said Nicholas, smiling, and they all started to laugh. Itch had lost his eyebrows twice before – the last time just weeks ago, when the Fitzherbert School had burst into flames. Itch and his cousin Jack had been lucky to escape with their lives.

'OK, I admit it: it did look pretty impressive . . . which doesn't make it right,' Nicholas added quickly. 'You should have told me what you were doing, Itch. I thought you might have had your fill of danger for a while.'

Itch started walking over towards the explosion site, his father and sister following. 'I wasn't planning it really, but the store in town was selling the potassium nitrate and I just thought now would be a good time to try it out. Better than at home, anyway.'

They all stared at the small crater that had been left by the 'stump removal'.

'Better than at home is about right,' said Nicholas, 'but I promised your mother I'd make sure nothing "bad" happened. I assume she meant nothing explosive.'

There was silence then as the three Loftes kicked around in the dust. Jude Lofte hadn't been mentioned by their father since they came to South Africa. After discovering Nicholas's secret life working for an undercover energy research organization, their mother had walked out. She had returned on Christmas Eve, but it had been a tense, unhappy time. When Nicholas offered to take Itch and Chloe on a mine examination in South Africa, she had reluctantly agreed, saying that she'd spend the New Year with their eldest son, Gabriel, and his girlfriend before he went back to university in January.

Itch and Chloe glanced at each other. Itch thought his sister seemed upset and tried to look reassuring. 'I won't tell her if you don't,' he said.

His father nodded. 'Fair enough,' he said. 'But that's it, Itch, OK? You plan any more experiments, you tell me beforehand – don't wait for me to hear a ground-shaking explosion before I know anything. Agreed?'

Itch nodded, and another small cloud of dirt fell out of his hair.

2

Itch, Chloe and their father had flown to Cape Town three days after Christmas. Their destination was the small town of Vanrhynsdorp in the Western Cape. Picking up a Land Rover at the airport, they had driven all day to the deserted mine. This was the 'Old Copper Way', a part of the country with as rich a mining tradition as their native Cornwall. In the semi-desert, they had set up camp in one of the old mine buildings. It had been abandoned in the 1960s when the price of thorium had dropped, but Nicholas and some of his colleagues were convinced that there was more to be found.

'We are really excited about this, Itch!' he'd explained as they drove north. 'The only reason more hasn't been made of thorium as a nuclear fuel is because you can't make weapons from it. But there's loads of the stuff in the ground – almost as much as there is lead. No one wanted this old mine, but Jacob thinks we should have a look at it.'

Dr Jacob Alexander was the director of the West

Ridge School of Mining and had been the only one to analyse the rocks of element 126 that Itch had found; he still treasured the printouts proving that he had actually tested the mysterious element. Spectacularly radioactive, it was dangerous beyond measure. He had seen its potential as a new energy source; it was a nuclear start-up kit in a bag. When Itch first hid the eight pieces of rock, Alexander had tried to persuade him to divulge their whereabouts, but to no avail. Now they had been destroyed, and Jacob Alexander had to resume his search for new energy sources without them.

'I'm looking for some europium, Dad – don't they have some of those rare earth elements in these mines?'

'Right, stop,' said Chloe. 'Excuse me? *Europium? Rare earth elements?*'

Nicholas laughed. 'You want to take that, Itch?'

'This is pretty basic, Chloe – don't you know anything?' Itch reached for his rucksack.

'No!' said Chloe. 'Nothing from there! No rocks, no gases, no nothing! Just tell me, Itch. In words.'

Itch sat back in his seat, leaving his rucksack by his feet. It boasted 118 pockets, one for each element on the Periodic Table; Itch used it to house his collection. Many of the pockets were for show – a joke from the MI5 agents who had watched over Itch – as so many of the elements were either unobtainable or too dangerous to keep in a nylon bag.

'All right, calm down,' he said. 'I had to leave

most of the stuff at home; didn't think customs would appreciate it. All I was going to show you was the chart – so you can see where the rare earths are.'

'Not interested,' said Chloe. 'You've got two sentences. Then I'm back to Rihanna.' She waved her headphones at her brother.

'OK. Mainly, they're the ones down the bottom of the Periodic Table – the bottom two lines. They're all very similar to each other and they're used in laptops, mobile phones—'

'That's enough,' interrupted Chloe, and she pushed the small white ear buds into her ears.

'And probably your iPod . . .' Itch trailed off.

'Nice try,' said Nicholas, laughing again. Itch sighed. 'And to answer your question, Itch: yes, there may well be some europium there, along with a host of other rare earths. Why the interest in europium?'

'It's what a lot of the 126 would have decayed into when I blasted it at the ISIS labs. I'm glad we destroyed it. And when I get the europium, I want to display it. To show what we managed to do.'

His father nodded. 'You guys were quite some team. Have you heard from Jack or Lucy? What are they up to?'

'I think Jack said that Lucy had invited her to a New Year's do in town,' said Itch.

'Wish you were there?' asked Nicholas.

'What do you think?!' Itch grinned. 'No way! I'm element-hunting! And you're here. And we're making Chloe come too; that beats some party which is bound to be a fail.'

Nicholas was checking the fuel gauge. 'Let's fill up.' And he pulled into a petrol station. 'I've also brought you both a present. You need it before we get to the mines.' Sitting in the warmth of the afternoon sun – a welcome change from the grim winter at home – Nicholas produced two identical packages, handing one to Itch and one to Chloe.

Wiping hamburger grease off his hands onto his jeans, Itch weighed the parcel in his hand. Paperback-book sized, it felt heavier, and he felt movement in the box under the Christmas wrapping. It was strange to be unwrapping presents with Santa Claus decorations in twenty-two-degree heat, with farm trucks thundering along the R301 to Stellenbosch. Itch and Chloe stared at the boxes, then at their father. Itch grinned, while Chloe looked puzzled.

'They're radiation detectors,' said Nicholas. 'State of the art. And we've set them to look for certain X-rays and signatures which you need to be aware of. They'll click like fury if there's a big surge in radiation. You both need to be careful – but, Itch, you know the dangers. After your bone-marrow transplant, you might not get a second chance.'

Itch opened the box and took out a black and yellow metal case with a yellow cord attached. At the top was a circular window showing a needle and a colour-coded display going from blue to red.

'I've had them made. Smart, huh? Made from cerium tribromide, the latest hi-spec compound, if you're serious about detecting radiation. While we're near the mines, you wear them all the time. There'll be low-level radiation everywhere, of course – you'll hear it click when it registers a decaying particle. It measures roentgens per hour—'

'Dad,' interrupted Itch, 'we know this stuff. The 126 sent Geiger counters crazy.'

Nicholas nodded. 'Of course. I'm just reminding Chloe that if the clicks coming out of the speaker start to get anything close to rapid, it's time to move. And tell me.'

'Why are we even going there if there's a danger?' asked Chloe quietly, not opening her box; uneasy at this reminder of the dangers of radiation poisoning.

'There isn't a danger where we are staying, Chloe,' said her father. 'We are some way from the mine itself, which is where the radiation is. It's just an extra precaution. And they're waterproof too – Jacob made them, look.' Nicholas pointed to Itch's name, etched into the silver reverse of the counter: *Itchingham Lofte. Keep those clicks low! Your friend Jacob.*

'Wow. The world's only personalized radiation detectors. Didn't need the message, but I've always wanted one of these things.' Itch strung the counter round his neck. 'Whaddya think, Chloe?'

She shrugged. 'Suits you, I suppose.' She gathered

up her detector and its wrapping, stuffing it all into her bag. 'Can we go now?' she said.

They had arrived in Vanrhynsdorp in the early evening, the sun already disappearing over the low, rocky hills. They had driven through the town, all neat hedgerows and bed-and-breakfasts, and Nicholas took the last few kilometres slowly.

'Glad we're not staying there!' said Itch as they left the trim, tidy lawns behind. 'Looked like the dullest place ever. Come on, Dad, let's get there before it gets dark.'

They were all excited to be arriving at last, the tiredness of the day disappearing as the car climbed the dusty, pothole-filled road. Their windows down, Itch and Chloe leaned out, ignoring the clouds of dust thrown up by the four-wheel drive.

'*Palmeitkraal mine. Danger. Keep out,*' Itch read from a small sign by the side of the road. 'This'll be it, then!'

'Four-star or five-star hotel, do you think?' said Chloe.

They were still laughing when Itch and Chloe jumped down from the Land Rover, detectors swinging from their necks. They stood looking at the dilapidated, once-white house, the buzz of the crickets interrupted by occasional clicks from the two detectors' tiny speakers.

'The white bosses stayed here,' explained Nicholas as they carried their suitcases inside. 'There were a number of houses where the mine owners lived. The black workers lived in crummy little huts nearer the mine. Then, in the sixties, everything got shut down, and nothing's really happened since then.'

The main living space had been cleared and swept, but that was as far as the luxuries went. At one end a battered sofa and two sagging armchairs were arranged round an old television; at the other, three camp beds leaned against the far wall, bedding bulging out of an old carrier bag.

Chloe checked her phone. 'This is weird,' she said. 'Like camping indoors. No wi-fi, no signal. Nothing.'

They found a basic kitchen and usable bathroom, but the upstairs rooms seemed to have been home to too many birds and small animals.

'Think we'll be mostly downstairs,' she said.

3

The morning after the stump-removal explosion, the Loftes were back in the car and in high spirits. This was their first trip to the mines, and even Chloe seemed to be looking forward to it.

'This is a weird way to spend New Year's Eve. I don't suppose you've planned a party, Dad . . . There's plenty of room in that house!'

'We could invite all the neighbours,' said Itch. 'Which based on the upstairs rooms would be all the local wild dogs and a few springbok.'

Their father laughed. 'You're right, it does stink a bit up there,' he said as they bounced along the track, away from the house. 'Maybe we'll have a quiet one on our own. We could have a braai!'

'You what?' asked Chloe.

'A barbecue,' said Nicholas. 'We can't leave without tasting some local Boerewors sausage or ostrich. We could get some tips from this guy we're meeting; he's one of Jacob Alexander's guys from the local university. His father used to be the foreman here when the mines were cranking out small amounts of thorium. He's going to show us around. There are a number of old shafts here which are best avoided – they're sealed off anyway – but he's told me there's one that might be explorable. Might pick up some europium, you never know!'

'So does Dr Alexander own these mines, then?' asked Itch. 'Is that why we can just drive where we want around here?'

They drove in silence while Nicholas thought of his answer. Eventually he said, 'Well, you know, this is all supposed to be secret – but I've probably kept enough from you guys, so . . .' He sighed. 'Essentially we've more or less bought the mines for study by the local university. There's a few paper-work issues to sort out, but I think the deal is pretty much done. There's a lot of buzz around the gold and platinum mines, but not much here. No one is interested because they're – officially – clapped out and dangerous. But our man here reckons other-wise. And there he is!'

Their father pointed to the T-junction ahead, then waved at a man standing by a flatbed truck. A boy sitting in the back stood and waved as Nicholas pulled up just behind them.

'Themba, good morning! Thanks for meeting us!' called Nicholas as he climbed out.

The other man smiled warmly. 'Nicholas! Good to see you again!' He was thin and slightly stooped, with tightly curled black hair that was going grey at the temples. 'This is my son Sammy.' The boy jumped down and stood, hands by his side, grinning. 'Well, say something, Sammy – this is the Mr Lofte from England who I was telling you about.'

'Hello, Mr Lofte,' said Sammy, still smiling. 'It is nice to meet you.'

They shook hands formally, and then Itch and Chloe came over.

'Itch, Chloe, this is Themba Motsei and his son Sammy. Themba's going to head up our work at the mines here.'

They all shook hands and nodded politely.

'How old are you both?' asked Themba.

'I'm twelve and Itch is fifteen,' said Chloe. 'How about you, Sammy?'

The boy squirmed and smiled some more. 'I'm thirteen,' he said softly. Then, 'Do you like Manchester City?' He pointed to his pale blue football shirt.

Nicholas and Themba started laughing, but Itch and Chloe looked baffled.

'I don't really follow football,' Itch said awkwardly. Sammy looked disappointed. 'I don't dislike it,' he added quickly. 'I just don't really have an opinion one way or another. Some boys at school like them, I think. And Manchester United. And Chelsea . . .'

'Itch, don't try and talk football,' said Chloe. 'We'll find other stuff to talk about.'

They all climbed into the truck – Nicholas and Themba in the cab at the front, Sammy, Itch and Chloe in the open box at the back. An assortment of packing cases was strapped down at the far end.

The truck's progress was slow; the holes in the road made any speed above five mph extremely dangerous. Itch and Chloe clung to the sides of the truck.

Sammy smiled again. 'You ridden like this before?'

Itch and Chloe both shook their heads.

'It's the best way. Even if the whole mine area is full of holes and very bad roads.'

'Do you know where we are going?' said Itch.

'My father says we are going to the Hewitt B mine. That's OK – at least you don't need the radiation suits there.'

Itch and Chloe glanced at each other. 'Is there a Hewitt A mine?'

The smile again. 'Yes. An A, C and D. We don't go there too much. But B is fun. You'll see. Why are you wearing those Geiger counters?'

'You know about these things?' said Itch, holding up his yellow, clicking metal box.

'Sure,' said Sammy. 'Dad brings that stuff home all the time. We've played around with them, but you're wearing them like necklaces.'

'It's a long story,' said Chloe, tucking hers away down the front of her T-shirt.

Sammy took the hint and didn't question them further.

The truck pulled up, and they turned to see

Themba unlocking a huge padlock and unwinding a chain that linked the two large iron gates. A large sign screwed to the bars said, HEWITT B MINE. CONTROLLED AREA. NO UNAUTHORIZED ENTRY. Nicholas joined him to push the gates open, and when both men had returned to the truck, they trundled slowly into a rock-strewn field.

Itch and Chloe knew a deserted mine when they saw one – they had plenty back home in Cornwall. There were the telltale spoil heaps of earth and stone that had been dug up and left, unwanted, in loose hills by each shaft. Rusty and decaying winding towers stood by a series of ugly concrete buildings. However, the sheer scale of the operation was new to them – it extended for miles, mostly downhill from where they stood. Areas of dense dark-green shrub were littered with patches of brown, broken rocks. A number of burned-out houses stood a few hundred metres away.

'That where the miners lived?' asked Chloe.

Sammy shook his head. 'Whites only. The miners were in shacks.' He pointed to heaps of corrugated iron and wood nearby. 'They all fell down. Even my grandpa's.'

The road, such as it was, circled round to a concreted area which looked new. Clean and swept, it too was surrounded by barbed wire, iron posts and NO ENTRY signs. An irregular double *click* from under Chloe's T-shirt made her jump and she caught Itch's eye.

'That won't be anything, Chloe – we aren't near enough any rock—'

'I'm still telling Dad,' she said, and as the truck slowed to a stop, she was the first to jump down.

Nicholas and Themba listened as Chloe told them about the extra clicks from the radiation detector.

Themba nodded. 'The thorium-rich mines are on the other side of the hill, Chloe. Many, many years ago there were tiny amounts of thorium here, but now the mine has been cleansed and tested and given the all-clear. The old buildings are being torn down and buried under clay because of their radioactivity. I've taken my Geiger counter right down this mine and there were no surprising readings. The shaft is completely restored. I wouldn't bring Sammy if it wasn't safe.'

Chloe looked reassured. 'OK. What happens now?'

'Themba and I are going to do some tests on some of the rock about fifty metres into the mine here,' said Nicholas.

'What are you looking for?' asked Itch.

'It's monazite,' Themba told him. 'Looks like this.' He produced a small reddish-brown pebble from his pocket. 'I got this from here. Should contain some lanthanum and almost all the rare earths.'

'And thorium? That would make it radioactive, wouldn't it?' Chloe stepped back. 'That's where my extra click came from!'

'Give me your radiation counter,' said Nicholas, and she pulled it out from under her T-shirt. It swung on the end of her hand and he caught it. Themba held out the monazite as Nicholas closed in with the detector.

'Listen,' he said. At a distance of one metre, there was a click every ten seconds. He stepped to within ten centimetres of the rock – still no increase in clicks. It was only when the counter and the rock were almost touching that the frequency increased.

'Probably just a little more radiation than a banana!' said Themba.

He was expecting surprise from Itch and Chloe, but instead got only rueful smiles. They had been told about radioactive bananas by an element dealer called Cake.

Chloe took the counter back, and Themba threw the monazite to Itch. 'Have a look,' he said.

'OK – well, is it valuable, then?' said Chloe, glancing only briefly at the pebble in Itch's hand.

Themba laughed. 'Actually, most rare earth elements aren't rare; they're just difficult to tell apart and isolate—'

'Wait – so they're not even rare?' said Chloe, incredulous. 'What's the big deal, then?'

'Well, they might be difficult to extract – but, for example, the magnets they give us are used in electronic devices . . . computers, phones, electric cars . . . You only need tiny amounts, but they're very powerful.'

Itch could tell that his sister had lost interest; it

was only the presence of Themba and Sammy that had stopped her going back to the truck.

'Could I help?' said Itch. 'You said it was safe . . .'

His father and Themba looked at each other. 'Sure,' said Nicholas, smiling. 'Why not? Bring the boxes from the truck and we'll get started.'

'And what are Sammy and I doing, then?' asked Chloe.

'I'll show you round if you like,' said Sammy. 'It's more interesting out here anyway – some of the bosses' houses have still got old equipment in. I found an old assegai there once . . . A spear,' he added, seeing Chloe's puzzled face.

'Cool,' she said, suddenly interested, and followed him towards the burned-out buildings. 'Hey, Sammy, catch!' she called, and threw her ball at him.

Itch climbed up into the truck and lifted the first crate.

'Careful, Itch,' called his father. 'Portable spectrometers are expensive!'

Itch had seen an X-ray fluorescence spectrometer used to analyse the 126, but that machine had been huge. 'Really? In here?' he said, and gently placed it on the floor of the truck. He jumped down, then eased the box into his arms.

The entrance to the mine was housed in a new steel building, and Itch set the spectrometer down in the doorway. He emptied the contents of the truck in a few trips, and walked back for the last few tools. He glanced at Chloe and Sammy: they were some distance away now, chasing her ball down the slope. They had passed a number of small spoil heaps, and were now throwing the ball around the bottom of a fifteen-metre mound of mine rubble. He had run over one himself back in Cornwall, and he remembered how precarious they were. As he watched, Chloe missed a catch and the ball bounced and rolled onto a ledge of small rocks, halfway up the heap.

Itch was suddenly filled with foreboding and took a step forward. 'Chloe!' he called. 'That's not safe! You should—'

The spoil heap sagged and, as he watched, a slash of black appeared below the ledge. The ball, ledge and Chloe dropped out of sight as though a trapdoor had opened.

4

It was over in seconds. One minute Chloe was on the side of the spoil heap; the next, it had swallowed her up. The crevasse that had opened was instantly filled with rocks that poured down from above. The surface already appeared smooth again – it was as though she'd never been there.

'CHLOE!' yelled Itch. '*Dad, now!*' He grabbed a spade from the truck and ran for the spoil heap, his detector swinging wildly. His eyes never left the patch of brown earth and stones where his sister had been playing just seconds before. Sammy was already scrabbling his way up the side of the heap, but the loose rocks kept giving way beneath his urgent feet; he would climb two metres, then fall back three.

'Chloe, we're coming!' Itch shouted as he leaped onto the first stones, but he was making the same mistake as Sammy. The loose rocks, stones and soil gave way beneath his steps, sending him crashing to the ground. His hands and knees took most of the impact and he dropped the spade. As his body scraped the rocks, a torrent of clicks came from the radiation detector.

Itch froze.

Radiation.

After his prolonged contact with the 126, Itch had come close to receiving a lethal dose of radiation. Blood transfusions, antibiotics and a bone-marrow transplant had saved him, but he had been warned that any future contact could be fatal – he just wasn't strong enough to take it. Face down on the jagged stones, his heart rate matched the rapid clicks. He heard his father's pounding feet and pushed himself up.

'Dad! It was a landslide! Chloe's in there!' He pointed to where the ledge had been. 'But this is all radioactive – listen!' He held his counter on the ground, and the click-barrage began again.

'Get off the heap, Itch,' shouted his father. 'And throw me the spade!'

Itch half ran, half slid back to the ground, then threw the shovel. Nicholas caught it in one hand. For a moment he watched Sammy, who was making progress up the slope on his hands and knees, then he copied him. Dropping onto all fours, Nicholas crawled up the spoil heap, metre by metre. Themba arrived, breathless and running with sweat, and threw another spade up the slope.

It landed near Sammy, who scrambled across to reach it. 'She was just there!' he cried. 'Just there . . . and then the ground . . . opened up! Dad, help me!'

Themba was about to start climbing, but Nicholas held up his hand. 'Quiet! Everyone shut up!'

Itch was beside himself with frustration. He kept stepping onto the spoil heap and then off again. He took off his detector and held it just above the stones at his feet; the clicks rattled from the speaker and he swore.

'Itch, shut that thing up,' yelled his father.

Itch switched it off and they all stood, crouched or lay motionless. Apart from the occasional clatter from an eddy of stones finding a way down the spoil heap, they heard nothing.

'Dad! *Do* something!' shouted Itch.

'Chloe!' yelled his father. Then they all joined in, their voices desperate. Nicholas, spreading his weight as much as he could, spidered his way up the hill of rocks. His arms and legs worked furiously as he tried to keep his purchase on the unstable surface.

'More to the right!' shouted Itch. 'Near where that darker sand is.'

Nicholas glanced back at his son, and corrected his direction, heading right, towards the spot his daughter had been occupying just a minute ago. He knelt up. 'Quiet again! Quiet!' he called. He started scooping rocks away with his hands, pushing them down the slope.

Now Themba and Sammy had reached him, they heaved and swept the debris away from where they thought Chloe was.

'No spades!' said Nicholas. 'She could be just below the surface!'

They were all scooping furiously now, the larger rocks flung with force by Nicholas and Themba.

Itch, pacing around the base, was desperate.

'Shall I call for help? Do we need a digger or something? Dad, answer me! Do—'

Themba held up a hand. 'Stop digging! Listen . . .' He put his ear to the surface of the spoil heap, and Nicholas and Sammy followed suit.

After a moment's silence they all heard it: clicks, and lots of them. A radiation detector doing its work.

'Chloe! Hang on!' called Nicholas. 'We're here!'

Sammy was nearest. He turned and heaved more stones away with both hands. Nicholas and Themba slid lower and, directed by the clicks, started their bare-hand digging again.

'She's here!' shouted Sammy, and Itch couldn't wait any longer. Radiation or no radiation, he couldn't just stand there. He raced up the spoil heap, stones flying everywhere. Sammy was kneeling by the hole he had dug . . . and there was the top of Chloe's head – brown hair sticking up through the soil.

Itch gasped and started pushing the debris away. The clicks were loud now. 'Chloe, we've got you. Hang on!' Looking at his father, he added, 'Dad, she's not moving!'

Nicholas nodded and bent to his task again.

With Itch and Sammy higher up and Nicholas

34

and Themba lower down, every one of them trying to combine gentleness and urgency, Chloe slowly emerged. She was hunched over, her body arched as though protecting something. She wasn't moving, but she was breathing.

It was Itch who brushed away the final debris from his sister's face. 'Chloe . . . Chloe . . . Chloe, can you hear me?' He wiped the earth from her nose and mouth, and she started to shake.

Nicholas appeared at his side and, reaching long arms deep into the soil, lifted his daughter free. The radiation detector fell silent. 'Itch, get off the spoil heap,' he said quietly, and Itch nodded, running and sliding to the ground.

He watched as they stepped gingerly down the steep, shifting slope. Chloe was shaking hard now, sand and small stones falling from her clothes and hair with every step her father took.

'You're OK now,' Nicholas said in her ear, then realized that it was still full of earth. She nodded anyway, and Itch sighed with relief.

Chloe tried to speak, but had to spit and then retch. 'Thanks,' she managed, then started to cry.

Sammy shot off in the direction of the truck.

'He's getting an old rug from the truck,' said Themba. 'She's in shock. We need to wrap her up, but only once we've got all the debris off her. Nicholas, that'll be thorium making the detectors go crazy. I am sorry – I had no idea there was so much radioactivity in that heap. I thought they'd all been checked – the nearby ones certainly have. But it will have been burning the skin. There's a shower at my house, but that is half an hour away.'

Nicholas's eyes narrowed. 'We'll talk more about this – but not now.'

'Back to our place then,' said Itch. 'The shower's rubbish, but it works.'

'OK. Themba, get the truck,' said Nicholas. 'You need to get as much of the debris off as you can, Chloe. We'll all look away. Wrap yourself in the blanket. Let's get you cleaned up.'

Back at the house, they sat on the old sofa, waiting for Chloe to finish her shower.

'She should go to hospital,' said Itch. 'Her skin looked red and she'd obviously breathed in some stuff. That could be dangerous.'

'Agreed,' said Themba. 'But the nearest decent hospital is more than an hour away. Forget the ambulance – we'll do it ourselves. Once she's clean.'

Chloe emerged in an old T-shirt and tracksuit bottoms. She managed a small smile. 'All right – don't stare,' she said, and sat in one of the armchairs.

Her face and arms were blotchy; Nicholas studied the marks carefully. 'You'll be OK, I think. You can't have been under for more than ninety seconds, though God knows it felt like an eternity. But if you breathed in radioactive material, we should get you checked out – and you need something for your skin.'

'I know all that,' she said. 'I've learned a bit about

radiation recently.' She smiled at her brother. 'But I kept my mouth shut. I tried to create an air pocket. Hopefully that was OK?' She looked around for support.

'You were amazing,' said Itch, 'really amazing. But it's been a few weeks since we were all in a hospital, so we should probably visit one. Just to be sure.'

Chloe nodded.

'Mum would say, *This family!*' Itch laughed.

Their father looked awkward. 'Best not mention this to your mother just yet, I think. You watch some TV and I'll get our things together. Sammy, you might want to stay – I just want to have a few words with your dad.' He switched on the old television and left the room with Themba.

Sammy sat rather awkwardly on the arm of the sofa and watched the images from a news channel of New Year celebrations around the world.

'Well, this will be a different New Year's Eve,' said Itch. 'Bet the hospital won't have too many thorium-burn patients to deal with.'

'We do like to be different—' said Chloe, but broke off as the sound of Nicholas's raised voice came through the open window. She and Itch glanced at Sammy, who was staring at his feet. They could all hear the dressing-down Nicholas was administering, and the use of some of his old oil-rig language added to the awkwardness. Sammy went and stood by the window, his face expressionless but his fists clenched.

Embarrassed now, Itch turned up the TV. He was just going over to talk to Sammy when Chloe said, 'Itch, look at this.' There was an urgency in her voice, and he turned to see what had caught her attention.

The small screen was showing night-time images: blue flashing lights illuminated a large saloon car, doors open, the paintwork and windows riddled with bullet holes. Police stood around it.

'What's this, Chloe? What is it?'

She pointed at the screen, and the scrolling words came round again:

BREAKING NEWS . . . LAGOS, NIGERIA. MISSING GREENCORPS BOSSES BELIEVED KIDNAPPED OR MURDERED IN ROADSIDE HIJACK.

Itch stood dumbfounded. He waited for the words to roll past again. 'Turn it up.' He'd shut out the sound of the TV to hear what his father was saying to Themba, but now this story had his full attention.

A reporter in a sharp suit and expensive haircut was explaining what he believed had happened: *'The men who run this vast oil company had only just landed in Lagos and, I am told, were on their way to a meeting. A meeting they never reached. According to the police, they got as far as this dock road when they were ambushed by what police are saying was a six-vehicle attack. Who attacked them? Well, the police say they are following several lines of enquiry, but obviously attention will turn to the Greencorps oil spill of three years ago, which cost the lives of seventeen oil workers. The only convicted Greencorps employee was Shivvi Tan Fook, who escaped from jail this July, only to die in a fire in an English school earlier this month. Police are asking for witnesses . . .'*

'Go and get Dad,' said Chloe.

'How far from Nigeria to South Africa, Sammy?' said Itch.

Sammy shrugged and said nothing.

'Sammy?' Itch repeated. 'How far away is Nigeria?

This time Sammy answered, but his tone had changed, his voice flat. 'Three thousand miles maybe.'

Itch and Chloe looked at each other.

'That sounds way too close,' said Itch.

In a small, smelly, noisy cabin, a man lay on a bunk, his head wrapped in bandages. He was motionless apart from his right hand, which was trying to roll a coin between his fingers. He worked it as far as his middle finger, then winced and dropped it. The coin rolled across the lino floor and disappeared under the toilet door; the man cursed loudly and reached for his whisky.

The room was sparsely furnished: a small bed, an overturned crate for a table and a laptop sitting on top of a small cabinet. The porthole above the bed showed only that it was night. In the unlikely event of the man receiving a visitor, the smell would have been described as a mixture of engine oil, medical astringent and garlic.

With an enormous effort, the man struggled off the bed, each small movement accompanied by a yelp of pain. He limped stiffly across to the bathroom, where he found some painkillers, then back to his glass of whisky to wash them down.

He sat on his bed, his feet still unsteady while the ship was rolling. Judging his moment, he lurched for the laptop, then was pitched back again as the vessel corrected itself. He lay sprawled uncomfortably on the thin blankets as he checked emails, blogs and websites, irritated by the ship's erratic wi-fi connection.

Suddenly he sat upright. Repositioning the laptop, he clicked on a headline and read the story that appeared underneath. It offered him a video to watch, and he risked the internet connection. He watched as images from the aftermath of the Lagos attack played on his screen.

'Well, well. What do we have here, Nathaniel?' he said to himself. 'What do we have here?' Smiling for the first time in many hours, his lips cracked and bled. He replayed the fifty-second video time after time, now on full screen, examining it closely. 'You were down by the docks – and both of you together! This was important, boys, wasn't it? And now it has all gone wrong – so wrong . . .'

He fidgeted with the bandage over his ear and watched again as the report concluded with a photo of the two Greencorps chairmen. They were smiling at the camera in happier times, and as the camera zoomed in on their faces, Dr Nathaniel

Flowerdew shaped his damaged hand into the shape of a gun.

'*Bang,*' he said, pointing it at Christophe Revere. He shifted his aim to Jan Van Den Hauwe. '*Bang.*' He chuckled softly as he closed his laptop. 'Good riddance.'

Three hundred miles from Flowerdew's ship, in a cramped underground storeroom, handcuffed to the metal bars of an old fire grate, the Greencorps bosses listened as their captors squabbled. It was an argument that had raged for the best part of two hours.

'If we don't kill them, what was the point of all this?' Aisha waved her knife at the two trussed and sweating men. 'Who wants prisoners? It really is very easy. They killed Shivvi; we kill them. An eye for an eye . . .'

A woman in an oversized plaid shirt held up her hands. 'Enough! This is going round in circles. We aren't killers! And they didn't kill Shivvi – that's the point – but they *did* let her go to prison. It should have been Flowerdew, of course, but that would have been too embarrassing for them. Let's keep them here for a few years, see how they like it.'

'You're a fool, Dada. You really think we can hold them here? Under Leila's flat? They'll be found. The police or Greencorps security teams won't be far behind. We need to sort this out now.'

'Tobi's right,' said Leila. 'I told you we should have decided this earlier. We've been offered a ransom from Greencorps – a million US dollars, and twice that from a mafia gang. We vote now.'

Christophe Revere was trying to attract their attention but was hampered by his gag and handcuffs. He flapped his bare feet about like windscreen wipers and made what noise he could with his own socks in his mouth.

'See what he wants,' said Leila.

Dada came over and pulled the socks out. 'What?' she asked.

Revere coughed and spat out some loose cashmere threads. 'We can get you Flowerdew,' he said. 'If it's him you want, we should work togeth—'

The socks went back in his mouth. 'Yeah, sure,' spat Dada.

'No, let's hear what he says,' said Leila. 'Let him speak.'

Dada pulled a face and took out the spittle-soaked socks again.

'We leave you a million dollars,' said the Greencorps man, pitching again. 'I can transfer it now if you wish. We accept we did wrong. You can spend it how you like – maybe set up a school or something – and we get you Flowerdew. We have security teams in many countries . . . we'll find him in the end. Then we'll call you.'

Aisha had heard enough. She snatched the socks from Dada and pushed them back in his mouth, then spun round to face her friends. 'They're within remember! *Oilmen!* And oilmen lie! Do you really think any of this will happen?'

From the corner of the room, a woman in skinny jeans and crop top raised a hand. 'Go ahead, Sade,' said Leila. 'We haven't heard from you yet.'

A slender Nigerian woman stood slowly to make her point. 'How about this?' she said. 'They issue a statement saying they were responsible for the oil spill, the deaths of the workers and Shivvi. They leave two million dollars for a school. And they resign from Greencorps. Then we let them go.'

Leila looked around at her friends. Some were nodding.

'OK, we vote,' she said.

5

Cornwall, England
January

The Lofte kitchen was buzzing with the smells and noises of cooking and conversation: Itch and Chloe were taking turns to tell everyone about their South African adventure. Gabriel was nursing his first coffee of the day while their mother, Jude, was assembling a pile of bacon sandwiches. Nicholas, brewing up yet more tea, was waiting for what he assumed would be a slightly amended version of the spoil-heap story when the doorbell rang.

'Jack!' shouted Chloe, and ran for the door. She returned hand in hand with their cousin, who was grinning widely.

'Hi, you guys! I missed you all so much!' Jack was tall, like all the Loftes – just a centimetre or so shorter than Itch – with black, pixie-style hair. She embraced her aunt and uncle, high-fived Itch and Gabriel over the table, then pulled up a chair. Just put a mug of steaming tea down in front of her. 'Well, it sure was quiet without you,' said Jack, still smiling. 'Apart from New Year, which got a bit stupid.'

Gabriel spun his laptop round. 'Do you mean this, Jack?' He showed a Facebook page that was full of photos: an assortment of partygoers pulling stupid faces, people lying in a garden, then dancing on the beach.

Jack laughed. 'Yes, that's some of it! It got worse later, apparently, but I was back home by then.'

'You should have been with us – we had a riot on New Year's Eve,' said Itch. His father shot him a warning glance. 'We watched the news on the oldest television ever, then Chloe . . . got a rash or something and we went to the local hospital. Which was like a thousand miles away.' Nicholas returned to the pouring.

Chloe's skin had been slightly burned by the thorium, but most of the redness had been covered by a combination of clothes, fake suntan – and now, embarrassment.

'Is it painful, Chloe?' asked Jude. 'Dad told me it was probably some weird plants you were playing near . . .'

'It's OK – a bit sore. I got some cream.'

'Let's see those pictures,' said Itch, changing the subject. He noticed Jack frowning, but carried on. 'Oh my God, is that Darcy Campbell dressed as a witch?'

Jack nodded. 'Suits her, don't you think? There

45

was a whole coven of them at the party, all waving wands and pretending to have dark powers.'

'Which in Darcy's case is almost certainly true,' said Itch.

Jack laughed and sipped from her mug.

'Should we ask the police if they want some tea or something?' asked Nicholas.

'I'll do it,' said Chloe, and headed for the front door.

After Nathaniel Flowerdew's escape, it had been decided that the local police would provide a 'presence' outside the house. In ones and twos, either sitting next door in the Coles' old house or in their cars, policemen had taken four-hour shifts; Itch thought it must be the most boring police work in the whole of Britain.

'Two teas, milk, three sugars,' called Chloe, and Jude reached for more tea bags.

The Lofte family ate and drank their way through brunch until Gabriel got a text and excused himself.

'Girl trouble, I think,' said Chloe, after he'd left the kitchen.

'Really?' said Itch. 'How do you know?'

'He told me. She thinks he's working too hard; he thinks she's lazy.' They started to clear the plates from the table.

'Well, they should split up, then,' said Itch. 'Obvious, isn't it?'

Everyone laughed. 'And what would you know about it?' said Chloe.

'Well, I was just saying . . .' said Itch defensively. 'That's how it sounds to me.'

'Well, tell him when he comes in, then. See what happens.'

'Which reminds me,' said Jack. 'Lucy inboxed me. She says sorry she couldn't come round, she's doing some boring jobs for her mum. She'll see us at the CA tomorrow. Maybe come round after.'

'Why is everyone looking at me?' asked Itch. 'Fine with me. That OK with everyone else?'

The others nodded, and Chloe smiled and started on the washing-up. Lucy Cavendish was in the year above Itch and Jack at the Cornwall Academy. Just last month they had discovered that she was the daughter of Cake, Itch's element dealer who had been killed by the radiation from the rocks of element 126. He had been absent from most of her life, but the knowledge that he had given her about the workings of the ISIS laboratory in Oxfordshire had proved crucial. It was Lucy who had known about spallation, the process by which Itch had managed to destroy the 126, by blasting it with a high-energy proton beam. Or 'death ray', as Jack had called it, much to his annoyance. For Christmas, Lucy had given Itch some of her father's sample of silicon, followed by a kiss on the cheek.

Itch had found himself thinking of that moment many times since then.

When the washing-up was done, Itch was left alone in the kitchen with his mother.

'Glad you're back,' he said, head in a cupboard, putting mugs away.

'Glad *you're* back . . .' Jude was staring at a steamed-up window.

'No, really,' said Itch. He took a deep breath. 'Dad said you wanted some time or something . . . And that it wasn't my fault you went away. Or Chloe's.'

'No, not really . . .' There was a pause.

'*Not really?* What does that mean?' said Itch.

'What I mean is . . .' Jude sighed again. 'It's complicated, Itch, you know . . . Everything was just too much. Your dad hadn't been on the rigs like he said he had . . . you nearly killed yourself with those rocks . . . and then we had a house full of guns and spies. So . . .'

'So it *was* a bit to do with me, then,' said Itch quietly.

Jude came and put her hand on his shoulder. 'You're safe, Itch. Chloe's safe and we are all together. It feels good like this.'

Itch waited for her to say more, but nothing came. 'OK,' he said, and went to find the others. He found Jack in Chloe's room; his sister was pulling her sweatshirt back on.

'Just been finding out what really happened on that spoil heap,' said Jack. 'Nasty burns.'

'Yeah . . . Dad went mad with this guy Themba, who'd told us it was all safe,' Itch told her. 'By the time we reached the hospital it was obvious that Chloe wasn't going to be sick, but the

48

burns needed treating. They getting better, Chloe?'

She nodded and showed him her arm; the redness was fading now. 'I'm fine. Really. And school tomorrow, so the sweatshirt can cover most of it. And some long socks, I think.'

Itch slumped onto Chloe's bed. 'Really? Tomorrow? I thought we had another day.' He felt his stomach tighten and the butterflies start. 'That's so unfair. Was there some work we had to do? I forget . . .'

Jack smiled. 'Of course you did. But we did miss the end of term, remember.'

'This term is really going to suck,' he said. 'I'm sure people will say all sorts of stuff they never dared to when we had the team with us. Potts and Campbell must be rubbing their hands with excitement.'

Chloe had been packing her school bag, but even she was looking uneasy now. 'It'll be odd to start with,' she agreed, 'but we actually only had MI5 around for a few weeks. Won't it be good to get back to normal?'

Jack nodded. 'Normal would be nice. Give it a few days, Itch, and everyone will have calmed down.'

Itch and Chloe hadn't walked to school on their own since the summer.

'This is weird,' said Chloe as she pulled their front door closed behind them. The day was cold and damp, her breath billowing in clouds as she spoke.

'Yup,' said Itch. 'No one to give us the all clear, no one to ask permission from, no one to check in with.' He looked around. 'Where's the police car, by the way?'

'Dad said they're only here sometimes. When they have a car free or something.'

Itch laughed. 'Don't see the point then, really.'

They headed down the hill towards the golf course.

'Do we still need protecting from Flowerdew, Itch?' Chloe asked. 'I still have dreams about the ISIS labs, when we were all lined up and the shooting started . . .'

He looked at his sister, and she smiled thinly. 'I know, that was bad,' he said, 'and given that he escaped, then yes, maybe we do still need protecting. He's still out there somewhere, unless he died of radiation sickness.'

'Which he *so* deserves,' said Chloe.

Itch laughed. 'Agreed! And I hit him in the face. And he got burned in the fire.'

'And you poisoned him with the tellurium!' added Chloe.

Itch was about to deny that the tellurium was poison when his phone rang. A grinning image of their cousin appeared on the screen. 'Hi, Jack. Happy new term and all that,' he said grimly.

'I can see you. Hurry up,' she said, and hung up.

Looking across the golf course, Itch could see her waving. And next to her, leaning against her bike, was Lucy. She was waving too.

'Wow, what's Lucy doing? This isn't her route to school,' said Itch as they hurried up the hill.

The girls all hugged, and Lucy – her hair as wild as ever after her cycle to the course – gave Itch a big smile. 'Happy New Year! How was South Africa? Gabe put some of your pictures on Facebook – looks amazing!'

'Er, it was great, thanks. How come you guys are here?'

'Itch!' said Chloe in a stage whisper. She raised her eyebrows.

'Oh yeah. Happy New Year too.' He looked at Chloe again, who just shrugged and smiled. 'How come you guys are here?' he tried again.

'Well,' said Jack, 'if the start of term is going to be weird, which it will, I thought we should all arrive together. We might not have Moz, Kirsten and the others, but Itch, Chloe, Lucy and Jack are a pretty good team anyway.'

They all grinned at each other.

'Nice speech,' said Lucy as they stepped off the golf course.

'Thanks,' said Jack, and they hurried to the academy.

As soon as they turned into the drive, Itch realized things had changed.

6

'Hey, there's Lucy!'

'Hi, Jack!'

'Look, there's Itch!'

'Chloe, over here!'

Even before they reached the front door, they had gained a following of fellow pupils, all eager for stories from their ordeal of the previous month. Most of the details seemed to be known, even if the final showdown at the ISIS labs was still shrouded in some mystery.

'Did you really burn down a school?'

'Was Mary Lee a terrorist?'

'Did she make you a suicide bomber?'

'Is it true you killed Flowerdew?'

Itch called a loud 'No!' to that one as they eased their way down the corridor. Lucy and Chloe peeled off to their respective classrooms, leaving Itch and Jack to get to the 10W form room. Except that it wasn't 10W any more. They had forgotten that John Watkins, their form teacher for the last two years, had decided to retire with immediate effect. Having been attacked by Shivvi Tan Fook, he had decided to quit.

Jack and Itch stopped at the form-room door, staring at the new plaque. 'Ten H,' said Jack. 'So he really did it. He really *did* quit.'

'Who's the H?' Itch pushed the door open. The room was already full, but there was considerably less noise than normal. Their appearance caused a few heads to turn; then a small ripple of applause started. As everyone realized who had walked in, the clapping became louder.

Itch and Jack looked at each other in amazement. 'Is this for us?' said Jack, blushing. Itch busied himself unpacking his school bag.

In front of them, Ian Steele turned round. 'Nice work at the school, you guys!' he said, still applauding. 'Sounds like some fire you started.'

As Tom Westgate wandered past, he leaned in close. 'Is it true that Flowerdew killed Mary?' he said. 'Or Shivvi whatever-her-name-was?'

Itch nodded. After she escaped from prison, Shivvi Tan Fook had joined the Cornwall Academy as a Year Thirteen student under the alias Mary Lee.

At this, Tom called out, 'It is true, Natalie!' At the front of the class, Natalie Hussain opened her mouth wide, and then started typing furiously into her phone. Tom perched on Jack's desk. 'Did she try to kill Mr Watkins? Is that why he's resigned?'

Itch didn't see any point in denying it, so he

nodded again. 'Yes, she hit him with a baseball bat,' he said.

Tom whistled. Then the whole class had questions, and Henry Hampton, the head of science, who was standing by the smartboard, had seen enough.

'OK, guys, thank you! Back to your desks please.' The American's voice boomed around the room. 'Itch, Jack, it's good to see you back in class. I'm sure you have lots to tell us, but not just now.' He looked around as everyone shuffled to their desks.

Itch stole a glance at Darcy Campbell and James Potts, who had always led the attacks on him and Jack. They both had their heads down, seemingly deep in a textbook. 'Wow,' he said in Jack's ear. 'Even the bullies are quiet.'

Jack smiled. 'Let's enjoy it. Won't last.'

'As you know,' Hampton continued, 'Mr Watkins has decided to retire – I'm sure we all, er, understand why.' Quite a few heads turned to look again at Itch and Jack; they just stared straight ahead. 'Dr Dart has asked me to take over here as form teacher . . . I know I'm new to the school, but I reckon we'll get along fine.' He smiled, then added, 'As long as you all sign up for my science club!' He laughed, took registration, then gathered up his papers. 'Have a nice day!' he called, and strode out of the room.

'How come teachers always laugh at their own jokes?' said Jack as they headed towards ICT. 'It's not as if they're funny or anything.' They were caught up in a large crowd swelled by Year Seven and Eight pupils.

'Maybe other teachers find them funny,' said Itch. 'Maybe when they're in the staff room, they spend their time laughing at each other and trying out jokes.'

As the other students crowded round, the questions started again:

'What happened to the MI5 team, Itch – they were cool!' shouted one voice.

'Is it true they let you fire their guns?' came another.

'Was Mary a spy or something?'

Itch felt Jack's hand on his shoulder. 'Come on, let's speed up,' she said, and steered him through the throng. They arrived at the stairs at the same time as Campbell and Potts, now with fellow Lofte-baiter Bruno Paul. They stood staring at each other; this was the moment Itch had been dreading. With no MI5, no Colonel Jim Fairnie, to give them protection, and with no teachers in sight, they were sitting ducks.

The stairs had always been a flashpoint; it was here that Itch had been slapped, tripped or simply made fun of. Now Potts stood in front of Campbell and Paul, who were waiting for his lead, but they seemed uncertain. Campbell said something to Potts, but he shook his head.

Then Jack whispered in Itch's ear, 'We've faced a lot worse than them. Next to Flowerdew and Shivvi, they're not even slightly scary. Come on.'

Itch followed her up the stairs. They climbed in silence; for a few seconds the stairwell was empty, so they could hear the footsteps start behind them.

'Faster, Jack?' suggested Itch.

But she shook her head. 'Slower.' Within seconds Potts was right behind her.

Itch glanced back. Potts's eyes narrowed; Darcy Campbell glared. Then a stream of Year Sevens appeared above them, running and shouting on their way down to their next lesson. When they saw the Lofte cousins, they nudged each other and called out.

'Hi, Itch! Hi, Jack!'

'Say hi to Chloe!'

'Add me on Facebook, Itch! Please!'

As they streamed down the stairs, Jack stopped, tugging Itch's sleeve to keep him with her. Surprised, Itch turned and noticed a sparkle in her eyes. She bent down and retied her shoelace. Itch knew it hadn't been undone, and guessed Potts did too, but the effect was an instant roadblock.

'Jack, come on!' said Itch urgently, afraid she was pushing her luck. Potts, Campbell and Paul, now with others crowding behind them, were backed up behind Itch and Jack, waiting for the Year Sevens to pass or Jack to finish with her laces.

Potts was waiting his turn. He opened his mouth to say something – but shut it again. The shout came from the foot of the stairs.

'Move along up there! You all have lessons to get to!' It was Dr Dart, the CA principal, the owner of the loudest voice in the school.

Jack and Itch took her advice while it was still reverberating around the stairwell. Taking the remaining steps two at a time, they shot to the next floor turning right for the ICT room.

'They actually waited for us, Jack! They waited for us!' Itch was running down the corridor, his eyes wide with surprise. 'I thought you'd totally lost it, making them wait like that. Maybe that story about me killing Flowerdew is quite useful after all!'

Jack laughed as they burst into the ICT room.

School finished at 3.45, and Itch, Jack and Chloe met in the entrance hall. While MI5 had been escorting them home, they'd had to wait until most of the pupils had left. Now they were on their own, they relished the freedom to leave when they wanted.

'You can come back to mine if you want,' said Jack as they stepped out into the damp and gloom. 'I could make you an omelette or something.'

Chloe nodded, but Itch wasn't listening. 'That was weird,' he said, 'not having Mr Watkins around.'

'That and being clapped when we walked into the classroom!' added Jack.

'I heard about that,' said Chloe, smiling. 'Hey, Itch, you got applauded! That must have been great!'

'Well, it's certainly never happened before,' he said. 'It was embarrassing, really. But better than being made fun of, I guess. It would just have been better with Watkins around, that's all. He's just always been there – every day I've been to the CA. And he was my form teacher for two years. I mean, Hampton's OK, but . . .' He tailed off. 'And it's my fault really.'

'That's stupid,' said Chloe. 'It's Shivvi's fault Watkins has retired. She's the one who smashed him with the bat, not you.'

'She's right, Itch,' said Jack. 'You know she is. Now, you coming for some food or not?'

'Let's go and see him,' he said, catching up. 'Let's go and see Mr Watkins – call in on our way home. See how he's doing.'

'Good call,' said Jack. 'I'll text my folks and tell them where we are. They're a little more nervous than they used to be about what I'm doing.'

'Which you have to say is fair enough,' said Chloe. 'I'll call Dad and tell him what we're doing too.'

Ducking out of the main flow of the students who were heading home through town, Itch, Jack and Chloe turned left towards the canal. John Watkins lived in a small group of houses that had been built at the end of the towpath, just a few metres from the sea. As Itch's form tutor and geography teacher, Mr Watkins had been Itch's biggest supporter at the academy. He had stood up to Flowerdew too, challenging him after the chemistry teacher had stolen Itch's first piece of 126.

A light drizzle had started, and was in the process of turning the towpath into a mudslide. They picked their way along it with care, the only light now from two weak streetlamps.

'Happy without your rucksack?' asked Jack. 'Must seem a bit strange . . .'

Itch shrugged. 'Just seemed easier for everyone if I left it at home. And I wondered if some people are actually scared of it − like it's a bag of potions or something. Seems stupid, but I thought I'd use Gabriel's bag. I was going to try and make some friends, if you remember.'

Jack laughed. 'Yeah, I remember! Well, that wasn't a bad start. Where's the element collection now?'

'Some of it is still in my room!' said Chloe. 'He came back from South Africa with loads of stuff, and it was too heavy for one bag. So me and Dad had to share the weight. Anytime you want to come and collect—'

'We only arrived back yesterday, Chloe!' Itch said. 'Give me a chance. I'm sort of running out of space − don't know where to put everything. They're all rare earths, I think . . . I'll sort them out tonight.' He looked ahead to see if Watkins's lights were on. 'Maybe we should have called him first. Looks pretty dark down there.'

They slithered up to the front door and a safety light clicked on. Up close they heard soft classical music coming from inside. Itch smiled at the others and rapped the iron door knocker twice. Seeing no sign of movement inside, he knocked again.

'Wait . . .' said Jack. She put her ear to the door and started to mime the actions of a pianist, running her hands across the keys. 'Coming up . . .' she said. 'Sounds like it's finishing any moment now . . .' She gave a great flourish, her fingers hitting a series of invisible chords. 'Try again, Itch!'

He knocked loudly – three times this time – and within seconds a silhouette appeared behind the frosted glass.

'There you go!' said Jack. Itch and Chloe started to applaud her, and she bowed theatrically.

'Who's there?' called the figure from inside. Itch, Jack and Chloe immediately stopped their pantomime and a look of concern crossed their faces.

'He sounds really scared!' said Chloe in a whisper.

'Sir – it's us, sir! Itch, Jack and Chloe Lofte!' called Itch hurriedly.

They heard, 'Oh my goodness – oh, thank heavens!' through the door and then the sound of three locks being undone and a chain unhooked. The door opened, and John Watkins, the recently retired head of geography at the Cornwall Academy, peered out at his visitors. Then he smiled. 'Come in, come in!' he said breathlessly, and stood aside as the Loftes all trooped in. 'Were you outside long? I was, er, listening to some music.' He pointed to his study, where the piano and orchestra had started up again.

'Is it OK, sir?' said Itch. 'We thought we'd call in on our way home to see how you are . . .'

'Yes, yes – of course!' Mr Watkins seemed flustered. 'I get a little nervous these days, I'm afraid. After the attack – you know . . . Anyway, come into the kitchen.' He quickly pulled his study door shut, and the music faded.

'Nice tune,' said Jack.

'Do you like it?' Watkins followed them into the kitchen. 'It's Mozart's twenty-first piano concerto – marvellous stuff!'

'We didn't mean to interrupt your work,' said Itch.

'No, that's OK,' said Watkins. 'I was wondering how everyone was getting on. It felt strange not being there with you all, I must say. Missing the last few days of term was fine, but not being there for the start of the Easter term has made me rather sad, I'm afraid.' He bustled over to the kettle. 'Tea and toast OK?'

They all nodded, and Itch watched as he lifted the lid of his bread bin and got out a small loaf. He looked stooped and tired, Itch thought, and he could see a flesh-coloured plaster above Watkins's left ear where Shivvi's baseball bat had met his skull. His voice sounded thinner, more frail too. At least he was still wearing his yellow corduroy trousers and salmon-coloured cardigan – not everything had changed.

'Do you wish you were still at the CA, then, sir?' asked Itch.

'Why, yes, of course . . .' Mr Watkins sighed. 'But it was the right decision to go.' He felt for the plaster and pressed gently around its edges. 'My head still hurts every morning – I have more tests due soon. But it could have been worse, much worse . . .' He gazed distractedly through the window. 'Anyway, now you have Mr Hampton, Itch – and you, Jack, of course – and a fine man he is, I believe.'

The kettle boiled, and Watkins made the tea. Chloe and Jack had moved to the kitchen table, which was strewn with papers and files.

'Keeping busy, then, sir?' said Jack as she pulled up a chair. And Watkins suddenly moved faster than Itch would have thought possible.

'Ooh . . . yes. Let me just tidy this up . . . How messy of me!' He swooped and quickly gathered up all the table's contents into his arms. Some sheets of paper fell to the floor and Chloe picked them up. 'Ah, Chloe, thank you. Yes, I'll have those,' he said, snatching the sheets of A4 from her.

The cousins exchanged glances as he dropped the papers into a dresser drawer and slammed it shut.

'Secret work, sir?' chanced Jack. 'An autobiography maybe?'

'Ha! Nice one, Jack . . . No, that would be really, really dull. It's . . . well . . .' Itch thought he was trying to work out whether to tell them or not. 'It's just that . . . Well, it is – as you say – secret. For now, anyway.'

'Oh, come on, sir!' said Itch.

'And any further questioning is totally pointless. It's just some research, that's all. Now, let's pour the tea.'

Itch shrugged and changed the subject. 'Did you see the news about the Greencorps bosses getting killed or kidnapped, sir? We saw it on South African TV. Who would do that?'

'Yes, I saw that too,' said Watkins. 'And we all know someone who might want to have them . . . "done in", shall we say. But it's very lawless in parts of Nigeria – there are shootings and robberies all the time. And Greencorps must be very unpopular in Lagos as they were responsible for that oil spill, of course. Maybe it was revenge? Who knows . . .' He forced a smile. 'Anyway . . . who's for jam?'

The walk home was as swift as they could manage. The drizzle had turned to sleet, and whichever direction they walked in, it seemed to be blowing into their faces. The town was almost deserted, and the shops were shutting.

'What was all that about?' Itch pulled his jacket collar up as far as it would go. 'What could be so secret that Mr Watkins had to hide it as soon as we went in?'

'And he didn't want us in the front room either – did you see the way he shut the door?' said Jack.

'*Mining deaths 1800 to 1877*,' said Chloe.

'You what?' said Itch.

'*Mining deaths 1800 to 1877*. That's what it said on the piece of paper I picked up. That's all I saw, anyway.'

'Mining deaths? Why would that be such a secret?' wondered Jack. 'Why couldn't he just tell us?'

'Dunno . . .' Itch shrugged. 'Maybe he's gone a bit funny. Anyway, see you tomorrow, Jack. Come on, Chloe – let's see if we can walk past a golf bunker without it blowing up.'

The phone was answered on its first ring.

'Osiegbe,' said the voice.

'Flowerdew.'

There was a silence of many seconds. 'I thought you were dead, Nathaniel.'

'So did I. It was close. I'm still here, but the 126 is gone. I had it, but it was stolen from me and is now gone for ever. I'm sorry, Abu, but I have quite a lot of work for your people.'

'Where are you? Sounds noisy.'

'Afloat,' said Flowerdew. 'Moving around.'

'How can I help you?' said Abu Osiegbe. 'What is the nature of your business?'

'Revenge,' said Flowerdew. 'For now, just revenge . . .'

There was a throaty laugh from the other end of the phone. 'I have helped with such matters in the past, it is true.'

'I heard of the, er, package in Lagos last week,' said Flowerdew. 'It sounds as if your famed "postal service" is still in operation.' There was silence at the other end and he pressed on. 'What is the usual, er, contents of the parcels?'

'Well, now, let me see . . . Some filings. A hint of a sparkly powder. Special ingredients . . . and extra toppings if you need them.' A deep chuckle from the Nigerian.

'Of course. Do you deliver to England?'

'I could if needed, yes. But why – apart from the money you'll be paying me – should I help you?'

'Because' – Flowerdew's voice rose slightly – 'these are the people responsible for you not having the 126. These are the thieves who took what is ours, Abu. The Greencorps men have been dealt with – Revere and Van Den Hauwe got what was coming to them – but the others are still untouched. That is why you should help.'

'How many?'

'I'll email the details. How long will it take?'

'Patience, my friend. As long as is necessary. But you won't be disappointed with the results, I assure you.'

'Payment will be made in the normal way?' asked Flowerdew.

'Yes, of course. But I must correct you on one thing before you go, Nathaniel. The Greencorps men have not been "dealt with", as you say. In fact, I happen to know that there are . . .' He paused to choose his words carefully. 'There are many options being considered.'

Flowerdew cursed loudly. 'OK. So I have to do everything myself. I'll clear this up.' And he broke the connection.

7

On the walk from English, Itch and Jack bumped into Lucy; her face lit up.

'Hi, you guys! What's happening? Coming to Hampton's science thing?' It was the first of the science club meetings of the new term, and Mr Hampton was particularly keen for everyone to be there.

'Yes, I'm in,' said Itch, 'but it's not really Jack's thing.'

'Got that right!' agreed Jack. 'One of us has to stay normal!'

Lucy punched her lightly on the arm and laughed. 'Thanks a lot, Jack. Anyway, who wants to be normal?'

'Actually, a bit of normal would be nice for a bit, don't you think?' said Jack. 'And yesterday was weird – tell Lucy about going to Mr Watkins's place.'

'You did *what*?' said Lucy, astonished.

Itch described the events of the previous

afternoon: how John Watkins had clearly been keeping a secret from them, and how Chloe had got a glimpse of something about *Mining Deaths 1800 to 1877.*

'Ooh, interesting,' said Lucy. 'Let's Google it.' They had arrived outside the chemistry lab, and Jack made as if to leave, but Lucy linked arms with her. 'Just come in and see what we come up with, Jack.'

Taking a seat at the front bench, she typed into her phone, and the three of them stared at the screen.

'*History of Ireland, the Act of Union and the Great Famine,*' read Lucy. '*Colorado Mining Disasters, Special Pizza Deals.* Hmm . . . not really what we were after.'

'Add *Cornwall* to the search,' said Jack, just as Mr Hampton strode into the lab. He acknowledged the small gathering of pupils and then noticed his new arrival.

'Hi, Jack! Knew we'd get you in the end.' He smiled and came over.

'Actually I was just leaving, sir . . . I was talking to the guys here and—' She broke off, distracted by the sight of a small pink butterfly earring sparkling from Hampton's left earlobe. 'Er, sir, that's gross,' she said.

'What is?' he asked, and Jack pointed to his ear. 'Oh, that! I thought it was rather cute. My daughter gave it to me.' He pulled at the butterfly and it came away in his hand. 'I could have tried this . . .' he said, and fixed it to his other ear. 'Or this . . .' When he had removed his hands from his nose, the butterfly was fixed to its side.

'Is it glue, sir?' asked Lucy. 'I can't see any piercings!'

'No, it's a tiny neodymium magnet. Itch?'

'Er, neodymium . . . it's one of the rare earths. Symbol Nd, number 60 on the Periodic Table. And the strongest magnets we have.'

Mr Hampton grinned. 'Well done, spot on. These are the smallest I've seen, but they still work through skin.' He showed them the small magnetic backing, and how it and the butterfly jumped together. 'You don't want to be around larger neodymium magnets – they could easily mess up your hand. Here, watch this.'

He hit the YouTube app on his phone and found a video called *Death Magnet*. They gathered round the small screen and watched as handlers with gloves and protective glasses used small, shiny, circular magnets to smash cans, cigarette lighters and fruit. The cherry was particularly spectacular: as the two magnets flew together, they destroyed their target, sending skin and juice splattering onto a nearby wall. Someone whistled their admiration.

'Now, who wants to wear a pink butterfly for a few minutes?' Natalie Hussain's hand went up and Mr Hampton threw her the earring. 'But a warning – nothing bigger, ever. There have been cases of students using a neodymium magnet to attach ornaments to themselves and then finding they needed surgery to get them off again.' Almost everyone winced.

'You got any neodymium?' Jack asked Itch.

He shook his head. 'No, but I'm thinking about it!' he said.

'Thought you might. That's your birthday present sorted.'

At the end of the session, Mr Hampton cleared his throat to attract everyone's attention. 'Now, I've got something you *really* want to hear about,' he said. He stood at the front of the lab, looking pleased with himself. 'Dr Dart has given me the go ahead to organize a CA trip to the science museum in Spain. It's in Madrid . . . It's not normally a must-see, but they have some new exhibitions. There's one on nanotechnology, another on 3D printers and, for the element hunters amongst us, a collection of Spanish silver, and how its mining was the start of the modern world. It'll be at Easter, and you'll get letters shortly.'

'Why Madrid, sir?' queried Itch. 'It's not exactly the best science museum we could visit. Munich's much better.'

Mr Hampton looked unsettled. 'Well, it's been, er, updated recently. You may have missed that news. And there's a good deal on at the moment . . .' He paused as though he had more to say, but then continued, forcing a smile.

'Who's up for it? Assuming your folks all say yes? There are only a limited number of spaces. And it is warmer than the UK!

70

Itch looked around – there were lots of hands up. He only vaguely recognized most of the others, but he knew Tom Westgate and Craig Murray from his form – and Natalie Hussain, with the butterfly earring fixed to her left ear, who had put both hands up.

'Sir, can we bring friends? Please?'

'Depends on you guys,' said Mr Hampton. 'There are ten places, and priority goes to those who come to this science club. If there are still spaces, then yes, of course. I'll be in touch soon on this. Thanks, everyone.'

As they stood to leave, he added, 'Itch and Jack – a quick word before you go, please.'

The cousins looked at each other and shrugged. 'Tell me later,' said Lucy, joining the others as they filed out. Mr Hampton closed the door behind them and came over to their bench.

'Good spot, Itch,' he said. He was speaking softly, as though afraid of being overheard. 'The Munich museum is way better. Of course it is. However, there's another factor which I shouldn't really share with you, but ... I don't think the normal rules apply here.'

Itch glanced at Jack; her raised eyebrows indicated that she was as surprised by this as he was. 'You remember my old colleague, Tom Oakes? The American who helped you at ISIS? I knew him from our days at the Mountain Path mine in California ...'

'Sure we do,' said Itch. 'He showed us how to

71

destroy the 126. He's the one who said, "Let's whomp this sucker," before we pressed the button.'

'Yeah, he showed us how to fire the death-ray thing,' said Jack. Itch was about to correct her, but Mr Hampton did it for him.

'I'm sure you mean "operate the neutron beam".' He smiled kindly and sighed. 'Well, Tom has disappeared. He was being given a hard time by his bosses for the meltdown at the target station, and he quit.'

'But that's so unfair,' said Jack. 'Poor man, he was just trying to help us.'

'He should be rewarded, not punished,' agreed Itch.

Hampton paced to the front of the lab, then back again. 'He called me, looking for work.' He shrugged. 'I didn't have any. He said something about an offer from Madrid, but he didn't sound himself. And he didn't say anything to his wife.'

'And you want to look for him,' said Jack.

'I should have noticed his distress' – Hampton was almost whispering – 'but I didn't. So when Dr Dart approved a science trip, I thought I should see what I could do.'

'So it's Madrid,' said Itch.

Mr Hampton nodded. 'It's Madrid.'

After school the following day, Lucy wheeled her bike up to Itch and Jack, who were waiting for Chloe in the reception hall. 'Hey! Been thinking about that Watkins' secret you were talking about.

We should call in at the library on the way home. If the "mining deaths" search doesn't come up online, we should try there. There's a big local history section I used once for a tourism essay.'

'OK,' said Itch, 'but I'm not a member. Never been in there.'

'Me neither,' said Chloe.

'Same,' said Jack.

'But I have!' said Lucy. 'Follow me . . .'

The walk to the library saw them all in high spirits; the term had started a whole lot better than they had expected. They were laughing as they passed a rather surprised librarian and dropped their bags around the 'Local History' table. There were four bookshelves in two facing rows and they stood looking at the hundreds of books.

Lucy headed for the nearest shelf. '*Old Parish Churches of Cornwall, Smuggling in Cornwall, Old Cornish Inns* . . . All fascinating, I'm sure, but not helpful. Where do we start?'

'Why don't we ask her?' said Itch, pointing at the librarian. 'It's her patch.'

'Good idea,' said Jack, and they all approached the woman sitting behind a vast table covered in books, leaflets and posters.

The librarian was younger than Itch expected a librarian to be, but was at least forty; her badge said MORGAN. She smiled as they approached and dabbed her mouth with a napkin. 'Hello. How can I help?'

The three girls all looked at Itch.

'Er, we have, erm, a school project on mining, and we were wondering if you had any books covering the period 1800 to 1877.'

'Sure. We've got quite a few on mining – and Cornish mining in particular.' She led them to a two-shelf run of books. 'These bottom shelves go from pre-history to the present day. You should find everything you need here, but it is a popular section – some books may be out. Good luck!'

They all sat on the floor and started to pull out a variety of books.

'Remind me what we're looking for . . .' said Chloe.

'No idea,' Itch replied, 'but something that explains why Watkins has gone all secretive on us.'

'Anyone heard of the Ding Dong mine at Land's End?' said Jack from behind the covers of a large book. 'Apparently there's a legend that says Jesus is supposed to have addressed the miners there.'

'Don't think it'll be that, Jack,' said Itch.

'Cornish miners led the rebellion of 1497 against Henry the Seventh?' offered Lucy from her book.

'Arsenic was found with copper ore at the Callington mine, and the dust often killed the miners,' read Chloe. She looked at her brother. 'These guys were the original element hunters really – this is all your stuff, Itch: copper, tin, arsenic, silver.'

Itch nodded. 'I know. And it was dangerous – there were loads of accidents. But everyone knows about that, so why should Watkins be doing more work on it?'

'Could we see if he's taken any books out recently?' wondered Lucy.

Itch smiled at her. 'Now that's a good idea. But the librarian won't tell us just like that, will she?'

'Let's see . . .' said Lucy, and walked back to Morgan the librarian. 'Hi again,' she said. 'Sorry to trouble you. Our teacher, John Watkins – you might know him, I think he comes here sometimes – has recommended a book, but none of us can remember the title. Or the author! We're all feeling a little dumb, but we don't want to get into trouble . . .' Lucy smiled and pulled an 'I'm-in-trouble' face.

The librarian nodded. 'Of course I know him. I'm not allowed to give you anyone's borrowing history, of course . . . but there are a couple of books on the returns trolley that might be what you need. Mr Watkins brought them back yesterday.' She gestured towards a chunky wooden shelf on wheels, piled high with books of all sizes.

'Thanks,' said Lucy. 'We might get our project done now! Hey, over here, guys!' She called to the others, and raced for the trolley. 'Two books in here somewhere,' she said when they'd gathered round. 'Watkins dropped them off yesterday.'

Chloe found one first. 'There!' She pointed to a hefty hardback. '*The Black Seam: Mining Stories.* That must be one.' She pulled it out. 'Nearly nine hundred pages, Itch,' she said, flicking to the end. 'Here – you have it.' The others scoured the trolley's shelves, but couldn't see any more mining books.

'It's getting late, you guys,' said Lucy, 'and I need to cycle home. Let's get this one for now and try again tomorrow.' She took the book to the librarian, who stamped it and smiled.

'Looks like it's going to be a big project!' she said.

''Fraid so,' said Lucy, and they all filed out onto the street.

'I'll take it,' said Itch. 'You can't ride home with that in your bag. You'll never get up the hills.'

'OK. Thanks, Itch. See you guys tomorrow!'

They watched as Lucy cycled off into the gloom. 'Say hi to your mum,' called Chloe, and Lucy waved in acknowledgement.

'You really going to read that?' said Jack as they walked home.

'Sure,' said Itch. 'Suppose I should finish *The Great Gatsby* for the Brigadier first . . .'

'Which you haven't started,' said Chloe.

'I've looked at the cover,' protested Itch.

Itch wasn't sure what had woken him. It had, as usual, taken him a long time to get to sleep – his brain refusing to shut down the way everyone else's did – but his clock said 3.10 a.m.

Way too early. He listened to the sound of the house. He could hear the pipes and radiators start-ing to warm and the creaking sounds that had alarmed Chloe when they had first moved into the house. While they had the MI5 team next door, he had slept well, knowing that he and his sister were being watched, being protected. Now they were gone and he found himself analysing every sound for danger.

His mind raced. The 126 was gone, but Flowerdew wasn't. He was out there somewhere, and Itch was sure he would hear from him again . . . But, Itch reasoned, the injuries he had sustained – the burns in the Fitzherbert School fire and the blows to the head at the ISIS labs – would put him out of action for some considerable time. Whatever noises the house was making, he was sure it wasn't related to his old science teacher.

Itch got up and stood on the landing. All the lights were off apart from a faint glow from Chloe's nightlight. He put his head round her door – she was fast asleep, of course, her breathing deep and steady. He walked silently back to his room and put on his light. He sat on his bed and picked up his copy of *The Great Gatsby*; he had managed three chapters last night. In fact, now he thought of it, it was this that had finally brought on sleep. Maybe it would work again, he thought; he found his place and started to read.

But he was bored within a page and thought about sending Jack or Lucy a message on Facebook to see if they were up. He opened his laptop and checked his inbox – and to his surprise Lucy had left him a message.

Thanks for taking Mining Tales! Bring to school if you can bear it, and we'll check it at lunch. Lx

77

He reached for his rucksack and pulled out the library book. *I should at least have started it,* he thought and, propping himself up with his pillows, began to read.

It was divided into counties, each section giving a short history of local mining, together with ancient photos and eyewitness accounts of life in and around the pit. Itch found the chapter on Cornwall and immediately recognized some of the photos. They were of the mines at South Carreg and the pit that had become South West Mines, where he and Jack had briefly worked last year. The coastal setting and the position of the winding tower were instantly recognizable, and Itch studied the old black-and-white images.

Rows of miners, their faces set, stared out at him. Some wore protective helmets; others wore caps or were bare-headed. Underground images of rock faces and primitive drilling machinery filled the next few pages, and then Itch noticed a page with a corner folded. The section told how the lift machinery, operated by a 'man-engine', had collapsed and thirty-two miners had lost their lives. There was an image of the mine and an account of how the disaster had unfolded. Itch was gripped by the story of an unnamed miner, aged only fifteen, who had lost his brother and uncle in the disaster. He read the next sentence and then sat up straight.

He read it again, out loud: '*There was much grieving in the village as the boy had only recently lost his father to the vomiting disease.*' The words had been faintly underlined in pencil. In the margin – in what Itch was sure was Mr Watkins's handwriting – were the words *Cross-check with FLOW*.

If Itch's mind had been racing before, it was turbo-charged now. Sleep was forgotten as he read furiously through the entire section on Cornish mining. There were no more folded pages, but one other paragraph had been underlined. It told of a mine near Land's End, where recent casualties had been attributed to *rock falls, drill-slips* . . .

'Ouch!' said Itch out loud. '. . . and the vomiting disease.'

That phrase again.

Again, Watkins – he was sure it was him – had written *Cross-check with FLOW* in the margin. *Flowerdew?* thought Itch. *But that makes no sense* . . . He read on until he reached the section about mining in Wales, but there was nothing of interest, nothing underlined. He flicked through every page, but found no more pencil marks.

Itch shut the book and stared at the Periodic Table on his wall. Getting out of bed, he stood in front of it. He traced his finger down the column which started with *Fe, Iron,* passed through *Ru, Ruthenium, Os, Osmium, Hs, Hasmium,* and ended where his father had handwritten *126, Lt, Lofteium.*

Surely not.

No way.

It was Mr Watkins who had told him that the rocks of 126 had been traced to South West Mines at Provincetown. They had been dug up and thrown out on a spoil heap. To disguise their illegal deep mining, the company had scattered the 'waste' over three counties; it was thought that the 126 ended up in Devon, where it was bought by Cake, the element dealer. He had later died from radiation sickness, the rock's fierce radioactivity then causing a violent illness that had nearly killed Itch, Jack and Chloe.

And it had been to Mr Watkins that he had asked why the rocks had come out of a mine. Itch had hoped that they were like the last of an endangered species and that, once they were disposed of, the 126 would be gone for ever. He understood its power and its potential for good but had seen first hand what it could do to people. With the 126, guns and violence were never far behind. He recalled Mr Watkins's words then and spoke them out loud, softly: 'Maybe they've been thrown away before.'

Even though it was only 5.30, Itch got dressed. He suddenly felt cold.

In a London sorting office, a brown-uniformed parcel delivery service employee was approaching the end of his shift. It had been busy – the New Year sales had meant a rush of packages needing delivery. Most seemed to be the size of books and DVDs, but there were larger parcels too. The man checked the addresses, felt their weight and enjoyed guessing the contents: clothes, tools – food maybe.

His last four packages were identical. Slightly larger than A4-sized padded envelopes. Heavy. No movement inside. Typed address labels. *Reference books*, he guessed. *Encyclopaedias maybe, if anyone still buys them.* One to Didcot, three to Cornwall. Two were for doctors, one for a man with lots of letters after his name. *Professional* – he nodded to himself. *Exactly the type to have encyclopaedias. Classy.* The addressee of the last one was a strange name he'd never seen before. He'd seen every name under the sun; characters he recognized from *Star Trek*, *Star Wars* and sometimes *Twilight*. He thought he'd seen everything, but he'd never seen a name like this one.

'*Itchingham Lofte* . . .' He shrugged and placed it in the pile for CORNWALL/OVERNIGHT.

'Oh well. Enjoy!' he said.

8

Itch woke Chloe at six a.m. It was a few seconds before she realized that he was already in his uniform.

'Itch, what's wrong?' She sat up, alarmed.

'When does the library open?' he said.

'You what?'

'When does the library open?'

She flopped back onto her pillow. 'I heard what you said – I just couldn't believe you'd said it, that's all. Itch, it's six o'clock in the morning. Go away.' She closed her eyes, but when Itch didn't move, she opened them again. 'What is it?'

'I've been reading the mining book.'

Chloe waited for him to continue, but he just sat on the edge of her bed. 'And?' she said at last.

'I think I know what Watkins is being secretive about. There are two passages about miners getting a sickness – a *vomiting disease* – and dying. Watkins had underlined them and written *Need to cross-check with FLOW*. But I don't know who or what FLOW is. Obviously it isn't Flowerdew . . .'

'Maybe it's something he wrote . . .' Chloe sat up again. 'You mean, he thinks it's the 126? But the book's about stories from hundreds of years ago, isn't it?' Itch nodded, and she pulled her T-shirt over her knees. 'Wow.'

When she was dressed, Chloe crept into Itch's room. He showed her the underlined passages and the *FLOW* sections. 'Maybe *FLOW* is the other book,' he said. 'The one we couldn't find. When's the library open?'

'Itch, you've asked me that three times already and I have no idea. Look it up maybe?' she suggested.

'Have done. Can't find it. We'll just have to be there when it opens.'

'Excuse me . . . why?'

'Because if we get there before they put those returned books back, we might find the FLOW book.'

'Might not be a book at all,' said Chloe. 'Might be a person. Even if it isn't Flowerdew. Member of staff or someone.'

Itch shrugged. 'Maybe. But I'd like to be at the library when it opens. I've messaged Jack and Lucy. Come on, let's get some breakfast.'

They were outside the library by 8.30.

Itch read the sign on the door and kicked the wall. 'Opens at ten?' he said, exasperated. 'What kind of useless operation is this? How can it only open at ten?'

Chloe laughed. 'Itch, until yesterday you'd never been inside. You're not even a member . . .'

'I joined online this morning. While you were getting dressed. Can you see the trolley?'

They both peered through the glass of the front door, their breath steaming it up. 'I think it's in front of the desk,' said Chloe, wiping the condensation away with her hand. 'All piled up . . . But you can't wait till ten – registration is in fifteen minutes.'

There was a shout, and Jack arrived, running. She was flushed from the cold and her exertions, sweat running from under her beanie hat.

'Hey. Just saw your message at breakfast. What's up?'

Itch told her about his night-time reading and pointed at the returns trolley. 'I need to be here at ten.'

'We're in English, Itch. Think the Brigadier will notice if you just disappear to go shopping.'

They walked back up the hill, as Lucy arrived at full speed, braking hard as she drew alongside the others. 'Hi! Came as quickly as I could!' She got off her bike and removed her crash helmet, trying to flatten her hair at the same time.

Itch explained again about the vomiting illness in the mine stories book, then stopped as the colour started to drain from Lucy's rosy cheeks.

She stared at her friends. 'You mean you think . . . those rocks had killed before . . . before Dad?'

'I don't know, Lucy, really. I just think it's what

Watkins is looking at—' Itch broke off as he saw the tears in Lucy's eyes. He hadn't thought about her reaction. When Cake died, he had lost a friend, a mentor, but Lucy had lost her father. He was annoyed with himself. 'Sorry . . .'

'I never thought . . . how can that even be possible?' she said, so quietly they nearly missed it.

Chloe and Jack linked arms with Lucy as they all walked into the CA and Itch told them about the conversation he'd had with Mr Watkins in hospital.

'*Thrown away before?*' they chorused. All four stood staring at each other, causing other students to detour round them.

'You never mentioned it,' said Jack.

'Haven't really thought about it since he told me . . .'

'What are you going to do about the library?' asked Chloe.

Itch shrugged. 'Dunno.'

'I do,' said Jack. 'I know exactly what you're going to do.'

Lucy and Chloe left for registration, and Itch and Jack filed into Mr Hampton's class.

'Go on, then – what am I going to do?' said Itch, smiling slightly.

'We'll go to English. And then you'll think of a reason to disappear. Then you'll reappear with a book by someone with the initials FLOW. How am I doing so far?'

At 9.45 English teacher Gordon Carter – known as

'the Brigadier' for his constant marching around the school – was deep in the pages of F. Scott Fitzgerald's *The Great Gatsby*. He hadn't noticed that Itch's hand was up.

'Sir,' said Natalie Hussain, 'Itch wants you.'

The teacher looked up, annoyed by the inter-ruption. He raised an eyebrow. 'Well?' he said.

'Not feeling too good, sir. Think I might be sick.'

The memory of the arsenic-infused wallpaper incident from the previous year was fresh enough in everyone's minds to trigger a wave of groans. A few hands covered mouths, and there were calls of 'Better let him go, sir!' The Brigadier nodded at Itch and he grabbed his bag.

'Good luck!' whispered Jack, and he ran for the door.

He went into the toilets first, in case anyone followed him, but he knew he couldn't wait there long. He needed to be at the library when it opened, needed to get to the returns trolley first. Instead of risking a departure through the front door, he ran into the grounds from the science corridor, then to the coastal path through a crack in the fence. This had only appeared since the departure of the MI5 team, but Itch had seen it used and was thankful for it now.

The wind off the sea was biting. He hadn't had time to get his jacket, and anyway it would have raised suspicions if he'd worn it while 'feeling sick'. He cut back to the road that led to the town centre and ran towards the library. He wasn't sure how long he had before someone asked where he was – the Brigadier would probably have already forgotten about him.

He crossed the high street, pausing briefly to allow the passing of a brown UPS delivery van heading down the hill. He glanced at his phone: 9.58 a.m. He was on time.

He tried the library door; still locked. He could see movement inside and waved, then knocked. Morgan the librarian was talking to a colleague; she looked up, smiled at Itch, then mouthed, 'Two minutes,' and tapped her watch. She went over to her desk, and Itch watched as she fired up her computer and poured herself a cup of tea. She checked her phone for messages, then placed it in a drawer and rearranged some leaflets, then said something to her colleague.

Itch realized he'd been concentrating on Morgan; and now he turned to look at her colleague. With a sharp intake of breath he saw that the woman was at the returns trolley. It was half empty, and she had a pile of books under her arm. 'No!' he shouted from outside and banged on the glass. 'Leave those! Please, leave those!'

Both Morgan and her assistant looked alarmed, then annoyed. Morgan came to the door and unlocked it. 'Excuse me – how dare you bash on our door like that! We open at ten . . .' She glanced at her watch. 'Which is now. What is so urgent that you couldn't wait two minutes?'

He pushed past her. 'I need a returned book!

From yesterday. Please don't put any more away – I need to check them first.' He ran over to the trolley.

It didn't take long to check the thirty-odd titles and authors. There wasn't a 'FLOW' amongst them. He ran to the two shelves of mining books, looking for the 'F's. Finding none, he tried the local history section. There was a Felix and a Foster, but he couldn't see any name like Flow.

'What's the panic?' asked the assistant.

'How many books have you put back?' said Itch, ignoring the question.

'Er, I don't know. Maybe eighty – a hundred tops,' she said. 'Can I finish my job now, please?' and she waited for him to step aside.

'What? Oh, sorry – yes.' He checked the time again. He had to go.

'Shouldn't you be in school?' she said.

'Er, yes, they know . . .' He opened the door to leave, then tried one last option.

'You don't remember a book with—'

Itch never finished his sentence.

The sound of an explosion ripped through the town.

He ran outside. The few early shoppers had all stopped in their tracks, looking around, staring at each other. A few ran into the road as Itch had done; some gazed up at the sky. A familiar sense of dread was settling in Itch's stomach.

He headed up the hill, where a small group had

gathered to stare seawards. Itch saw hands pointing and heard cries of 'Look there!' He quickly glanced over his shoulder to see what they were staring at, but the shops obscured everything. He ran faster.

There was a small area at the top of the hill – actually the first tee of the golf course – where you could look out across most of the town. Itch saw golfers and shoppers standing together and heard their cries of alarm. Heart pounding, the sound of the explosion still playing in his head, he reached the brow of the hill and spun round, looking seaward.

He saw the dark plume of smoke first. Then he saw the flames.

The cottages by the canal.

The end cottage.

John Watkins's cottage.

Itch blanched as panic gripped him. Around him, he could hear 999 calls being made, but he stood staring at the house by the canal.

'Yes, fire brigade, please . . . The canal. There's a house on fire . . . Explosion, I think. Yes, my name is . . . No, I don't know if there's anyone inside . . . Here's my number . . .'

Some of the onlookers then started to run in the direction of the canal. On the towpath Itch could see people heading towards the fire. Next to him a woman in a duffel coat and cap murmured, 'Oh my,' and started sobbing. It broke the spell.

Itch headed right, tearing down the one-way street. It had no pavement – it wasn't intended for pedestrians – so he ran in the road. The traffic wasn't heavy, but there was enough to cause a slew of swerving cars and angry horn blasts. Itch kept to the edge until an oncoming motorbike forced him into the middle of the road. With cars now flying past him on both sides, he looked for the left turn that led down towards the towpath.

Please don't let it be Watkins . . .

A break in the traffic, and he jumped the barrier onto the pavement. He landed awkwardly, but quickly regained his footing and picked up his pace. Itch's whole body was hurting – his head and hand were throbbing badly – but he couldn't let that slow him down. In the escape from the Fitzherbert fire and the fight with Flowerdew, his body had taken quite a hit. And with his bone-marrow transplant only six months ago, Itch now felt every bruise, every stitch, every broken bone.

Don't let it be him . . .

He dodged the shopkeepers and householders who were emerging onto the street, a few locking their doors and heading for the canal. Watkins's cottage was obscured, but black smoke was now clearly visible above the houses.

Itch felt his phone ringing, but ignored it as he hit the towpath and turned right. Ahead of him, a procession of running, shouting people merged, with helpers crossing the lock gates. And at the end, by the rocks, Itch saw the orange and red flames of a house on fire.

Oh God, it is him

From somewhere, large buckets had been found and were being used to throw canal water onto the flames. A human chain from the waterway to Watkins's garden had been formed but was ineffective; the flames had really taken hold now. As the heat grew more intense, the makeshift fire-fighters were forced to back off until they were too far away to throw any water at all. The smoke billowed towards the crowd, and when a moored longboat started to smoulder, many people ran for safety. On a crowded, slippery towpath, two men fell into the canal. There were shouts and screams, but they both managed to swim to the other side, where many hands hauled them out of the freezing water.

Itch fought his way through the crowd. At the first of the six cottages he took the path that forked left and led round to the back doors and the sand dunes. A handful of helpers had had the same idea, but they were watching and assessing, not doing.

'Mr Watkins! Mr Watkins!' Itch's voice sounded shrill and shaky as he ran. He tried again as he passed the deserted properties. 'Mr Watkins, are you in there?' he yelled, but the noise of the fire drowned out his words. In the distance he registered the wail of a fire engine. *It won't be here in time*, he thought. *I need to do something now.*

He approached the back door with caution. Most of the flames were at the front of the house, but even so he could feel the heat.

'What are you doing, lad?' called one of the

onlookers. 'Wait for the firefighters – they'll be here soon!'

But Itch wasn't listening. He ran at the back door and kicked hard. A panel splintered and he tried again. This time the whole door fractured, and Itch found that he now had a few companions at his side.

'Is John in there?' shouted one.

'I think so!' yelled another. 'Someone saw him take in a parcel.'

Itch felt his stomach lurch again.

'John!' yelled the first man.

'I'm going in,' shouted Itch. But the flames had reached the kitchen now, and when a spark caught a flapping tarpaulin next door, the little rescue party had to admit defeat. They backed away up the sand dunes.

Itch stood there, coughing, as he watched the approaching fire engines. It was going to take too long. Everything was taking too long. If Mr Watkins was in there, he needed rescuing right now, not in five minutes' time. He ran to meet the first truck. The driver had his window down and was talking furiously to his colleagues.

Itch shouted, 'You need to hurry! There's a man in there. Please come now!'

'We're on our way, son,' came the reply. 'I'm getting as close as I can.'

Itch ran alongside the truck as it parked. He heard voices from inside.

'Another explosion?'

'That's what the report said.'

'The other truck will have to take it.'

'We'll need back-up fast.'

'This looks bad . . .'

Another explosion? thought Itch as he headed back to the dunes. He climbed the highest mound, which was high enough to see into the cottage bedrooms. He wanted to shout again. He wanted to see Mr Watkins's face at the window. The dread and terror in his heart told him that it wasn't going to happen.

His phone vibrated again. Jack. He took the call.

'Where are y—' she began.

'Jack! Watkins's house is on fire! I'm there now! I heard an explosion and . . .' Itch's eyes filled with tears. 'Jack, I think he's inside. I've gotta go . . .'

The fire crew were now running a hose along the towpath. 'Everyone back away,' yelled the leader. 'We need a clear path! Go now!'

The crowd edged back towards the boulders that marked the end of the canal and the start of the beach. Two more firefighters with breathing equipment arrived at the back of the house.

'Please hurry . . .' whispered Itch. 'Please still be alive.'

The whole ground floor was burning fiercely now, thick black smoke gusting into the sky. Itch followed it as rolled inland; it seemed as if half the sky was filled with ash and embers. Suddenly he realized that it wasn't all coming from the canal. There was another column of smoke, high above the cliffs.

He ran to the end of the dunes and climbed onto the boulders. Away from the sheet of smoke coming from Watkins's house, the second plume was clearer. Others had noticed it too, arms raised again.

It could be anything. It could be from anywhere . . . But Itch knew. Deep down inside, he knew that all this was about him. *He* was the target.

And that was *his* house burning.

9

Itch's legs had turned to lead. He was running, but he didn't seem to be moving. He was freezing, but he didn't feel cold. Surrounded by the din of the fire and the shouts of the firefighters, he heard nothing. He staggered over the dunes. He needed to get home, but he wasn't sure he could make it.

He noticed that the second fire engine was reversing: it was leaving. He ran alongside and waved at the driver, who ignored him, continuing his manoeuvre. Itch stood in front of the vehicle and raised his arms in the air. A blast of the horn and angry shouts didn't move him.

Two firefighters, their faces grim, jumped down from the cab. Before they reached him, Itch shouted, 'That other fire is *my house*!' He pointed at the now clearly distinct second column of smoke. 'That's where I live! I need to get there now!'

The two men looked at each other, and nodded. 'It's Nicholas Lofte's kid!' called one of the men, and the driver beckoned them inside. Hands reached out to Itch and hauled him into the fire engine. The crew, all helmeted, nodded and made space for him. As he squeezed in beside them, Itch realized that he was shivering uncontrollably. The nearest firefighter produced a spare jacket and draped it around him.

'What's h-happened?' he stammered through chattering teeth. 'What's happening?'

The siren blasted through the cab as the fire engine gathered speed out of the car park. 'We don't know,' said a man from the front, 'but sit tight – we'll be there soon enough.'

The journey from the canal to Itch's house was a short one; in a speeding fire engine with siren wailing it was even shorter. But to Itch, his mind in torment, it seemed the longest journey ever. He needed to be there, but he dreaded getting there. Every imaginable horror played through his mind.

He took out his phone. Five missed calls – one from Jack, four from Chloe. He rang his sister. She answered on the first ring and Itch heard a muffled voice say, 'Can I be excused, miss?' then rustling.

He waited. After a few seconds he heard her panicked voice. 'Itch? Where—?'

'Listen, Chloe . . .' He suddenly wasn't sure what to say. 'I'm in a fire engine. I think there's a fire at our house . . .' and he ran out of words.

'You mean at Mr Watkins's house? Jack said you were down by the canal . . .'

'I was. It was on fire, and then I noticed smoke and . . . We'll be at our house any minute. Chloe you need to go and find Dr Dart and tell her . . . tell her all this is happening.'

'Itch, was Mr Watkins in the house?'

Either she hasn't understood, or she's more together than I am, he thought. 'Someone said they saw him receive a parcel. So . . . I think so . . .'

'OK,' said Chloe. 'I'll go and find Dr Dart.'

Itch sat back in his seat. At least Chloe was safe.

Chloe ended the call, her heart racing, and started running. She took the stairs three at a time; mid-lesson there was no pupil traffic. She got a 'Slow down, Chloe!' from Craig Harris, the games teacher, but merely said, 'Sorry, sir!' and carried on. She reached Dr Dart's office in seconds, and knocked loudly on the door.

Miss Hopkins, the school secretary, opened it. 'What is it, Chloe? You look upset. Come in.'

Chloe was breathing heavily, but managed, 'Itch says Mr Watkins's house is on fire. He's with the fire brigade going to our house. I think there's a fire there too! I need to go now, Miss Hopkins. I need to go home. Please get Dr Dart!' She looked pleadingly at the shocked secretary.

'Of course. I'll find her straight away,' and she bustled out of the room.

Chloe checked her phone. No messages. She stood up and paced to and fro. Fear, worry and horror in equal measure coursed through her.

Dr Dart's phone rang. Chloe wondered if, under the circumstances, she should answer it. What if it was about the fire? What if it was about Itch? With no school secretary and no principal to pick up, maybe it was her duty?

She walked round the desk. A large brown parcel addressed to Dr Dart was propped up next to the phone. She'd have to move it to pick up the handset.

Which was still ringing.

She reached out for the parcel . . .

There was a knock on the door, and Jack burst in.

'Chloe! What's happening? Text from Itch to find you and go home. Said you'd be here. I told Mr Logan I was feeling ill.'

The phone stopped ringing.

'Miss Hopkins is getting Dr Dart,' said Chloe. 'I spoke to Itch. Oh, Jack, he says there's a fire at our house!'

'At *your* house? As well as at Mr Watkins's? What's happening, Chloe?' Jack peered out of the window towards the town.

'My God. *Look* . . .' Chloe hurried over too, and saw black smoke above the beach. Both girls looked at each other, eyes swimming with tears.

Dr Dart hurried into the office, the secretary close behind. 'Chloe? Jack too?' She sat down. 'Tell me what's happening. Where's Itch? And what's this about a fire?'

The firefighter in the front seat spun round, removing his helmet.

'What did you just say?' he shouted above the siren. His name badge said CALLIER.

Itch was nonplussed. 'Er, I was talking to my sister. She asked me about Mr Watkins's house. Whether he was in or not.'

'You mentioned a parcel . . .'

'I heard someone say they thought he was in because he had just received a parcel.'

Itch sensed the mood in the cab change.

'It's too early for Royal Mail,' called a voice behind him. 'They deliver in the afternoon. Must be a parcel delivery firm.'

He sat up straight. 'I saw one! Brown with, er, yellowy-gold letters!'

'Call UPS!' said Callier. 'Get their delivery schedule now!' The firefighter next to Itch got on his phone.

'You think the parcel might have—' Itch began.

'We don't know. Our job to check,' said Callier.

The fire engine sped round the one-way system that Itch had run down earlier. Lights flashing, it crowned the hill at fifty miles an hour; cars and vans pulled over as they heard the siren. As they flew down from the golf course, Itch, slouching low, could clearly see the black smoke now – clouds of it being blown inland, swooping low and then dispersing in the wind. The firefighters had seen it too. In the cab, no one spoke.

Next to Itch, the firefighter listened to someone from the parcel delivery service and tensed. He repeated the information, his voice strained and loud.

'Three parcels delivered this morning. Recipients as follows . . . Mr John Watkins . . .' He paused, swallowed. 'Itchingham Lofte . . .' Itch gripped the arms of his seat. He felt a reassuring hand on his shoulder, but it was what came next that sent ice through him. 'And Dr Felicity Dart. At the Cornwall Academy.'

Chloe's phone rang. 'It's Itch, Dr Dart!'

'OK, take the call.'

She hit the button. 'Itch! Tell me—'

'Chloe, this is Sergeant Wes Callier from the Cornwall Fire Service. It's very important that you listen to me. Are you with the principal, Dr Felicity Dart?'

'Yes, but—'

'Put her on please. Now.'

Chloe handed her phone to Dr Dart. 'It's the fire service, miss. They want to speak to you.' She saw Jack and Miss Hopkins tense.

The principal took the phone. 'This is Dr Dart – who am I speaking to?'

The fireman had one of those voices that, even through a phone, everyone could hear; Dr Dart held Chloe's phone a few centimetres from her ear. In the pin-drop silence of the office, they could hear the siren in the background.

'Have you had a delivery from a parcel company this morning, Dr Dart? In the last half-hour?' the fireman asked.

'A parcel? I don't know . . .' She looked at her

secretary. Sarah Hopkins nodded and pointed to the large brown jiffy bag propped up against her phone.

'Ah, yes. It's here on my desk. I hadn't noticed. Do you want me to open it?'

'*No!* Touch nothing!' The fireman was shouting now. 'Dr Dart, please leave your office now. Do not touch the parcel. Do I make myself clear? *Do not touch the parcel*. Leave your office and evacuate the school. Hit the fire alarm. Do it now. Stay on the phone. Tell me what you are doing.'

The principal was flat against the window and was staring at her desk. 'Is it a . . . bomb?' Her voice was no more than a whisper.

'LEAVE YOUR OFFICE. EVACUATE THE SCHOOL. NOW. DO IT NOW.'

Before she had even moved, Chloe and Jack ran out of the office. The nearest fire alarm was outside the staff room, and Chloe smashed it. As the sound of the bells filled the school, Jack ran into the staff room. Miss Glenacre was the only occupant. She looked up in surprise.

'Tell Dr Dart that Chloe and I have gone to the fire at her house,' Jack shouted. 'We've gone to find Itch.'

And they ran.

Sergeant Callier was still shouting down the phone when the fire engine tore into Itch's road. The smoke was thicker now, and rolling towards them, checking their progress. Small groups of neighbours and passers-by stood on the pavements, a few spilling onto the road. As they heard and then saw the fire engine, they scattered, clearing a path.

Itch had started shaking again. 'There's a parcel at the CA too, isn't there? Is my sister OK?' he asked. 'What are they doing?'

'Yes, there's a parcel there. And yes, she's OK,' said Callier. 'They're evacuating the school. At least, that's what I've told them to do.' He grabbed the truck's radio to report events at the academy to his HQ.

Itch wanted to call his mum and dad, but realized that he was scared of them not answering. And they hadn't called him . . . But he was here now – it was too late. He could talk to them himself.

Maybe.

As the truck screeched to a halt alongside an empty police car, the firefighters called advice, encouragement and support to each other.

'All right, let's go!'

'Equipment check! Oxygen check!'

'Back-up coming from Launceston; more police here in two minutes!'

'Fire's at the back! Ground floor!'

As they jumped from the cab, Callier grabbed Itch by the shoulders. 'You stay here till I say. Got it? You stay *right here*.'

Itch nodded. He watched as the crew ran straight towards the flames. The fire looked every bit as terrifying as he'd expected . . . with one major qualification: it wasn't his house. The adjoining house, which had until recently been occupied by the MI5 security team, was the one that was burning. For a few seconds, waves of relief flooded through him.

Then, as the firefighters ran in, his father staggered out. It took a fraction of a second for Itch to realize that the figure over his shoulder was his mother.

Itch found the door handle and jumped out of the truck. 'Dad! Dad! Is she OK?'

'It's the smoke,' he shouted. 'She'll be OK, I think. Got to her in time.' He laid her down against the garden wall, and a passing firefighter handed him his oxygen mask. Nicholas placed it over Jude's mouth; her breathing steadied and she opened her eyes.

'Hi, Mum!' said Itch, and she smiled and nodded. She tried to say something but started coughing.

'Hush,' said Nicholas. 'Just breathe deeply.'

'At least you're all out,' said Itch. 'Will our house be OK, Dad?'

Nicholas turned to look at him, his face smudged with soot, his eyes red. 'There's a policeman in there, Itch. He took the blast. We were trying to get to him. We came close—' Then he too began to cough and broke off.

Horrified, Itch looked again at the burning house.

The ambulances arrived, with three police cars behind them. The road was now blocked with emergency vehicles, their flashing blue lights stark against the black smoke. Itch, Nicholas and Jude watched as the fire crews rushed to douse the flames. The vast pipes pumped gallons of water into what Itch still thought of as the Cole house, and within ten minutes the fire was out.

Jack and Chloe arrived, terrified and exhausted . . . then relieved as they saw their family safe. They all sat against the wall of the house opposite. Jack's father, Jon, arrived, briefly embraced his daughter, then sat down next to Nicholas. There was much to say, but once they had been told that the policeman had died, they all fell silent. When his body was brought out, the rescue workers paused; some removed helmets. Led by Nicholas, the Loftes all stood and bowed their heads.

'What happens now, Dad?' said Chloe.

'We'll be told soon enough,' said Nicholas.

A paramedic came over with some blankets; he talked to Jude, but she waved him away. 'I'm fine really. It was just the smoke. I've had some oxygen.' She smiled weakly, then turned to Nicholas. 'This family has seen the inside of too many hospitals. I'm not going unless I'm out cold!'

'Fair enough . . .' He managed a brief smile.

Chloe and Jack's phones were buzzing constantly; they typed replies as quickly as they could. Then Jack stopped and held her hand over her mouth.

'What is it, Jack?' asked Jude. 'Are you OK?'

Jack showed her screen to her aunt.

'Oh my!'

The phone was passed along in silence, but Itch, at the end of the line, refused to look.

'I know what it's going to say,' he said, his voice tight. 'Don't need to see it.'

Sergeant Callier emerged from the house and walked over to where the Loftes were sitting. Before he could speak, Nicholas said, 'What was his name?'

Callier nodded. 'Tony Marston. PC Tony Marston. His family are being told now.' He paused. 'And I'm afraid it's bad news from the canal fire. My colleagues found a body there. They're certain it's John Watkins. I'm sorry – I understand you knew him. Thought you should know.' Chloe and Jack started to cry silently as the fireman put his helmet back on. 'You got somewhere to go?' he asked Nicholas and Jude. 'Your house is fine, but we need to check everything before you're allowed back in.'

Jon Lofte put up his hand. 'They can stay with us. Plenty of room.'

'Of course,' said Callier. 'We'll let you know when you can return.' He walked to where Itch was sitting and crouched down. 'You probably saved some lives today,' he said.

Itch, stony-faced, looked at the firefighter.

Callier continued, 'You told us about the package at Mr Watkins's house. If we hadn't warned the CA, that package would have gone off too. Someone owes you.'

'OK. Thanks,' said Itch numbly. *But Mr Watkins is*

dead, he thought. *And that's my fault. And whatever anyone says, I'll always know it was my fault.*

When the firefighter had gone, Jack and Chloe came and sat with Itch.

'So let's get this clear,' said Jude softly. 'Someone has just sent you a parcel bomb, Itch. Someone has tried to kill you.' Nicholas put his arm around her.

Itch nodded. 'We know who it is, Mum. It's not a *someone*. It's Flowerdew — it *has* to be. But he killed the policeman who was checking the mail, not me.'

'And a package arrived at school,' cried Chloe. 'I saw it! It was addressed to Dr Dart. The academy was evacuated . . .'

'And a fire has killed poor John Watkins,' finished Jude.

'He got a parcel too,' said Itch.

'Are there more?' asked Chloe. 'Have they stopped now?'

Jack tensed, but Itch held her arm. 'There were three packages,' he said. 'They checked with the parcel firm.'

'So we're safe now?'

Itch stared at the charred house and at the sombre police and fire crew, quietly going about their business.

'Doesn't really feel like it,' he said.

10

The six divers stood in front of the two oilmen. Leila, Chika, Aisha, Sade, Dada and Tobi took it in turns to tell their stories. In the heat and stink of the basement, they spoke of how they had come to work for Greencorps, fallen in with Shivvi and become the best diving team in the company's history. And then how they had been disbanded, sacked and their leader punished.

'We know she was a bitch,' said Leila. 'We know she was a criminal – but she looked after us better than you did.' She crouched in between the sweating Revere and Van Den Hauwe. 'Imagine that. A convicted criminal looking after Greencorps employees better than the company itself. You must be so proud.'

A muffled sound came from the Dutchman. It was the best he could manage with his socks in his mouth.

Leila nodded. 'I'll take that to mean you're very sorry and wish to make amends for your sins.'

He nodded.

'And that the two million dollars will be transferred today.'

He nodded again.

'And that you'll resign from Greencorps. Also today.'

They both nodded.

She stood up and faced her colleagues. 'We are done here. Dada, stay and watch them. Let's get to work.' The divers filed out, Chika making sure she kicked both men on her way out.

Revere and Van Den Hauwe stared at their remaining captor; with shaved head and large hoop earrings, she stared straight back at them. It looked as though both men wanted to talk, both straining against their ropes.

'I wouldn't bother,' said Dada. 'Divers know how to tie knots. It'll all be over soon anyway.' She sat on a stool and picked up a magazine. Eventually the men were silent.

Outside, the Lagos traffic was a distant rumble. Inside, the only sounds were the oilmen's heavy breathing and the rustle of Dada's magazine. The temperature was stifling and both men appeared to be asleep. Until a voice said, 'I'd leave, if I was you.' Then they were wide awake.

Dada jumped up, dropping her magazine, a diving knife appearing in her hand. 'Who the hell . . . ? Oh God . . . no.' She shrank back into her chair, reaching for her phone.

'Most unwise, sweetheart,' said Nathaniel

Flowerdew, and pointed a gun at her head. She looked at it, then at the heavily bandaged face, and dropped the knife. Both hands went in the air. 'Better,' he said. 'Which one are you, by the way? Shivvi did tell me about her little gang of divers, but I never took much notice . . .'

Dada swore viciously in Malay and Flowerdew laughed.

'Ah yes, I remember Shivvi telling me to do that too. Oh well – no matter,' and he turned to the trussed and panicking oilmen. 'You can still tell who I am, then . . .' He indicated his bandaged face and arm. 'Despite my . . . clever disguise.' He grabbed Dada's stool and placed it in front of Revere and Van Den Hauwe. 'I am Dr Nathaniel Flowerdew, and you are both about to sell me your company. How's that for a fun day?'

'Thought I'd find you here.'

Itch nodded without looking up. He didn't want company, but Lucy had already sat down; the beach-hut door gave a little as she settled against it. They sat in silence watching the crashing surf. It would be high tide soon, and the larger waves covered them with a fine spray of salt water.

'How long have you been here?' said Lucy.

Itch shrugged.

'You're shivering – let me get—'

'I'm fine,' said Itch, and Lucy watched the sea some more.

'Give me two minutes . . .' She ran back to the

car park. She reappeared with two steaming poly-styrene cups and handed one to Itch. 'Cup of tea,' she said. 'Car-park café's finest.'

'I don't like tea,' Itch said, but took the scalding cup anyway.

'You do now,' said Lucy. 'H_2O plus tea leaves plus heat equals . . . er, feeling better. Something like that, anyway.'

'OK. Thanks.'

They sat in silence again.

'My dad liked it here,' said Lucy. 'He brought me here several times. He loved the surf, the beach – the whole thing.'

'And this is where he gave me the 126,' said Itch. 'Just the one rock. From that satchel he had.' They both smiled at the memory and were silent again. Itch squeaked the lid from the cup and sipped some of the tea. He pulled a face and Lucy laughed. 'It really is disgusting, you know,' he said.

'Yes, I know. But it's hot, so drink it anyway.'

'OK – thanks, Mum . . .'

Lucy put her hand on his arm. 'Listen, Itch, I know you were close to Mr Watkins. I'm so sorry. He was a great teacher.'

'The best,' said Itch. 'And he'd still be alive if I hadn't started this whole thing.'

'You can't think like that, Itch—'

'Yeah, well, I *do* think like that,' he snapped. 'I do think like that because it happens to be true. If I hadn't taken the 126 to school, none of this would have happened.'

'Yes, that's true,' said Lucy. 'But why were you into this element-hunting in the first place?'

'Excuse me?'

'Why are you an element hunter? Who started it?'

'Er, my dad gave me a book—'

'So it's your dad's fault, then. Who got him into it?'

'My grandad said—'

'So blame him, then.'

'That's ridiculous.'

'Maybe,' said Lucy. 'But Mr Watkins died because someone sent him a parcel bomb—'

'I think we all know who did it.'

'OK . . . Watkins died because Flowerdew sent him a parcel bomb. And you. And the CA. But he did it. It's his fault and no one else's.'

'Maybe,' said Itch. 'Maybe.' He sipped and winced again. 'Don't suppose I'll have a teacher like him again. He always listened, Lucy. He was always . . . there. Always the same. Stood up for us against Flowerdew. And Shivvi. That beating he took from her is the reason he—'

'Stop,' said Lucy. 'You're doing it again.'

Itch's phone rang. He glanced at the screen and answered it. 'OK, see you in five.' He turned to Lucy. 'That was Mum. The police want to talk to me. And I have to go to the police station as the press are outside Jack's place. My dad's on his way.'

★   ★   ★

'Have you caught him?' said Itch as two police officers walked into the interview room. 'Have you caught Flowerdew?' He and his father had been sitting at a plain wooden table, but he had jumped up as soon as the door opened.

'I'm DCI Abbott – Jane Abbott.' A woman with shoulder-length grey-flecked hair smiled briefly at Itch. 'And this is DCI Underwood . . .' An over-weight man with glasses and a beard nodded. Itch wanted to say that he didn't look like a policeman but thought better of it. They all shook hands.

'You must be Nicholas Lofte?' said Abbott.

Nicholas nodded.

'Now, then . . .' She turned to Itch. 'Have we caught who?'

Itch looked at his father, then back at the policewoman. 'Well, Flowerdew obviously. The man who sent the parcels. The man who killed my teacher . . . the man who tried to kill me.'

'And sent the bomb to the Cornwall Academy?' asked Abbott.

'Yes!' said Itch, sounding exasperated. 'Of course!'

'Well, I think we're getting just a little bit ahead of ourselves, aren't we?' Abbott gave a tight smile, and Itch sensed his father bridle.

'My son is fifteen, not five. Someone has tried to kill him today, my neighbour's house got blown up instead, and one of your colleagues was killed taking the blast. So try keeping that patronizing tone from your voice, if you don't mind.' Nicholas sat back and glared at the woman across the table.

Her eyes narrowed. 'OK, I'll try again . . .' She checked some papers in front of her. 'PC Marston died opening a package he had taken to your neighbour's house to check. He had a wife and baby.' She stopped and looked up at Itch and Nicholas. Itch felt something was wrong. *That sounded like she's thinking it was our fault.*

'I'm sorry for your loss,' said Nicholas quietly.

DCI Abbott nodded and continued. 'His colleague was burned in the fire and has gone to hospital.' Again the look up, and Itch fidgeted in his seat. 'According to the fire team, the rear of the next-door house is smoke-damaged and will need major work. Your house is fine, and you can return as soon as the investigations are complete.'

Itch nodded. 'Would you like to know about Flowerdew now?' he said. 'You must—'

Abbott held up a hand and produced another sheet of paper. 'Wait, please. The fire team have told us that when they returned to their station, they went through the usual checks and discovered something rather odd.' She looked at Itch now. 'Their protective gear – their helmets, uniforms and so on – all tested positive for radiation. It wasn't strong, but it was there. They were radioactive. Do you know why that might be?'

'Was . . . the bomb radioactive?' said Nicholas, astonished.

'No, we don't think so. Just the usual sort of explosives. The radiation came from somewhere else . . .'

Itch was aware that not only were both police officers staring at him; his father was too.

'We know something of your, er, adventures, Itch,' said Abbott. 'And that you collect the Periodic Table. You've got quite a collection, I'm told. Might you have had something that could have been released in the fire?'

Itch looked at the floor. This was a familiar feeling. *Of course . . . Of course, it was me.*

'But this was next door to us—' began Nicholas.

'Yes,' said Itch, slightly too loudly. 'Yes, there was some thorium next door.'

'There was some *what*?' This was the first time Underwood had spoken. He sat down next to DCI Abbott.

'Itch?' said Nicholas.

Itch took a deep breath. 'Thorium, named after the god of war. Atomic number 90, melting point 1750 degrees C. It's where most of the Earth's heat comes from. It's silvery—'

'Is it radioactive?' said Abbott flatly.

'Yes,' said Itch. 'It's weak, but yes.'

'And this was part of your . . . collection?' asked Underwood.

'Yes — it's not illegal, is it?'

Abbott shrugged. 'We'll check. But in general, last time I checked, boys aren't allowed to have radioactive material.' That thin smile again.

'What — you mean, like bananas?'

'Itch, don't do this,' said his father softly. 'Not now.

'Bananas are radioactive,' said Itch, ignoring his father. 'It's the potassium, you see. Your bones are radioactive. Not illegal at all. Radiation is everywhere. If your house is made of granite, it'll release some radon gas. That's radioactive.'

'OK, enough of the science lesson,' said Abbott. 'I take your point. Where do you buy thorium, then?'

Itch looked at his father. 'We've just come back from South Africa. We visited a thorium mine and I brought some back.'

'Is that even allowed?' said Underwood, busy looking up thorium on his phone.

'How much did you bring back? Did you tell customs?' Abbott was looking at Nicholas.

'I . . . I didn't know he had it. I'm sorry,' he said.

'It's only a small amount. It was stored safely. Or I thought it was. But the parcel explosion must have—'

Abbott leaned in towards Itch. 'Do you have anything else that we should know about?'

Before he could answer, Nicholas leaned in too, their faces close. 'Excuse me . . . this is all wrong. We can come to the thorium and whatever else Itch has in his collection later. But someone tried to kill my son. Have you forgotten again? His teacher was killed, and a bomb was sent to his school. That's what you should be talking about.' He sat back and glowered.

'Ah yes, the package at the school.' Abbott

produced yet another sheet of closely typed paper. 'Itch, can you explain why you left your lessons – left your school, indeed – moments before the bomb was delivered by the parcel company?'

There was silence in the interview room. Itch looked pale and flushed at the same time.

'Your teacher said that you felt unwell and asked to be excused. But seconds later you were seen running from the school. Just as the bomb was delivered. Where were you going in such a hurry?'

'Itch?' said Nicholas, his brow furrowed. 'What's going on?'

'I can explain!' said Itch, flushed and rattled. 'It's not what you're thinking! I was going to the library in town . . .'

Underwood frowned. 'You ran out of school to go to the library? Really? What was the hurry?'

Itch looked from face to disbelieving face. 'There was this book that Mr Watkins had got out and I was trying find it. He was doing some research into mining accidents or something, and he wouldn't tell us what it was.'

'I didn't know you'd joined the library,' said his father.

'I just did. Last night.' Itch's head was spinning. He had hoped that the police might be close to finding Flowerdew. Now he was being interrogated as though he was the bomber. 'I think I need some help,' he said.

'You'd like a lawyer?' said Abbott, her eyes wide.

Itch shook his head and reached for his bag. Finding a small card, he handed it to his father.

'I think we should call Colonel Fairnie.'

It was dark when Itch and his father left the police station. The wind blew hard off the sea and the freezing rain stung their faces, but neither of them hurried to the car. The cold was a refreshing blast after the stale heat of the interview room, and they stood on the steps, inhaling deeply. Itch knew from Jack's texts that the journalists were still camped outside her house.

'How many does she think are there?' said Nicholas.

'She says about eight. And a TV crew. And a policeman . . .'

Nicholas sighed. 'Maybe we could just go back to ours anyway,' he said.

'No point. Chloe says they're there too.'

'OK. Uncle Jon's, then.'

'I'm sorry, Dad. I should have told you about the thorium.'

'Yes, you should, but in the greater scheme of things, on a day when someone's tried to kill you and Dr Dart and actually succeeded in killing John Watkins, it hardly matters.'

They were pulling out of the police station car park when Itch's phone rang. 'Hello, Colonel Fairnie,' he said. 'I'm putting you on speaker. I'm in the car with Dad.' Itch put his phone on the dashboard.

'Good evening to you both. Nice to hear your voice, Itch. I'm shocked by what's happened today – really shocked. I'm so sorry about Mr Watkins. He was a good man.'

There was a long silence . . . Itch couldn't think what to say.

'Yeah, well . . .'

'Colonel Fairnie, it's Nicholas Lofte here. What did you say to the police?'

'What I had to. Explained what, and more specifically who, we are up against.'

'You mean Flowerdew,' said Nicholas.

'Of course. We need to reconsider the threat level again, I'm afraid; he's clearly still active, and has resources at his disposal. You heard about the fourth package?'

Itch and Nicholas looked at each other, horrified.

'No . . . Who . . . ?' said Itch, hardly daring to hear the answer.

'Bill Kent at ISIS. The guy who helped show you round the target station – the guy Flowerdew no doubt blames for helping you to destroy the 126. He'll be OK. He realized there was something wrong and turned his back on it. It went off, but he only suffered minor burns to his neck. I told your DCI Abbott enough for her to be impressed with you, Itch, instead of suspicious. Given the targets of the bombs, there can be little doubt about the perpetrator.'

'Thank you,' said Itch and his father together as they drove past their house.

Then Nicholas added, 'Any advice on dealing with a media scrum?'

'Ah. I'd restrict your comments to expressions of sadness about John Watkins. Say nothing of the bombs addressed to Itch and Dr Dart. And get Itch indoors quickly.'

'Pretty much what I was thinking,' said Nicholas as he turned into his brother's road. The gathering of reporters was larger than Jack had reported and they had all spotted the approaching car; two bright TV lights swung in their direction.

'Oh, and Itch,' said Fairnie, 'keep your head down and get inside. Let's do this one day at a time. If I were you, I wouldn't say anything at all.'

As Nicholas parked, the car was surrounded, cameras flashing.

Itch nodded. 'That's easy. I never want to say anything to anybody anyway.'

Fairnie laughed. 'Well, good luck. Call me any-time. I'll always speak if I can.'

Itch ended the call as his father killed the engine.

'Ready, Itch?' he said.

'No.'

They sat for a second as the car was circled, questions shouted through the steamed-up glass.

'How is your son, Mr Lofte?'

'Were they trying to kill him?'

'How you feeling, Itch?'

Itch looked at his father. 'Can't we go somewhere else? This sucks.'

For a moment it looked as though Nicholas was

considering it. Then he shook his head. 'We'd have to get your mum and Chloe out of there first. And then they'll follow us. So let's just get this done.' The front door of the house opened slightly and he saw his brother Jon peering out. 'Come on, Itch. Let's go.'

With the assistance of a policewoman who cleared a path for them, Itch sprinted for the door. He heard questions coming from all around but ignored them. As he approached the house, the door swung open and he ran in. A smiling Chloe was waiting with Uncle Jon.

'Come in, come in!' he cried, ushering them inside. 'Your mum's in the kitchen.'

'Itch, come and see,' said Jack from the front room.

He walked in to see Jack and her mother watching TV. It took a moment for him to realize that the twenty-four-hour news channel was showing pictures of Jack's house; and another to realize that his dad was fielding questions. Itch heard his voice outside the door, then the satellite-delayed version on screen a few seconds later.

'. . . of course it's been a terrible day . . . We just want to be left alone now . . . We are all very upset about what happened to John Watkins . . . My son's fine really, just shaken . . . Now, if you'll excuse me . . .' They watched as Nicholas, looking tired and tense, turned and pushed his way through the pack. Moments later he was in the hall. The TV picture had switched to a reporter, who was standing next to their car.

'This is weird,' said Chloe as her father appeared in the room, her mother and uncle close behind.

'Can someone turn that down?' said Jon, pointing at the television. 'Tell us what happened, Itch. What did the police say?'

Itch slumped onto a large sofa next to Jack and was about to answer when she nudged him. 'Itch, look.' She was pointing at the TV. They both sat bolt upright. The Greencorps company logo had appeared, along with pictures of its co-chairmen.

'Turn it up, turn it up!' said Itch, and Chloe found the remote. The room fell silent.

The report had cut to footage of a badly lit, grimy basement and what looked like bloodstains in the dirt. The caption across the bottom of the screen said: *Oil executives found 'executed' in Nigeria.*

Chloe came and sat by Jack and Itch.

'*Van Den Hauwe and Revere had been missing since the end of last year,*' said the reporter, '*and it was believed negotiations for their release were well advanced. But both men were found with a single gunshot wound to the head. Police are saying they believe the execution was the work of a local gang and have issued photos of the women they want to question.*'

'Women?' said Jude.

'Women . . .' whispered Jack as a photo of six women, all in diving gear, appeared on the screen.

Itch felt his flesh creep. 'Shivvi's diving gang . . . weren't they all women?' he said. Jack nodded.

Suddenly Itch's phone rang. 'It's Lucy,' he said. 'Come on.'

The three cousins jumped up and found the kitchen empty.

'Itch, it's Lucy. Were you watching the news? When you weren't on it, I mean?'

'Yes, we're all at Jack's.'

'Itch, that picture . . . they must be Shivvi's divers! When I broke into her house, she got a Skype call from someone called Leila. After she left, her screen-saver came up. Itch, it was that photo! The version on the news was cropped, but standing behind them was Shivvi Tan Fook.'

11

Itch had never been to a funeral before. When his grandfather died, he had been declared too young to attend, so John Watkins's was to be his first. He had woken even earlier than usual, when the house was still dark and cold. As he thought about the day ahead, the leaden feeling in his stomach returned as it had every day since the bombs. Maybe he would always feel like this. Maybe it would go after the funeral. He didn't know. He wondered who would be going – did Mr Watkins have any family? He didn't think so. He wondered who would speak – presumably Dr Dart would say something. He wondered if he would cry – he didn't want to but he couldn't be sure. Was it OK to cry at funerals anyway? Would it look bad if he *didn't* cry? He didn't know that either.

There was a knock on his door and Chloe peered in. 'You awake?' she whispered.

'Yup. As ever.' He switched on his bedside light.

Chloe was already in her school uniform. 'That what we wear?' he asked.

Chloe nodded. Her eyes were red, as if she'd been crying. 'I've been reading the plans on the CA website,' she said. 'And school's opening again.' She found the relevant pages on Itch's laptop. 'Tomorrow. They were obviously waiting for the funeral. Sounds like the whole school is going.'

Itch stared at the ceiling. 'Won't fit. It might be the biggest church in town, but it won't take 1,200 pupils. Maybe just those he taught will go.'

'Well, I'm going,' said Chloe quietly, 'even if he never taught me.'

'I'm sure that'll be fine.'

'Have you seen this page?' She wiped her eyes on her sleeve and held the computer up to Itch. 'It's for messages about Mr Watkins. *So sorry you've gone, we'll always remember you. Thanks, Mr Watkins, you were the best.* Sam Jennings left that. *We'll miss your stories – RIP.* That's from Natalie.' She looked at her brother. 'Should we leave one?'

He shrugged. 'Not bothered.'

'Yes, you are.'

'Not going to make a difference to anyone, is it? So what's the point?'

'Just a way of leaving a message, that's all. Sure there's nothing you want to say?'

'To him, yes. To a website? What's the point?'

Chloe was still holding out the laptop.

'OK, OK,' he said irritably, and sat up to read the

comments. 'They're all so lame, Chloe. It's like their pet hamster died or something.'

'No one knows what to say, Itch, that's all.'

He sighed. 'I'm not going to write anything.' His voice was thin and he swallowed hard. He closed the laptop. 'But if I did, it would be something like: *You were the . . .*' He cleared his throat. '*You were the greatest. You were funny, you were kind. You had the worst dress sense ever, even worse than mine. You would always listen. You made geography interesting. When my dad disappeared, you didn't. When Mum didn't smile very much, or talk to me much, you did both.*'

'Itch, don't . . .' said Chloe quietly.

'*And when Darcy Campbell and James Potts were in my face and being foul, you spotted it and stopped it. When Flowerdew needed standing up to, it was you who had the guts to do it. And that's what got you killed and I'm sorry . . .*' Itch's voice cracked, and the tears rolled down his cheeks. 'I'd say something like that, Chloe. But I'd like to say it to him. Not leave a dumb message on a dumb website.'

'Shall we just leave it, then?' she said.

Itch nodded. 'I'll get dressed.'

Itch sat on the hard wooden pew staring at the floor. It was easier that way. He didn't want to see anyone, talk to anyone, even acknowledge anyone. He thought if he kept still enough, maybe no one would notice that he was there. He could hear the sounds of the church filling up: shuffling feet, creaking pews and whispered, respectful conversations; he just didn't feel the need to watch.

The Loftes had arrived early; they sat together – his mother and father at one end of the pew, Jack's parents at the other. Lucy arrived soon afterwards and joined Jack and Chloe and Itch. They had all tried to say a few words to him, but he just nodded, said nothing and counted the hymn books. The heaviness in his gut was almost overpowering now; a physical pressure that was making him feel sick. He dreaded the service starting but at the same time couldn't wait for it to be over.

He heard Jack say, 'Everyone seems very nervous.'

'There's loads of police outside now,' said Lucy. 'Everyone's walked past them. It's set everyone on edge. And we haven't been together since the bombs, so . . . hell, I'm nervous too.'

'Fairnie's here!' said Jack, and now Itch *did* look up. She pointed back at the door, and he craned his neck to see the MI5 man standing by the ornate, carved oak entrance, dressed in a black coat with a black tie. He nodded at Itch and Jack.

'Are any of the rest of the team here?' whispered Jack.

Itch scanned the congregation. The front pews were full of staff from the CA. It looked like everyone was here. By the curtained-off side entrance, Jim Littlewood sat talking with Gordon Carter; Sunil Masoor and Jimmy Logan, the maths teachers, were both deep in conversation with Craig Harris, who for once was not wearing his Scotland tracksuit; and a tense-looking Dr Dart sat reading the order of service and checking through her notes.

Itch could see most of his class, some sitting together, others with their parents. In front of him, Sam Jennings, handkerchief in hand, sat with her eyes shut. Natalie Hussain had her head on Debbie Price's shoulder. Tom Westgate, arriving late, nodded at Itch and squeezed into a pew in front, Ian Steele shuffling everyone along to make room for him. The two policemen who had interviewed Itch sat stony-faced in one of the back pews. He looked away before they noticed him.

'Can't see any of them, Jack,' said Itch. 'Reckon Fairnie's the only one.' He saw a movement at the back of the church: the arrival of the coffin. He spun back round, eyes fixed on the floor, just as the organist began playing and everyone stood.

But suddenly Itch didn't want to stand. It was as if, by standing, he was accepting everything that had happened; by staying seated he was keeping Watkins alive for a few more minutes. He squeezed his eyes shut and clenched his fists, choosing to concentrate on the ringing in his ears, not the funeral march playing in the church.

'Itch! Stand up!' He heard Chloe's rebuke and felt her tugging his arm. 'Itch, people are looking!' He opened his eyes and turned to Chloe; tears were running down her face. 'Please?' she mouthed.

He nodded. There was no point in adding to his sister's grief and he slowly unfolded himself; he felt Jack's hand helping him up. By the time he was standing, the four pall-bearers had reached the front of the church and were lowering John Watkins's coffin onto a stand. The white-robed priest stood silently at the front holding a large green book. She waited for the men to make the final adjustments. The organ finished playing.

'Please sit down,' she said, her words echoing around the church and bouncing off the high ceiling.

Everyone took their seats again and Itch picked up his order of service. *The Funeral of John Gordon Watkins*, it said, with a black-and-white photo on the front. It showed Mr Watkins smiling broadly, dressed in a large waterproof, on top of a mountain somewhere. A field trip presumably, thought Itch. He had one hand raised; it looked as if he was about to launch into one of his famous stories. Which they'd never hear again.

Before he knew it they were standing again, and the organ was playing the introduction to the first hymn. He heard the Brigadier start singing the words a fraction early, and glanced up. Other members of staff were smiling and nudging him, but Itch's attention was taken by movement behind the curtain. The side entrance to the church was a smaller door with a porch, and a thick red curtain that could be pulled across it. Itch and his family had used this entrance earlier for a more discreet arrival, away from most of the journalists who had gathered to cover the funeral. The door had been shut and the curtain drawn soon after the Loftes had arrived, but now Itch was sure that someone else was there.

As the hymn continued, he watched the curtain. For most of a verse it didn't move, and he began to think he had been seeing things. But then the heavy fabric twitched again, and Itch leaned forward. He saw four fingers holding it open, presumably to give someone a view of the funeral, and held his breath.

That can't be right . . .

The hand twisted slightly, and now Itch was sure. The hand was bandaged.

The hymn continued, but Itch wasn't singing. He wasn't listening. He didn't hear anything apart from the ringing in his ears which had started up again. He looked around him. No one else had noticed the movement behind the curtain, and he hesitated before alerting the others. He looked again, but the hand had disappeared, the velvet curtain hanging straight.

He felt a tug on his sleeve and looked round. The hymn had finished and he was the only one still standing. 'Sit down!' said Chloe, and he quickly took his seat again as the priest continued with the service.

'What's up?' asked Jack quietly.

'There's someone behind that curtain . . .' Itch pointed his order of service towards the side door.

'So?'

So, thought Itch. Maybe that was right. Why shouldn't there be someone there? A churchwarden maybe, or some other official. Maybe a reporter had followed them in. But a reporter with a bandaged hand?

The curtain was moving again, and this time he nudged Jack. The hand held the curtain away from the wall, and this time they both gasped. A face had appeared between the stone wall and the velvet. A face swathed in bandages.

Lucy and Chloe followed Itch and Jack's gaze. The four of them were sitting close enough to each other to feel that they had all tensed.

'It can't be him!' whispered Jack. 'Not here!'

'He'd have his face bandaged, though, wouldn't he?' said Lucy.

'Itch?' Chloe sounded scared. 'You don't think it's him, do you?'

I don't know . . . What do *I think?* wondered Itch. It would be madness for Flowerdew to turn up at the funeral of the man he had hated and then murdered. But then, he is mad, isn't he? Watching the final humiliation would be exactly what he would enjoy.

Itch glanced round and caught Fairnie's eye. The colonel noticed for the first time that while the whole congregation were watching the priest, Itch, Jack, Chloe and Lucy were looking the other way, over at the side entrance. Itch saw the colonel frown.

Itch decided that he wanted a closer look. He couldn't see the man's head clearly, but the image of Flowerdew's burned face was still vivid. He remembered how Flowerdew had hinted that he was

130

going to kill Jack; how he had once bashed Itch's head against a wall and tried to expose him to a lethal dose of radiation.

He needed to move to another pew. The easiest route was past Jack, Lucy and his aunt and uncle at the end. He started to edge his way along the pew.

'Itch, come back!' said Chloe in a tense whisper.

'Itch, no. Let Fairnie deal with it!' hissed Jack.

'I'm not going to do anything!' he snapped, then, 'Excuse me,' as he edged past his Uncle Jon. Crouching, he made his way to the pew nearest the side entrance. There was clearly no room for him there, so he squatted in the side aisle.

Dr Dart, midway through her eulogy, paused, distracted, as she watched Itch on the move. She waited for him to stop as she would in a school lesson, and was just about to resume when she noticed that the MI5 man was moving too. Fairnie had eased away from the main entrance and was walking across the back of the church to see what Itch was doing. The congregation picked up on the principal's unease and, following her gaze, started murmuring. There were enough CA pupils and staff present to know that Fairnie didn't act like this without reason. They sensed the danger.

Nicholas leaned over to Chloe. 'What's Itch doing? What's happening?'

'There's someone behind that curtain,' she said. 'He's got a bandaged face and hand. I'm sure Itch thinks it might be Flowerdew.'

'Here?' said Nicholas, incredulous. 'But that's ridiculous.'

If Itch had turned round, he would have seen his father stand up, closely followed by DCIs Abbott and Underwood. Over his other shoulder, he'd have seen Fairnie closing on him. But he was staring straight ahead. He had caught the smell of antiseptic surgical cream and he recognized it instantly. It was the smell of Flowerdew's flat; it was the smell of Flowerdew's burns.

It really *was* him.

Itch straightened up. His body awash with adrenalin, grief and rage, he ran for the curtain.

12

'Itch, step away!' yelled Fairnie, now sprinting down the aisle. As he ran past them, rows of the congregation stood up to see what was happening.

Nicholas was edging past his family, eyes focused on his son. Chloe had grabbed hold of Jack, and Lucy was following Nicholas.

Itch was metres from the velvet curtain. He heard nothing of the increasing commotion around him; only the whooshing, pulsing rush of blood in his head. The smell of the surgical cream was stronger now, and as he skidded to a halt in front of the porch, he grabbed the folds of heavy red fabric.

As he did so, Fairnie rugby-tackled him. Itch went sprawling onto the stone floor, but his hand still held onto the curtain. The ancient metal rail above the porch gave way and the curtain collapsed to the ground. Around them, parents, pupils and teachers got to their feet; some shouted, a few screamed. Itch sat up and stared into the porch. A distressed young woman in a smart suit stood, arms held wide, shielding a man with bandaged face and arms. Her eyes were wide with shock.

'What?' she wailed as she looked out at the faces all turned to her. 'What have we done? What are you looking at?'

Itch stared at them, uncomprehending. He looked at Fairnie, who still had his hand placed firmly on his shoulder.

'Stay where you are,' Jim Fairnie said.

Police were streaming into the church now; DCI Abbott was leading them towards the porch. She ran up to Itch, eyes blazing with anger. 'What the hell do you—?'

'He thought,' said Fairnie sharply, 'that he was going to be attacked. He thought Nathaniel Flowerdew was behind the curtain.'

'Did he now? And who might you be?' Abbott's eyes flicked from him to Itch and back again.

'Colonel Jim Fairnie, MI5. We spoke on the phone.'

Abbott's eyes narrowed. 'So we did. You told me what a good boy Itch was, really. Well, that isn't your bad ex-science teacher, as I'm sure you've realized. That's the officer who was injured opening your post. The one who didn't die. His name is Martin Graham. That's his wife, Grace.'

Itch was horrified. He watched as police officers comforted their colleague and his distressed wife. Many of them threw reproachful glances at Itch, still sitting on the church floor.

'I'm so sorry—' he began, but the DCI interrupted.

134

'PC Graham wanted to come today, but thought it better if no one saw him. He didn't want to upset anyone, you see, so he chose to sit behind the curtain and watch the service from there.'

'I thought that—'

'It doesn't really matter what you thought, does it?'

'I think you should calm down, DCI Abbott,' said Fairnie. 'This was an unfortunate mistake. I'm sure Itch will want to apologize and then we can move on.'

'Colonel Fairnie,' said Abbott, barely controlling her fury, 'I'll calm down when I want to. We'll "move on" when it is appropriate to do so. I don't take orders from you. And either you take this boy out of the church or I will.'

Nicholas, Jude, Jack, Chloe and Lucy had all arrived now.

'I thought it was Flowerdew. I'm sorry,' Itch said quietly.

Around them, people were resuming their seats, and PC Graham and his wife were being led out through the now curtain-less porch.

'Come on, Itch,' said his father. 'We'd better go home.'

'Dad, that's not fair,' said Chloe.

'It's all right,' said Itch. 'I'll go.'

'We'll come too,' offered Lucy.

'No. Please – everyone stay,' he said. 'It's Mr Watkins's funeral.' He scrambled to his feet. 'Tell me what happens.'

★   ★   ★

ELDRAKE59 I'm looking for Roshanna Wing.

RWING You've found her. Who's this?

ELDRAKE59 Your saviour.

RWING Didn't know I needed one.

ELDRAKE59 You do now.

RWING Do I know you?

ELDRAKE59 You owe me.

RWING Unlikely.

ELDRAKE59 Well, let me try this. You kidnapped me. Took me from the British police, handed me back to Greencorps.

RWING Flowerdew?

ELDRAKE59 Are you still as focused? I was impressed. You seemed to know what you were doing.

RWING What happened to Revere and Van Den Hauwe?

ELDRAKE59 Good question, but more of a theological issue now.

RWING Where are you?

ELDRAKE59 Nearer than you think. I have a job for you. If you want it, I'll be in touch.

RWING Sure. Possibly. What sort of job?

ELDRAKE59 has logged off.

The first few days after the funeral were amongst the grimmest Itch could remember. Even worse, he concluded, than his dismal first days at the CA after the family moved from London. Then he had at least been allowed to stand alone and ignored in the corner of the playing field. He would have settled for that loneliness now. The weight of grief in his stomach had been replaced by something else: the fear of any conversation with anyone.

'Even the teachers hate me,' he said as he trudged out into the evening gloom. Jack and Chloe exchanged glances. 'The Brigadier made a point of telling me how disappointed he was with me. Even Mr Hampton called me "spectacularly stupid".'

Chloe hooked her arm through his as they turned out of the drive. 'It'll die down, Itch,' she said. 'They'll get bored with it.'

'Chloe's right,' said Jack.

'She isn't, actually,' snapped Itch. 'She's totally wrong. This is the way it's going to be. It's a new game for everyone – see how many comments involving curtains and hiding everyone can come up with. Today's total is seventeen – up from fifteen yesterday and twelve the day before.'

An unidentifiable anoraked cyclist overtook them, shouted, 'Beware the boogie-man!' and disappeared down the road, his laughter billowing steam into the freezing air.

'New total: eighteen, then,' said Itch. 'See what I mean, Chloe?' His sister nodded and they walked on in silence.

The girls fell behind. 'He's bad,' whispered Jack.

Chloe nodded. 'I know. He doesn't really talk at home at all any more,' she said. 'Mum and Dad are just hoping he'll come round.'

At the golf course, Jack started to say goodbye.

'Can we come back to your house?' asked Itch.

'Sure,' she said, surprised. 'Everything OK?'

He shrugged. 'Sort of. Mum and Dad just argue

a lot, that's all. The last one was about security again. Mum has refused to have MI5 back, so we just have police outside like before.'

'OK. Yeah, come on back,' she said. 'Oh – Lucy gave me this for you. She said you'd know what it was.' She produced a small parcel the size of a paperback.

'Oh right, yeah . . .' He shoved it deep into his bag.

'Itch?' said Chloe.

'None of your business.'

'Why is Lucy giving you parcels?' Chloe persisted.

'If you must know,' said Itch, 'it's because I can't really get post at home any more. For obvious reasons. Everything has to go to a special check-point where everything is opened and analysed. This is just easier.'

Jack's mother, Zoe, welcomed them into her kitchen. She was as tall as her daughter, and had the same high cheekbones. She smiled as she put the kettle on, pushing her glasses up to sit on top of her brown shoulder-length hair. As if acting on some silent code, Jack and Chloe left the room, leaving Itch alone with his aunt.

'I imagine you're feeling a bit rubbish,' she said, putting a plate of biscuits in front of him.

'S'pose.'

She rattled around with some washing-up as she spoke. 'You must have been very upset about what happened at the church.'

Itch really didn't want to be having this conversation, so he ate the biscuits instead. He nodded occasionally while she made a pot of tea.

'I think, Itch, that you must feel as though you haven't said goodbye properly to Mr Watkins. Everyone has had the funeral, apart from you. And maybe you needed to be there more than anyone.'

And suddenly there were tears in Itch's eyes. *Yes, that's exactly how it is, and it's taken my aunt to explain it to me.* He needed to get out.

He cleared his throat. 'Thanks for the biscuits, Aunt Zoe. Could you tell Chloe I'll see her at home?' He grabbed his bag and ran for the door.

'Itch, I hope I didn't—'

He spun round, his hand on the door latch. 'No, you didn't. You were dead right,' and he was gone.

He was in no hurry to get home and was wondering about going via the beach, when he noticed a familiar figure leaning against his garden wall. The streetlight silhouetted Lucy perfectly, her hair sticking out from under her enormous parka.

'Hey, Lucy,' he called. 'What are you doing here?'

'Give you two guesses,' came the voice from under the hood.

'Thanks for the parcel,' said Itch.

'That's what I've come about . . .'

'Did you get into trouble?'

'Can we go inside? I've been waiting for you.'

'We were at Jack's. You should have come down,' said Itch.

'I know, but I wanted to talk to you, not them.' Lucy smiled, realizing that might have sounded a bit weird.

'Sure, let's go in,' said Itch, feeling awkward. 'My parents are in, I think. It might be a little, er, tense.'

There was no sign of his father, but Itch could hear his mother working in her study. A local solicitor, she often did a lot of her research at home.

'Kitchen OK?' he said.

'Sure,' said Lucy, unzipping her coat. 'You could make me a tea if you like.'

'Oh, right,' said Itch, and made for the kettle just as Jude appeared in the doorway.

'Lovely to see you, Lucy.' She smiled. 'I hope Itch is being a good host. Tea for me too, please, while you're at it.' Itch made another trip to the taps as his mother settled in at the table. 'Do you two see each other at school much? Year Elevens don't often hang out with Year Tens, I imagine.'

Lucy shrugged. 'Yeah, I see Itch around. And at the science club Mr Hampton runs.'

'Ah yes,' said Jude. 'You going on that Spanish trip? I think Itch here is waiting to see who else is going.'

'Yes, my mum says it's OK. Maybe we could all go, Itch? Would Jack and Chloe be up for it?'

'Where *is* Chloe?' said Jude before Itch could answer.

'She's at Jack's,' Itch told her. 'Me and Lucy were . . .'

'. . . talking homework,' finished Lucy. 'Some of

the stuff Itch and Jack are getting set I did last year. Itch has got this English essay, and I was going to see if I could . . .'

'. . . write it for him?' suggested Jude.

'No, course not,' said Lucy. There was an awkward silence. 'He missed some of the lessons, you see, and I thought I could help.'

Jude smiled her tired smile again. 'Of course, I'm sorry. I wasn't suggesting . . . Why don't you guys go upstairs? I'll call you for food.'

Itch and Lucy balanced tea and school bags all the way up to his room.

'Hang on a sec,' he said, darting through his door.

'Can't be worse than mine,' Lucy called through the door as he grabbed discarded clothes and shoved them in a drawer. He opened the window.

Itch felt himself redden and hated himself for it. 'OK, come in. Er, the chair should be fine for you. I'll sit here.' Itch sat on the bed, flustered.

'Itch, listen,' said Lucy. 'I didn't mean to make things tricky. I just wanted to talk.' She slid down the wall and sat on the floor, sipping her tea. 'I'm fine here . . .' she said.

Itch moved off the bed and sat on the floor too, facing her. 'I haven't got an English essay, have I?'

'How would I know?' laughed Lucy. 'I just didn't want to talk in front of your mum. It's the package, Itch. I worked out what you're doing. And I don't think you should, that's all.'

Itch stared at her. His classmates had never

141

known or understood anything about him. Everybody had either thought him stupid and crazy, or – more usually – they just ignored him. He wasn't used to having another friendly scientific mind around, but now, with Lucy, all that had changed. Itch knew he was blushing again, and looked away.

Above Lucy's head was his Periodic Table; he ran his eyes along the familiar rows and up and down the columns. He took in the symbols, numbers and images, and counted again the marks that showed he had added another element to his collection. He felt himself grow calmer. He had done this before when his thoughts were in turmoil; he found comfort in the order and timelessness of the universe's building blocks.

'Open the parcel, Itch.' Lucy had sat quietly, sensing what Itch was doing. When he didn't move, she stood up and took a pen from her bag. Standing in front of the poster, she ran her finger down the left-hand column.

'Hydrogen, lithium, sodium, potassium, rubidium. Five down.' She looked at Itch. 'Then three across: rubidium, strontium and yttrium. Can I cross it off, then?'

Itch nodded. She took her pen and put a line through the Y39 box.

'Yttrium,' she said, reading from the chart. 'Symbol Y, atomic number 39, atomic weight 88.90585—'

'Boiling point 3338 degrees C. I know,'

interrupted Itch. 'And it's it-ree-um, not why-tree-um.' Lucy stared at him. Itch looked away first. 'Sorry,' he said.

'Just open it, Itch,' she sighed. 'I ordered it − I know what it is. I just did some homework on it too, that's all.'

Itch removed the package from his bag and prised the cardboard open. Inside was a circular tin. 'I hadn't planned on opening this with anyone around,' he said quietly.

'Well, you reckoned without me, then,' said Lucy.

He twisted the lid and lifted a bundle of tissue from its centre. He unwrapped a small egg-shaped purple crystal and held it up to the light.

'Well, compared to all the grey metals you've got,' said Lucy, 'you have to say it's a riot of colour. That's yttrium? Really?'

Itch looked sheepish. 'Yes. Well . . . mixed with fluorite crystals, actually.'

'And why would you want that?' she asked.

There was a long silence. Itch stared at the purple crystal, but he knew that Lucy was still staring at him.

'You know why,' he said eventually.

A folded leaflet had fallen on the floor. 'You want to read that, or shall I?' asked Lucy.

Itch picked it up, took a deep breath and read from the cheaply produced flyer. He scanned the paragraphs. 'Wow, that sounds crazy,' he said.

'Can I see?' said Lucy. Itch hesitated, then handed the paper over. She read aloud: '*Your crystal*

143

of purple fluorite is maybe the most valuable purchase you'll ever make. It is perfect for channelling messages from those who have passed over to the other side. You want to contact them and they want to contact you. It will radiate light and mystical insight throughout your body.' She looked up. Tears were rolling down his face. 'Oh, Itch,' she said, and put the sheet down.

'No, carry on!' he said. 'Read it all. Let's hear it.'

'Are you sure?'

'Do it.'

Lucy picked up the sheet again. *'Hold the crystal in your hand while trying a psychic reading. The crystal will cleanse and stabilize your aura, absorbing and neutralizing negative energy and stress. The message from beyond will be clearer. Try it and be amazed.'*

There was silence again as she folded the leaflet.

'I just thought,' said Itch quietly, 'that maybe I could say thanks. And sorry, and goodbye. That's all. And maybe it *does* work. How do *I* know?'

Lucy came and knelt in front of Itch, holding the crystal in front of him. 'You know because you're a scientist. This rock is CaF_2 – calcium fluoride. I've looked it up. It melts in a flame, and is used to produce hydrochloric acid and fluorine gas. It's very common, Itch, and it looks pretty. And that's it.'

'I know . . .' he said.

She grabbed the paper again. *'Perfect for channelling messages?* No it isn't. *They want to contact you?* No, they're dead. *It will cleanse and stabilize your aura?* No it won't. Itch, when my dad died, there were so many things I needed to say to him, it really screwed me up. I was mad at you guys, but I was mad with him too. I was desperate to talk to him, but . . .' She took a breath and wiped her eyes. 'You've got me going now . . .'

'Go on,' said Itch.

'Then I realized that if Dad had anything to say to me, he'd said it already. He hated all the psychics and healers he saw at those fairs he went to. Some people thought he was part of that scene, but he was the opposite of all that. You said you sometimes asked yourself, *What would Cake do?* Well, ask now.'

'I don't know . . .'

'Yes, you do.' Lucy reached for Itch's hand. 'He'd say, *Mr Watkins knew what you thought about him. And now he's gone. It's a shame what happened at the funeral, but it was a mistake and you apologized to the policeman and his wife. Don't waste your breath on the dead; concentrate on the living.* He'd say something like that.'

Itch looked away, then nodded and smiled.

'What?' said Lucy.

'You looked just like him then.'

'Really?'

'Just a bit, yeah.'

They were still holding hands when Jude called them down for food.

At the allotted time, his computer screen flashed into life.

Skype call from RWING was written across the centre of the screen. He clicked the microphone icon.

'Hello?' said a voice, only slightly distorted by the thousands of miles of fibre-optic cables.

Flowerdew leaned closer to his screen. 'Roshanna Wing?'

'Yes. But I can't see you.'

'For now, let's stick to that,' said Flowerdew. 'You only need to listen, anyway. I have a proposition to put to you. You will either be interested or you won't – you will not need to think about it.'

'OK, speak.'

'I remember you from the mining school when you oh-so nearly caught the Lofte children but lost out to me. I also remember how you got me out of the clutches of the British police and handed me over to Greencorps.' There was no reply from Wing – just the familiar squelchy noise of digital communication from the computer's speakers. 'I made you an offer. Suggested that we could be good partners, but you chose to stick to the rules. I wonder if you've reflected on that?'

'What do you want, Flowerdew?' Her tone was flat, bored even.

'I want you to run Greencorps.' He sat back, knowing that he had surprised her, and enjoyed the silence. He wove a coin back and forth between his fingers.

Eventually she said, 'Could I have some details on that?'

'Certainly,' said Flowerdew. 'There is a vacancy at the top of Greencorps due to the sad demise of Dr...... and Van Den Hauwe. Before they left us, they sold the company to me. Now, I have a criminal record, Ms Wing, as you well know; I am something of a wanted man. So I need someone to front this operation; to be the public face of Greencorps. To all intents and purposes, you will run the show.' He paused, then added, 'But I will write your script. And there will be a few company policy changes to implement. There may well be some unpleasantness along the way. I am after *redress*. I seek *satisfaction*. I want *vengeance*, Miss Wing. Should I go on?'

A second's pause; nothing longer.

'Yes, go on.'

Flowerdew could now smile without his lips bleeding. He hit the camera icon.

13

As far as most of the CA was concerned, things had quickly returned to normal. The routine of lessons, homework, tests and exams meant that there was little time to dwell on the events of the beginning of term, however devastating they had been. The police had hung around for a few weeks, but the patrol had become increasingly irregular. Dr Dart had held a special assembly for everyone who couldn't attend the funeral; counselling had been made available for any staff and pupils who wanted it. A tree had been planted in front of the school with a plaque that read: IN MEMORY OF JOHN WATKINS. A GREAT TEACHER AND FRIEND. A few small ornaments had been placed there, resting against the trunk.

Itch had felt better after his chat with Lucy. Caught up in his own grief, he had forgotten about hers. He knew what her father would have made of his purple fluorite. He could hear Cake saying in his London drawl, *You've turned stupid, Master Lofte, and* smiled. He'd decided to keep it for its yttrium content, and put it in the shed where most of his collection was stored.

Mr Watkins's lessons were now being taken by Jennifer Coleman, who had joined the geography staff the previous year. Itch knew Mr Watkins had been involved in her appointment so knew she'd be OK eventually. She was not much older than the Year Thirteen girls, and seemed to Itch to be a bit too jolly and silly.

'She's trying to be our friend,' concluded Jack.

'Well, she could try to be a teacher first,' had been Itch's response.

Miss Coleman arrived in class and wrote *Half-term project* on the smartboard. Everyone groaned.

'Thought you'd like it!' she said, and Itch was reminded again of one of the reasons Mr Watkins would have approved of Miss Coleman. She was very Cornish and knew her local geography. Next she wrote: *Rocks, stones and magic*, and Itch sat up.

'We live, as you know, in God's own county, and this half-term you will be exploring it to the full. In teams . . .' Itch's heart sank. 'Three is perfect; two is OK.' He relaxed again.

'Who'd want to collect rocks with us?' he said to Jack.

She smiled. 'Maybe no one . . .'

'The stones of Cornwall are as old as time itself,' continued Miss Coleman. 'About 300 million years ago, a great mass of molten granite welled up in a line from Dartmoor to what is now the Isles of Scilly.' Various photos and diagrams appeared on her screen. 'Since then it has been constantly eroded away, and we have been left with some wonderful rock formations which the ancient people here thought had magic powers.'

'Well, they were stupid, then,' said Darcy Campbell – to a few giggles.

'And you'd have been thought stupid then too, Darcy,' said Miss Coleman, 'because that's just what everyone thought in those days.'

'Stupid then, and stupider now,' said Jack quietly. Itch suppressed a laugh.

'I'll be writing to your parents with details. There's a new page on the CA website where you can register your teams – each one will get a different site to visit. By the end of the week please.'

'While you're online, you could check Facebook again,' said Jack at lunch time, pushing Itch into the ICT room. 'You can't stay off for ever.'

After the parcel bombs, Itch had quit all social media. He'd never been as obsessed with it as everyone else, but after becoming the centre of a big news story he'd been asked to be friends with hundreds of people he didn't know. It was easier just to ignore them.

Now he sighed. 'Do you think . . . ? *Really?*'

'Yes, Itch, *really*. Sign up for the stones thing, then just log on and see. If it's mental, you can always duck out again.'

When a computer became available, Itch logged on to Facebook. It was Jack who gasped the loudest. Above the FRIEND REQUEST icon was a bubble with the number 5,000. Above the MESSAGES column the number was 144,876.

'No kidding,' said Jack in awe. 'Five thousand friend requests! That's the most you're allowed, isn't it? Why don't you just say yes to all of them. That would be so cool.'

'Jack, are you mad?' said Itch. 'They're nothing. Anyone can have Facebook friends. Sure it *looks* as though I could have five thousand "friends"; but we all know who I actually have. And that's you two. Facebook sucks. I hate it.' He walked off, sat at the nearest table and pulled out some books.

'Can I see who wants to be your friend?' asked Jack, glancing at him.

'Sure . . .' Itch shrugged. 'Help yourself. I need to finish this maths sheet.'

'The one for yesterday?' said Jack, scrolling through the friend requests and messages. 'Mr Logan will be thrilled.'

'Logan is never thrilled. Not ever.'

They worked though the lunch hour, with Jack calling out names, countries and messages: 'Thomasina Flavia in Italy wants to be your friend, Gerhart Hölde in Austria wants to be your friend, Shunishi Kimura in Tokyo wants to be your friend—'

'Tell them I'm busy,' muttered Itch.

'And . . . Itch, you should look at this,' said Jack, stepping back from the screen.

He came over and she pointed.

'*Mary Lee*,' he read, a shiver going down his spine. 'There must be millions of Mary Lees.'

'Though one fewer than there used to be,' said Jack.

There was a tiny photo next to the words, and Itch clicked on it. They gasped together. There on the screen was the photo Lucy had seen on Shivvi's computer; the image that had appeared on the news showing the gang suspected of killing the Greencorps bosses. Six divers smiled out, with Shivvi Tan Fook, or 'Mary Lee', as she had called herself at school, standing behind them.

They both stared at the screen.

'But we know she's dead, don't we? Didn't Fairnie say they'd found her body?' said Jack.

'Yup. We can check with Fairnie, but there was no doubt. I'll text Lucy.'

'Unless they were so busy chasing Flowerdew they messed up,' said Jack. 'Maybe they couldn't identify her properly after the fire.'

Itch shook his head. 'Anyone could have used this photo – it's all over the news.'

'But, Itch, it says *Mary Lee*. Did she use that name anywhere apart from here?'

Itch was silent until Lucy came running in.

'What's up?' she said, a little breathlessly.

Itch pointed at the screen. 'Someone called Mary Lee wants to be my friend.'

'Another one?' said Lucy as she leaned over.

'Well, that's the question,' said Jack.

'Wow . . .' Lucy looked at the photo. 'Them again.'

'But anyone could have used the image,' Itch repeated.

'No, they couldn't,' said Lucy. 'This isn't the same picture. The girl with the dripping hair wasn't at the end of the row – they've all moved round.'

'You sure?' said Itch.

Lucy nodded as she clicked around the page. 'This Mary Lee has been on Facebook for a week. This is the only image; no messages, no notifications, no activity at all.'

'What's the point, then?' Itch wondered.

Lucy and Jack both shrugged.

'Doesn't feel good, though, does it?' he said. 'Can we just go back and register for this geography trail thing, Jack? You need to sign me up as a partner before the rush.'

That night, Itch was on the verge of sleep when his door opened and Chloe put her head round.

'You ill or something?' he said, his words only slightly slurred.

She sat on the end of his bed, wrapped in her dressing gown. 'I've been thinking about that Facebook photo – the Mary Lee one you showed me.'

'Thought you were asleep,' said Itch.

'I think you should accept them – her – whoever it is as a friend,' she said.

Itch propped himself up. 'I think so too.'

153

Even though the only light in the room was coming from the landing, Itch could see the surprise on his sister's face. 'Really?' she said. 'I assumed you'd think I was mad.'

'Well, that's quite possible' – Itch smiled – 'but on this you might be right. You go first.'

Chloe sat cross-legged on Itch's bed. 'Well, it's simple really. If it *was* a fake, they'd have used the same picture that's all over the news. Also, it's someone who knew Mary Lee was the name Shivvi was using. So chances are it's one of the divers trying to get in touch.'

Itch nodded. 'Pretty much what I was thinking.' He reached for his laptop, opened it and put it down between them. 'But why get in touch? Why bother with all this stuff?' The light from the screen filled the dark room and the smiling wet-suited figures appeared again.

'If it turns out that they're as nasty as her' – Chloe pointed at Shivvi – 'we can just tell Fairnie. But why would they go to all this trouble while they're being hunted for killing those Greencorps guys?'

'Shall we find out?' said Itch. Chloe nodded. He clicked ACCEPT. 'What now?'

'Probably nothing,' said Chloe, swinging her legs off the bed. 'See you in the morning.'

She'd been back in bed barely a minute when Itch walked in, laptop open. 'Look at this,' he said.

Chloe stared at the screen. The words: *Is that you, Itchingham?* had appeared

Chloe's mouth dropped open. 'Wow.' She switched on the light. 'What are you going to say?'

'That they've spelled my name wrong,' he said. But he typed: *Who are you?*

My name is Leila.

Not Mary Lee then, typed Itch.

No. Sorry. She was our friend.

Itch swore quietly. *She tried to kill me. She was cruel and mad.* There was no reply to that, so he added: *What do you want?*

We didn't kill the Greencorps men, came the reply.

Itch glanced at his sister. *Why are you telling me?* he typed.

Because the man who did was Nathaniel Flowerdew.

Itch closed his eyes.

Chloe inhaled sharply. 'You have to be kidding . . .' she said quietly.

The bus to Bodmin Moor was leaving shortly, and Itch and Chloe both needed a packed lunch. Jude was asleep and Nicholas deep in an animated phone call which he was having in the garden, so they were making it themselves.

'Dad's lost it,' said Chloe. 'Why is he outside? It's cold and miserable . . .'

'Something I'm sure he's noticed,' said Itch, slicing bread. 'I think this call has been going on for some time. I heard him talking downstairs very early. Maybe he's keeping himself awake.' The light from the kitchen illuminated the first few metres of the garden and they watched as their father paced up and down.

'He looks stressed,' said Chloe. 'Who needs to be shouting at eight o'clock in the morning? Pass the tinfoil, Itch.'

'It's aluminium foil, Chloe – big difference.'

'Actually, they're the same.'

'Aluminium is 13, tin is 50. You can check—'

'They're both shiny and keep sandwiches fresh,' said Chloe. 'Which makes them the same. So pass, please.'

Outside, the onset of hard, swirling rain was forcing their father to shelter near the house. As he walked past the window, they picked up snippets of conversation.

'I think he's talking to Themba from the mine in South Africa,' said Itch. 'Something isn't right . . .'

He saw that Nicholas *did* look stressed. His brow was furrowed, his eyes closed in exasperation as he listened. Eventually he hung up and slumped onto a garden chair. Chloe knocked on the window and beckoned. He smiled and nodded and, seconds later, came in, dripping and weary. Chloe put a mug of tea in front of him and he grabbed it gratefully.

'Thanks, Chloe, exactly what I needed.' He inhaled the steam, took a sip, then a mouthful.

'What's up, Dad?' asked Itch.

Nicholas sighed. 'That was Themba from the mine at Palmeitkraal. I'm still trying to work out what happened, but it seems that the sale of the mine didn't go through. There was a new bid from somewhere at the last minute, so the university won't be getting it after all.'

'Poor Sammy and Themba,' said Chloe. 'Where will they go?'

Nicholas shrugged. 'Not sure, Chlo . . .' He looked at their food preparation. 'You off somewhere?'

Chloe pointed at a sheet of paper stuck to the fridge. 'You signed the form. It's Itch's "Rocks of Ancient Cornwall" project, remember? He and Jack are off to look at some stones on Bodmin Moor. Me and Lucy are going along too – she says they're actually pretty cool. We're meeting up at the bus stop.'

Nicholas glanced outside as the rain hit the windows with a renewed force. 'Of course I remember. And you've picked a lovely day for it. Bring me back a spoon or something.' He followed them to the door. 'And Itch, remember to text that number you were given.'

Itch nodded and Chloe herded him through the door. 'I'll remind him,' she said, and kissed her father goodbye.

The bus to the moor took a long time; the roads were slow and there were many stops. Itch, Jack, Chloe and Lucy sat at the back, Itch already eating a roll from his packed lunch.

'It's only ten thirty,' said Chloe. 'You'll have nothing for lunch.'

'It's breakfast,' he said, his mouth full.

'Well, if *you're* starting . . .' said Lucy, and she produced a huge packet of crisps. 'Anyway, this isn't my project, or Chloe's . . . We can do what we want.' She handed the bag to Chloe, who grinned. 'And I did all this last year. If they hadn't changed the questions, I'd tell you the answers.'

The windows were steaming up, and Jack drew a rudimentary map with her finger. 'This is the road to Launceston, and this is the one to Minions.' Her finger left a dripping zigzag trail on the window, water running down the glass as it pooled where her finger stopped. 'And these are the Hurlers.' She stabbed her finger in a circular pattern.

'They are pretty amazing actually,' said Lucy. 'They're stone circles like Stonehenge. It's supposed to be impossible to count them.'

'Why?' said Chloe.

Jack stood up and wrote *Rock, stones and magic* in big swirly writing. 'It's the devil's work!' she said, laughing. 'They're cursed or something. My dad has a song about them – I might put it in the project when we write it up. He was singing it this morning. Something like:

'Come take this warning,
Cried the priest:
All good hurlers
Are the devil's feast.
He will curse where you stand,
Mark his circle upon our land.'

Chloe and Itch applauded and Jack bowed. 'I used to think hurling was like being sick,' she said. 'Then Dad showed me the game on YouTube. It was pretty neat, actually. The hurlers on the moor were cursed for playing on a Sunday and turned to stone. That's the legend, anyway.'

'We have to take photos and answer some questions. That's it, really,' said Itch.

'And report to the police,' added Chloe.

'And that,' said Itch. 'I told them about the trip and they seemed fine about it.'

Since Itch had told Fairnie about the contact with one of Shivvi's divers and her claim that it was Flowerdew who had killed Revere and Van Den Hauwe, security had been stepped up. No one wanted a return to the intense MI5 patrols of the previous year, but the colonel had insisted that action be taken. Itch had to report every trip he made to the police, along with any suspicious social media contact. This would apply to his school trip to Spain too; the local police had already been alerted. Itch guessed that his phone, emails and Facebook were monitored anyway, though Fairnie had been evasive on this point.

As the bus arrived in Minions and turned into the car park, Itch texted the number he'd been given. He received a *Confirmed. Thank you*, and they all trooped out into a howling gale, the rain now horizontal across the moor. They pulled their hoods down over their eyes and followed the signs.

'Let's make this quick,' Jack shouted into the

wind as they walked single file up the track towards the stones. She pointed at some old ruined buildings that loomed out of the low cloud. 'I know there are old mine works here, Itch, but not this time, OK?'

He nodded and, heads bowed, they almost missed the people hurrying in the opposite direction. They looked up as the first one splashed past holding onto his peaked cap, his waterproof flapping in the wind. He was followed by three others, a woman and two men, all of whom looked shaken and upset.

'It's terrible, what's happened!' wailed one of them. 'Never seen anything like it!'

'It's shocking, really shocking,' called another. 'We've called the police!' And they hurried back down the hill, helping each other pick their way through the rapidly expanding puddles.

Itch, Jack, Chloe and Lucy stood and stared after them. Itch took his sister's arm. 'Come on, Chlo – it'll just be a dead sheep or something. They're probably panicking because they're low on fudge, or haven't eaten a pasty for five minutes . . .' He steered her up the track, their trainers now squelching through what was becoming a stream, and noticed a small group of people standing just off the path, huddled together and pointing.

Itch followed their gaze to a scene of chaos. Through the swirling, drenching low cloud they could see the Hurlers – three rings of large granite slabs . . . but every stone had been upended. Each one had fallen, leaving a large earthy hole where it had been rooted for millennia.

'It's like a battle scene,' said Jack.

As they headed towards the stones, Itch thought his cousin was absolutely right – that was precisely what it reminded him of. The dead and injured of this battle were the ancient stones of the moor; they had stood in an organized pattern, but were now thrown down in disarray. The first one they came to had stood at least two metres tall, but had been prised from the ground, exposing a darker, less eroded base. Itch peered into the gaping hole it had left, expecting to find a clue to its fate of some kind, but found only the gritty, peaty soil of Bodmin.

The Hurlers lay at regular intervals and Itch led a procession that trooped from each lichen-covered granite slab to the next. At each one, scuffed and broken soil seemed to be evidence of the effort that had been needed to topple each monolith.

'Who would do this?' wondered Chloe.

Before anyone could think of an answer, there were shouts from behind them, and a man in a cagoule came running over. 'No one touch anything!' he bellowed breathlessly from under his hood. 'This is a crime scene! Come away from the stones!' He rushed up to Itch, his eyes darting everywhere, rain dripping off his glasses. 'You'll have to leave,' he said. 'This is terrible. Please go!' And he ran from stone to stone, becoming more agitated at each one.

'Itch, come and look at this . . .' called Lucy. She was standing by a slab on the opposite side of the circle, and he ran over. It too was grey and weathered, but now had large red letters sprayed on it. Some of the paint had run off the granite and onto the grass.

'*Meyn Mamvro*,' read Itch. 'Is that a name or something?'

Chloe and Jack joined them, as did the breathless man in the anorak.

'Who are you?' said Lucy.

But the man just stared at the stone, mouthing the words, 'Meyn Mamvro . . .'

'Excuse me,' said Lucy. 'What does that mean?'

'It makes no sense,' he replied. 'No sense at all . . .' And, hearing an approaching siren, he ran off towards the car park.

'Do you know what?' said Itch. 'I don't fancy being here when another police investigation starts. I think they've seen enough of me too. Let's disappear before they get here.'

Jack took some final photos of the stones, and they followed anorak man back in the direction of the main road.

There was no phone signal on the journey back; they had to wait till they reached Jack's house. They had dried out a little on the bus, but Zoe insisted on hanging up their jackets and throwing their sweatshirts in the dryer. Jack produced her laptop and they sat round the kitchen table.

She typed *Meyn Mamvro* into the search engine, and they all read the first entry that came up: *Cornish: Stones of the Motherland.* There was silence in the kitchen.

'*Stones of the Motherland?* What's that about?' said Jack.

'Doesn't really help much,' said Itch. 'It might mean nothing, anyway. Let's see your pictures, Jack.'

She uploaded her photos and they stared at the images. 'Well, it's not going to be the project Miss Coleman thought she was getting,' said Jack. She added a picture of a fallen stone to her Facebook page and added the *Meyn Mamvro* stone too. 'Might as well put it out there. Someone will know what it's all about.'

Zoe Lofte produced mugs of tea and hot chocolate, and they all took it in turns to explain what they had seen. She shook her head. 'What a shocking thing to do,' she said. 'It's Cornish, but seems a bizarre thing for the Cornish Nationalists to do. They'd want to look after the stones. Maybe it's just vandals . . .' She walked away as Jack's phone bleeped.

'Text from Debbie. She says to look at her page,' said Jack, already clicking on it. Debbie Price and Natalie Hussain had been given a different site for their project: Carn Kenidjack at the far southern end of the county. Debbie had volunteered for it as her family planned to be there for half-term anyway. Her photos made everyone gasp, and Zoe turned round.

They were more images of scattered stones and broken granite. Kenidjack had been a meeting point, a local curiosity that became known as the 'Hooting Carn' because of the weird noise the wind made as it swirled around the rocks. Now it was a pile of rubble.

'But that's terrible,' said Zoe, looking over their shoulders.

'And look at that . . .' Jack scrolled to another picture. A broken slice of rock lay propped up against some rubble, red letters sprayed across it.

'*Meyn Mamvro*,' said Lucy.

'This is going to get nasty,' said Itch.

14

Itch was right. Over the next week there were reports of ancient sites across Cornwall being destroyed. Images of overturned granite, piles of scattered stones and toppled slabs filled first the local news, then the national bulletins. In each case the words *Meyn Mamvro* had been scrawled somewhere on the site. Theories were everywhere: an anti-capitalist demonstration; an individual with a grudge against the county; even a witches' coven.

'The truth is,' said Nicholas over breakfast, 'no one has a clue. No one has heard of *Meyn Mamvro* before – it doesn't make sense.'

'It does if you believe in aliens,' said Chloe. 'There's a Facebook group that think these places are landing sites for spaceships.'

Her father laughed. 'Well, it makes about as much sense as anything else,' he said.

Itch came into the kitchen and poured himself some orange juice. 'Been any more attacks?' he asked.

Nicholas shook his head. 'Police have closed most of the sites and roped off the tors. But some are so remote, it's impossible to protect them properly. Volunteer groups are camped out on some of them apparently. Police are checking owners of tractors and JCBs – it's clear that heavy lifting gear was used; deep tyre marks were found at most of the sites.'

'Good luck with that,' said Itch. 'Should take most of the year . . .'

'Got a theory?' asked Nicholas.

'Nope. You know Miss Coleman got a visit from the cops?'

'You're kidding!' said Chloe.

'Lucy just messaged me. Apparently they turned up at school yesterday. It was a staff training day or something, and they wanted to know about our half-term project. They said that so many of our year had posted images of the *Meyn Mamvro* rocks, it seemed a bit of a coincidence.'

'Well, if they think your class is athletic enough to shift all these rocks, they clearly haven't seen you do games,' said Chloe.

'That's definitely what she would have told them,' said Itch, smiling. 'And shown them that the CA has done exactly the same work many times before. Lucy's still got hers somewhere.'

The sound of an incoming email came from three devices at once: Itch's laptop, and Chloe and Nicholas's phones.

'It's from Gabe!' said Chloe as they all opened the message.

'What's he sending that we all need to see?' said Nicholas. He read aloud: '*Saw this in Coventry and thought of you! Your news travels fast. G.*'

Itch had the picture on his screen first. 'Dad, look!'

Chloe and Nicholas moved swiftly and stood behind him. They saw the battered wreck of a car in what looked like a multi-storey car park. It had lost its tyres, its windows were smashed, and across the side in red spray paint were the words *Meyn Mamvro*.

Nicholas spoke first. 'I get the feeling that it doesn't mean "Stones of the Motherland" any more. It just means random violence. Or destruction. Or anarchy.'

Chloe leaned in front of Itch and typed *Meyn Mamvro* into Google images. 'Just a thought,' she said, and hit ENTER. The screen flashed white, then filled with lines and lines of images. The first few were of the defaced Hurlers and other rocks around Cornwall, but then came houses, furniture, walls, caravans, shops . . . All were damaged and broken. And all had the words *Meyn Mamvro* scrawled across them in red letters.

When the CA returned after half-term, it was the only topic of conversation. A story that had started life as a Year Ten geography project had gone viral. Everyone had seen different versions of the graffiti. Before lessons started, Itch and Jack had been shown T-shirts, tattoos and screensavers. Debbie

Price and Natalie Hussain came over with photos from their trip to the Hooting Carn, but Itch had already seen most of them on websites and in local newspapers. Ian Steele had found the words on the Great Wall of China, but most people concluded that the words had been photoshopped.

The buzz of excitement lasted until Mr Hampton walked in; their new form teacher did not look happy. His soft-spoken, genial tones had an added touch of steel this morning.

'Welcome back, Ten H. You should know that some graffiti has appeared on school property. Some idiots have deemed it acceptable to scrawl the words of the moment in the school hall. It happened this morning. Dr Dart is understandably furious. The culprits have been sent home. Any repeat of this idiotic behaviour will be dealt with severely. I hope you all understand the seriousness of what I'm saying.' He looked at his class, challenging them. 'Well?'

'Yes, sir,' mumbled most of 10H.

It was soon clear that the 'culprits' were Darcy Campbell and Bruno Paul; they'd been temporarily suspended. Their parents claimed that Dr Dart had overreacted because of the press attention after the parcel bombs, and had been embarrassed by the publicity that came with the *Meyn Mamvro* graffiti. Headlines like IS THIS THE COUNTRY'S MOST NOTORIOUS SCHOOL? and ACADEMY OF HATE had certainly not helped, and the school governors were apparently taking the appeal seriously.

An emergency meeting with the CA's sponsors had been called, and it was then that Itch noticed the new school board. As before, it showed the school crest and the name of the principal, followed by a list of the companies which had contributed to the building; until recently this had included the oil multinational Greencorps. This had now been removed.

'That'll be Fairnie's doing,' said Itch as he and Chloe stood in reception. 'He must have told Dr Dart what they'd been up to.' He hadn't thought about Greencorps and the murdered bosses for some time; now he wondered about Leila and her claim about Flowerdew.

'What are you guys staring at?' asked Jack, arriving with Natalie and Debbie.

'Greencorps are no longer sponsors of our fine academy.' Itch pointed at the board.

'Don't know whose reputation is lower,' said Jack gloomily. 'Anyway, Deb has found a real nasty on Facebook, Itch, so I wouldn't go there.'

'I don't anyway,' he said, 'but you might as well tell me. I'll find out soon enough.'

Debbie Price twisted uncomfortably. 'Someone took a photo at the church, Itch. Of you on the ground after you pulled that curtain down. And the comments say that it's you who should have been excluded. And . . .' They waited for her to finish.

'Go on . . .' said Itch.

'And that the school was bombed because of you. And that Mr Watkins—'

'OK, that's enough,' said Chloe. 'It's full of garbage – clearly the work of that cow, Campbell.'

'You've seen it?' asked Itch.

'Of course.'

'Why didn't you tell me?'

'You'd be amazed what I don't tell you!'

'Apparently a poster-sized version of the photo went up outside yesterday,' said Jack. 'It didn't last long, but you get the idea . . . There could be more today. We need to report it.'

'I wish Fairnie and the team were here,' said Chloe.

'Yes – a marine with a gun can sort most things,' said Itch, 'but in the long run I'm going to have to cope without spooks to look after me.'

'OK,' said Jack, 'but if this gets any rougher, you should call him.'

In the weeks that followed, there seemed to be a never-ending supply of Cornwall Academy stories turning up on blogs and local news sites. Some were rumours, some gossip, others completely made up. But the CA was the story of the moment, and anything that mentioned it, and preferably Itch, was sought after. Its academic results, its sporting fixtures and the private lives of its staff were all considered interesting enough for what appeared to be a local army of reporters to write about. Itch guessed it was actually just Darcy and Bruno filling their recently acquired spare time, but that didn't seem to matter.

The atmosphere in the CA was tense. Now that

members of staff were the subject of scrutiny, they became irritable and prone to issuing random punishments. The day a story came out about Craig Harris's 'high jinks and emotional behaviour' at a wedding, he had the whole of Year Nine running laps of the school grounds. Chris Hopkins had handed out extra homework on electromagnetism after a rumour about him and the school secretary led to wolf whistles in his class. A pink fluffy heart with *I love Sarah* had been the final straw.

The image of Itch on the floor of the church at Mr Watkins's funeral wouldn't go away. Itch knew that James Potts had it as a screensaver and suspected others did too; a few Year Eleven boys had started to throw themselves to the floor as he passed. Whenever he walked into a classroom, someone would pretend to faint.

'I'm not calling Fairnie!' Itch said to Jack after a particularly theatrical fall of six pupils in an ICT class. 'I can't just run to him whenever bad stuff happens here. They'll get bored soon, anyway.'

Jack wasn't so sure. 'I know that's the way it's been in the past, but this is different, Itch. The CA is a pretty messed-up place at the moment and this isn't getting any better. Dr Dart looks pretty stressed. No one dares talk to her in case she explodes.'

'Yeah, well, she's got that hearing soon. Campbell and Paul's appeal. Maybe they'll be thrown out for good. Then some other school can enjoy their poison.'

The only place Itch felt safe was Mr Hampton's science club. No one fell over, no one joked about curtains, no one thought element-hunting was a strange way to spend your time . . . He even started to use his 118-pocket rucksack again. Itch knew he wouldn't be expected to talk football or pretend to know anything about *Britain's Got Talent*. He didn't need to explain anything. He found he was looking forward to the trip to the Spanish science museum.

And then there was Lucy. The science club was the only thing in school they did together, and he looked forward to each session knowing she would be there. He was still embarrassed about the whole purple fluorite incident, but was grateful for the way she had talked him round. And not told anyone. Not even Chloe and Jack knew about his attempt at mystical insight. He shuddered.

'Hey, Itch, over here!' Lucy had arrived early.

He sat down next to her, dropped his rucksack and reached for the pocket marked *25*.

'Stop! Don't tell me,' she said, closing her eyes. 'Chromium? Vanadium?'

Itch shook his head.

'Close?' she asked.

'Very . . .' Itch pointed to *23* and *24*.

'Ah, so close! I give in.'

Itch took out a small, roughly cut, slate-grey stone. 'That's manganese. I think it's from Bodmin Moor – they mined it there. That's what I was told, anyway.'

'Hi, y'all,' called Mr Hampton, striding into the

172

lab. 'Or *Hola* maybe! Time to start thinking Spain, everyone.' He spotted Itch's stone and wandered over. 'May I see?'

Itch handed it over. Hampton smiled. '*Manganeso*, Itch. Still named after Magnesia in Greece, but that's what the Spanish call it.'

'Thought the Periodic Table was the same everywhere,' said Lucy.

'The shape is. The grouping of elements is. But some of the names are different. Here's a poster with the whole thing on – you can have it, Itch, if you like.' He unrolled a sheet of A3 that showed the familiar squares of numbers and letters arranged in rows and columns. 'At first glance it's the same. Some of the names are the same; some are very similar: helium is *helio*, zinc is *cinc*. Some are different . . .' He took a felt tip and circled two squares in the eleventh column, one above the other. 'We say silver, they say *plata*; we say gold, they say *oro*, and so on. And speaking of valuables, please make sure you all have enough euros to last the five days. Miss Coleman and I will not be buying you souvenirs if you run out of money.' He handed the poster to Itch.

'Why is Miss Coleman coming, sir?' asked Tom Westgate. 'Thought you'd have another scientist.'

Mr Hampton smiled. 'One of Miss Coleman's hidden talents is a reasonable fluency in Spanish. I have some too, having lived in California, but Miss Coleman studied in Madrid for a year. I have your information packs here – our flight is at the somewhat inconvenient time of 04.15 hours, and I warn you, I am not at my best before breakfast. Jack and Chloe have taken the last two spaces, so no room now for pets or parents!' He laughed loudly. 'Itch and Lucy, could I have a word before you go?'

As everyone wandered out, Itch and Lucy approached his desk.

'Any news of Tom Oakes?' asked Itch.

Mr Hampton paused briefly, and winced slightly. 'I'm afraid not – after the bomb at ISIS, he may want to stay hidden for longer. All things considered, I'd be grateful if you could keep our chat to yourselves. I shouldn't have said anything, really. This trip is complicated enough!'

'Is there a problem?' said Itch. 'I thought everything . . .'

Hampton raised his hands. 'No, of course all is well if your folks are happy. But your safety is paramount. For the moment we just have to inform the police of our movements – flight details, hostel, that kind of thing. And we get a police escort from the airport.' He looked from Lucy to Itch and back again, clearly expecting a smile.

'Another joke, sir?' suggested Itch.

15

Mr Hampton and Miss Coleman called it the Museo Nacional de Ciencias Naturales, but everyone else called it the science museum. The verdict of the CA students, having spent the best part of a day there, was that it wasn't a patch on the one in London. If it hadn't been for the new exhibits Hampton had told them about, they'd rather have gone shopping. It was also incredibly stuffy; despite the unusually warm spring weather, the museum's radiators were all blasting out heat.

Itch spent all his time, as expected, absorbing silver. He knew that it was the shiniest substance in the world, and the best electrical conductor, but that was about it. However, here were rows of coins going back centuries. You could (under supervision) pick them up, spin them, even smell them. The display showed how the Spanish went to the New World looking for gold, but found silver. In brutal conditions they had forced the workers to use a refining process which used mercury; the result was

175

a vast increase in productivity and global trade. Silver knitted the global economy together for the first time – it was an international currency. There were some cool by-products too, and while there was a queue for the coins, Itch was the only one looking at and making notes on silver salts.

When they met up in the café on the cavernous ground floor, Tom Westgate had an alternative reason for their trip to Madrid.

'I reckon this is all so that Hampton and Miss Coleman can, you know, have a romantic few days away together,' he told them.

'Are you kidding?' said Itch. 'Really? That's disgusting.'

Natalie and Debbie laughed.

'Haven't you seen the way they look at each other?' said Tom. 'She never takes her eyes off him.'

'Isn't she a bit young for him?' said Jack.

'They're all teacher-age,' said Itch. 'Don't suppose it matters, really. As long as we don't see them holding hands or anything . . .'

'Here they come,' said Lucy as both teachers appeared from the lift.

'What's everyone laughing at?' asked Miss Coleman, flushing slightly as they walked over.

'Oh, er,' said Tom, 'Lucy told a joke. About the sequencing of human DNA.'

Lucy shot him a 'thanks-for-nothing' look.

'Like to share it?' said Mr Hampton knowingly. 'Not sure I know of many DNA jokes.'

'Oh, it wasn't that good anyway. Can we visit

the shop before we go?' Lucy asked, changing the subject.

Hampton looked at his watch. 'Fifteen minutes is all you have; you won't want more – it's even hotter in there. Miss Coleman and I will stay here. We've already seen what there is on offer.' This produced another bout of giggles, and everyone hurried away to cover their embarrassment.

As soon as they were out of earshot, Jack said, 'Oh my God! Tom, you are so right! That was excruciating. Now they know that we know. And it'll be all over Facebook. Maybe that's why they made us leave our phones at the hostel – so we couldn't report back to anyone.'

'Well, they said it was a security thing because of thefts and street crime,' said Chloe.

'Itch – you've got yours, you must tell everyone,' said Natalie.

Itch shook his head. 'If the Spanish police are watching out for messages from my phone like they said, I think it'll be for security reasons. I don't think they want to read about an American science teacher getting off with a geography teacher.'

'Boo,' said Debbie. 'Spoilsport.'

As they split up to browse the shop, Jack whispered, 'You need to check Facebook soon and see if those divers have been in touch.'

'Maybe,' said Itch. 'When we get home. You going to buy anything?'

'Hey, Itch!' called Chloe. 'Look at this!' She held up a T-shirt with the Periodic Table in Spanish.

'Cool!' said Itch. 'It's just like the poster Hampton gave me. How much?'

Chloe checked the label. 'Twenty-five euros,' she said, 'which is outrageous as it was probably made in some sweatshop for a few cents. But it is you, Itch, and it's your size.' She threw it to him and they walked to the tills, Itch pointing out the elements that were different in Spanish.

Chloe laughed. 'If that information ever proves useful, Itch, I'll buy you any element you like. As long as it's safe. And legal. And not a grey-silvery metal – you've got way too many of them.'

There was a long queue at the tills, and they were just wondering if they'd have time to buy the T-shirt when there was a shout from the front.

They looked up to see smoke coming from behind the counter. The queue dissolved as everyone crowded forward to see what had happened. A startled museum employee was staring at the till: blue flames seeping through the sides. He pushed a button to eject the cash drawer, and it shot towards him, a cloud of smoke billowing upwards. When it had cleared, he cried out in alarm: all the banknotes were on fire. He flapped his hands ineffectively till one of his colleagues threw a souvenir tea towel at him and he smothered the drawer with it.

A security man with a fire extinguisher appeared on the scene. Aiming the nozzle at the till, he succeeded in blasting its contents all over the watching customers. Partially burned euros and foam flew everywhere.

Itch looked at the soggy T-shirt he'd been about to buy. 'Is there time to get another one?' he said. 'There are other tills, if we hurry.'

'But there's no one there, Itch,' said Jack. 'Look . . .' All the shop staff had gathered to look at the steaming mess of what was left of the burning till, leaving the others unattended.

Itch looked from till to till and nudged her sharply. 'Look, Jack! They're on fire too!'

She turned to see wisps of smoke coming from two other tills. 'Hey! Look!' she cried, pointing and waving her arms to attract the staff's attention. 'Fire!'

Jack's call was echoed by many voices but now with a discernible increase in tension. The staff rushed back to the burning tills, while the remaining customers decided they didn't want their souvenirs after all; or at least, they didn't want to wait around to pay for them. They headed for the exits. The security man found his extinguisher again and directed more foam at the smoke, causing both tills to short circuit. When the general fire alarm sounded, there were cries of concern everywhere.

'Everyone back to me!' yelled Mr Hampton, just making himself heard over the clanging of the museum's bells.

Lucy grabbed Chloe and Jack. 'Everyone back to Hampton and Coleman! Itch, come on!'

They ran together, pushing against the exiting flow of visitors, and then waited for the rest of the party to return. The Year Elevens were last back, led by a pasty-faced student called Luke Lieberman. They were holding coffees, and had a 'what's-the-panic' look on their faces.

Mr Hampton stood on his chair. 'Right – the bus is due in two minutes. Follow me, and please stick together. This is going to be one hell of a bunfight.'

'Or bullfight,' muttered Lucy, and they followed the teachers towards the exit.

Outside it was dusk, but the air was still warm. They fought their way to the bus stop marked PLAZA LUCENZA and found their bus nearly full. They showed their travel cards to the driver and they all stood along the aisle, holding onto the seats. As the bus pushed its way into the evening rush hour, cars blasted their horns in irritation.

'It's only a twenty-minute ride,' said Mr Hampton, looking at the tired faces around him. 'We've got the best tapas you've ever tasted waiting for us at the hostel.'

'Can't we get pizza?' asked Natalie.

'Or KFC? I saw one on the ride in. We could—'

'In Madrid, we eat like Madrileños!' said Hampton, smiling. 'You can eat pizza at home.'

'Nice try, Natalie,' said Jack.

'Sir, you ever seen exploding tills before?' asked Tom.

'Nope,' he said. 'That was quite something, wasn't it? An electrical fault, I suppose. It'll have wiped out their takings, that's for—'

There was a sudden lurch, and Mr Hampton shot

backwards, hitting the seat behind him, then falling in a heap. The loud metallic crunch and splinter sound was followed by a torrent of shouting from the driver, who leaped from his bus. While Miss Coleman helped Hampton back up, all the students ran to the front of the bus. Looking through the driver's windscreen, they could see that the bus had hit the back of a taxi – its boot had crumpled and popped open. The cabbie and passenger had leaped from the car, but seemed oblivious to the bus that had just crashed into it. A squat man, with a REAL PASSION REAL MADRID T-shirt stretched across his body and a taxi driver's licence bouncing from a chain around his neck, was shouting at a terrified-looking man in a suit and waving what looked like part of a twenty-euro note. The suited man tried to talk back, but it only seemed to enrage the taxi man further.

'He's going to make a run for it,' said Lucy, watching the suited man. 'You watch.'

And, on cue, he turned and fled. Surprised, the taxi driver took a few seconds to respond, but then set off in pursuit, leaving the bus driver waving his arms at the pair of them.

'We're not going anywhere here,' said Mr Hampton. 'The taxi has blocked the road. Every-one out.'

They filed out of the bus and looked around. A bank and a few local shops were closed, but one coffee bar was still open, its lights shining brightly into the gloomy street.

'Come on, let's regroup in there,' said Mr Hampton. 'We'll work out a new route.' He led the way inside, his map of Madrid already in his hand. The place was busy, and they had to spread themselves out over a number of tables. Behind the counter, a large screen showed a La Liga match, the sound muted.

'I'll get the drinks,' said Miss Coleman, having taken their orders. 'Itch, could you help me?'

As they waited in the queue, Itch picked up some bottles of water and juice. 'Is it far to the hostel, miss? Should we get food here?'

Miss Coleman laughed. 'Any excuse to avoid the tapas! No, we'll be fine, I think. No need to stock up. We'll find another bus soon, I'm sure.' She ordered a selection of teas, coffees and hot chocolates in what sounded to Itch like perfect Spanish, paid and went to talk to Mr Hampton.

'Don't worry, miss, I'll bring them over – you go talk to your boyfriend,' muttered Itch. He beckoned Jack over to help him, and between them they ferried the drinks to the tables. On the last trip, the barman said something in Spanish and, pointing at Miss Coleman, indicated a small plate of notes and coins sitting on top of the coffee machine. He nodded and carried it over to his teacher.

'Miss, you forgot your—' Itch stared at the euros he was carrying. He was sure they were changing colour. 'What the . . . ?' He looked closely at the blue, red and grey notes. Slowly but unmistakably, they were all turning brown 'Sir . . .'

Now they started to smoulder, and by the time he'd dropped the plate in front of Mr Hampton, small wisps of black smoke were rising into the air.

'Itch, what have you done!' cried Miss Coleman in alarm.

'What? Nothing! I just brought them over!'

Now small glowing circles appeared as the reaction ate away at the centre of the notes; the holes opened quickly as the flames caught. Within seconds, the euros had turned to ash. Everyone stared at the remains of Miss Coleman's money.

'You forgot your change,' said Itch quietly.

The smell of burning had caused heads to turn, and one of the waiters came rushing over, shouting in Spanish.

'He says it is against the law to burn money in Spain,' said Miss Coleman, who replied with some fast talking of her own.

'Why do you need a law to tell you that?' said Chloe. 'What kind of a loser burns their money?'

The waiter was joined by a woman wiping her hands on her apron, who appeared to be the manager. She listened to what had happened, then angrily pointed to the door. Now both Mr Hampton and Miss Coleman joined in; all four were shouting over each other when a cry cut across them. A small boy of no more than eight was wailing and holding out his reddening fingers to his mother. At his feet, a five-euro note burned furiously.

'What's going on, sir?' said Lucy as the manager and waiter hurried over to the crying child. The mother was now shouting too, and some customers started to leave. The smell of freshly roasted coffee had now been replaced by that of freshly burned paper.

'I've never seen anything like it,' said Mr Hampton. 'Money just doesn't self-combust like that. Maybe there's some chemical in the till . . .'

'The plate was pretty warm when I picked it up, but that note looked like it was under a magnifying glass or something,' said Itch. 'Took a while to catch, but when it did, it was gone in seconds.'

'You're right, Itch, that's exactly what it looked like. Maybe we should drink up and find a bus,' said Mr Hampton, gulping down his coffee.

'Should we check our money?' asked Debbie, who was looking alarmed. 'Everyone else is . . . look.' They all glanced around, and sure enough, most customers had started to look suspiciously at their purses and wallets.

'So at the science museum, it wasn't the tills catching fire, it was the money,' said Lucy. 'And that taxi we crashed into – the cabbie was waving a note, wasn't he? I bet that had caught fire. That's why they looked freaked out. No wonder the other man ran off.'

'Maybe it's all a big joke,' said Natalie, 'and we're being filmed for TV.'

At nearby tables students were looking at news websites on their laptops; one called to the waiter to change the TV channel. A remote control was found and the football switched to a news network. Images of fire filled the screen. The volume was now on full, and everyone turned to watch.

'What are we looking at?' asked Jack nervously.

'Trouble in Valencia,' said Miss Coleman. 'And some looting in Barcelona too.' Three men then appeared on screen, each with a handful of ashes in their hands. They were shouting at the camera.

'No!' cried the students next to Itch, hands over their mouths. It didn't need translating. The burning money was not just happening in Madrid.

More interviews followed, each word loud in the silent café, even if the CA students barely understood a word. 'They are saying the banks have taken their money,' said Miss Coleman; 'that all their savings will be burned.'

The report now showed hooded men throwing bricks at a shop window. The focus was erratic and the camera wobbled, but there were gasps of recognition from the watching customers. The students immediately grabbed their belongings, pocketing their phones and packing up their computers. One of them turned to the CA students, clearly trying to choose the right words.

'We must leave,' he said in heavily accented English. 'You must leave. That' – he pointed at the TV pictures of looters – 'that is here. They are here.'

And then the café window shattered.

16

The air was full of flying glass. The customers screamed as a thousand fragments blew in on them. Itch felt little daggers hitting his neck and dropped to the floor, pulling Chloe down with him. Her cheek was bleeding, and she was breathing in short, panicky gasps. He grabbed hold of her jacket.

When the looters ran in, yelling and kicking over tables, he held her closer. Itch watched as the men, all with scarves round their faces, made their way over to the food counter, stuffing their pockets with wraps and sandwiches. They heaved the glittering coffee machine to the floor and swung a chair at the bean jars, scattering coffee and glass over the terrified customers. With more yells and chants, they ran from the café.

When he was sure they were gone, Itch looked around. All the customers had dived to the floor, some under tables, and most were wide-eyed and blandly. He saw that Miss Coleman's eyes were closed, blood pouring from a wound in her head; a brick lay nearby.

'Everyone stay down,' shouted Mr Hampton. 'Is everyone OK? Let me hear you call your names! Go!'

One by one, the students called out their names, some falteringly, others loudly.

'Jack.'

'Natalie.'

'Chloe.'

'Debbie.'

'Lucy.'

'Tom.'

'Craig.'

'Luke.'

'Russell.'

'Itch. Sir, Miss Coleman looks bad.'

Mr Hampton crawled over. He exclaimed when he saw the blood. Miss Coleman was conscious now, but she'd started to shake; he propped her up against an overturned table. The manager who, moments before, had been threatening to throw them all out now arrived with a first-aid box and some water. Miss Coleman nodded her thanks, then winced; she was already sporting an enormous bruise and her jacket was red with blood.

'We'll get you to a doctor. But first we have to leave,' said Mr Hampton. Miss Coleman nodded again and struggled to her feet.

Everyone was standing now, pale and scared, Chloe holding onto Itch's arm. Through the smashed window they could see groups of people running in every direction. Across the road through lines of parked cars, a group were kicking at a shop front. When it gave way, the alarm blasted to life and they disappeared inside.

'Sir, might it be safer to stay put?' asked Lucy. 'We don't know what's happening out there.'

Mr Hampton found his map and, sweeping away glass and coffee beans, spread it out on the floor. 'We are here,' he said, pointing. 'Paseo del Doctor Vallejo Nágera. We have to cross one of the bridges over the Rio Manzanares and make it back to the Plaza Lucenza, here . . .' He stabbed his finger at a small square. 'That's maybe forty minutes' walk – I don't think we'll find a bus now. I think we should go. It doesn't feel safe here.'

They left the café, nodding their thanks to the manager, who was tending to one of the other customers.

'*Buena suerte,*' she said.

'What's that, sir?' asked Jack.

'Good luck,' said Mr Hampton. 'She said good luck.'

'Where are the police?' said Miss Coleman, a bloodied souvenir tea towel held to her head as she scanned the road. 'You'd think they'd be here by now.'

'Well, if the news was anything to go by, they'll be busy,' said Mr Hampton. 'We can't rely on them.'

'Sir,' said Itch, 'why don't I text that number we were given? I know it was just for keeping the police up to date with our movements, but—'

'Yes. Do it,' said Hampton. 'In case any of them are watching their screens—'

He was interrupted by shouts from the looters leaving the shop, arms full of trainers.

'They did all that for shoes?' asked Chloe in amazement.

'They've only just started,' said Lucy. 'Look, they're all on their phones. There'll be more coming.'

'You know you said we should leave our phones at the hostel, sir,' said Jack. 'Well, what if we get separated, what do we do then?' Itch could hear the tension in her voice as she watched the looters coordinate their next move.

'We won't get separated,' said Hampton. 'We stay together. We look like tourists – no one will think we're looters – you're too young, and Miss Coleman and I look too old. We're going to the hostel – we'll be safe. Let's go.'

With Mr Hampton on one side and a patched up Miss Coleman on the other, they walked in a tight group down the middle of the road.

'We're being watched,' said Chloe, looking up at the top windows of the buildings, where silhouetted faces could be seen staring down at them. Scooters buzzed backwards and forwards, some with passengers riding pillion. After a couple of drive-pasts, one pulled up alongside them; its rider had a scarf around his mouth, his hood pulled low, and he studied them one by one.

They all increased their pace and closed ranks, the girls linking arms.

'What's he want?' wondered Chloe, not taking her eyes off the road ahead.

Itch shrugged. 'Who knows? Money? Our passports? Your trainers maybe.' His attempt at cheery humour didn't register, and when two more scooters arrived alongside them, everyone tensed.

Miss Coleman removed the tea towel from her face. '*Soy inglesa*,' she said. '*Habla inglés?*' None of them acknowledged her question, but one by one they peeled away. 'I asked if they spoke English. Guess the answer's no.'

'Fire ahead . . .' said Itch. 'At the crossroads.' Flames had burst from a wall and a crowd had started to gather. As the CA students approached, they saw that the building was a bank; a cash point was on fire. A weird high-pitched whistle filled the air.

From every direction, more people were coming to see the spectacle. The crowd already numbered around fifty and almost all of them were filming the fire at the ATM. The two who weren't, Itch noticed, were staring straight at him. They were standing in the doorway of a darkened newsstand; unnerved, he turned to attract Jack's attention, but when he looked back, they had gone.

More flames burst from the cash point; more cries from the crowd.

'No wonder these people are mad,' said Jack. 'That's their money that's burning in there.'

'No, it isn't . . .' said Itch, still looking around. 'It's just money. I think they're just mad at the banks

Mad at everyone. Did anyone see those guys at the newsstand just now?'

A bottle smashed above the cash point and some of the crowd cheered. Itch's question went unanswered.

'Come on,' said Mr Hampton. 'Let's not hang about.' He steered his group around the crowd and down a street called Paseo de las Acacias. 'Did you send that text?' he asked Itch.

'Tried to,' said Itch. 'No signal. Maybe it's the network. Everyone else seems to be using their phones, though.'

'The police might have shut the phone networks down. I expect the demonstrators are using the BlackBerry messenger system. Can't stop that without killing the internet.'

'But what are they demonstrating about?' said Chloe.

'Everything,' said Mr Hampton as they strode quickly past department stores; the remaining staff pulling down shutters as fast as they could. 'Unemployment. The government. America. Poverty. All of it. If you haven't got much money to start with, your euros catching fire is a disaster.' Hampton pointed at the end of the street. 'That's the bridge ahead. Puente de Toledo, the Toledo bridge. We need to cross there.'

Ahead, the wail of a siren; behind them, the sound of breaking glass. Itch glanced over his shoulder just as a car went up in flames. The wave of heat caught them by surprise, and Natalie swallowed a scream. They paused to watch a Renault disappear in the inferno; within seconds the Fiat next to it was engulfed too. Scores of chanting rioters in scarves and balaclavas ran to join in. Brandishing stones and bricks, they attacked car after car; windscreens shattered, doors were stoved in, boots looted.

'We seriously need to keep moving,' Jack shouted above the din.

'Too right,' said Lucy. 'Those guys look like they might do anything – like they're high on something.'

They closed on the bridge entrance. As the riot gathered pace behind them, they moved faster, held on tighter. Even the boys linked arms, Itch hooked up with Chloe on his left and Jack on his right. Lucy had Jack and Tom. It might have been the dropping temperature or the rising tension but Itch was aware that they all seemed to be shaking.

The bridge was around fifty metres across, raised slightly in the middle, with ornate walls and carvings along its sides.

'How far, sir?' asked Debbie, her black knitted hat pulled down low over her wide eyes.

'Not far,' said Hampton, in a manner that did not invite further questioning. 'Itch, any signal on your phone yet?'

Itch checked. 'Nothing,' he called.

Hampton glanced at Miss Coleman, who had been checking hers too, but she shook her head.

As they approached the bridge, they realized

they had company: a few people were, like them, trying to get back to the city centre, but most were running towards the riot. And amongst them were TV crews with lights and cameras under their arms, ready for action. A man in a suit and with well-coiffed hair glanced at them as they ran past.

'Spot the journalist,' said Hampton.

'How do they get their hair so it never moves?' wondered Itch.

'Wax and vanity,' said Hampton. 'A potent combination.'

Suddenly, behind them, they heard glass breaking, then loud cheers. They turned to see that flames were shooting out of the department store windows. The crowd stepped back from the inferno, but they were exultant, those at the front jumping up and down and chanting.

The arrival – 'At last,' said Hampton – of blue flashing lights and piercing sirens changed the mood instantly. Scores of the demonstrators turned and ran from the police and straight for the bridge.

'They're coming this way!' shouted Lucy, and they all started to jog.

Itch tried to concentrate on keeping in step and holding onto Chloe but the volume of the crowd was increasing and he needed to see how close they were. What he saw made him cry out, 'Faster! We need to go faster!'

The demonstrators were running at a speed that indicated they were being chased. Across the width of the bridge they came, some still with scarves on their faces, others waving them like flags. Behind them, Itch saw the police cars, herding them across the Toledo Bridge like sheep.

The shouting, the sirens and the sounds of rioting were beginning to create panic: in the school party Natalie tripped, Tom falling over her and crashing to the ground. They all stopped to help, but by the time everyone was up and moving again, the running crowd was nearly upon them.

It was a stampede.

Staying still wasn't an option.

They ran.

17

The students and staff of the CA on the Toledo Bridge soon realized that you can't sprint holding hands. With the fleeing demonstrators metres away and closing fast, they broke ranks. The Year Eleven boys were already sprinting away, while Mr Hampton and Miss Coleman frantically tried to keep track of the dispersing group.

'Itch! Stay with me!' yelled Chloe, already falling behind. He checked his stride and they ran together, but now they were barely keeping ahead of the demonstrators. Jack and Lucy were out in front and so were the first to brake; they stopped dead.

With a wall of noise and flashing lights, white vans with POLICÍA emblazoned on the side screeched to a halt, and lines of black-clad riot police ran to face them. They wore black helmets with visors pulled down, black padded jackets, and in gloved hands carried shields and batons.

The crowd struggled to stop, a few losing their

footing and disappearing headlong into the crush. They backed up a few metres, but there were police cars behind them too. Shouts of rage and frustration erupted as they looked first one way, then the other. Itch thought Mr Hampton and Miss Coleman looked frozen, terrified. Natalie and Debbie started to cry.

'Sir, we can't stay here,' shouted Itch. 'We look like rioters. We're with rioters. They'll treat us like rioters.'

'He's right, Henry,' said Miss Coleman. 'They're not going to bother sorting out the tourists from the rioters.'

'And we go where?' shouted Mr Hampton. 'In case you hadn't noticed, we are being "kettled" – controlled, surrounded. They'll keep us here for as long as they need to. No one's going anywhere.'

'But we need to tell them we're not a part of all this!' insisted Itch.

'Do they look like they're interested in chatting?' Hampton turned to see lines of mounted police arriving behind the vans. A battery of camera flashes accompanied their arrival.

'No, they don't,' admitted Itch. 'They really don't.' He checked his phone again – still no signal.

'Maybe try him,' said Jack, pointing at the journalist with perfect hair. He was in the middle of the crowd, being jostled and pushed but still managing to speak into the camera.

Itch smiled briefly at Jack and pushed his way into the crowd. The demonstrators were so densely packed, it took five minutes to get anywhere near the TV reporter. But as everyone else was shouting, Itch couldn't attract his attention.

Suddenly Lucy was by his side. She grabbed his arm and leaned in close. 'What are you doing?' she yelled.

'I'm gonna talk to him,' said Itch, indicating the reporter. 'Someone needs to say we don't want to be here and we aren't rioters. That's all.'

The man had started interviewing those around him, and Itch dived in, Lucy following close behind. He knew he was being sworn at as he shoved his way through, but it was in Spanish and he didn't care.

The powerful TV light was shining at two young women with burning euros in their hands. Even though they'd seen it before, the watching crowd were clearly stunned: the spontaneous combustion illuminated shocked faces. Someone produced a T-shirt bearing the Spanish flag and, dangling it above the flames, set it alight. The cameras followed the blaze, and the reporter looked pleased, nodding at his cameraman.

He was about to move on to a woman with a Guy Fawkes mask when Itch shouted, '*Habla inglés?*' It was what he had heard Miss Coleman say meant 'Do you speak English?' He knew his accent was terrible, but it worked: the reporter turned away from the demonstrator and raised his eyebrows at Itch.

'*Si!* Yes. I speak some English. Why are you here?

What is it you want?' He pushed his microphone at him, and the powerful light made Itch squint.

'We are on a science trip here from England and we want to get home,' he shouted. 'We got caught up in all this – our money started burning at a café and it got looted. We are not campaigning or marching or fighting . . .' He looked around. 'There's a lot of scared people here who just want to get home!'

The reporter turned to the camera, speaking in Spanish, and Itch peeled away to find Lucy behind him.

'You were great,' she said. 'Let's hope he translates that.'

They had started to push their way back to the others when a man with a ponytail wearing an army-style camouflage shirt grabbed Itch by the arm. Itch winced.

'You got a problem with this?' he said, his English only slightly accented. He gestured to the demonstrators. 'I heard what you said to the TV. We don't need doubters and deniers. This is a battle. They've stolen our jobs and now they're stealing our money.' Others around them started watching and when the camouflaged man spoke to them in rapid Spanish, there were nods of approval for his words. When he reached for Itch's other arm, Lucy pushed her way through in front of him.

'Leave him alone! We are just on a school—'

Without warning the man head-butted Itch hard and, lights popping in his head, he dropped to his knees; someone pushed him over and a boot pressed down on his back. He felt strong arms wrap around his waist; two more took hold of his ankles.

What the hell is happening here? thought Itch. *Someone's trying to drag me away!* He twisted and kicked just as the crowd surged and the hands were torn away, releasing him. With hundreds of closely packed people and the possibility of a police charge, Itch knew that he had to get up fast. He tried to ignore his splitting headache, and he writhed and spun away from the legs around him. A sudden gap in the crowd appeared as a fight broke out, and he found Lucy helping him up.

'Come on, let's get out of here,' she said.

'What happened?' said Itch, his head ringing. The camouflaged man was now exchanging blows with two other men.

'Some guys started fighting with him. Let's not be around when it's over.'

'And someone else tried to grab me . . .' said Itch. 'I'm sure of it.' He looked around frantically, but the crowd was too dense for him to see anything. He shrugged; he didn't know what or who he was looking for anyway. 'You OK?' he asked Lucy as they tried to push their way through.

'Fine. Are you? That was some head-butt you took . . .'

'Once my head stops throbbing, yeah.'

The few benches and bins on the bridge were being broken up, attacked with whatever the demonstrators could find. The sound of splintering wood and rupturing metal was everywhere.

'Ammunition?' said Lucy.

'Guess so,' said Itch. They watched graffiti being daubed along the walls and the pavement; most of it made no sense to them.

'Don't suppose that's going to be in our phrase book,' said Lucy.

They had progressed only a few metres when a man in front of them found a stone on the ground and after encouragement from those nearby, hurled it towards the police. It fell short, but others now found projectiles and threw them with greater success; the clatter of glass and stone landing on riot shields was heard by everyone.

'This is bad, Itch,' said Lucy, pushing him though the crowd. 'This lot are pretty hard-core.'

'Agreed. Feels like it's building up to some-thing . . .'

More stones and bottles were launched into the air, each followed by an exultant two-arms-aloft salute. Suddenly there was a deep thud, and a man in front of them collapsed, holding his head. Someone screamed and, looking up, Itch saw missiles falling everywhere.

'They're throwing them back, Lucy!' yelled Itch, crouching and pulling her down as low as the crowd let him.

All around them the crowd were being peppered with the projectiles they had just launched at the police. Blood and screaming were everywhere. As demonstrators fell, spaces opened up in the crowd and Itch and Lucy stepped gingerly around the stricken, a path opening up back to the CA group.

They looked up and spotted their teacher. 'There's Hampton!' cried Lucy. 'He's waving at us. But I can't see the others! Come on!' Eyes on their teacher, who was calling and beckoning them furiously, they dodged, weaved and shoved their way back. As they got closer, they could hear what he was saying, and Itch's stomach seized up.

'Itch! It's Chloe! She's been hit!'

As they reached the group they saw Chloe lying on her side, her bloodied head cradled in Jack's lap. Miss Coleman was kneeling next to her, holding her phone to her ear.

'Trying the emergency number!' she said. 'Maybe that'll get through. She needs medical help fast!'

'The stones just came at us out of nowhere,' cried Jack. 'She didn't stand a chance.'

Itch knelt at his sister's side. She looked deathly white and the cut was deep and ugly. A bystander gave Jack a handkerchief and she pressed it gently against Chloe's forehead. It turned red in an instant.

'We need to get her to a hospital, Jack,' Itch cried. 'And we need to do it now. Help me get her up.'

'Are you sure it's OK to move her?' she asked.

'No, not really . . . But either the police are going to charge or the demonstrators are. We need her on her feet.'

Jack nodded. 'OK, that makes sense.' She and

Miss Coleman lifted one shoulder, Itch and Mr Hampton the other.

'Chloe!' called Itch. 'We're getting you help! Hang on in there!' He ducked and put his arms under his sister. 'OK, I've got her,' he said, scooping up her limp body. She was heavier than he expected, but he knew exactly what he was going to do. Balancing his sister as well as he could, he stepped forward, away from the crowd.

'Itch, stop right there!' called Mr Hampton. 'We stay together . . .'

'Itch, what are you doing?' cried Lucy.

'Quickest way out is straight ahead,' he said, glancing back. 'When they see Chlo, they'll have to let me through.'

Lucy held his sleeve. 'Itch, they don't have to do anything.'

'No, but *I* do,' he said.

'OK . . .' Lucy paused and added, 'And . . . Itch?' She waited till he had turned to face her. 'Don't trust anyone. Try not to be scared.' She managed a smile.

Itch recognized the words immediately. It was how Cake, Lucy's father, had finished his letter to Itch just before he died. Itch's mouth went dry. The unexpected memory shocked him: the spoil heaps of Cornwall and the 126 seemed so far away. He realized he was staring at Lucy and looked away, back towards the lines of shields, batons and flashing blue lights.

'This is what Cake would do,' he said, and before

anyone could stop him, he began his walk towards the police lines.

The no man's land between the demonstrators and the police was thirty metres wide. Itch walked slowly, every step deliberate and focused. This was partly because his sister was bleeding and un-conscious, but also because he wanted the police to see what he was doing. The first voice he heard was Mr Hampton's.

'Itch, you need to wait. You should come back!'

'Chloe needs help *now*,' he shouted back.

'Well, wait for us, we should all go!' His teacher sounded agitated again.

'It's better this way!' Itch yelled and carried on walking. He heard the sound of the crowd change behind him as they stirred, seeing what was happening. He saw the ranks of riot police shift as they watched a boy with a wounded girl in his arms approach. Some shields were lowered; others raised. Through their visors, Itch saw them shouting to each other – they seemed unsure as to how to react. Camera flashes popped all around him and new TV lights trained on him.

Twenty metres from the police, Itch glanced back. He saw Jack and Lucy had started to follow him, tentatively edging forward; Mr Hampton and Miss Coleman calling them back. He didn't want anyone else to get involved – didn't want the police to have any excuse to attack – but he wasn't turn-ing back now. Chloe still hadn't regained consciousness and the blood from her head had continued to flow.

Ten metres out and Itch could sense the nervousness in the ranks of the police. Some of the helmeted figures were shouting at him, and Itch wanted to slow down, but Chloe's breathing was growing shallower and his concern for his sister overpowered his fear of the riot police.

Don't trust anyone. Try not to be scared.

'My sister is injured!' he yelled. 'She needs an ambulance. Now!' His arms were shaking with the effort of keeping her still but at least his legs were steady. He kept walking. They were smaller steps now but he thought if he stopped, he might topple over. The riot police were pointing their batons and shouting at him. Some were staring at the crowd beyond and Itch feared that if his friends – and others – were following, it might look as though he was leading some kind of charge. A painfully slow charge, but a charge nonetheless.

Don't trust anyone.

'English!' he yelled. 'We are English! Please let us through. My sister needs help!' He heard the desperation in his voice. *Surely they'll let us through*, he thought. But the ranks of black-clad police hadn't shifted; no path had opened up. If anything, they were bristling. Poised, ready for battle, waiting for an excuse. It was as though he had a battering ram in his arms, not an unconscious girl.

Itch guessed there were two lines of thirty riot police and counted six on horseback. Behind them were lines and lines of police cars. Flashing lights, camera lights and street lights all illuminated what seemed like an immovable wall of authority ahead; while behind was an unpredictable wave of anger.

Try not to be scared.

'You have to help me! Look!' He tried to hold out his arms, but they had locked, the muscles in spasm. He looked at Chloe. Her face was now deathly white, and in spite of everything, he stopped. Three metres from the first baton, he hesitated. A barrage of flashlights caught the moment and he squeezed his eyes shut. His arm muscles were screaming, and his head was spinning – he knew he was swaying . . . And then, from what seemed like miles away, he heard Jack's voice.

'Take her home, Itch! Don't stop there!'

And he started walking again. Itch heard the blaring of the police radios, and the shouting of instructions or encouragement – he couldn't tell which. At two metres he realized that it was him they were shouting at. At one metre a gloved hand grabbed his arm.

Itch tried to look through the riot policeman's visor but it obscured all detail of the man's face. However, his grip told him everything he needed to know: this was an arrest, not an offer of help. He held Itch in one hand and his baton in the other, ready to strike. Itch pulled his arm away, but the policeman was unyielding and shouted, incomprehensibly. Itch heard the crowd start a new chant, and all around him, shields were raised and batons drawn.

'I just need a doctor!' he yelled. 'She needs help. Can't you see?'

He heard smashing glass, then a bottle hit the policeman's helmet, showering Itch and Chloe with an explosion of shards. The policeman reeled and, still holding his sister, Itch sank to his knees and closed his eyes. He was aware of running boots, of stones hitting shields, of screams from the crowd, but he ignored it all: he simply leaned over Chloe, protecting her with his body.

Hunched over like a fallen jockey protecting himself from the stampede, Itch felt every muscle tensed or screaming with pain. Someone tripped over Itch's legs and he took a blow in the ribs; he knew he needed to get to his feet. He opened his eyes and, through the melee, saw two figures moving towards him, trying to create some space, holding demonstrators and police at bay. While one blocked the path of a man waving a metal barricade, the other knelt in front of him.

'Itchingham Lofte? We've been looking for you. Come this way – hurry please.' Dressed in a thick overcoat, the man looked as though he had just emerged from a business meeting, not walked into a pitched battle. 'Here – let me help you.' He reached out for Chloe, taking the weight from Itch's trembling arms. 'Félix Blanco, Centro Nacional de Inteligencia. We should go.'

Itch struggled to his feet, his arms immobilized by pins and needles.

Don't trust anyone.

'Wait,' he said. 'How can . . . ?' He felt a hand in the small of his back, gently but firmly steering him away.

'We'll explain. But first, let us get off the bridge.' The man's colleague was now using the metal barricade to clear a path for them. They walked round the police lines, past the police cars towards an ambulance, waiting with its doors open.

'No, wait,' said Itch, stopping. 'What's happening here? Where did you come from? Was that *you* back there? Did you try to grab me?'

The man who called himself Blanco turned round, Chloe still unconscious in his arms. 'We're Spanish secret service, like your MI5. We knew you were here, but lost your phone signal when the riot started. Then you turned up on television, and we saw exactly where you were. And no, we haven't approached you until now.'

'You just happened to be close by?' said Itch.

The man smiled. 'When things like this happen . . . ?' He glanced in the direction of the fighting. 'Yes, we are always close by.' He glanced at Chloe; her short brown hair was now thick with blood. 'Your sister?' Itch nodded. 'She needs help. We need to get away.'

Itch felt he had no choice. 'OK. I'll travel with her.'

Félix Blanco spoke quickly with his colleague. 'All right, let's go,' he said, stepping into the ambulance and handing Chloe to the waiting paramedics.

Itch glanced back at the fighting on the bridge. 'Our school party is out there, my cousin Jack . . .'

'We know,' said Blanco. 'We'll get them. Now, will you sit down? You need to get cleaned up.'

As the ambulance set off, Itch looked at his reflection in one of the darkened windows. He had forgotten about the flying glass – his face was covered in cuts. 'OK, you're right,' he said. 'But only after her. Will she be OK?'

Chloe was on a stretcher, an oxygen mask strapped over her mouth; a paramedic was carefully cleaning the head wound. Blanco translated the question, and the medic shrugged and muttered a few words without looking up.

'He says she's lost a lot of blood.'

'I know that,' said Itch, looking at his jacket. 'Most of it is on me. But will she be all right?'

The agent didn't translate again. 'Let him do his job. You'll find out soon enough.'

Itch watched the dressing on his sister's head turn red and closed his eyes tight.

Try not to be afraid.

18

The route to the hospital was not a straightforward one. Every street seemed full of drama: burning cars, smashed shop windows, burning wheelie bins. Itch heard the driver curse as he had to detour around another makeshift barricade. He held Chloe's hand as the paramedic attached a drip.

'Is this all because of the burning money?' he asked the Spanish agent, who sighed.

'Yes,' he said. 'On top of everything else. It's the same in Barcelona and Valencia. People are panicking. It happened to me earlier.' He reached down and picked up half a ten-euro note from the floor of the ambulance; it had the usual pinkish-red archway design, with a big number ten, but there was a jagged black edge where the rest had burned away. He held it up to the harsh ambulance strip light. 'Imagine if this is your savings! What kind of country has a currency that bursts into flames for no reason? These people know they can't trust the politicians or the bankers. Now they can't trust their money.' He handed it to Itch. 'Here. A souvenir of your time in Spain. To go with the scar your sister will have.'

Silver coins seem so much safer, thought Itch. He took the burned note and they both looked at Chloe.

'Do you think she'll be OK?' said Itch.

'I do,' said the agent. 'I'm not a medic, but head wounds always bleed a lot, and' – he shrugged – 'I've seen worse.'

The ambulance was picking up speed now, and the paramedic spoke to Blanco. 'He says we'll be there soon. My colleague and I are to stay with you until you leave the country.'

Itch nodded. *Here we go again*, he thought. 'Thanks.'

'We don't normally look after kids.'

'Right.' Itch didn't know what else to say.

'We were told someone sent you a parcel bomb. Is that right?'

Itch nodded and Blanco whistled. The agent clearly wanted more detail, but Itch didn't feel like telling his story again and stared resolutely through the window. He noticed a road sign that said, HOSPITAL 2.

The paramedic tapped Itch on the leg, and nodded at Chloe.

Her eyes were open.

'Chloe!' Itch shifted along the seat into her eye line and she managed a feeble smile. 'You got hit by a rock,' he said. 'We're on the way to hospital.' He smiled at her 'Another one,' he added.

Chloe cleared her throat and the medic offered her some water. She sipped slowly. 'Mum's going to go mad,' she whispered.

Itch had rung home as soon as Chloe was delivered to the doctors at the hospital. His sister had been wrong – Jude Lofte had seen the news of the riots in Spain and watched in horror as the cameras focused on the image of the boy with the bloodied, lifeless girl in his arms. For the media it was the definitive image of the night; for Jude it was her son and daughter in mortal peril. When Itch rang to say that Chloe was awake and talking, Jude broke down in shuddering sobs of relief. She said she or Nicholas would fly out soon, and Itch had promised to be back in touch.

It was after midnight when Chloe returned from having her wound stitched up and was shown into a private room. Jack and Lucy arrived soon afterwards with a fraught Mr Hampton. They described how they had survived the battle on the bridge, avoiding most of the brutality by being nowhere near the stone throwers. Craig Murray had bruised ribs, and Luke and Russell, the two Year Elevens, had suffered cuts and were treated at the scene. Miss Coleman was back at the hostel with the rest of the party. The cut on her head was not deep, but she was sporting a large plaster. They had been told that they would be flown home the next day, Chloe and Itch joining them only if the doctors said it was safe for her to fly.

Jack and Lucy took it in turns to use Itch's phone and call home; Mr Hampton's had run out of battery hours ago. Everyone's parents knew what was happening as Jude had rung Jack's dad and Lucy's mum, and they had then contacted all the other parents. Mr Hampton asked to borrow Itch's phone too, and walked away down a corridor.

Itch, Jack and Lucy sat around Chloe's bed while Félix Blanco waited outside.

'It's chaos out there,' said Jack. 'The hospital's as bad as the streets. So many injuries – people waiting to get their heads stitched up.'

'Think I was the first,' said Chloe.

'And one of the most serious,' said Lucy. 'That's some pretty fancy stitch work you've got there.'

'Fifteen, they said.' Chloe gingerly touching her head. Most of the blood had been washed from her hair, but some of the more congealed patches still showed through from her scalp. 'Lucky they saw Itch.'

Lucy and Jack looked puzzled. 'Lucky *who* saw Itch?' asked Jack.

'Turns out the police or secret service people saw that interview on the bridge and came and got me,' said Itch. 'They're going to fly us out with you guys, if Chlo's OK.'

'Well, the airports are pretty stuffed up,' said Jack. 'They told us at the hostel that apparently, two planes had to make emergency landings because money caught fire on board. And the airports had lots of burning cash too. Loads of flights have been cancelled.'

'Wow,' said Itch. 'Mum said that she or Dad would fly out, but it sounds like they might not make it after all.' He looked around. 'I wish none of this had happened, of course, and I'm pleased Chlo's going to be OK . . . But I'm glad I didn't cause it. Bad stuff usually has something to do with me – but not this time. It's nothing to do with us!'

'That's true, Itch,' said Lucy, finding her camera, 'but you remember that graffiti we saw on the bridge just before the bottles and stones started flying?'

'Yes. Don't remember what it said, though.'

'Well, look at this. I took it after the fighting, while Hampton was trying to find everyone. I'll send it to you.' She showed Itch a video of the bridge, showing scores of demonstrators lying or sitting on the road. Then the film focused on the words sprayed in purple on the bridge wall. There were several in Spanish that he remembered but then one phrase he didn't. Lucy had zoomed in on two words that had appeared alongside the slogans.

Itch read them out loud, astonished.

'*Meyn Mamvro* . . .'

Itch slept at the hospital – in a makeshift bed on the floor of Chloe's room – while the rest of the CA party returned to the hostel. The next morning Chloe was given the go-ahead to return home; the stitched-up wound was starting to heal, though the left side of her face was badly bruised. A plane was summoned to take them home, and by the end of the day they were touching down in Cornwall.

'Didn't know you could fly from Madrid to Newquay,' said Jack as they snapped off their seat belts.

'You can't,' Itch replied, 'unless they want you out of the country. Then people like Blanco talk to people like Fairnie, and it's amazing what can happen.' As they all walked to the terminal – Chloe had refused the offer of a wheelchair – Craig Murray and Tom Westgate came to thank Chloe for the plane-ride home. 'Saved us that boring trip to London – thanks!'

'How are the ribs, Craig?' asked Itch.

Even though the night air was cold, the boy pulled up his jacket and shirt to reveal a swathe of bandages wrapped around his chest. 'Sore but OK,' he said. 'Got a bit crushed when the police waded in, that's all. But I might claim it was a baton or something – just to make it more exciting.' He hurried to catch up with the others, and Itch leaned over to Jack and Lucy.

'Imagine needing to make life more exciting!' he said.

They both smiled at him, and then they followed the weary party into the terminal building. At the luggage carousel, Jack spotted a familiar figure.

'Wow, look – it's Colonel Fairnie,' she said as the MI5 man strode over to them.

He smiled as he shook their hands. 'Hello again,' he said. 'Wasn't expecting to see you so soon.

Sounds like a nasty riot you got caught up in. How's that head, Chloe?'

'Sore and throbbing,' she said, 'but I've got painkillers. I've got to go for a check-up tomorrow.'

Fairnie nodded as Mr Hampton came over. 'Colonel Fairnie . . . checking up on us again?' Itch thought their teacher sounded irritated as well as exhausted.

'Not at all. I just need a quiet word with Itch, if I may. Before he goes through immigration. I've arranged a room . . .' He indicated an open office nearby.

Hampton sighed. 'OK, I'll get Miss Coleman to take the others through. I'll wait for you, Itch.'

Itch hesitated as Fairnie led the way into the fiercely lit interrogation room. 'Can the others come please? I'll need to tell them everything anyway.'

'Of course, if that's easier,' the colonel replied, and Itch beckoned them over. There were only three chairs at a cheap plywood table so Itch, Jack and Lucy stood and Chloe sat, while Fairnie closed the door behind him.

'Firstly, you need to know that the press are here. It's quite a scrum, I'm afraid.' He spread a few newspapers on the table; they all carried photos of Itch approaching the police lines with Chloe in his arms. The headlines screamed: SAVE MY SISTER! or TERROR BOY IS A HERO! One proclaimed: THE SCHOOL TRIP NIGHTMARE – MORE PROBLEMS FOR 'DISASTER ACADEMY'!

'You will have to say something,' said Fairnie, 'and then maybe they'll leave you alone. But I wouldn't count on it.' He paused and Itch thought he looked weary; exhausted even.

'Is there something wrong?' asked Jack, sensing the unease.

Fairnie sighed. 'To put it bluntly, yes – though my bosses would say no. Here's what happening.' He leaned against the table in front of them and folded his arms. He looked at each of them in turn, and then, with a thumb and forefinger, stroked his moustache. 'I'm being moved to another case and will not be in contact again. This is partly because I have important work elsewhere, but also because Greencorps are going legit.'

'They're *what*?' said Jack.

'They are going legitimate. They are going legal. They know their reputation is mud and – they say they're going to do something about it. Everyone is keen to expose the bad practices in the oil industry, and this is their chance. The new boss of the company has said – publicly – that she wants Greencorps to be the whistle-blower, to be the company that exposes the criminality and price fixing. And people have got very excited about that.'

'But this is *Greencorps*, right?' said Itch, astonished. 'The company that caused the oil spill in Nigeria, that hired Flowerdew and Shivvi . . . Does anyone believe a word they say? I heard from one of the divers that Flowerdew was in charge. He'd killed the old guys and taken over himself! That's going *legit*?'

Fairnie spread his arms and nodded. 'Precisely. But the desire to "get" the oil industry is greater than the desire to "get" Greencorps. They say they have changed. They have a new CEO to replace Revere and Van Den Hauwe . . .' He checked some papers. 'She's called Mary Bale apparently, and she says they'll tell all in return for immunity from prosecution; governments around the world are willing to take her up on it. They are doing a deal with the prosecutors. There's no sign of Flowerdew having anything to do with it, I'm afraid. So you see, this has got way, way bigger than anything I can do. I have argued that they cannot be trusted; that they – more than any other company – should be prosecuted for all the misery they've caused. But I have lost, and it is important that you know – that you all know – how things have changed.'

There was silence in the room. Lucy swore.

'Precisely,' said Fairnie.

'And the hunt for Flowerdew?' said Itch. 'He's still a wanted man, right?'

'Right.'

Itch waited for more detail, but none came, and Fairnie looked uncomfortable. 'Colonel . . . ?'

'Look, yes, he's wanted; yes, there are still agents on the case. But is it a priority?' He shrugged.

'But he sent the letter bombs!' cried Jack. 'We know he did! He killed Mr Watkins, tried to kill Itch and blow up the school. And killed Shivvi!'

'Which is why he is still wanted,' said Fairnie. 'But it's a question of priorities, Jack. And priorities can change. Have changed.' He looked at them, his face set and unblinking. 'I'll argue the case whenever I can, of course, but it's the police you should report to in future. I'm sorry, but that's the official line. And this comes from very high up.' He looked as though he was about to say something else, but checked himself. 'Good luck,' he said, and marched out of the room.

The four stared at each other as the noise of the airport filled the room again.

'Sounds like we're on our own,' said Jack.

Jude and Nicholas Lofte, along with Jack's parents, arrived soon afterwards, followed by a tearful Nicola Cavendish. Itch was pleased to be back; he was glad that everyone was safe, but the sense of betrayal stayed with him through the bewildering, chaotic airport press conference. He knew he should be concentrating on the questions and trying not to look stupid, but the image of Fairnie walking away wouldn't shift.

'Did you think your sister would die?'

'What do you feel about the demonstrators?'

'Would you ever go back to Spain?'

He had assumed that Fairnie would always be there if he needed him. He had saved him from kidnap, rescued them at the ISIS labs and stood by him after the fiasco of the funeral. Now he was gone.

'Smile for us, Chloe – show us your stitches!'

'What's wrong with your school, Itch?'

'What do you think about it being called the Disaster Academy?'

The flashguns were firing constantly, and Itch closed his eyes and put his head in his hands; for some reason that made them flash all the more. He had assumed that Mr Watkins would always be there for him too, and the images of the fire that had killed him filled his mind, merging with burning euros and exploding cash points. He'd had enough.

Itch stood up. 'Come on – let's go,' he said to Jack. 'This sucks.'

'Is there anything you'd say you have learned from the last few days?' called a voice from the throng of journalists.

Itch couldn't see the reporter who had asked the question, but realized he had an answer anyway. He leaned back down to the microphone.

'Yeah. Don't trust anyone,' he said.

19

Itch had forgotten that it was Easter. When they eventually made it home, they found Gabriel slouching at the kitchen table, his long legs crossed at the ankle. He had a steaming mug of tea in his hand.

'Hey, it's calamity girl and disaster boy!' He hugged his sister and high-fived his brother. 'Good trip?' he asked, grinning. His long wavy hair might have looked like his brother's, but his smile was definitely his sister's. His laptop was open, and he spun it round for everyone to see. The news website had their return as its lead story, ahead of the continuing chaos in Spain. A short piece of video showed Itch, Jack, Chloe and Lucy flanked by their parents and lit by a hundred flashguns.

Chloe couldn't watch. 'I look hideous,' she said, turning away.

'Not true,' said Gabriel. 'If anything, it looks pretty impressive. Let's see the wound?' Chloe lifted some hair up to show him the stitches and he whistled. 'I have a battle-hardened sister, with a war wound courtesy of the Spanish police. Many of my student friends would kill to have that to show off!'

Chloe looked puzzled. 'Maybe you have weird friends, then. How is uni anyway?'

He shrugged. 'Same. Exams, soon. Bit behind – you know how it is. But tell me about the burning money – that looked really scary! Did it happen to you?'

Even though it was after midnight, they sat around the table, talking. Jude and Nicholas – sustained by a fresh pot of tea – joined them. Itch and Chloe described how the euros had caught fire in the museum and café, and how the cash points had burst into flames. When they got to the battle on the bridge, Jude was open-mouthed.

'When we heard the reports from Madrid, we feared you might be caught up in the trouble, but then we saw the pictures . . .'

Gabriel put his arm round his mother as she faltered. 'Mum called Dad and me in to see that shot of you two in front of the police line,' he said. 'It did look bad, guys, I have to tell you.'

They all looked at Chloe and she managed a weak smile. 'I'll be OK,' she said. 'Though some more painkillers would be good.'

Jude stood up. 'I'll get them.'

'Was it your money that burned, Itch?' asked Nicholas. 'I got the euros here in town, and they sat in my wallet for a couple of days without any trouble.'

'No, they were fine.' Itch fished his wallet out of his jacket. He cleared the mugs and spread the notes on the table; everyone recoiled, then laughed at each other.

'Should I have a bucket of water ready?' asked Jude, only half joking.

They stared at the notes for a while before Gabriel said, 'This feels really silly.'

When nothing happened, Itch remembered his souvenir from Blanco. 'The Spanish agent who rescued us gave me this.' He produced the charred ten-euro note and passed it round.

Nicholas took it first, holding it up to the light and then sniffing it. 'You know who you should take this to, don't you? Jacob Alexander at the mining school. He's got the tools to find out what's happened here.' He offered the note to Gabriel. 'I could run you there in the morning, Itch. You can bet your life the Spanish government and banks will be doing all the tests they can right now to find out what's happened. There's talk of calling it a terrorist attack; their government might not survive the week. Why don't we see what Jacob's lab can tell us?'

Itch nodded. Testing the euro was a good idea; analysis and facts had been in short supply so far, but he wasn't sure about going back to the mining school. It was there that Alexander had identified the rocks of 126; there that they had fought off three Greencorps agents before being kidnapped by Flowerdew. There was a knot forming in his stomach, but that wasn't a reason to stay away.

'Sure. Why not?'

'I'll send him an email now,' said Nicholas.

'By the way . . .' said Gabriel. 'Bit random, I know, but what did you make of the car video I sent you?'

It took a few moments for Itch and Chloe to remember the wreck covered in graffiti.

'Yeah, that was weird,' said Itch; then, remembering the video Lucy had taken, added, 'But look at this! Lucy took it on the bridge in Spain.' He played the clip with *Meyn Mamvro* scrawled alongside the Spanish slogans.

'Wow,' said Gabriel, 'it really is *everywhere*. And there's been more while you were away – a really big one.' He typed something into a search engine, and up came the familiar image of St Michael's Mount. The headline was IS NOTHING SACRED? above pictures of a wrecked chapel and a smashed shrine. *MM* had been sprayed over a Cornish flag. 'They've gone mad down there,' he went on. 'They're saying it's like an attack on Cornwall itself. There are groups of locals patrolling the streets. No one seems to know who's responsible, but they looked pretty angry to me.'

Jude frowned. 'What's going on?' she said. 'St Michael's Mount, Madrid, the Hurlers, the parcel bombs . . . Everything's gone mad.'

And suddenly Itch wanted to see Mr Watkins again; to see him at school on Monday – mad clothes, weird tea and everything – just so he could ask him. He would have had a good theory about the attackers, one based on reason and evidence, not wild stupid speculation. His eyes welled up, and he left the table to cover his embarrassment.

He ran up the stairs, his head crammed with the unfairness of it all. He shut the door and leaned against it. Watkins was gone, Fairnie was gone, and Flowerdew was still out there somewhere . . . What was he supposed to do — just pretend nothing had happened? Go back to school and carry on? At least his dad was around now, but he wasn't sure how long it would be before his next trip . . . or whether he and his mum would still be speaking.

Instinctively, he reached for his old rucksack. His element collection was scattered now, but there were still plenty of items to study and sort. He emptied out the rocks, tubes and tins, arranging them in columns on the floor; as each found its place, he muttered its name and number. The europium he had brought back from South Africa was placed in the bottom two rows, along with nearly all the rare earth elements.

Itch's most recent acquisition had been left in his room; ordered with and opened by his father. A small box lay on his bedside table, sealed in plastic. It contained a clear bag of tiny grey beads. He read from the small sheet of paper: *Iodine, non-metallic solid. Chemical symbol I, atomic number 53, melting point 114 degrees C.* He stood in front of his Periodic Table, and held the bag by the square for iodine, second to last column, third from the bottom

It sat in between tellurium and xenon, and Itch allowed himself a small smile. 'Two old friends,' he said.

Tellurium had been added to Flowerdew's whisky; it made him stink of garlic – an unusual by-product but one that had alerted Itch to his presence at the ISIS labs. And Itch had once used a canister of xenon gas to anaesthetize Flowerdew so that he and Jack could escape from his car.

He continued reading:

Discovered as a result of the Napoleonic Wars of the nineteenth century. Desperate for more potassium nitrate to make gunpowder, a French cottage industry grew, producing it from heaps of rotting manure from latrines and cesspits. Mixed with soil and ashes, it produced potassium.

'Neat,' said Itch.

A local chemist then added sulphuric acid, and the purple fumes condensed to form beautiful crystals. He had discovered a new element – iodine. More explosives can be found by researching 'fulminates'.

Never able to resist the word 'explosive', Itch did just that, making notes and checking facts in his father's old *Golden Book of Chemistry Experiments*. He found details of old experiments, together with comments his father had made when the book had been his.

Itch studied the ordered rows and columns of numbers and letters that represented everything that existed, anywhere, and felt himself calming down. Everything in his life seemed to be out of control, but in front of this poster he found the order he wanted. He knew it seemed ridiculous to everyone else, with the exception of Lucy, but he didn't care.

There was a knock on his bedroom door, and Chloe put her head round. 'You OK? I was just off to bed.'

'Yeah, just wanted to think some stuff through, that's all.'

She sat down on his bed. 'New element?'

'Yup. Iodine. Want to see?'

'Not really.'

'Oh. OK.'

'Just wanted to say thanks for getting me to hospital, that's all.'

He shrugged. 'You're welcome. Any time.'

'Well, I'll need to go to the head-injuries clinic in Exeter apparently. So then would be good.'

He shrugged again. 'Sure.'

There was another knock and Gabriel came in.

'And you're welcome too,' said Itch.

'Am I missing a sibling meeting?'

'Yes, but you've missed quite a few over the years,' said Itch.

'Fair point,' said Gabriel. 'Anything dangerous?' He pointed at the iodine beads.

'Er, according to this' – Itch waved the information sheet – 'only if you add it to ammonia.'

'Are you planning to add it to ammonia?' asked Gabriel.

'Doesn't feel like the time really,' said Itch quietly.

Itch thought he'd be asleep within seconds, but it was wishful thinking. The events of the last few days had sent his head spinning; just when he thought he was drifting off, images of a burning note, Chloe's stitches or a crashing baton filled his head again. When sleep finally came, it was all too brief. For a moment he thought his vibrating pillow was part of a dream, but when his head cleared and he heard the accompanying grinding sound, he realized that it was his phone. His clock said 3.10 a.m., and he reached under his pillow. In the darkness, the illuminated screen's image of his cousin filled the bedroom and Itch squinted in the glare.

'Jack?' he whispered, disappearing under the duvet for soundproofing.

'Itch! You awake?' She was whispering too.

'Yes. What's up?'

'There's something happening at the church! I was just outside and I saw a light—'

'Wait,' said Itch. 'You were outside at three o'clock in the morning?'

'I left some toiletries in Dad's car. I didn't want to wake anyone so I just crept out. You know how you can see the corner of the church from our drive? Well, there was a van and some guys there.'

Itch thought for a moment. 'What were they doing?'

'To start with they stayed in the van. Then a couple of them got out and went into the church-yard. That's all I could see. Should I wake Dad? Call the police?'

Itch hesitated. He knew that the correct answer was *yes* and *yes*, but the desire to find out and see for himself was strong. 'Maybe.'

'Itch, I know what you're thinking . . .' she said.

'I'll be outside in two minutes. If they're still there, we'll call the police then.'

He dressed hurriedly and was on the point of leaving his room when he checked, turned back and scribbled *At church with Jack* on a sheet of paper, leaving it on the floor. When he clicked the front door shut behind him, he thought briefly of the last time he had slipped out of his house. That had ended in Shivvi strapping caesium tubes to him and Jack, their kidnap, and Shivvi's murder at the hands of Flowerdew and his henchmen. *This is different,* he told himself. *These are just vandals and we need to find out who they are.*

It was cold, the air crisp; the clouds had cleared since their return, and the moon was out. Itch's breath billowed as he ran the short distance to Jack's house. She was already sitting on the doorstep with a woolly hat pulled down over her eyes. As she saw Itch approaching, she waved, clearly relieved to see him.

'This is mad!' she said as he ran up to her.

'We'll be fine. We're just watching,' he said, panting slightly.

'And not getting kidnapped.'

'Definitely not getting kidnapped.'

She pointed down the hill at a small dark van parked in the shadows before the lights of the main road. The orange sodium streetlamp illuminated a corner of the churchyard, but nothing was moving.

'That's the van,' said Jack. 'No one's come back yet – could they be in the church?'

'It'd be locked,' said Itch. 'There might be someone still in the van. Let's loop round the other side. Maybe we'll see what's happening from there.'

Jack nodded, and they jogged along the street that ran behind the church. Every house was dark, every curtain drawn as they passed the parked cars. Despite his exhaustion, Itch felt alive, his heart racing with adrenalin.

Turning sharp right downhill, they trod carefully, quietly, and immediately heard noises ahead. Beyond the church wall, about six houses away, in a small group of trees, there was a faint light – a torch maybe; they dropped to a crouch, tucking themselves in by a garden gate.

Once their breathing had slowed and their hearts stopped hammering, they heard sounds coming from the churchyard: a slow, methodical crunching followed by regular, perfunctory scraping. They both looked at each other incredulously, and Jack mouthed, 'Digging?'

Itch nodded – that was exactly what it sounded like. It would last for a minute, stop, then continue again. The occasional low grumble of indistinct voices could be heard. 'We need to get closer!' he whispered, but Jack held him back.

'We go closer – fine, but not so that they can see us.' She held up her phone. 'I can call the police anytime.'

Itch nodded and, stooping, led the way along the garden wall. A lone car passed along the road in front of the church, and all noise from the church-yard stopped. As the sound of its engine receded, the scraping continued and Itch edged closer.

The moonlight gave the trees a wet, metallic look; it also lit two figures bending over as they worked. They were merely silhouettes amongst the trees, but one was clearly digging while the other appeared to be sifting or measuring. Occasionally the sifter would stop, and a torch beam would briefly illuminate the scene.

'Gravediggers?' mouthed Itch, and Jack shrugged, her eyes wide.

'Film them!' whispered Itch. Jack looked horrified. 'Go on! Let's film them!' he repeated.

'No way!' she said, too forcefully.

They both held their breath, afraid they'd been overheard, and stared into the trees. When the digging didn't stop, they relaxed, but Jack looked determined now, her expression fixed. She leaned close to Itch's ear.

'If they catch us filming them, we are dead. Just for once, Itch, let's not push it. We watch, that's all. Or we can ring the police.' She looked at Itch, her eye-brows raised, challenging him to disagree with her.

But he looked away; he had to admit she had a point – after Madrid, his energy was running low. 'Fine,' he whispered. 'But what now?'

Crouching on freezing paving stones above the 'gravediggers', Itch and Jack knew they couldn't be seen through the trees, but equally they had no way of seeing who the diggers were. 'We could be here for hours!'

The crunching and shifting continued; and then a new noise. A noise so familiar yet so out of place, it took Itch a while to work out what it was. The digging had stopped, and in its place, from the middle of the trees, came a quiet, irregular clicking. Jack got it first. She looked at Itch in astonishment.

'It's a Geiger counter!' she said, grabbing his wrist. And Jack was right. As they sat in the freezing stillness, the only sound they could hear was the clicking caused by the detecting and counting of nuclear radiation.

20

Itch stood up. Jack tried desperately to pull him back, but he simply grabbed the phone and walked towards the clicking Geiger counter. *This is all wrong*, he thought. It wasn't that the radiation reading sounded high; on the contrary, the occasional and sporadic nature of the clicks indicated readings that were entirely normal. It was the fact that there was a Geiger counter at all that had spooked Itch. You might expect vandals smashing things up, or drunks sleeping against a headstone, but people with Geiger counters are only looking for radiation.

Itch strode along the church wall. He found the phone's video function, pressed the red button and held the glowing screen up in front of him, pointing it at whoever was working amongst the trees.

'Itch, no!' called Jack. 'Just call the police!' But Itch kept filming.

'Hey, you!' he shouted at the men, his voice sounding unbelievably loud. 'That's right, you!

We've found you! Caught in the act!' He heard Jack curse behind him but he carried on, his head buzzing. Somewhere he registered a nano-particle of thought that suggested he was being unbelievably stupid, but he kept filming.

He saw the men freeze; then panic. They grabbed some of their equipment and took off through the churchyard towards their van.

'And I'm calling the police too!' Itch called after them, then jumped as a hand wrapped itself round his mouth.

'For God's sake, shut up,' said Jack angrily. 'Have you lost it completely?' She glared at him, her hand still firmly over his mouth.

From the other side of the churchyard came the sound of slamming doors, an engine starting and squealing tyres.

'Good, so they've gone,' she said, her eyes still blazing. 'But what if they had run at you, rather than *from* you? What then? And maybe, just maybe, they'll know who you are given that your face is plastered over every newspaper. Honestly, Itch, you can be really stupid sometimes.'

Itch was reeling. Jack had never spoken to him like that before; he found he had absolutely nothing to say. They just stared at each other until, behind them, they heard a front door being unlocked. They jumped over the wall and ran round the church, registering a can of purple spray paint lying amongst the trees.

As they neared Jack's house, a police siren,

scarily close, made them jump. Jack fumbled for her key, and finding it deep in her pocket, eased them both into the dark sanctuary of her hallway. They stood panting, facing each other, wide-eyed. Fighting for breath but desperately trying to keep quiet was making them both faint. They stumbled into the kitchen and sat on the floor, listening to the siren, expecting a knock on the door at any moment. For a long time they didn't speak. Two more sirens and more flashing lights passed by. They sat there without moving until everything was quiet again.

'I'm sorry,' he whispered, handing her the phone.

Jack snatched it back. 'Don't ever do any-thing that stupid again,' she said, her voice only slightly calmer. 'Promise me, Itch – you need to tell me that.'

'OK, I promise. But it was a Geiger counter, Jack, in the churchyard!'

'I know – *I* told you that!' She played back the footage from the churchyard and Itch leaned over to watch it.

'You can see their faces,' he said.

'And their surprise that anyone could be quite so stupid,' added Jack.

There was silence before Itch swivelled to face her. 'But you realize what this means?' he said.

'No, but you're going to tell me.'

'It means they weren't vandals at all. Maybe none of them were. They're not wrecking stuff, Jack; they're *looking* for stuff. And on the basis of what we've just seen, they're looking for radioactive stuff.'

The kitchen was silent for a few moments.

'Itch, I'm getting scared again,' said Jack.

Itch took a deep breath. 'Me too.'

The following morning Itch slept so long that Chloe had to come and check up on him.

'I'm awake,' he grunted as the door squeaked open.

'Getting worried,' Chloe said. 'Not like you to be in bed after nine.'

He peered at her blearily, pushed the hair out of his eyes and slumped back onto the pillow. 'Bit late last night,' he said, still groggy.

Chloe looked puzzled. 'But you went to bed when we did,' she said. 'You online or something?' She saw the note on the floor where Itch had left it and knelt down to read. '*At church with Jack?* Itch? You went to church?' She handed him the piece of paper and he crumpled it into a ball.

Sitting up, he motioned for Chloe to shut the door. 'Jack called me. There were men in the churchyard. We went down and they were digging—'

'Wait, wait,' said Chloe, her hand raised. 'Last night, after Gabe and I left you, you and Jack were at the church?'

'She called me! Get this: they had a Geiger counter. They were looking for radioactive stuff in the churchyard. That's what all this destruction has been about.'

'And this note,' said Chloe, 'was instead of a text to that police number, I suppose?'

'You sound just like Mum.' Itch flopped back onto his pillow. 'But at least I left you a note. I learned that from last time.'

'What does Jack think?'

Itch sighed. 'Jack's mad at me because I filmed them on her camera. And they noticed.' He pre-empted Chloe who, he knew, was about to shout at him. He held up his hands. 'I know it was stupid – OK? I wasn't exactly planning to do it, you know.'

'But, Itch, they could have attacked you . . .'

'I know,' said Itch defensively, 'but I was in shock. It was the sound of the clicks, I think. I just wasn't expecting to hear that in a churchyard.'

'Where exactly were they digging?'

'The far corner, under the trees.'

'What's there?' asked Chloe.

'No idea,' said Itch.

'Well, get dressed and we'll find out.'

'Your head OK?'

Chloe nodded. 'It's fine.'

Itch was up in a matter of minutes. There was a note from Jude saying she'd be back from work to get dinner, and one from Nicholas explaining that he'd had to return to South Africa on some urgent business but that Jacob Alexander had said yes to a visit to the mining school.

'There goes the lift to the hospital,' said Itch.

'Gabe's passed his test,' said Chloe. 'He might take us.'

'We'll ask,' said Itch as they shut the front door, 'but let's see what the vandals were sniffing around last night.'

'You said you'd recorded them?' said Chloe.

'On Jack's phone. We could put it on YouTube. Then they won't try to mess around anywhere else.'

Chloe shook her head. 'How about the police? Shouldn't they see it?'

'I was thinking that. But you know how they reacted last time. They thought I might have been responsible for the parcel bombs. If they find out I was in the churchyard when the place was being vandalized, they'll be far more interested in what I was doing there than in the guys with the Geiger counter.'

They turned the corner – and stopped. A police car was parked near where Itch and Jack had been crouched the previous night; police incident tape was stretched across the road.

'C'mon, let's see how close we can get,' said Chloe. They walked down the hill towards the church and heard running footsteps behind them.

'Hey, you guys!' said Jack, catching them up. 'Saw you walking past. So Itch told you about last night, Chloe.' She linked arms with her cousin. Itch looked sheepish.

'Yup,' said Chloe. 'Classic Itch. We were discussing what to do with the video he took.'

'Maybe nothing,' said Jack. 'I'll show it to you. Doesn't look like we'll get anywhere near the church again, though.' She nodded at two policemen and a priest, who stood staring into the trees where the vandals had been the night before.

'We saw nothing, we say nothing,' said Itch. 'Last thing we need is to be part of another police enquiry. They'll blame me if they get the chance.'

One of the officers looked up and called them over. 'Itchingham Lofte, isn't it? Saw you on TV.' He nodded at Chloe. 'This your sister?'

Chloe bridled. 'Yes, I'm his sister, I'm Chloe,' she said. 'This is our cousin, Jack.'

The officer nodded. 'You looked like you were in a bad way.'

'I'm OK now, thanks. What's going on here?' Chloe was keen to change the subject.

The policeman glanced back at the trees. Between the trunks they could see a weathered granite wheel-headed cross, now leaning at a precarious angle and held up by one of the trees. 'More attacks, I'm afraid. You live close by – did you hear anything last night?'

Itch looked at the ground and Jack said, 'What sort of thing?'

'Anything out of the ordinary. Anything unusual?'

All three of them shrugged. 'No,' said Chloe. 'We'd have been asleep, I guess.'

A tall thin man with an angular, lived-in face came over, his clerical dog collar visible underneath his coat. He managed a smile at Chloe.

'We were all shocked to see what happened in Spain. Your brother is very brave. We could have done with you here last night. Some vandals attacked our Cornish cross in the trees there, but ran off before they could spray those wretched words. They left their can of graffiti spray behind, though.'

Jack and Itch exchanged the briefest of glances. 'Is the cross damaged?' asked Jack.

'Yes, it looks as though they were trying to dig it up, but they were interrupted, thankfully,' said the priest. 'It's the oldest part of the churchyard. It's thought that the cross was assembled hundreds of years ago from some ancient Logan stones and had supernatural powers. It could either heal you or turn you into a witch . . . I forget now.' He smiled. 'Bunkum, of course, but historic bunkum, so thank God someone scared them off. Whoever it was has done us a service.'

To which the police officer added, 'And should come and tell us about it. We'd like to talk to them.'

Itch started to pull at Jack's arm. 'Don't we need to get back . . .'

'Yeah, we should go,' Jack said. 'Hope you catch them . . .' And they turned and walked back up the hill. They exchanged wide-eyed glances, but no words until they had turned the corner.

'Oh my God, they were talking about *us*!' said Jack. 'They must know!'

'But how could they?' said Itch. 'There was no one else around, and if they suspected me they'd take me in for sure.'

'But the "whoever it was has done us a service" stuff . . .' said Jack. 'Was that just a coincidence?'

'I think so,' said Itch slowly. 'Probably.'

'I never knew about that cross,' said Chloe. 'More stones with special powers . . .' She grinned at Itch.

'Ideal,' he said. 'Just what we need.'

'And that can turn you into a witch,' said Jack. 'Maybe Darcy spent time here once.'

They were still laughing when they walked into the Loftes' kitchen.

Gabriel was sitting exactly where he'd been when they returned the day before: legs crossed, but with coffee this time, he looked up from his laptop. 'No news stories about you guys today, as far as I can see. Losing your touch, Itch. Where've you been, anyway?'

'Another *MM* attack. At the church here,' said Itch, not sure how much to say. He knew he was looking awkward, so he went and rummaged for some biscuits.

Gabriel sat up. 'Really? Got any pictures?' He missed Chloe's glance at Jack.

'Er, no,' said Itch. 'But go have a look. Police are still there.'

Gabriel sipped more coffee. 'Might do that,' he said. 'Want to see the news sites? You've left behind more chaos in Spain. More burning money, and riots. Some of the bad euros have turned up in France and Portugal too.' He showed them the latest footage, which looked identical to what they'd watched the day before. 'The markets are going mad, the euro's plunging and everyone's panicking Apart from that, all quiet.'

'You know Dad's gone again . . .' said Chloe.

'Yes, I saw the note,' said Gabriel. 'Jacob Alexander called him early, apparently.'

Jack nudged Itch. 'Oh yeah. Could you drive us to the mining school, Gabe? Dad was going to do it, but obviously he can't now. Jacob said he'd take a look at my burned euro. Do some tests.'

'What's in it for me?' asked Gabriel, smiling.

'The thrill of being part of family life for a change.' Itch mirrored his brother's expression.

'OK, well argued,' said Gabricl. 'When do we go?'

Within ten minutes Itch, Jack and Chloe were sitting in the family car – to be driven by Gabriel for the first time.

'He was easier to persuade than I thought!' whispered Jack in Chloe's ear on the back seat. She smiled as Gabriel started the engine and retuned his parents' radio.

'Let's call by for Lucy,' said Jack. 'Is that OK, Gabe? She's sort of on the way . . .'

'Ah yes . . . The beautiful and mysterious Lucy.' He smiled at Itch, who was sitting next to him. 'Sure we can call for her.'

'She's not mysterious,' said Itch, flushing slightly.

'Well, she kept that whole Cake's daughter thing quiet, didn't she? Last time I saw her was at the hospital in London after you guys had burned down the school with the well, and she was just about to tell you who she was. Seemed mysterious to me.'

Loud music filled the car, and Chloe leaned towards Jack. 'Notice he didn't dispute the "beautiful" bit!' she whispered, and they both grinned.

'I'll text her,' said Jack.

Chloe led a round of applause as they pulled out onto the road and accelerated up the hill. Despite the trauma of the previous days, their mood was light as they all started singing along to the song that was pulsing from the car's speakers.

There was no reason for them to pay any attention to the hire van that, fifty metres behind, had started to follow them.

21

As the car turned into Lucy's road, Gabriel's phone rang and a picture of Jude appeared on the screen. He threw the phone to Itch to answer.

'Hey, Mum, Gabe's driving. What's up?' he said.

'Had a call from the clinic in Exeter. They've had a cancellation today and were wondering if Chloe would like to take it. Could Gabriel take her?'

Itch's heart sank. 'Well, we're on the way to the mining school now . . .'

'Which is hardly as important as getting your sister's head sorted. They have a specialist there who wants to see her.'

Gabriel had parked up. 'I'll talk to Mum; you go in and get Lucy,' he said.

Itch handed the phone back, and Jack and Chloe followed him to Lucy's house. Nicola Cavendish, Lucy's mother, greeted them. Middle-aged and stocky, she was all smiles as she opened the door.

'Itch! And Jack and Chloe too! Well, this is a

treat.' She showed them into the kitchen. 'Chloe, I'm glad to see you looking better . . .'

'I feel OK, thanks, but I need check-ups. There's a clinic in Exeter I need to go to—'

'Hi, guys!' called Lucy, pulling on a jacket. 'We going straight away?'

'There's a kettle just boiled if you fancy a tea,' said Nicola. 'Lucy said you were heading to West Ridge . . .'

'Might be a change of plan,' said Itch. There was a knock at the door. 'That'll be my brother Gabriel. He's driving us.'

Lucy let him in and made the introductions.

'Mum thinks I need to take Chloe to Exeter, and I guess it does make sense,' said Gabriel. 'Sorry, Itch – maybe leave the euro-testing for another day.'

Itch sighed. 'OK, I suppose it can wait. Not sure when Alexander will be able to help next, though. He has some lab time this morning, that's all.'

'Sorry,' said Chloe. 'You're making me feel guilty. You don't all need to come, you know.'

Their plans disrupted, they stood around wondering what to do next.

Nicola Cavendish brandished her kettle. 'Why don't I take Itch to West Ridge and Gabriel take Chloe to Exeter?' she said. 'That way everyone's sorted.'

'Really?' said Itch. 'Aren't you busy with . . . something?'

'Nothing that can't wait,' she said. 'It's been many years since anyone mentioned "lab time" to me. Lucy's father was always obsessed with booking it whenever he could. We had to arrange our dating around it.' She smiled ruefully and Itch was taken aback to hear Cake discussed in this way.

The Cake of his memory was the worldly-wise drifter, selling elements to whoever he could find; not a domesticated boyfriend arranging dates around his experiments. He realized it had never occurred to him to ask Lucy's mother about Cake, but now didn't seem like the best time to start.

So he said nothing.

'Why don't I go with Mum and Itch to the mining school,' said Lucy, breaking the silence. 'Jack? West Ridge or Exeter?'

Jack shrugged. 'Maybe I'll be more use with Chloe,' she said. 'Some female companionship!' Her cousin smiled appreciatively.

'Sorted,' said Gabriel. 'Let's go.'

The two cars left Lucy's drive within seconds of each other, both heading inland. They passed a hire van, a Renault, parked in a bus stop, the occupants apparently busy with a large map. In the Cavendish car, Itch watched it in the mirror as it rejoined the road, a good hundred metres behind them. He remembered to text his destination to the police.

At the dual carriageway, Gabriel turned left, waving farewell. Nicola, Itch and Lucy turned right. He waited to see which way the Renault turned. He thought he detected indecision: neither indicator was flashing and for a moment he thought the car had stalled. Then it went left, heading for Exeter, and Itch wasn't sure whether to feel relieved or not. He sent Jack a text.

Nicola shifted in her seat, and drummed her fingers on the steering wheel. 'Itch, I hope you weren't embarrassed when I mentioned Lucy's father back then in the house. I've realized that I got out of the habit of talking about him with her and that was a mistake. So I'm trying to make up for it now.'

She glanced in the mirror, but Itch wasn't sure how Lucy was reacting and didn't want to turn round to check. He realized he needed to say something, but no words would come. It was Lucy who helped out.

'Itch bought loads of stuff from him, didn't you?'

'Oh, yes,' he said, eyes fixed on the road ahead. 'I got all my cool elements from Cake. There aren't too many element hunters around, so we got on great. He just seemed to know stuff. He got it; he understood. I didn't have to explain why carbon is interesting – he knew that anyway.' Itch realized he actually had lots to say. 'When I asked him about lithium, he knew about it being one of the three elements around after the Big Bang. He knew that burning magnesium is impossible to put out, and that my sulphur sample came from a volcano . . . and that it is mentioned fifteen times in the Bible and blew up Sodom and Gomorrah. We talked about the Periodic Table, and the stuff you weren't allowed to have, even if he seemed to know how to get most of it . . .' Itch trailed off.

'Which is where the 126 came in,' said Lucy quietly.

'I guess so,' said Itch.

They had turned off onto the twisty lanes that led to West Ridge before Nicola tried again. 'Did you talk about anything apart from chemistry?' she said.

Itch thought about that. 'Not really. He did ask about my family sometimes, and he met Jack and Chloe.'

'Did he seem happy?' She had stopped drumming on the steering wheel, and was gripping it tightly.

Itch hadn't thought about that, either. 'Yes,' he said eventually. 'Actually, very happy. Probably the happiest person I knew. He loved just drifting around. Unless he was shouting about governments, pollution and not trusting anyone. Then he was quite noisy.'

Nicola smiled and nodded. 'Yes, that sounds familiar . . .' She was silent for a while; then, as if she'd had enough of reminiscences, asked, 'Who are we meeting in West Ridge?'

'Dr Alexander – he's the boss there. He analysed the 126 – he's got all the kit at his labs. Nice guy with some weird ideas about the planet, which he'll probably mention.' Then, remembering a conversation he'd had in his garden at home, 'And he says he knew Cake too.'

'Really?' chorused Lucy and Nicola.

'Yes, he said he was really called Mike. Is that right?'

'Wow, he really *did* know him, then,' laughed

Nicola. 'Hardly anyone remembered that – he was always Cake. I was even Mrs Cake to some people, though I soon put a stop to that.' Itch saw her smile to herself, a private memory. 'He'd have been fantastically proud of you both, you know.'

She glanced at Itch, who was surprised to be referred to in the same breath as Cake's daughter. He nodded his thanks, looking away. Lucy had told him that before, but somehow it was all the more telling coming from the woman who had been Cake's partner.

Itch, Lucy and Nicola walked into the reception area, and immediately heard Dr Alexander's greeting as he strode round the corner.

'Why, Itch, how good to see you again!' His smile was broad and his eyes sharp. He held out his hand and Itch shook it, then introduced Lucy and Nicola.

'Of course. Cake's family. I'm so sorry for your loss . . .' He paused, rubbing his greying, closely cropped hair. 'We met a few times, you know. He came to a couple of events here and we saw each other at some science fairs – that kind of thing.' Nicola nodded as Dr Alexander struggled for what to say next. Then he smiled at Lucy. 'And Itch's father tells me it was you who knew how to destroy the 126 – spallation and the ISIS labs.'

Lucy nodded. 'We used to hang out there,' she said. 'I just remembered Dad's conversations about neutron capture and stuff.'

'Well,' said Alexander, smiling, 'that science gene

of your father's has most certainly been passed on.' He smiled at Nicola, then switched his gaze to Itch. 'And your father, Itch, tells me you have one of those burning euros for me to look at . . .'

Itch reached into his pocket and pulled out the charred ten-euro note.

Alexander's eyes lit up. 'Come! Come! Let's get it under the Raman microscope!' And he strode off down the corridor towards the labs.

'I'll wait here for you,' Nicola told Lucy. 'You don't need me. I'll catch up on some emails. You carry on.'

Lucy nodded, and she and Itch ran after Alexander. 'You all right, Itch? You look a little green,' she said.

'I'm OK, really. Last time I was here was when Jack and I got kidnapped by Flowerdew, that's all . . .'

'And I took a kicking from that Greencorps thug,' called Alexander over his shoulder. 'Served me right for talking to that woman who said she was a reporter for the *International Herald Tribune*. Too vain! I was far, far too vain! A problem not unique to scientists, but we have more than our fair share, I think.'

The corridor ended in a T-junction, and Alexander turned right, walking and talking. They entered a brightly lit room, filled with benches and lined with overflowing shelves. Itch wandered over and peered at the jars, tubs and bottles that looked as if they had been left mid-experiment; tubes and assorted glassware stood next to bowls and a calculator.

'Those rocks were the temptation, you see,' said Alexander. 'A previously unknown energy resource – and sitting in my lab! Look, I still have the readings.' He pointed at a notice board; pinned in the centre was a printout of a spectrum. 'The data from the spectrometer – the only proof that they were here! I stare at them most days, and wonder. You know I wanted the rocks, Itch – we could have done great things with them.'

'Yes, I remember,' said Itch. '"Earth's last chance" or something.'

'I thought so, yes. For a few moments I thought so. A way of getting through the new hot age. The Earth is a living organism, you know, and this was a spectacular way of showing that it has a regulatory mechanism.'

Itch had glazed over but Lucy was intrigued. 'You mean, like a thermostat?'

'Kind of, yes,' said Alexander. 'If it's cold in the morning, you'll put on a jumper or turn the heating up. If it gets warmer, you can open a window. We do it all the time. This Gaia theory I told Itch about basically says the Earth does the same: the biosphere regulates the environment to suit itself. Stops us from freezing or boiling, basically. That's what I think the 126 would have done.'

'I think we've sort of done this bit, Dr Alexander,' said Itch, impatient to test the euro.

The director turned slowly to face him. 'I know. And we'll doubtless do it again. Then one day, maybe when you're a more eminent scientist than I am, you'll remember what I told you, and you'll walk in and tell me I was right.'

He gazed steadily at Itch, then nodded. 'But we move on. Lab Two here is for microscopy, and I have the Raman ready to go.' He indicated a white, black and silver microscope that was connected to a large cream-coloured circular box set up on the lab's front bench. 'A Raman microscope. A lovely thing! An ordinary microscope, but with a spectrometer attached. You remember the X-ray fluorescence spectrometer next door?'

Itch smiled. It was the machine that had fired X-rays at the rocks of 126, then analysed the ones that bounced back, telling Alexander precisely what he was analysing. It had caused the director – despite being in his early sixties – to dance around like a crazed teenager.

'I'm not likely to forget it really, Dr Alexander. Or your cool moves afterwards!'

'Yes, well . . . it was one of those moments, wasn't it? So, with this machine, you load what you want to study under the microscope in the conventional way. Then, when you've got it in the middle of the crosshairs, you flip the microscope to spectrometer mode. If you don't, you'll shoot its laser straight into your eye, which might limit your career prospects as a microscopist a little!'

Lucy laughed at that. 'So what do you see, Dr Alexander, once it has gone to spectrometer mode?' She pulled her hair back, fixing it with a small band.

'Well, it uses the vibration of the molecules it's analysing to produce a spectrum – a plot with peaks and troughs. The waves have numbers, and you match the peaks to a library held on a computer. That tells you what you're looking at.'

'Is it pretty instant? Like the X-ray spectrometer next door?' asked Itch.

Dr Alexander nodded. 'Yes, we'll know straight away what caused the money to burn. It's an analysis that the Spanish will be doing right now, so we may as well find out too. Ready?' Itch nodded and handed over the ten-euro note. Dr Alexander rubbed his hands together and smiled. 'This is my favourite bit,' he said. He placed it on the sample slide. Then, with the briefest of glances at his audience, he bent down and put his eyes to the binocular-style eye-pieces of the Raman microscope.

The head-injury clinic of St Michael's Hospital in Exeter proved more difficult to find than anyone would have thought possible. Chloe, Jack and Gabriel had walked through what seemed like miles of corridors before pushing through some double doors and arriving at the reception area, marked by plastic flowers and large posters of trees and flowers. A family sat in a corner looking bored; opposite them, an elderly man was busy with a newspaper crossword.

'Anyone with a real head injury would have died long before actually finding this place,' said Gabriel.

'What do you mean, "real" head injury?' said Chloe, punching him on his arm.

252

'I mean someone who's bleeding and every-thing!' said Gabriel defensively. 'Obviously yours was bad, Chlo – I just meant . . .'

'Who are you seeing?' said Jack, gazing at the directory board. 'They have neuropsychologists, a neuro-rehabilitation specialist or a neuro-otolaryngologist. Whatever that is.'

'I'm not sure,' said Chloe, and she approached the woman seated behind the reception desk. Her badge said SANDRA, and she managed a rather bored smile as she looked up Chloe's appointment.

'You're early,' she said. 'You're due to see Mr Schaffer at three. Take a seat and fill out this form, please. Do you have an adult with you?'

Gabriel put his hand up. 'Me,' he said, smiling. 'I am. Well, most of the time, anyway.'

Sandra didn't look impressed. 'You sign too, please.' She returned to her computer screen while Gabriel and Chloe sat with Jack by a low table piled high with a selection of the dullest magazines they had ever seen.

'Missed two texts from Itch,' said Jack. She showed her phone to Gabriel and Chloe.

'*You being followed? Check out the Renault behind you*,' read Gabriel. The second text gave its registration number. He shrugged. 'No use now,' he said. 'I didn't notice anything, but then my instructor always told me to use my mirrors more. Sorry. You see anything?'

'Call him,' said Chloe.

'Really? But we're here now!' Gabriel was

about to protest further, but Jack just stared at him.

'Call him,' she said. 'If Itch is concerned about something, then *I* am.' Catching a look from Chloe, she amended, '*We* are.'

'OK, calm down,' he said. 'I'm on it.' He got out his phone, dialled and listened, but gave up after a few seconds. 'On divert.' He looked from his sister to his cousin and back again. The carefree atmosphere seemed to have gone: they both looked tense.

Jack checked the time on her phone. 'Three o'clock seems like a long time to wait now,' she said.

At the reception desk, Sandra broke away from a phone call, cradling the handset on her shoulder. 'Anyone got a Ford Galaxy reg number GYU 129K?' she called.

'Gabe, that's us!' exclaimed Chloe.

'Oh,' said Gabriel. 'Yes, that's me. What's up?'

'Parked illegally. Going to be towed.' He swore and Sandra shook her head. To the caller she said, 'Yes, he's here. He'll be five minutes.' To Gabriel she said, 'They said you had two minutes.'

'Damn, damn, damn,' he said and headed out of the reception. 'Which way?' he yelled, turning back.

'Follow the signs for *car park*?' suggested Sandra, and he was gone.

The bored family were called through to another waiting area; Jack and Chloe watched them go, feeling jittery. Chloe called Itch, but it diverted again. She called Gabriel, but he didn't answer. 'I was going to suggest he check the car park for that Renault Itch mentioned,' she said. 'As he's out there anyway.'

'Good idea,' said Jack. She fell silent, then suddenly put her hand on Chloe's arm. She spoke quietly and slowly. 'Chlo, why did they call here about the car? Why did they call this reception? Why not the main desk?'

'Maybe they did,' suggested Chloe unconvincingly. 'Maybe they work their way round the different departments till they find the car they're after?'

'Maybe,' said Jack. 'Do you remember where we parked? It's just that I don't remember any red lines or disabled bays.'

'Jack, stop talking like this,' said Chloe. 'You're scaring me!'

'Well, something's not right, that's all.' Jack tried Itch's phone again, then Lucy's. 'Must be the lab they're in,' she said. 'I'll leave a message.' She waited for the message to play out. Then, 'Lucy, it's Jack. We're worried about that car Itch said was following us. And Gabe has gone to reception and I'm not sure . . . Oh, this sounds stupid now I'm saying it out loud . . . Oh well, just call when you can.' As she hung up, she saw that Sandra was escorting the crossword man to his appointment. 'That sounded really lame,' she said. 'Maybe we're fine after all.'

'Maybe . . .' Chloe was still nervous. She looked around. 'But we are on our own now. We need to be with people, Jack. We need company.'

As he waited for Dr Alexander to analyse the burned euro, Itch suddenly felt worried. With all that had happened – the Geiger counter in the graveyard, the journey with Gabriel, the talk of Gaia – he hadn't given much thought to the note he'd brought back from Madrid. But whatever it was that had caused the money to spontaneously combust, it had led to Chloe's injury and countless others. The riots and panic had now spread across Spain. The director was right: this same piece of analysis was no doubt being conducted right now in labs across the country; maybe across the world.

He glanced at Lucy and she looked up at him, smiling and shrugging at the same time. She tucked some loose strands of hair behind her ears. Itch remembered the words from his old banned text-book, *The Golden Book of Chemistry Experiments* . . . *There is hardly a boy or girl alive who is not keenly interested in finding out about things.* Itch had found that, in this respect at least, its author had got it wrong: most of his fellow pupils didn't appear to be even slightly interested in 'finding out about things'. That was what he liked so much about Lucy. She got it. She wanted to find out about things. And looking at her now, eyes wide and restless, Itch realized that she was as excited about the chemical analysis of the euro as he was.

Dr Alexander worked silently, and with the minimum of movement: a repositioning here, a small adjustment there (a complete contrast, Itch thought, to his demented whirling after the analysis of the 126). He stood up to stretch his back, but then bent forward again without comment. At first, Itch and Lucy were happy to stand and watch him work, but after a while they started fidgeting.

Eyes still glued to the eye-pieces, Alexander held up his hand. 'Desist. Please.'

Itch and Lucy froze, grinning at each other. They had been told off for sure, but the thrill of an imminent discovery overrode any embarrassment they felt. They stood like bodyguards on either side of their employer, waiting for their next instruction.

Suddenly Alexander straightened again and stepped away from the microscope.

'OK, your turn. Itch, it's your banknote – tell me what you see. We have quite a story here, I think!' He rubbed his hands together again, then waved Itch over to a computer screen next to the microscope. It showed a graph that looked like a stormy sea.

'OK . . .' Itch smiled nervously at Lucy, then peered at the screen. 'It's a graph,' he said after a few seconds. 'Peaks and troughs. Different colours, different waves . . . black mainly, but red, green and blue. There are numbers at the top of each peak.'

Dr Alexander nodded. 'That's the wave number along the horizontal axis and the Raman intensity along the vertical. See that cluster of peaks there? They're small, but not present when we compare it with a spectrum of a clean euro note. So those, I would suggest, ladies and gentlemen of the jury, are from your culprit!'

Itch stood up and allowed Lucy to peer at the screen. She gave it the briefest of examinations.

'OK,' she said. 'I see the graph, but what does it say?' She was now hopping from one foot to the other. The director was enjoying the moment, like a talent-show host about to announce the long-awaited winner. He paced as he spoke.

'The smaller wave is europium oxide – which is a puzzle . . . I'll have to check it out. But the big beast you can see in the middle, the large cluster there, is picric acid!' If he expected any reaction from Itch and Lucy, Alexander was disappointed. They both stared back at him, waiting for more information.

'Picric acid?' asked Itch, puzzled.

'Also called 2,4,6-trinitrophenol,' said Alexander. 'It was used as yellow dye for silk; also as an anti-septic, I think. But it became famous as a military explosive. The French, Russians and Japanese liked it particularly, but it fell out of favour eventually. It's still used in fireworks – that screaming some of them do . . . that's burning picric acid.'

'The noise from the cash machine!' said Itch. The director looked puzzled. 'The cash points in Spain were exploding,' he explained, 'and there was one giving out a high-pitched whine. I thought it was weird, but there was so much else that was weirder at the time, I didn't give it much thought.'

Alexander nodded. 'That confirms it. These euros have been treated with picric acid. It is sensitive to heat or shock; it would lie dormant in the dark and cool, but then kick off when coming into contact with light, warmth or someone chucking it about.'

'Do they use picric acid in the banknote printing process?' asked Lucy. 'Might it have been an accident?'

He removed the charred euro from the microscope. 'Unlikely, I'd have thought. Very unlikely. It's either a very expensive mistake – a chemical contamination somewhere – or it was deliberate.'

There was silence in the lab for a few moments. 'But who would want to make money burn like that?' asked Lucy. 'What would be the point?'

Dr Alexander leaned back against the bench and stabbed a finger at her. 'That is precisely the question that needs answering. This bit with the microscope is the easy part. Scientists everywhere will have discovered the picric acid and the in formation will be out soon, if it isn't already. But quite *why* it's there, that's a whole new game. And that game can get nasty.'

'Do you mean like the kicking you talked about?' asked Lucy. 'When that Greencorps woman turned up, pretending to be a reporter?'

'It wasn't her,' he said. 'It was the goons she was with. They did her dirty work.'

And the blood drained from Itch's face. 'Wait!' he exclaimed. 'Just wait! No one say anything!' He stood still, staring into the distance, focused on nothing.

Lucy and Alexander exchanged glances, then waited.

'Oh my God . . .'

'Itch, what is it?' Lucy was alarmed now.

Itch's face was white, his hands in front of his mouth.

When he spoke, his voice was strained and surprisingly quiet. 'That woman . . . The Greencorps agent pretending to be a journalist,' he said; 'the one who came here. What was her name? She called it through the glass.'

Dr Alexander thought for a moment. 'Mary Bale, I think. Well, that's what she claimed, anyway. She said she was from the *International Herald Tribune* and I foolishly believed her. But so what, Itch? What's the problem?'

Itch took a breath. 'When we landed yesterday, Colonel Fairnie met us at the airport. He explained why he wasn't going to be around any more. Basically Greencorps are going all legal and decent and want to expose price fixing in the oil industry. Stupidly, everyone believes them. He mentioned they had a new CEO after those two guys were shot – I think by Flowerdew. I thought at the time that the name was familiar in some way. Dr Alexander, I think Mary Bale now runs Greencorps.'

Alexander led the way to his laptop and searched for *Mary Bale + Greencorps*.

The screen flashed with a photo that looked like it came from a press release. He clicked on it, and they all stared at the image of a tall, stylish Asian woman in her twenties with a discreet, controlled smile.

'Is that her?' asked Lucy.

Dr Alexander cursed viciously and nodded. 'This is extraordinary.'

'But so what? Sorry, but I don't get it. What if she is in charge?'

'It means that Greencorps have a criminal at the top,' said Dr Alexander. 'Another one. And that their new image is a sham!'

'No surprises there,' said Itch. 'I'd better call Jack and Chloe.'

The doors of the head-injury clinic opened and a smiling, broad-shouldered man in a white coat and crocs appeared. He looked at his clipboard.

'Chloe Lofte? This way please!'

Chloe stood up, acknowledging the doctor. 'Yes, that's me,' she said. 'Come on, Jack, we're up.'

But her cousin didn't move, her hands in her lap, eyes staring straight ahead. The doctor shifted impatiently in the doorway.

Chloe tapped her cousin on the shoulder. 'Jack?'

There was a second's pause, then Jack leaped to her feet, dashed round Chloe and kicked hard at the doors, trapping the doctor's outstretched arm. He yelled with surprise and pain, dropping the clipboard, his arm was pinned just below the elbow. Jack kicked again at the door, harder this time, and there was a snapping, crunching noise as the man's radius bone snapped. He slumped to the floor on the other side of the door.

'Jack!' screamed Chloe. 'What are you doing?'

But Jack grabbed her hand and ran. 'Just stay with me!' she yelled, and they took off down a corridor. The sign said CONSULTING ROOMS AND X–RAY.

'Jack, you broke his arm!'

'Yup!' She started opening doors; all the rooms were empty. 'We need people – where *is* everyone?' She reached for her phone, but saw that there was no signal. Behind them they could hear the man's groans and then sharp words exchanged. The injured man sounded German, the other American.

'Chloe, it's the burned-hair man!' Jack pulled Chloe along as she spoke. 'It's the guy who attacked us at the mining school. I recognized his voice – he's a Greencorps man! After Itch got on the train to Brighton, he followed me and I only just got away. He's the guy who attacked Dr Alexander. I *know* it's him!' She opened another door to another dark, empty room.

'Should we hide?' said Chloe.

Jack pulled her in, and they shut the door as quietly as their racing hearts and shaking hands would allow. The only light came from the small opaque window in the door and the glow of green and red monitor lights – not really enough to see by, but they didn't have time for their eyes to adjust to the dark. They dived underneath what looked like a desk and crouched there. Over their panting breaths they heard their pursuer trying all the doors, just as they had.

'I could lock it!' whispered Chloe, and before Jack could pull her back she ran towards the door.

'Chloe, come back!'

Ignoring her cousin, Chloe felt for the bolts at the bottom. Her hands found the metal latch and forced the steel shaft down. It clicked as it was rammed home, and she winced at the noise. Suddenly they heard banging: their pursuers were searching the next room! Jack joined her cousin and reached for the top bolt, pushing it home. The light from the small window darkened as the two men passed by outside. Jack and Chloe heard more conversation, punctuated by gasps of pain.

'The other door!' hissed Chloe, and pointed at the flat thumb-turn latch that would lock the doors together.

'But they'll hear!' mouthed Jack, and they stared at each other, frozen with indecision and fear. Jack reached out and rested her fingers on the latch, ready to twist. They waited for the Greencorps men. They pushed the left door first, hard. It rattled against the bolts. For a terrifying moment Chloe and Jack thought it would give way, but it held fast and, under cover of the noise, Jack twisted the latch. It slid shut just as the push came. Both doors shook as the men pulled and pushed at the handle, but they stayed shut. A firm boot would have splintered them, but there were other doors to try and the pair moved on.

'We need Gabriel!' Chloe was crouched down, looking scared. 'We need to find Gabriel!' Then, with a dawning look of horror, she grabbed her cousin's arm. 'What if . . . ? Do you think he's OK?'

Jack shrugged and tried her phone again, but

there was still no signal. 'I think maybe we shouldn't depend on Gabriel . . .' She was choosing her words carefully and guessed that Chloe knew it. 'We need to deal with this ourselves. There are hundreds of people around, and just two Greencorps guys. We need to find some proper doctors and get help. We'll be fine.' She pulled Chloe up. 'We go back to reception, and if there's no one there, we run for the wards. They were back up the corridor, I think. OK?'

Chloe nodded.

Jack continued, her voice more urgent now. 'And if we run into those men, we shout and scream.' They stood listening by the bolted doors. A tannoy call for a doctor to attend an emergency reassured them that life in the rest of the hospital was carrying on as normal, and they nodded at each other. Jack unlocked the door, waited for a second and then opened it as silently as she could. She pointed left. 'We go that way,' she mouthed.

The man with the broken arm – burned-hair man – spotted them first. He had been standing in reception, sentry-like; now he called to his colleague. A second man, also dressed in a white coat, appeared at his side and sprinted towards the girls.

Jack and Chloe had to turn right, but the sound of the two men so close meant that drastic action was called for.

'Help! We need help!' Jack shouted as they ran, banging on doors.

Now Chloe joined in the shouting. 'Anybody help! Please!'

The first 'doctor' was only metres away now. He was powerfully built and moving fast, his eyes grimly fixed on Jack and Chloe.

At the end of the corridor a door opened, and Sandra appeared with a furious-looking man behind her. 'What the hell is going on!' he called. 'We have patients here!'

'You two should be back—' began Sandra, but Jack and Chloe flew past her into the consulting room. They stood behind her and the consultant, and turned to see his patient lying uncomfortably in a huge tunnel-shaped MRI machine.

'These men aren't real doctors!' shouted Chloe. 'They are trying to kidnap us!'

'They've attacked our cousin and now they want to get us too!' added Jack. 'Please help us call the police!'

The 'doctors' looked around the room. The one with two working arms smiled broadly. 'I'm Dr Waylon; this is my colleague, Dr Wallander. He has a broken arm, I'm afraid, after being assaulted by this girl here. They both have a history of violence, but we were hoping to deal with the matter quietly. We only wanted to take Chloe here for some tests.' 'Dr Wallander' tried a smile, but it was more of a grimace.

'I've never seen you before,' said Sandra. 'And you sound American. What department are you from? What tests are you doing?'

'We're from the Bains Hospital in Bristol,' said 'Dr Waylon'. 'We do most of our work there. Yes, I'm originally from Detroit, but really, this shouldn't take long . . .'

'What's happening?' called a muffled woman's voice from inside the MRI scanner, but everyone was focused on Drs Waylon and Wallander.

'Why would someone get a bone-marrow transplant?' asked Chloe.

'Pardon me?' said Waylon.

'Why would someone get a bone-marrow transplant?' she repeated. 'You're a doctor. That should be easy for you. It's a medical question. Come on, prove it!'

Jack joined in. 'Yeah, and if I had three broken fingers, how would you treat me?'

'This isn't a game' – the American tried another smile – 'and I'm not playing.'

'Oh, but you are,' said the consultant. 'I'm Mr Copeland, and this is my unit.' He was a short, grey-haired man with glasses on a string around his neck. 'Tell me what your business is here. The idea that these children are right and that you're out to kidnap them seems ludicrous, but . . . Your credentials, please, and then we can sort it all out. I have never heard of you, and we don't normally work with the Bains. Who is your head of department there? Maybe I know them . . .'

The hesitation was all the consultant needed. Not used to suffering fools – or anyone else – gladly, he strode over to confront the American. 'If you can't answer those questions, try this one. What are the main principles of neuropsychology? You're in my rooms – you'll know that, surely?'

Behind him, Mr Copeland's patient was easing her way out of the scanner; two wriggling legs were emerging from the tunnel.

Waylon and Wallander were now looking increasingly uncomfortable, and the consultant was reaching for his phone. 'What is your specialism, Dr Wallander? Where did you train?'

The German glanced briefly at his colleague. Jack hooked her arm through Chloe's. 'Berlin,' he said reluctantly.

'Very well!' said Copeland, holding up his phone. 'And I didn't catch your specialism . . .'

The MRI patient now appeared at his side, looking puzzled. 'What's happening? she asked.

'What's happening, Miss Chignell,' said Mr Copeland without turning round, 'is that these men are just about to be reported to the police for pretending to be doctors and trying to attack these poor—'

Sandra the receptionist and Miss Chignell the patient both screamed at the same time. The American had produced a pistol and the German kicked the door shut. The consultant swore loudly and backed away, but not fast enough to avoid a blow from the pistol butt.

The American had caught him on the crown of his head and the consultant slumped to the ground. 'Always the best way to win at games,' he said, and the German laughed. 'You, on the floor!' he shouted at Sandra. 'You, back in the tunnel!' to Miss Chignell. The receptionist scurried to the corner of the room, while the patient crawled back into the imaging unit. Chloe and Jack held each other tight. 'You might come to regret breaking Volker's arm like that,' the American said, more softly.

Now it was the German's turn to speak. Holding his damaged arm across his chest, he stepped forward. His voice shook slightly. 'At the mining school, you attacked me with that burning magnesium. I couldn't see properly for days. Today you attack me again, but you have lost. We have dealt with one of your brothers – he might be older, but he was far less troublesome. All we have to do is wait, and your other brother will come looking for you.'

Jack and Chloe hauled themselves up. They were shaking slightly, but their stance was defiant, their eyes fierce. 'We got you at the mining school because you attacked Dr Alexander then came for us,' Jack said with barely controlled anger. 'And I broke your arm because you're doing it again. You're a thug and a bully – we have people like you in school – it's just they don't have guns.'

Volker Berghahn had heard enough; with his good hand he hit Jack hard across the face. She fell backwards, her cheek split and bleeding. Chloe found a tissue and handed it to her before turning to face the Greencorps pair.

'My brother is smarter and braver than both of

you. And he doesn't have to hit girls to prove it.'

The American stepped forward now, his gun still in his hand. 'Don't you ever shut up?'

'Not unless I have to. And back at the mining school? That was phosphorus, not magnesium. You guys really *are* dumb.'

And the pistol butt came down again.

22

It was a silent trip with Lucy's mum. After trying and failing to raise Jack, Chloe or Gabriel, Itch had rung his mother, who had persuaded him not to go to Exeter, but to return home. He had told her about the car that might have followed them, and found the registration number from his text.

There were only bad explanations for the sudden disappearance of his brother, sister and cousin from the hospital, and on the journey home he went through all of them. Lucy tried to be reassuring, but Itch could tell that her heart wasn't in it. He wished his father was at home, not sorting out mines in South Africa.

In the kitchen he found that Jude – looking more gaunt than ever – had company. A teary-eyed Jon and Zoe Lofte, clearly just as scared as Itch, were at the table, and DCIs Abbott and Underwood were sitting next to them. The presence of the two policemen who had suspected him of bombing his own school filled Itch with dismay, but their tone was altogether more sympathetic now. They asked Lucy and Nicola to stay; surprised, they pulled up chairs too. The absence of Jack and Chloe and Gabriel filled the room.

'He's on the first plane he can get,' said Jude, reading her son's thoughts.

Itch nodded.

DCI Abbott cleared her throat. 'I don't want to speculate, so I will tell you everything that the Exeter police are telling me. Jack and Chloe have disappeared after being assaulted at the hospital.'

Itch, Lucy and Nicola gasped; the others had clearly been given this news before. Jon Lofte had one hand on his wife's shoulder, the other on Jude's.

The DCI continued. 'Gabriel was assaulted too, but was found in a store cupboard by a cleaner. He is bruised and shaken, but will be OK and is being driven here now. It seems the attackers wanted him out of the way – it was Jack and Chloe they were after. We know from witness accounts that they were deliberately targeted, and that their abductors were disguised as doctors. We're asking for the CCTV footage now.'

'I saw them!' said Itch. 'A van was following us when we left town. I texted the number to Jack, but she never got back . . .'

The policewoman nodded. 'Your mother passed on the number – thank you. It is a hire car, rented with false papers. Obviously we are trying to trace it now.'

Jude groaned, head in hands. It was a desperate

sound, unlike anything Itch had heard from his mother before, and his stomach tightened. 'Is this Flowerdew again?' she asked. 'Who else targets our family like this?'

'Course it is,' said Itch, and then addressed the police. 'I tried to tell you about him, remember? You weren't that interested, as I recall.'

Underwood – still, Itch thought, looking nothing like a policeman – consulted some notes. 'Apparently the two attackers were known to your sister and cousin.'

Now everyone looked up. 'Excuse me?' said Jon. 'They knew them?'

'That's what we think, yes. Apparently there was one who sounded German and one who sounded American. The German – according to the witnesses in the room – seemed to think *he* had been attacked before. And by Chloe and Jack.'

'But that's ridiculous,' said Zoe. 'They'd never attack anyone.'

'Something to do with phosphorus?' suggested DCI Underwood.

Itch swallowed. 'Burned-hair man,' he said softly. 'Of course.'

'Itch?' said his uncle. 'You know this guy?'

'Before Jack and I were kidnapped by Flowerdew, three Greencorps agents arrived at the mining school. They were trying to get the 126. They were with a woman who said her name was Mary Bale. If you look her up, she's the new CEO of Greencorps. The new "nice-and-legal"

Greencorps. Her two thugs attacked Dr Alexander, and I escaped by using some phosphorus that Cake had given me. It temporarily blinded one of them, and burned his hair. He nearly found us again at Victoria station, but the smell alerted Jack . . . and, well, you know what happened after that.'

It was clear from their expressions that the police officers had no idea what had happened after that, but reckoned this was not the moment for a general catch-up. Abbott's phone rang and she left the kitchen.

'Did anyone follow you to the mining school?' asked Underwood. 'Are you sure there was only one car behind?'

'Yes, I think so,' said Itch, glancing at Lucy and Nicola. 'There was just the car I told you about, and it turned to follow Gabriel. Maybe they weren't expecting us to split up. They wanted to get me, but had to decide which car to follow. Flowerdew will be seriously angry when he discovers that I'm not with Jack and Chloe.'

In some distress, Nicola Cavendish said, 'I don't think we were followed. I parked in the car park and sat in reception. I didn't see anyone else, I'm afraid.'

DCI Abbott came back into the kitchen. 'The hire van has been found at the docks in Bristol,' she said, avoiding eye-contact. 'We are checking it now. We have informed all immigration points to be on the lookout and have circulated photos of Jack and Chloe.' She looked up now and tried a smile. 'I'm sure we'll find them soon.'

Zoe Lofte had been sitting quietly, hands in her lap. Now her eyes blazed. 'No, you're not. You're not sure at all. You have no idea. Please don't treat us like fools, Detective. Our daughters have been taken and the car found at the docks. They could well be out of the country by now—' Her voice broke, and Jon Lofte reached for her hand. 'After the bombs,' she continued, 'Itch told you who was responsible. And now we are *all* telling you. Flowerdew has tried to kill our children before, and he is trying to do it again. Just tell Interpol or whoever it is that we know who did it . . . you just have to *stop* him!'

Nods around the table. 'Exactly!' said Jude.

Underwood had flushed slightly, but Abbott remained impassive. 'When we talked to Itch about Flowerdew, we did of course take his accusations seriously. And after certain representations—'

'You mean Fairnie,' interrupted Itch. 'We all know he talked to you . . . just say what you mean.'

Abbott bridled, but forced herself to continue. 'After representations from Colonel Fairnie and others, we did look into the whereabouts of Nathaniel Flowerdew. After his escape from the ISIS labs, we believe he received treatment at a clinic in London. Since then there has been nothing – no sightings, no activity on any of his accounts. And certainly no indication that he is back at Greencorps.'

'That's because he's not stupid,' said Itch, angry now. He stood up sharply, knocking his chair over. 'Of course he's not going to announce his takeover

– he's a *criminal*! What is it with you people?'

'Itch, this won't help,' said Jude quietly, but he ignored her.

'How many bombings have you had to deal with?' he asked, voice raised.

'Itch!' Jude tried again.

'Well?' he continued. 'Both of you added together?' He gestured to Abbott and Underwood.

'Just the ones here actually, but—' said Underwood.

'Just the ones here? Right. And when Mr Watkins was killed, and your colleague too, the first person you thought to blame was me!' Itch picked his chair up and rammed it back under the table. 'Maybe you'll understand if we aren't that thrilled with the police here. If we suspect that maybe you haven't a clue what you're doing. But here's the deal: I promise you this – if you find Chloe and Jack, you'll find Flowerdew holding them.'

Itch stormed out. Lucy whispered something in her mother's ear and followed him.

'God, they're useless, Lucy!' Itch had thrown himself on his bed, but then jumped up again, unable to keep still. 'How can we find Chloe and Jack when they're the ones in charge?'

'They won't be,' she said. 'They're just the local cops, Itch. This will go much higher now.'

'But not to Fairnie,' said Itch bitterly. 'He'd sort this out.'

'He would, but he can't,' said Lucy. 'Sit down,

Itch.' Reluctantly he sat back on the bed. 'Give me your laptop . . .' He handed it over, puzzled. She found his Facebook page and whistled. 'You are one popular boy!'

'You know that's not true. What are you doing?'

'You have a lot of people interested in you, Itch. Around the world, it must be in the millions. And after those pictures from Madrid, there are more all the time. If you ask them for help—'

'Lucy, it's Facebook. I know the police were rubbish just then, but surely when it comes to—'

She looked at him fiercely, her eyes wide, eyebrows raised. They looked at each other for a few seconds and the penny dropped.

'Don't trust anyone,' he said softly.

Lucy nodded and smiled.

'OK. What should we put?'

'Change your status. Say you're looking for your sister and cousin. Kidnapped from Exeter hospital, maybe taken out via Bristol harbour. Put it in your own words, say what you want to say. Tell the truth.'

Itch took the laptop and typed. He showed Lucy and she smiled.

A knock at the door and Jude appeared. 'You OK, Itch?' She came in and stood awkwardly in front of them. 'Dad says he'll be back tomorrow. I know how much you want to talk to him.'

Itch didn't notice the tone of hurt in his mother's voice, though Lucy did.

'Here – sit down,' she said. 'Have the police gone yet?'

'Not yet. They've requested a media blackout till they know what's happening. They asked me to tell you.'

'Too late,' said Itch. 'Just posted.' He showed her the status update.

Please help find my sister Chloe Lofte, 13, and cousin Jacqueline Lofte, 15. They are both tall and pretty. Kidnapped today from Exeter hospital by Greencorps agents. Possibly out of Bristol. Don't believe what Greencorps tell you – they'll come for me next.

Jude looked up from the laptop. 'I have a feeling the police are going to go crazy,' she said.

'Maybe . . .' Itch shrugged.

'But we need them, Itch! We need them to be as desperate as we are, not really hacked off because you're making them look stupid.'

'It was my idea,' said Lucy. 'Sorry, Mrs Lofte – it just seemed the best way to tell everyone, that's all.'

There was another knock at the door and DCI Abbott came in, flushed and clearly furious. 'Mrs Lofte. Itch and Lucy. I said a media blackout was in place! We asked the news organizations to wait before reporting this incident and they agreed. But if you're going to splash this about yourself, then I'm afraid we have lost control of the story already.'

Itch was up on his feet again. His room was small, the policewoman close. If he hadn't been taller than her, they'd have been eyeball to eyeball. 'OK . . . first, it's not about "losing control of a story", it's about finding Jack and Chloe. You can't control this anyway. And second, you didn't tell me till it was too late. I had already posted before Mum told me.'

DCI Abbott, fighting to control herself, snapped back, 'The purpose of controlling the story is to speed up the return of your sister and cousin. When we are ready, and we have all our stakeholders all working together, then we can get maximum impact and spread the net as wide—'

Now it was Jude's turn to struggle. '*Stakeholders?* What in God's name are you talking about? I'm sorry – I know we have to work together on this. I know you'll do your best. You know we're desperate to get our girls back, but please talk to us normally. And start by using words everyone understands.'

From outside came the sound of cars pulling up and doors slamming. Inside, the phone was ringing. Abbott held out her hands. 'That's the sound of a story *out of control*. There'll be trucks here soon – things will move fast. From now on we need to work *together*. Maybe we can use your Facebook account to help Chloe and Jack – but tell us first, OK?' She tried another one of her forced smiles, and Itch grimaced.

Later that evening, heralded by a barrage of flashes from the photographers, Gabriel returned from Exeter in an ambulance. He embraced his mother and brother and then broke down. Itch was shocked to see tears running down his bruised face; he had never seen his brother traumatized like this.

The words tumbled out. 'I'm so sorry, Mum! I don't know what happened. We were all in a waiting room, waiting for Chloe's appointment. I went to move the car, and . . . then I was coming round and a nurse was telling me that Chloe and Jack had been taken!' He was holding Jude's hands – something else Itch had never seen before.

In the harsh light of the kitchen, Jude inspected his injuries. Gabriel winced. 'One sharp blow to the temple,' he said. 'That's all it took. How embarrassing. Small cut, big bruise.' He looked at Itch. 'They said we were followed to the hospital. Sorry, buddy, but I missed that.'

'Hire van,' said Itch. 'Two Greencorps men. We met them before, at the mining school. Hacked them off by escaping with the 126.'

'I remember the story.' Gabriel felt his bruise and shook his head slowly. 'This is all my fault! If I could have protected them somehow . . . if I'd stayed with them, none of this would have happened . . . They must be so scared . . .' He trailed off.

'Yes,' said Itch, 'but they're tougher than you think, Gabe. And they've got each other.'

Gabriel closed his eyes together as if in prayer, but there were more tears running down his cheeks. 'I know that, you guys have been through a lot. But what do we do now?' said Gabriel. 'We have to do something. Do we all hold a press conference? Can we help the search somehow?'

Itch went to rummage for some snacks – and to

hide his feelings. Gabriel was asking him what to do next! It had never, ever been like this. Growing up, he had always deferred to his older brother, and always assumed he would know what the right course of action would be. Now Gabe was as lost as everyone else.

Lucy and her mother stayed the night. Once the media had set up camp outside Itch's house, neither of them fancied battling their way through. Jon and Zoe had faced a barrage of cameras and lights when they left, and Nicola was horrified.

'We've got lots of room,' said Jude. 'Please do stay. It would be nice to have some company. With Nicholas away, there's strength in numbers. It'll be no trouble, really.' She smiled sadly.

'Lucy can have my room,' offered Itch. 'I'll sleep on Gabe's floor.'

'If you're sure that's OK,' said Lucy.

'I might need to tidy a few things,' he said, 'but that'd be great.'

'I'll make up the spare bed,' said Jude, and she disappeared upstairs.

Itch was clearing the table, but he suddenly stopped and listened to the creaking of the floor-boards. He could tell that his mother had crossed the landing to Chloe's room. He waited for her to move on. He imagined her looking around at the posters, the make-up, her still packed bag from Spain. It was quite some time before the boards creaked again and Itch resumed putting the plates away. The house had plenty of people in it, and many more outside, but it was the missing Chloe who seemed to fill the house with silence.

While Jude and Nicola talked late into the night, Itch and Lucy moved bedding and elements around.

'I'm not bothered about your collection, Itch, really,' said Lucy. 'It's just for one night, and if there's some iodine or sulphur knocking about with your pyjamas, I can live with that.'

'Thanks,' said Itch, 'but they're better put away.'

While he worked, they listened to the muffled voices of their mothers talking downstairs. Itch froze each time he heard Jude sobbing.

'I'm glad we could stay,' said Lucy.

'Me too.' Itch stuffed some jeans into a drawer, then sighed and leaned his forehead against the wall. 'I can't stop thinking about what might be happening to Jack and Chlo.' He banged his head a few times. 'I didn't want to mention it to Mum, but I'm really scared for them, Lucy.'

She came and stood next to him. After a moment she put her hand on his shoulder. 'OK, stop. This is not helping. We're all thinking the same stuff, but here's the thing – we don't know anything. Not for certain, anyway. So it's laptop time again.'

Itch handed it over and Lucy looked at Itch's Facebook page.

'Two hundred thousand notifications. Roughly. Still five thousand friend requests.' She clicked and read, clicked and read. 'Support from all over the world, Itch. Tons from Spain – literally tons. All after

Madrid, I suppose. Loads apologizing for their burning money and the riots. They're saying they'll watch out for Jack and Chlo. You should accept all these requests, Itch. Who knows who might be able to help? Oh, and a message from Mary Lee again. Or Leila, as she says she's called.'

'Saying what?' said Itch, looking up.

'*Sympathies Itchingham,*' read Lucy. '*We tell everyone about Greencorps. We hope your family is reunited soon.*'

'They haven't been caught, then,' he said. 'Still evading the Nigerian cops.'

'Corrupt as hell, you said. Must help a bit.'

'Guess so.'

'And loads from school. Chloe's friends; Jack's friends. And that vicar from Mr Watkins's funeral says she's praying for them.'

'I think we'll take help from anywhere,' said Itch, yawning. 'Whether it's the vicar or Facebook. So yes to the friend requests.'

'All of them?'

'All of them.'

'OK, I'll sort it. Now you need to sleep,' Lucy insisted.

'I don't want to, I really don't. Feels like I should stay awake. Just in case something happens.'

Lucy pushed him to the door. 'Your dad's back tomorrow, Itch. Go to sleep. I promise I won't mess up your room.'

He hesitated a moment, then nodded and headed for Gabriel's room.

★ ★ ★

Itch had always been an early riser, but when your family is the lead story on the news, you wake when the first Breakfast TV lights go on. An unusually fierce brightness was shining through the curtains of Gabriel's room at 5.55 a.m. and, with a sinking, squirming stomach, Itch knew that his day had started.

Realizing that his brother was already up, he bounded down the stairs to find the kitchen already full. Jude and Gabriel were sitting with Jon and Zoe, neither of whom appeared to have slept a wink. DCI Underwood had returned, along with a policewoman he hadn't seen before. Lucy was there too, wearing one of his old T-shirts; she smiled at him and gave a 'flatten-your-hair' gesture.

'Any news?' asked Itch. 'What's happening?' He permitted himself a micro-second of anticipation, while at the same time knowing full well that if Chloe and Jack had been found, he would have been woken. And people wouldn't be looking so tense.

Jude shook her head slowly. 'Nothing, I'm afraid, Itch, no. This is PC Jade Greaves – she's a family liaison officer or something. She'll help with dealing with the press and—'

'Tell us about the search,' interrupted Itch. 'Where are you looking? Two people can't just disappear into thin air.'

PC Greaves had been about to speak, but now deferred to DCI Underwood. For a moment he looked uncomfortable at being questioned by a fifteen-year-old, but then produced a sheaf of notes.

'Well, as I said yesterday, Interpol is aware of Jack and Chloe's disappearance—'

'Kidnap,' said Itch and Gabriel together.

Underwood appeared to weigh the word for a moment, then accepted it. '"Kidnap" is the most likely scenario, yes. OK. But there have been no ransom demands to date. The CCTV at the hospital doesn't appear to have been working in the corridors we checked. The van the two men used has been searched and tested. It's covered in fingerprints, as you might expect, including those of your sister and cousin. There's no doubt they were there, just no clues as to where they were taken afterwards. It's been cleared of all papers, emptied of evidence. The hire company is accessing the documents this morning; we should have that information soon.'

Itch looked disappointed: the van had been the best chance of a clue.

Almost as an afterthought, Underwood added, 'We did find two numbers scratched into the plastic seats, but we don't even know how old they are. So they might mean nothing.'

'What are they?' said Itch.

Underwood accessed an email on his phone and found the attached photo. He passed it to Jude first. Everyone leaned in to see.

'Is that a *41* and a *19*?' she asked, passing it on to Jon and Zoe.

They squinted at the numbers. 'Could be,' said

Zoe. 'They're a bit on top of each other.' She handed it to Itch.

He looked at the numbers – a series of indentations made by what could have been a sharp fingernail. And Itch knew exactly what they were.

'It's not 41 and 19.'

'What?' said Lucy.

'Excuse me?' said Underwood.

'It's not 41 and 19,' repeated Itch. And, to the bewilderment of everyone in the kitchen, he sprinted for the door.

23

Itch ran up the stairs, taking them three at a time.

'So you *did* listen after all!' he shouted when he reached his room. He grabbed his bag and hurtled back down the stairs, jumping the last six and almost crashing into his uncle Jon. 'She *did* listen, Uncle Jon!' and he pulled him into the kitchen. Sweeping away numerous cups and mugs, Itch spread the Periodic Table poster Hampton had given him out on the table. 'They're in Spain!' he announced.

There was silence in the kitchen – looks of incredulity from the police and astonishment from the family.

'How do you work that out, then?' asked Gabriel. Jude and Zoe came over to get a closer look.

'Before we left for Madrid, Mr Hampton explained that some elements have different names in Spanish. When we were in the science museum, Chloe found a T-shirt with the same design. I was showing her, but I thought she wasn't paying attention.' He pointed to two elements Hampton had circled on the poster. 'Silver and gold. The elements I was telling her about. In Spanish, they're *plata* and *oro*, but obviously still on top of each other on the table: numbers 47 and 79. That's what she's carved into the car. Chloe must have heard where they were going and written the only thing she could think of which wouldn't alert the Greencorps men – it almost didn't alert you guys, either.'

He noticed Lucy and Gabriel wince at his final comment, and wondered whether he'd overstepped the mark. Jude inspected the photo on DCI Underwood's phone again.

'Well, you're right, Itch – it's a 47 and a 79. And they're clearly on top of each other. And Chloe has the nails.' There was a spark to his mother's voice which the others caught.

'Why else would you write 47 over a 79?' Zoe was looking over her sister-in-law's shoulder.

'It's not much to go on—' began Underwood.

'But it is, though,' said Lucy. 'It absolutely is. She couldn't have written *Gone to Spain* because her captors would have seen it. Chloe did the only thing she could. In four numbers. These are smart girls you're dealing with here; if they had a chance to get a message to us, they'd have taken it.'

Underwood looked again at the photo from the car. Sensing a quickening in his interest, Lucy leaned forward across the table and waited till he looked at her.

'It is just too much of a coincidence, and you know it – 47 over 79. Silver and gold, *plata* and *oro*, English and Spanish. Chloe and Jack are telling you where they are.'

There was a slight pause before the policeman nodded. 'I'll make a call.'

When the mayor of Madrid found out that the girl carried unconscious from the Toledo bridge was believed to be one of the two kidnap victims, he sent his expressions of regret to the Lofte family. When he found out that she and her cousin might have been forcibly brought back to Spain, he sent his private jet. A wealthy man, he had an eye on the forthcoming crisis-induced elections and saw himself as a future prime minister; Spain's saviour. The chaos caused by the burning money had been compounded by thousands of notes in circulation turning out to be fake. Taken to banks for testing in the wake of the recent conflagration, they had failed the teller's tests and been confiscated. Within hours the panic was nationwide. The demonstrations that had only just subsided ignited again. In cities and towns across the country, protest marches turned into riots. The police were overwhelmed, and there was talk of the army taking to the streets to restore order.

The Bank of Spain had performed the same tests as Jacob Alexander at the mining school. They too discovered picric acid, and wasted no time in saying so. The governor, along with the Prime Minister –

who was hanging on until fresh elections were held – denounced the sabotage as an act of terrorism. The euro plunged all over the world, but in Spain the collapse was spectacular.

The mayor believed that, in the absence of a proper working government, he had the opportunity to show that he could run things. With the Chief of Police, he invited the Loftes to come to Madrid and make a public appeal for help in finding the missing British girls.

It had taken a while to convince the Cornwall and Devon Police that the numbers 47 and 79 were a massive clue, but when the credit card used to hire the kidnapper's van turned out to have been issued by a bank in Spain, the arguments were over. By the time Nicholas returned from South Africa, grim-faced and pale, the Guardia Civil had already been contacted.

'Who's going to listen to us, Dad?' said Itch as they boarded the Cessna Citation. 'They have enough going on without helping us find Chlo and Jack.'

'No idea,' said his dad, 'but this mayor seems to think it's a good idea. And at least we'll be doing something, not just sitting on our backsides or being hounded by the moronic press outside the house.'

They strapped themselves in for takeoff, and Itch realized that his father was right: anything was better than staying at home.

The suggestion had been to send over as many family and friends as could fit in the plane. He twisted round and saw Lucy talking to his aunt Zoe, and Uncle Jon talking to his mother. Everyone looked exhausted and strained, but there was a buzz to the conversation that had been missing since the kidnap; a genuine belief that they were flying closer to Chloe and Jack.

As his father typed furiously into his laptop, Itch noticed that the email subject was 'Thorium' and chanced a question.

'Was the trip to Cape Town worth it, Dad? I was going to ask you before, but . . .'

Since his father's return, Chloe and Jack had been the only topics of conversation, with endless visits, phone calls and meetings. As each day passed, they had become more urgent, more frantic. All other concerns had disappeared.

Nicholas looked up. 'You're right – everything's been too hideous, hasn't it? And it was bad in Palmeitkraal too, I'm afraid. I was hoping to rescue the Hewitt mines sale, but a new company's been snapping up anything and everything they can get their hands on. Gold, platinum, rare earths – you name it. But the worst thing? It's not just losing the mine, though heaven knows that's bad enough . . . it's that I'm partly to blame.'

Itch was astonished. 'You, Dad? That can't be right . . .'

Nicholas shook his head, and spoke quietly. 'You remember I shouted at Themba after the, er, incident with Chloe at the Hewitt mine?'

'Which you obviously haven't told Mum about.'

Nicholas nodded. 'I also lost it a bit with him afterwards, and used some language which could have been seen as insensitive and patronizing. Apparently Sammy particularly felt that his father had been humiliated. He told Themba it sounded like an old white mine owner talking to his black staff. So when another buyer came sniffing around, Themba didn't fight it or tell us until it was too late. So we lost the mine, along with the lanthanum, terbium, europium and neodymium that came with it.'

'But the spoil heaps were dangerous—'

'Yes, they were, and he messed up, big time. But I got angry and made a mistake. So we keep looking. We still need to find new energy sources. It's just that, next to finding Chlo and Jack, it all seems utterly meaningless.' He slammed his laptop shut.

'I didn't mean to stop you working, Dad . . .'

'It's fine. My heart wasn't in it anyway, and I know we're going to have to do a big press conference. You ready for that?'

'No – but if it helps find them . . . Had to do one when we came back from the riot. Maybe it'll be like that.'

His father shifted in his seat. 'I have a feeling it'll be a bit bigger than that.'

Nicholas was right. They were met at the airport by the mayor – a powerful, broad-shouldered man with a bald head so shiny Itch thought it could almost be polished rhodium – and their every move

291

was recorded, photographed and filmed. He greeted them all individually, fully conversant with who was who in the Lofte family, and that Lucy – or 'Miss Lucy', as he called her – was a friend who had been caught up in the original Madrid riot.

'I am so sorry for your distress,' he said first to Jude, then Zoe, and then the others in turn, as a camera crew took close-ups of his concerned face. 'Maybe the people of Madrid, the people of Spain can help find your girls. Maybe you could tell your stories and we can see what sort of girls they are?' He performed a small bow, and Itch saw his father bridle; this was the sort of unctuous man that he knew he couldn't stand.

'They basically want us to cry for the cameras,' he snarled to Jude.

'That might not be difficult,' she said.

They were shown to a minibus and transported, with a police escort, to the Cibeles Palace in the centre of Madrid. It looked more like a cathedral than a town hall, which prompted the mayor to chuckle about 'our humble office' as they drew up beneath its huge white Gothic arches. No one said anything.

They were ushered into a small ornate lounge, and Itch spotted a familiar face: Félix Blanco, the Spanish agent who had rescued him and Chloe from the bridge, was making his way over.

'I hope we can help find your sister,' he said as he shook Itch's hand. 'The press conference won't be easy, but once you're done, I wonder if you and your school friend' – he pointed at Lucy – 'can help me? I'm still working on our little euro problem and you might be able to be of service.'

Itch shrugged. 'Can we see how this goes? Might need to help Mum and Dad.'

'Of course,' said Blanco. 'I'll wait. *Buena suerte.* Good luck.'

The smiling mayor was ushering them through to another room which was buzzing with people. Itch's stomach tightened: this could only be grim, he thought. He saw Jude grab Nicholas's hand – something he hadn't seen in years – and then felt his own hand gripped in turn. Lucy had hung back, not wanting to intrude in the family procession, but now, as they approached the pandemonium, she reached for Itch's hand.

They emerged by a long table with seven chairs and seven glasses of water. The chatter died down as soon as the Loftes appeared; cameras were hoisted, microphones held aloft, and then journalists began calling out questions. Itch couldn't see how full the room was: the lights were too fierce, and anyway, he was keeping his head down; but the *sound* told him it was full to bursting. And he was terrified.

If tears were what the media was expecting, they were disappointed. What they got was anger. Under the full glare of the world's media, with dazzling lights and rattling camera shutters, all four parents spoke about their daughters, Zoe and Nicholas even managing a few words in Spanish. Gabriel described the events on the day of the kidnap, and

Lucy testified to the bravery of her friends. Sitting at the end of the row, Itch watched his family as they fought to stay in control.

When it was his turn to speak, the noise from the cameras and the blinding light from the flashes reached a peak; then, all at once, there was silence in the room. *Oh help*, thought Itch. *It's me they're waiting to hear.* The image of him and Chloe on the bridge and the subsequent kidnap had made it the biggest news story of the day, even supplanting the ongoing euro chaos. The few TV and news radio networks that hadn't been taking the press conference live now joined to make sure they heard the words of the fifteen-year-old English boy who had carried his sister to safety just days before. Itch felt a squeeze of encouragement on his right hand.

For a moment he was silent. He had no idea what – if anything – he was going to say; he hadn't realized that he was going to have the final word. But as he stared into the white glare of the camera lights, he suddenly remembered watching the news on the tiny set in South Africa, then at Jack's house after the bombings, and then in the café in Madrid. And he realized that, actually, he had quite a lot to say.

24

'Er, hello. My name is Itchingham Lofte, and four days ago my sister and cousin were kidnapped in England. As you've heard, my brother Gabriel was attacked too. We know who took them. It was two men who are working for Greencorps – they have attacked us before. The company is run by a woman called Mary Bale, but the real power behind it is Nathaniel Flowerdew. He was my old science teacher at school, but before then he was responsible for the oil spill in Nigeria which killed seventeen people. He avoided prosecution because Greencorps allowed someone else to take the rap. Her name was Shivvi Tan Fook, and I saw Flowerdew kill her. He's been on the run since Christmas, but I believe it was him who killed the CEOs of Greencorps, Christophe Revere and Jan Van Den Hauwe, and not the divers who are being blamed.'

There were gasps and murmurs as Itch began his speech – it was clear this wasn't what the networks had been expecting at all. As his accusations continued, reporters started to look at each other, wondering if his comments were libellous. The mayor was looking nervous, wiping a handkerchief over his gleaming head. Itch, oblivious to what was happening on the other side of the lights, was just getting started.

'Flowerdew is positioning the company so that everyone thinks they've changed. Politicians are prepared to believe Greencorps because they want to use them to get inside the oil industry. But the truth is, they should leave well alone. Greencorps is now run by a criminal and a murderer and—'

The mayor had heard enough. He'd noticed a few networks switching off their cameras; reporters gathering their things together.

'Was there anything you wanted to tell us about your sister and cousin?' The mayor was steering Itch back to what he saw as safer ground.

Itch looked surprised to be interrupted. 'You know about my sister and cousin. My family have spoken about them. But you need to know who has taken them – otherwise they won't be found. This isn't a normal ransom—'

And Itch's mic went dead.

He carried on speaking for a couple more sentences before realizing that no one could hear him any more. The mayor announced that they were out of time and consequently there could be no questions. It was a close call as to who was the more furious – the mayor for having his press conference 'hijacked', or Itch for being silenced. As the family filed back out, they glowered at each other; only the presence of the camera crew preventing a shouting match.

'You rocked!' said Lucy in Itch's ear as soon as the mayor had gone. 'That was awesome. No one else was going to say that stuff so—' She broke off as she saw Jude coming over; Itch's mother did not look happy.

'What the hell was that?' she said. There were tears in her eyes now, and a tremor in her voice. She had kept it together for the media, but her son was not so lucky. 'We are trying to find Chloe and Jack, not make grand speeches! But you had to spoil it, didn't you? Instead of concentrating on getting Chloe back, you had to go grandstanding and make those . . . those wild accusations.'

'Mum, that's not fair!' Itch looked astonished. 'You'd said everything about Chloe and Jack – I'd have just been repeating the same stuff. And since when was talking about Greencorps and Flowerdew "wild accusations", anyway?'

Nicholas had appeared at Jude's shoulder and was trying to steer her away, but she shrugged him off. She was about to go on, but then thought better of it, looked hard at her son, and stormed off.

Itch's father leaned over. 'She'll be OK. I thought you were great. We might get sued, but you were still great.'

'But maybe she was right,' said Itch. 'This is all about finding Jack and Chloe. Did I help that?'

'Who knows, Itch? Who knows? But you certainly rattled some cages . . . Let's see what comes crawling out.'

Next came Félix Blanco, still in his overcoat, his face enigmatic, impossible to read. 'The most interesting press conference I've heard for a long time. The TV news anchors were busy issuing disclaimers as they pulled away. I could almost hear their directors shouting in their earpieces.' He allowed himself a smile. 'Quite amusing, as you might say.'

'Well, I seem to have upset my mother again,' said Itch. 'I think she was about to tell me that this is all my fault.'

'Do you need to stay . . . ?'

'I'll ask. What do you want me to do?'

The Spaniard looked from Itch to Lucy; his tone was business-like. 'You and your friends witnessed a number of crimes being committed while you were caught up in the riots here. Some of them are of interest to us. I know you're here to find your sister and cousin, but if you had a few moments . . . ? We have an incident room at the Fábrica Nacional de Moneda y Timbre – Real Casa de la Moneda.'

Itch looked blank.

'Ah,' said Blanco. 'Apologies. It is the Royal Mint. They are of course most distressed by recent events. It is ten minutes away.' He looked expectantly at Itch.

Itch looked at Lucy.

'We have some time, I think, before they fly us back,' she said. 'If your folks are OK with it . . .' She shrugged.

Itch nodded. 'OK,' he said. 'If you clear it with my parents.'

Blanco smiled and bowed slightly. 'Of course,' he said, and strode to where Nicholas and Jude were huddled with Jon and Zoe.

With the help of a wailing police siren, the journey through the rammed streets of Madrid took less than ten minutes. Blanco kept up a running commentary as they weaved their way along the Plaza de la Independencia and Calle de Alcalá. The signs of protest were everywhere – from scrawled graffiti and boarded-up windows to the protesters' tents in a park.

Their progress was halted briefly by a burned-out car being winched onto a transporter.

'Why are we doing this?' Itch said quietly to Lucy, as Blanco continued his chatter. 'We should be finding Chloe and Jack, not helping the police with their enquiries. Maybe we should go back . . .'

'He said it wouldn't take long,' said Lucy. 'We'd only be sitting in that room, making conversation with people you don't want to talk to. We might as well . . .'

And suddenly they were there. The police car pulled up by a vast, drab concrete building with square pillars, the words FÁBRICA NACIONAL DE MONEDA carved above the entrance. Blanco ushered them up the steps and into the marble reception area. Itch could actually see his reflection in the slabs under his feet, his face ghostly white, with dark rings around his eyes. Flashing an ID card at the security men, Blanco led them through airport-style security checks – pat-downs and metal detectors. When Blanco set off an alarm, it filled the hall with an echoing electronic howl, but he just nodded at the uniformed men, all of whom nodded back. When they were clear, he led the way down a hushed, carpeted corridor to a small office.

Three people looked up as they entered, and nodded as they recognized Itch and Lucy; a TV screen was still rerunning scenes from the press conference intercut with photos of Jack and Chloe. Itch and Lucy looked away.

The walls were covered in images of banknotes, most faded and worn. Rather than see himself on TV again, Itch went over to examine them. The pre-euro currency was the peseta, and a variety of notes featuring – Itch assumed – assorted Spanish kings and noblemen were displayed in frames. In comparison with the euro, he thought they looked like ancient documents. The frames ended with the latest issues, and a prominently displayed 500-euro note.

'The highest denomination we have,' said

300

Blanco. 'And unlikely to be stolen.' He indicated the security cameras in every corner of the room. 'There are alarms too, though maybe a fire extinguisher would be more useful today.' He didn't smile, but Itch thought he was joking.

Remembering the note Blanco had given him, Itch asked, 'Presumably you know what caused them to burst into flames . . .'

The agent paused briefly, exchanging glances with his colleagues. 'Yes, of course.' He spoke in Spanish and was handed a file of papers. 'This information is widely known, though not officially confirmed. There is much nervousness in this building about what can be revealed.' He went to shut the door. 'It is feared that once it is known how to sabotage the euro, others will try.'

'I've tested the note you gave me so I know what was on it,' said Itch.

Blanco's eyebrows raised. 'Of course you have – you are a scientist, so maybe we can share our information.' He studied the text. 'We have *acidio picricio* . . .'

'Picric acid,' said Itch.

Blanco nodded, running his finger down a list. '*Oxido de titanio.*'

'Titanium oxide,' said Itch. 'And maybe some nitrocellulose in there too? That's what we found, anyway. It's no wonder they burst into flames.'

Blanco was still reading. 'Plus europium and traces of gadolinium,' he said.

Itch was silent. He remembered now that Dr

301

Alexander had mentioned europium before telling them about the picric acid, and he had meant to follow it up . . .

'Europium? In a euro?' He turned to Lucy. 'Is that a joke?'

She shrugged. 'Science jokes are like teacher jokes. Not funny to normal people.'

'It *is* funny, though,' said Itch. 'That's the thing. But what's it doing on a banknote?'

Blanco looked surprised and pleased. 'Well, I can help Britain's greatest chemist, then. And it might be a joke to you, but it isn't to us. This is why we have had the new riots.' He called to a colleague, and a petite, dark-haired woman brought a lamp to his desk, plugged it in and switched it on. 'The europium is part of the security system of each note. If you hold a five-euro note under an ultraviolet light, the yellow stars glow an intense red.' He took a note out of his pocket and held it under the lamp.

'Wow,' Itch said, leaning in to study it. Blanco was right: the string of usually dull, faded yellow stars behind an ancient-looking arch were now a deep red. When the lamp was switched off, they were yellow again.

'Now, here's the problem . . .' Blanco held another note under the ultraviolet lamp. This time the stars turned from yellow to a dull orange. 'It's not much of a difference, but enough to trigger the security alarms – these are the notes registering as fake.'

'You mentioned gadolinium,' said Itch. 'Another rare earth. Is that normally there?'

'Apparently not,' said Blanco.

'I think europium decays to gadolinium,' Lucy told them quietly. Itch's eyes widened. Everyone in the room had stopped to listen now.

'Why would europium decay like that?' asked Itch.

'Someone's blasted it with neutrons.'

'And why would someone do that?'

'To make fakes!' said Blanco, reaching for his phone and barking instructions around the room. 'To undermine the euro! I will keep it a secret that two English schoolchildren told us more than our own scientists.'

When he stopped talking, Lucy asked, 'Excuse me, but we came to look at some images from the riot . . . Could we do that and then get back to the others?'

But Blanco persisted, 'The number of people who could have done this is very small. And the number of places it could happen even smaller.'

'And while your people work on that, could we see what you brought us here for?' said Itch.

'Oh – of course . . .' Blanco seemed to have forgotten the purpose of their visit. He stood by his desk – empty apart from a computer screen and keyboard. 'The police are investigating what happened with our currency. But, as it concerns the security of our country, so are we. The governor of the mint is a colleague of sorts. So . . .' He offered them both chairs. 'We have prepared a selection of photos and videos taken on the night of that first riot, when we rescued you and your sister. These are, in the main, people known to us. Faces which have been flagged. If you remember any of them, please tell us.'

Itch and Lucy pulled their chairs closer as the photos started to scroll up. An assortment of images appeared on the screen, some clear, other blurry. Hooded figures running; rioters launching missiles – followed by a series of individuals in extreme close-up. As each frame appeared, Itch and Lucy studied the screen, consulted and clicked to the next one. The first video showed a gang setting fire to a van; the second, flames from a burning cash point.

Itch paused the film. 'This looks like the bank we passed on the way to the bridge. Its ATM was on fire.'

Blanco leaned over to click on another video. 'Yes, we found you. Here . . .'

Itch and Lucy watched the enhanced CCTV film of their school party stopping briefly at the bank before hurrying on. Zooming in, it was possible to make out Mr Hampton, Miss Coleman and, with a gasp from Itch and Lucy, Chloe and Jack arm in arm.

'I didn't mean to distress you . . .' said Blanco. 'We picked you up on the bridge too.' A different film showed the melee on the Toledo bridge and, when

Blanco paused the images, the school party caught in the middle. Lucy put her hands over her mouth, and Blanco apologized again. 'I'm sorry, this was a mistake . . .'

'No, wait . . .' said Itch, holding up his hand. 'Can you zoom in just beyond our group? There – near where the TV crew are?' He pointed at the bright lamp that shone halfway across the bridge.

'What are you looking at, Itch?' asked Lucy.

He waited while Blanco enlarged the area. 'Can you keep that up and go back to the bank shot?' asked Itch.

In a separate box on the screen, Blanco ran the previous video.

'Stop it there!' said Itch, slightly too loudly. 'Zoom in behind Mr Hampton, next to me!'

Blanco leaned in, his head swivelling back and forth as he compared the images. He glanced at Itch. 'What am I looking at?'

'The same two men in each image. The guy with the cap, and the tall guy next to him.'

'So?' said Blanco. 'There was a big crowd. They were all surging onto the bridge . . .'

But Itch shook his head. Lucy and Blanco noticed him swallow nervously. 'No, that's them.'

'Who?' asked Lucy.

'I forgot all about it till now. I thought that maybe I was being followed that night. And someone tried to grab me on the bridge too, but I couldn't see who it was. Well, now I know, because

I've seen them before. They're the Greencorps agents who attacked us at the mining school.' He turned to Blanco and pointed to the screen. 'They're the men who kidnapped my sister and cousin. They were here!'

25

After everyone in the room had studied the faces of the kidnappers, Félix Blanco fielded a string of questions from his team. Itch and Lucy did their best to follow the animated conversation – they were both pointed at continuously – but had to wait for Blanco's brief summary in English before they realized what was happening.

'They think that this is one story, not two,' he said. In the silence that followed, he and his team stared at Itch and Lucy.

'What?' said Lucy. 'You think the kidnap and the riots are connected?'

Blanco shrugged. 'You are at the centre of both. That's one big coincidence.'

Itch had to agree. 'You're right. But to put the two together, Greencorps have to be behind the riots *and* the burning money. That doesn't make sense, does it? They're interested in oil, not anarchy.'

Blanco suddenly jumped up. 'Come with me,' he

barked, and almost ran from the room. Itch and Lucy jogged after him.

'What's happening?' asked Lucy. 'Where are we going?'

'They're not going to like this . . .' said Blanco, 'not going to like it all.'

'Who's not going to like what?' called Lucy as they followed in his wake.

'Security is tight here – for obvious reasons,' shouted Blanco as they ran up a sweeping carpeted staircase. 'They don't have visitors – they hate visitors – but they're going to have to put up with you two.'

As they approached a security arch, three uniformed men with silver earpieces blocked their path. Blanco yelled, 'Centro Nacional de Inteligencia,' and waved his ID card, and they fell back. He quickly spoke to them; then to Itch and Lucy: 'Better leave them your bags or they will get mad,' and they were swiped through steel doors.

They found themselves in a control room with screens showing every corner of the mint. Operators sat monitoring, recording, testing, but there was barely a sound in the darkened room. It was cathedral-quiet with any conversation conducted in hushed tones. Blanco went over to speak to a plump man in a dark suit and thick glasses who had started to get to his feet, his face distinctly unwelcoming. The agent oozed reassurance, but the other man wasn't buying it and steered his unwanted guest into a glass-walled office, snapping the door shut behind them.

Through the door Itch noticed that Blanco had unbuttoned his jacket, revealing the strap of a holster. He leaned close to Lucy. 'Blanco's got a gun!' he whispered. 'That's why the metal detector went off.'

She followed his gaze and nodded. 'I suppose he would have,' she said. 'Fairnie and his team had plenty of guns when they needed them.'

Fairnie, thought Itch glumly. *How we could do with you now.*

'Are they arguing about us?' whispered Lucy, pointing at the gesticulating men in the office.

'Given how many times we are being pointed at, I'd say that's a yes,' he whispered.

As the wrangle continued, Itch stared across what he guessed must be at least twenty screens. In front of him, the work of the entire Spanish Royal Mint was revealed. A number of screens seemed to show paper-making, although the process started with what looked like vast sheets of cotton being soaked, beaten, boiled and cut up. The workers they could see wore waterproofs and wellington boots – water was sloshing everywhere. Close-up cameras showed images of the enormous fabric sheets being dried in a tunnel of hot air, then bathed in what Itch imagined were chemicals, and dried again.

'This is awesome,' whispered Lucy. 'They're actually making money!'

Itch said nothing as he watched the rolls of cotton paper being split into four, then cut into manageable sheets – enough for maybe twenty notes each. More close-ups revealed that there were no numbers, no amounts – no words or letters at all; they bore only watermarks, which were either arches or bridges. The rest was blank.

The office door opened and the plump man emerged, seemingly placated; after one long stare at Itch, he eased himself back into his chair and picked up a phone.

Blanco came over to Itch and Lucy. 'I said they'd hate you being here. Didn't realize they'd hate me being here too. But we need to go. And that' – he pointed at the screen showing the watermarked, blank sheets – 'is where we are going. I've had a crash course in euro-production from my team, and I need to see this close up . . . with the help of the happy director here. Come.' And they stood by another set of steel doors, waiting for the director to finish his call.

'I think he's making a point,' said Lucy.

Eventually, just as Itch thought Blanco was about to explode with frustration, the director wandered over. He muttered a few incomprehensible words as he passed Itch and Lucy.

'He's a real charmer,' said Lucy as they watched him swipe his ID card on a security panel. A solid double click, and the doors swung open.

To their surprise they were now outside again; a

small buggy with a uniformed driver was waiting in front of them. The director jumped on next to him – the buggy swaying ominously; Itch, Lucy and Blanco sat behind.

'It's a huge complex,' said Blanco as the electric vehicle jerked into life. 'It's split into two. We're heading for the paper-mill section, where the notes are, er, assembled. The final printing takes place in a separate building.' They travelled at surprising speed along small walkways; staff and security ducked out of the way as the buggy approached.

'I know why we're doing this,' said Itch in Lucy's car, 'but this feels all wrong. We should be back with my folks now. We're not welcome here.'

Before Lucy could reply, they had parked up in front of a hangar-sized modern brick building, its huge metal doors open, and a large lorry reversing inside. The director jumped off and led them inside. They emerged into the noise and smell of industrial money making. Itch and Lucy grimaced at the heavy, cloying chemical odour, thick with moisture. In front of them bales of what looked like coarse cotton wool were being poured into a huge boiler that stood two metres off the ground.

'They pour in some cleaning agent and cook it all up,' said Blanco as they walked through clouds of steam. 'It's 140 degrees Celsius in there, and they get raw cellulose out of it. It's a messy business.'

Lucy looked impressed. 'You really *have* done your homework!'

Blanco shrugged. 'Well, I had to fight for every fact, so I might as well use them.'

The director led them past a huge vat, where he stopped to speak to the staff.

Blanco fidgeted, clearly impatient, and continued to play the tour guide. 'They add bleach here – get rid of the colour – then squeeze the pulp with a heavy roller. The director would tell you this himself, but he thinks it is all too sacred to explain to anyone, including me. He is an idiot. But an idiot who is in charge, which makes him dangerous. So we must wait patiently.'

'Why are we heading for the section where they print the watermark?' asked Itch.

Blanco glanced at the director, who was sharing a joke with a man in overalls and boots. 'Because that's where they add the security thread too. Before it gets any numbers, letters or signatures, they add the tricks to foil the counterfeiters.'

'Or picric acid,' said Lucy. The expression on Blanco's face suggested that this was what he was thinking too.

When they eventually continued, Itch noticed that they were being watched every step of the way. People working on the boiler, the vat, and a pulp conveyer belt scrutinized them as they passed. No one smiled.

'Don't like this much . . .' said Lucy quietly.

By a huge, twisting tank of circulating pulp, they stopped again, but Blanco had had enough. This time he didn't wait for the director. 'Stick with me. We'll find our own way.'

When the director realized that his guests were no longer waiting, he shouted loudly. You didn't need to understand Spanish to know what he was saying.

'Stick with me,' repeated Blanco. 'He'll catch up.'

As they rounded an enormous press squeezing gallons of water out of a sea of white mulch, they walked into a line of workers. Some wore overalls, some oversized aprons; all looked furious.

Blanco didn't stop. 'We don't need to talk here. Ignore them.'

The line of staff only parted after he had shown his Centro Nacional de Inteligencia accreditation; even then he was jostled as he pushed his way through. Blanco snapped. He grabbed the bearded man who had pushed him and rammed him into the steel walls of the press. A flurry of words followed, and the bearded man spat at Blanco. Behind him, the other workers reacted with fury, shouting and gesticulating. From around the mint, staff appeared to see what was happening. Itch, Lucy and Blanco were effectively surrounded.

Itch and Lucy moved closer together. 'There's going to be another riot if we're not careful,' said Itch.

'But aren't we all on the same side?' asked Lucy.

'Doesn't feel like it, does it?'

Itch glanced up at the security cameras which filled every visible corner. Their red flashing bulbs looked reassuring to him. 'At least someone else can see this,' he said, nodding at the ceiling. 'They'll be watching in the control room.'

'Yes, but whose side are *they* on?' said Lucy.

As Blanco wiped spittle from his face, the director ambled into view. He issued an order and his staff backed away, but his face was crimson. As he started another furious volley of words, Blanco turned away, ignoring him. Hooking Itch with one arm and Lucy with the other, he ushered them deeper into the mint.

'Do we need help?' asked Itch hesitantly. 'I mean, I know you're an agent and everything, but . . .'

'But they seem hostile?' finished Blanco. 'You're right there. But we'll be fine.' He patted his holster.

'Where are your colleagues?' wondered Lucy. 'They might help us.'

Blanco shook his head. 'Busy. And even if I wanted to call them, mobiles aren't allowed in here. They don't want any photographs.'

They stopped by another bulky machine with piles of roughly cut paper stacked like hay bales. Teams carried and loaded the raw money, watching as it disappeared on yet another conveyer belt.

'Where's it going now?' asked Lucy.

'To the printers, in the other building,' said Blanco. 'To the watermark team. But we need our friend the director again . . .' He nodded towards the two security guards who stood by a locked glass-panelled door with red and green lights above it. The red one was lit.

They heard the puffing director before they saw him. He was speaking into the tiny microphone of his headset, and as he approached the door, the green light came on. One of the guards pushed the door and it clicked open. The director turned to Blanco, beckoning him nearer; Itch and Lucy followed.

Up close, they saw that he was sweating. Rivulets of moisture ran down his forehead and into his eyes; his collar was drenched. It looked as though he'd been swimming in his clothes.

'This guy is very nervous,' murmured Lucy.

The man looked hard at her, then at Itch, and finally Blanco. '*Dos minutos,*' he said breathlessly, and checked his watch. 'You have two minutes only.'

On the other side of the door the climate changed. They walked along a wide tunnel lit by fierce halogen strips. Armed security men stood at every doorway; cameras watched every movement. Here the air was dry, the temperature cool. In the distance they heard the clatter of machinery, but no voices. The team responsible for watermarks and security threads had been expecting them. There were fifteen men and women, all dressed in white coats bearing the mint's logo. They had lined up as if for an inspection. Stacked on benches, waiting to be checked, were large chrome-covered plates, each containing the images of thirty-two 100-euro notes.

Blanco wasted no time. He spoke first in Spanish, then in English. 'My name is Félix Blanco. I work for the Centro Nacional de Inteligencia. I am speaking in English too so that our friends here can understand what I am saying.'

Either everyone knew who Itch and Lucy were or they didn't care; all eyes were on Blanco.

He continued, accompanied by mutters from some of the workers. 'I am investigating the criminal sabotage of our currency. The notes that burned were contaminated with picric acid, titanium oxide and nitrocellulose.' He spoke in Spanish again, before translating for Itch and Lucy, then continued. 'It is just about possible that this happened outside the mint, but it seems unlikely as all notes are – as you know – under armed guard as soon as they leave. Which means the crime happened here. Or somewhere near here. By people you might know. Or might have seen.'

The workers remained silent. In fact, it seemed to Itch that they had frozen there, arms folded, eyes fierce; not one had moved since Blanco started speaking. It was obvious that they resented every word.

'So I was wondering,' Blanco went on, 'if anyone had anything they could tell me which might help catch those responsible. I would like to speak to you all individually. The criminals have made this mint a laughing stock around the world.'

His words hung in the air, unanswered. There was nothing. No reaction at all.

Then the director looked at his watch. 'Time is up. I'm sorry your visit has been a waste of everyone's time. You see, we have already been asked these questions by the police. And they were more . . . respectful . . .'

'I'm sure they were,' said Blanco. 'And they got nowhere. So I am arranging for a full forensic testing of the mint – specifically these rooms. You know what we'll be looking for . . .'

The workers had started up again – their voices rapid, urgent.

'And if we find picric acid . . .'

The director spoke briefly into his radio.

'Or titanium oxide . . .'

The bearded man who had jostled Blanco bent down to tie his shoelace.

'Or nitrocellulose . . .'

Two security men came through the doors.

'Then we will know—' Blanco broke off, realizing that the power in the room had shifted: everyone felt it. He was no longer in charge. The bearded man walked up to Blanco. His walk was slow, controlled, head down; every step looked menacing.

He stopped a few centimetres away and raised his head. Blanco reached for his gun, but the man grabbed his arm and held it firm. 'I speak in English too so your friends can understand. We have more guns than you. Your time is up.'

Itch didn't see the head butt – it happened too fast – though he heard it. The crack of Blanco's nose as the man's forehead made contact sounded like a rifle shot. As the agent staggered, he got an elbow in his cheek; Itch heard it cave in.

Lucy screamed.

Itch glanced up at the security cameras just as their red lights went out.

26

Jack and Chloe knew they were on a boat. Underneath the blindfolds, they could sense the movement beneath them, hear the noise of an engine and smell the occasional tang of sea air. When the scarves were finally removed they saw their prison room was a cabin; the porthole had been blacked out, but through a couple of scratches they could just make out sunshine and sea. But Jack and Chloe, tied to opposite corners of the pitch-dark room, knew very little else.

To start with, they had been blindfolded 24/7. Even when their seasickness was at its height, they were told not to remove the scarves that were wound tightly round their eyes.

Once the seas had calmed, their two captors allowed them to remove their blindfolds. One provided them with towels for a shower. The men made no attempt to speak, and Jack and Chloe were quite happy to keep their silence. They waited until they were sure the men had gone before they risked any conversation.

'Would you say they are uglier than the German and the American?' asked Jack.

Chloe considered for a moment. 'Impossible as it seems, yes,' she said, smiling. 'And even stinkier.'

By the third day, they knew the routine. The cabin had two beds, one at each end, both screwed to the floor. With one hand cuffed to the bed head, their movement was limited, but once the blindfolds were off they could at least see and speak to each other.

'You look terrible,' said Chloe.

'So do you,' said Jack grimly.

Jack's cheek was no longer bleeding, but they both sported large bruises from the blows they'd received.

'You've got sick on your shirt,' said Chloe.

'I've got sick on my socks,' said Jack, her eyes shut. 'I've got it everywhere.'

'Me too,' said Chloe. 'Think I've stopped now, though.'

'Sea's calmer, that's why,' said Jack, coughing. She reached for her plastic bottle of water, which had been left with the towels. She emptied it in swift gulps and threw it at Chloe, bouncing it off her knees. 'Just keeping my aim in for when I get a chance to throw something hard and pointy at one of those scumbags. Can't even bring myself to look at them when they come in. Don't you look at them either.'

'I try not to,' Chloe said; then, with a catch in her voice, 'I'm so scared, Jack.'

Jack opened her eyes. Her cousin was biting her lip and she forced herself to sit up. 'Chloe, listen to me . . . Honestly? I'm scared too. But we've beaten them before. We'll do it again. And you can't just kidnap two girls and disappear. Someone will find us. Maybe someone will see those numbers you left. That was genius, by the way. We stay strong. We stay angry. We're better than them.' Jack sounded more confident than she felt, but it produced a flicker of a smile and a small nod from Chloe.

'Do you think he's here?' she asked. They had barely spoken of Flowerdew since they'd been snatched, but they both knew who was responsible.

'No. He'd have been down to gloat if he was.' Jack peered at the blacked-out porthole. 'But I don't suppose he'll be far away now.'

'Where are we, then?' said Chloe. 'We seem to be moving, then we stop for ages. Then we move again.' She paused, then answered her own question. 'We're hiding, aren't we?'

Jack agreed. 'Feels like it. Which means that someone's looking for us.'

'You haven't got an escape plan, I suppose?' said Chloe.

Jack pulled at the handcuff tying her hand to the bed. 'Well, let's make one now,' she said. 'OK, so we'll jump the guard guy – the really stinky one with the ear wax.' Chloe giggled. 'Run to the deck and dive into the sea. Swim to safety – maybe a luxury launch owned by some crack military outfit will pick us up. Simple.'

'Why don't we just push them all overboard?' said Chloe, joining in the fantasy. 'That'd be simpler. Then we could just drive this boat back home.'

'Nice one. I wish we had something from Itch's rucksack – bet he'd have something to gas them with, or make their skin go green.'

Chloe laughed again, but broke off. 'They'll be after him, won't they?' she said. 'They must have thought he'd be with us at the hospital.'

'Lucky he wasn't,' said Jack.

Chloe nodded, then whispered, 'Keep safe, Itch . . . Keep safe.'

The Spanish agent lay sprawled on the white tiles, a smear of blood marking where his face had hit the floor like a skid-mark. Itch crouched to check his breathing, then doubled up in pain as the bearded man's foot found his stomach. His vision full of popping lights, he felt Lucy's hands hauling him up again. He stood, leaning heavily on her shoulder and trying to focus on the faces of the staff.

Surely there must be some friends here, he thought. He could hear Lucy shouting, but he didn't understand the words; his rasping breaths filled his ears. Slowly, hearing and comprehension returned, but as he surveyed the row of hostile faces, he realized he was wrong.

We are on our own.

Lucy was still shouting, and now he understood what she was saying. 'What is this? *All of you?* You are *all* part of this?' she yelled.

The director spoke sharply in Spanish, and the bearded man placed his hand firmly over Lucy's mouth. He leaned in to apply further pressure – and Itch saw his moment. He had a fraction of a second to adjust his balance, then, with all the force he could muster, he slammed his knee into the man's groin. The man howled and dropped to the floor.

Itch grabbed Lucy's hand and turned to run, but two security guards blocked their path, guns drawn. Itch spun round and picked up a chromium plate. He saw the director's alarm and grabbed three more. Each was a massive sheet of 100-euro engravings, its value clear from the horrified reaction of the mint workers.

'Oh, so you do respond to some things . . .' said Itch, holding them up in front of him.

'Careful!' The director's eyes were following every movement of his plates. 'Don't drop them!'

'Get them to put their guns away!' yelled Itch. 'Or you lose these plates!'

The order was given and, reluctantly, the security team holstered their pistols.

'You must stop now,' said the director. 'There are too many guns here for you to get anywhere. You cannot escape – this place is a cross between a maze and a fortress. If we do this to your friend from the security services, imagine what we could do to you . . .' He didn't need to indicate the fallen Blanco; all eyes flicked there anyway. The bleeding had stopped but his face was a mess.

Itch felt Lucy's shoulders slump. 'He's right,' she said. 'You don't escape from here.'

Itch hesitated, then lowered the plates. 'We only wanted to find my sister and cousin,' he said quietly.

'And I'm sure you will,' said the director smoothly, stepping forward and easing the valuable etched plates out of Itch's hands. 'Unfortunately you have got involved in . . . something else altogether.' He turned to the watermark team, dismissing them with a sweep of his hand.

'What do you want with us?' asked Lucy. 'What use are we to you?'

The director found a handkerchief and wiped his face with it. 'Ah! No use at all,' he said. 'Not to me, anyway.' Itch and Lucy exchanged glances. 'But,' he continued, 'I think you should raise your hands where we can see them.'

As Itch and Lucy complied, the bearded man – still groaning – slowly got to his feet. Through narrowed eyes, he stared at Lucy, then Itch. He spoke rapidly in Spanish, the director interrupting when he could; then they started arguing at full volume.

Itch and Lucy had inched closer together, hands in the air. Neither understood what was being said, but none of it sounded good. Finally the director appeared to have had the last word, and the bearded man spat on the floor and turned away. As he passed one of the security guards, Itch saw him lean in to share a joke. The guard laughed loudly – and suddenly the bearded man made a grab for his pistol. Surprised, the guard reacted too late. The director cried out in alarm, but the man raised the gun. And pointed it straight at Itch's head.

'No, wait!' yelled Itch.

The director ran in front of the bearded man, waving his arms, but the gun stayed on Itch. Their argument resumed until the bearded man shouted, in the strangest American accent Itch had ever heard, 'C'mon, let's whomp this sucker!'

And suddenly Itch understood everything.

And his world went black.

It was the slowing of the engines that woke Jack; the vibrations in the cabin had dropped to a low rumble. Their room was dark – she must have been asleep for hours – but there were lights shining through the scratched porthole. She heard raised voices issuing commands, and distant answers drifting back.

Another ship.

'Wake up, Chloe.'

She heard her cousin stir, then jolt awake. 'What is it, Jack?' Chloe's voice was an urgent whisper.

'We've stopped,' said Jack. 'See those weird yellow lights out there? We've got company.'

They listened to the sounds of activity on deck and followed the faint beams of light as they danced around the cabin.

'Lots of lights,' muttered Chloe.

'A big ship,' Jack guessed.

'And getting closer . . .' Chloe watched the shadows in the cabin sharpen. 'This is where they're taking us, isn't it?' She was fighting rising terror, but not succeeding. 'He's there, isn't he?'

Jack couldn't lie to her. 'Yes,' she said slowly. 'Yes, I think this is where they're taking us, and yes, I think Flowerdew will be there. But Chloe . . . we've faced him before. And he lost. He's a loser and we should tell him that.'

'Maybe you should go first with that,' said Chloe.

And in their dark cabin cell, staring through the scratched porthole at their next prison, they both laughed. Quietly to start with, as though seeking each other's permission, then louder and freer. It became the hysterical laughter of the desperate – they both knew that – but it felt good; it sounded loud and it sounded defiant.

They were still laughing when – under the door – they saw the lights in the corridor flicker on and heard approaching footsteps.

'Well, this is it, Chlo,' said Jack loudly as a key turned in the lock. 'But remember – we are not quiet, we are not beaten and we are not forgettable.'

The door swung open; their two jailers switched on the lights from outside and came in. Chloe and

Jack blinked at the sudden brightness and stared at the men. Judging by the surprise on their faces, they had been expecting two cowering girls. What they saw instead were two furious hostages who were not going to go quietly.

Chloe went first. 'Wow – you must be so proud of yourselves,' she spat. 'Locking up two girls must be a real highlight for you.'

Jack joined in. 'Hey, *you*! The stinky one with the earwax problem!' Both men turned towards her. 'We know what's happening here. You are handing us over to a madman – you know that? You happy with that? If your mothers were here – here now – would they stay quiet or would they be deeply ashamed of you?' Both men glanced at each other, an involuntary action, but it was clear that they understood what Jack was saying. 'And when we escape and tell our story, they will disown you. You'll be in prison, but it'll be your family's shame—'

A large hand was clamped over Jack's mouth. It smelled of oil, beer and sweat.

Chloe took up the attack now. 'You have daughters? Sisters? Is this—'

The second man grabbed her hair and pulled. 'Shut up,' he said. 'Just shut up.'

Jack tried to keep talking, but her captor pressed harder, covering her nose as well. At last she fell silent, and the man produced a length of insulating tape, which he pressed over her mouth. He threw the roll to the other man, who did the same to

Chloe. She managed to curse him before she too was silenced. Both girls were then untied from the beds, their hands now bound with plastic cord. They both kept twisting round, seeking eye contact with the men – glaring, pleading – but their captors looked away.

Jack and Chloe were pushed, still struggling and defiant, out of the cabin and up towards the deck. As Jack climbed the stairs, her captor leaned in close. 'If I were you,' he said, in heavily accented English, 'I would stay quiet. And small. As small as possible. And maybe you get lucky.'

Itch and Lucy had spent no more than twenty minutes in the first vehicle. Hoods fastened tightly around their necks, hands tied, they had been bundled out of the mint and thrown into a waiting van. Or was it a truck? Or an armoured car? They couldn't tell. The driver was in a hurry; as he threw the vehicle around, Itch and Lucy were flung against boxes, metal partitions and each other.

After one particularly violent brake and swerve, the back doors were flung open. Within seconds, Itch felt strong hands grab him, and he was lifted, carried, then dropped again. Another running engine, another vehicle.

'Hey! Ow! What's happening? What are you doing?' cried Lucy as she was dumped next to Itch. Doors slammed and their new vehicle sped off, making them collide again.

'This is getting boring,' said Itch, rubbing his head through the hood and trying to wedge himself between the side of the van and what felt like a tyre.

'Boring?' said Lucy. 'Hardly the word I'd use. How about "terrifying"? Or "totally stuffed up"? Ever since I met you, my life has been anything but boring. I'd love a bit of boring, actually. God, this sack stinks. What do you think it contained before? My money's on cheese.'

'Sorry,' said Itch. He heard Lucy moving around, but she said nothing. 'Lucy?'

'What?'

'Sorry for putting you in danger.'

'Shut up, Itch. It's not you I'm scared of, believe it or not.'

'Oh, OK.'

He heard her tug at her hood and curse. 'I was just wondering . . .' she said. 'Do you think we're on our own in here? Apart from the driver, obviously—'

'Hey!' Itch called out to the front of the vehicle. 'Where are we going? Where are you taking us?'

Two voices shouted back; the only words they recognized were 'British' and 'shut up'.

'Just the two, then.' Lucy pulled at the straps around her hood again. 'But we're blind with these on. Might as well be ten of them.'

'Lucy, I think I know what's happening,' he said.

'I *know* what's happening, Itch. We've been kidnapped, that's what happening.'

'I don't mean that,' said Itch. 'Back at the mint. Just before they put the bags over our heads . . . what did that guy with the gun shout?'

There was silence.

'No idea,' said Lucy. '*I'm a violent criminal who shouldn't be allowed anywhere near anyone?* Was it that?'

'He said, "Let's whomp this sucker,"' said Itch. 'And we've heard that phrase before.'

Apart from the steady rumble of the tyres on the tarmac and the clatter of the engine, there was silence in the back of the van.

And then Lucy remembered. 'That guy at the ISIS labs . . .' she whispered.

'Tom Oakes,' said Itch. 'That's what he said just before we destroyed the 126. It sounded weird at the time, but what with everything else, I didn't get around to asking where he got it from.'

'Tom Oakes,' repeated Lucy. 'He worked with my dad. You said that according to Hampton, he got the sack from ISIS. Took the rap for losing a target station. Which was our fault, really. But maybe lots of people use that phrase, Itch. It doesn't necessarily mean it was him.'

'OK,' he said. 'But that is one hell of a co-incidence. I think Oakes needed work and found some sabotaging the Spanish euros. Flowerdew was at ISIS, remember – he knew who was helping us. The other guy, Bill Kent, got hurt with one of the letter bombs.'

There were irritated shouts from the front of the

vehicle: '*Cállate! Cállate!*' and Itch and Lucy fell silent.

'That probably doesn't mean speak up a bit, does it?' muttered Lucy. After a short pause she whispered, 'I know you haven't got your rucksack, but please tell me you have a pocket full of mercury or sulphur or something spectacular to get us out of here.'

Another pause. 'Sorry,' said Itch. 'Just a burned ten-euro note.'

Lucy cursed quietly.

By the time the van stopped, it was dark. As soon as the doors opened, Itch smelled the sea air.

Lucy took a deep breath. 'Great. A day at the seaside,' she murmured. 'Just what I needed.'

Still hooded, hands tied, they were herded along what felt like the wooden planks of a jetty. It was cool here, and a keen breeze blew in their faces – a welcome change from the stale air of the van. They had discussed making a run for it, but trying to fight blind seemed like a bad idea.

'Until we can see what we are doing, we're wasting our time,' Lucy said, and Itch agreed.

There was only intermittent lighting, and not much of it penetrated the fabric tied around their heads, so their steps were hesitant. Then powerful torches, raised voices and new hands grabbed them. Itch felt himself being frogmarched down steps, along what must be a ship's deck, then along narrow corridors. Blocks of light and shadow passed in front of him. He could hear Lucy not far behind, her protests accompanying their every step. He twisted round but received a sharp blow to the head for his efforts.

Itch heard a clinking chain and, with a sinking feeling in his stomach, felt the familiar snap of handcuffs around his wrist. He was panicked momentarily by the feeling of hands around his throat, but then his hood was whipped away. As his eyes were adjusting, he felt his hand seized, then cuffed to what looked like an old stove. Next their captors – two men in cargo shorts and hoodies – removed Lucy's hood; her face was temporarily hidden by a curtain of hair. She tossed it out of her eyes, and now it was her turn to blink at the fierce brightness of the room's strip lighting. Before she could protest further, the men snapped another set of cuffs on her, hooking her to Itch's other hand. Without speaking, both men left the room, pulling the door shut and locking it.

'We're going on a cruise,' said Lucy grimly. 'Always wondered what they were like . . .' She looked around at the old kitchen appliances and blankets. 'Do you think we could ask for an upgrade?'

'This isn't good, Luce,' said Itch as they felt the boat power move away from its moorings. He tugged at the cuffs. 'My hand's still recovering from the fire at the Fitzherbert School – I don't think I can get out of this one.' He looked around their cramped quarters. 'Looks like all the galley equipment they don't want any more.' They both slumped, exhausted, against the old oven door; it clanged shut behind them.

'Thought of a plan yet?' asked Lucy.

'Nope.'

'Me neither. How long do you think we have?'

Itch considered. 'A few hours maybe?'

'You'll think of something,' she said, and then, to Itch's surprise, fell asleep with her head on his shoulder.

He closed his eyes, but found sleep impossible. His mind was full of what might happen to them – what might be happening to Jack and Chloe – and Lucy's assumption that he would get them out of there.

He laughed bitterly. 'The genius strikes again,' he said. The truth was, he had no plan. He had no rucksack, no elements, and no idea how they were going to escape. He felt a cold despair in the pit of his stomach.

Lucy woke him with a sharp tug on the handcuff chain. It was dark, and it took Itch a few seconds to remember where he was. He had no idea how long he had slept for; his head was heavy and his clothes were wet with sweat.

'Itch, something's happening,' said Lucy. 'Everyone's running about.'

He sat up slowly and heard approaching steps; a

key turned in the lock and the door was pushed open. Fierce lighting flooded the room, and the same two men stood silhouetted in the entrance.

'You again?' said Lucy. 'Not room service, I suppose? Two teas maybe?'

Itch saw they each had the hoods swinging in their hands and felt the despair again. One of the men leaned over and unlocked his cuffs from the old cooker; the other ordered them to their feet. Still cuffed to each other, the black hoods were forced back over their heads and tied around their necks. Second time around, Itch found the darkness and smell of nylon even more terrifying; it was as though they were being summoned to their execution. A string of curses came from under Lucy's hood, and Itch smiled bleakly under his. 'That's pretty much what I was thinking,' he said.

'Don't trust anyone. Try to be brave,' whispered Lucy.

Itch nodded. 'I'm fine with the first part . . .' he said.

They were pushed out into the corridor. Lucy found Itch's hand and held it fiercely. They were clearly retracing their steps from . . . well, when exactly? Yesterday? A few hours ago? Up steps, through doorways, and into the noise of a powerful boat idling in a strong wind. The temperature dropped noticeably, and they saw only small pin-pricks of light through their hoods. Firm hands steered them around unseen obstacles until they felt a metal rail. From the sea below them they heard voices calling.

'Oh my God . . .' murmured Lucy.

'They're putting us in another boat,' said Itch. 'And listen . . .'

They became aware of another sound competing with the ship's engine. A deeper, heavier sound, coming from a short distance away. Itch turned to face it. Through the fabric of his hood he made out some faint lights higher than the sea but too low for stars.

Ship's lights.

There was no doubt in his mind now that this was to be their final destination, that this new ship was where Flowerdew would be. And Jack and Chloe too. With that realization, Itch felt more resolute. Terrified too, but stronger, angrier . . . and he took a deep breath.

'That's a big ship out there. It's him, Lucy – it has to be. So we might as well do this now.'

A voice from below shouted in English: 'Ready here!'

Another from behind said, 'Six steps to boat,' and uncuffed them.

Itch was pushed forward through a gap in the railings. Turning round, he heard Lucy say, 'Be careful,' and he edged his way down, feeling for each rung. He had a sudden memory of his descent into the Woodingdean Well, but he forced it away.

It's only six steps.

As his right hand slid down, it caught on a sharp

metal edge. Itch winced, but quickly leaned into the steps, his fingers guiding the fabric of the hood onto the sharp metal. He continued down, the hood catching, pulling, then tearing. It was only a small rip, too near his ear for him to see very much, but he could now make out the sea. If he twisted his head, his field of vision took in the small inflatable he was about to step into.

Hands grabbed his legs, and he allowed himself to be pushed into the bottom of the boat. Lying back, he could see Lucy's final cautious step before she too was shoved down next to him.

'I can see you,' he whispered. 'Tore the hood.'

He felt Lucy's shaking arm hook through his as the inflatable powered away. Hoping it wasn't obvious that he now had some limited vision, he twisted round to line up the tear with the direction of the boat.

It wasn't difficult to see where they were going. Through the jagged shreds, two hundred metres away and closing, Itch glimpsed sections of a large, industrial ship, its deck covered in cranes and what looked like drilling equipment. At the bow, he saw the name *Strontian* and metal scaffolding supporting a large flat platform. *A helipad?* he wondered.

Bright lights shone from the deck, and Itch saw a small bobbing craft pull up alongside. He watched surreptitiously as a figure was hauled up on deck. A figure about the size of . . .

Itch gasped and stood up. His hands reached for the rip in his hood and pulled sharply, opening the tear up further. He pushed his head through the hole. In an instant he took in the size of the drilling ship, the gathered hands on its deck – and the sight of his sister being hauled aboard.

'Chloe!' he yelled.

27

Itch's terrified, heart-stopping howl was heard by everyone. It carried loud and clear across the short expanse of water between the ship and the approaching inflatable. The men tying the small craft to the larger one froze, staring out across the water. Those on the inflatable leaped at him. Chloe, approaching the top of the ladder, twisted round to see where her brother's voice had come from.

'Itch!' she screamed, then disappeared from view as she was hauled up onto the deck.

Itch was struggling with two men who were now sitting on his chest, one trying to put his hood back on. 'That's my sister!' he shouted before some of the material was forced into his mouth, cutting off his reply.

'Itch, what's happening?' cried Lucy, her voice fearful. His smothered, wordless reply turned the fear to panic. She pulled frantically at her hood — but to no avail. She forced her fingernails along the side of the boat, deliberately tearing them. Ignoring the pain, she scratched at the hood, hoping one of the splintered nail shards might be sharp enough to penetrate the fabric. But they weren't, and she shouted and screamed in frustration.

The inflatable's engine revved as it accelerated towards the *Strontian*. One man steered; the others restrained Itch and watched Lucy rage. Itch could hear Chloe's shouts; each one gave him new strength. He wrestled, twisted and kicked against the dead weight on top of him, but the men were too heavy.

He stopped struggling, his desire to see Chloe and Jack stronger than his hope of escape. From the bottom of the boat, he saw the brown and orange hull of the ship loom above him; a rope ladder dangled down from the rail to the sea. He saw faces peering over the side, calling, then Lucy being man-handled to the side of the inflatable.

'Itch, where are you?' she yelled. He tried again to call out to her but his muzzled voice had no power. Her hands were guided to the ladder but she pulled them away. 'Take this hood off me now! I can't climb if I can't see!' She stood balancing on the bobbing craft, her shoulders rising and falling, her breathing rapid. A shouted exchange from the digger to the inflatable, and Itch watched as her hood was swiftly removed. Lucy whipped her head from left to right and, finding Itch lying gagged and restrained in the bottom of the boat, cried out in alarm. Itch tried to look as reassuring as possible, which, as he was pinned to the floor, he realized might not be very reassuring at all. Meanwhile Lucy's hands were forced back onto the ladder and she started her ascent, slowly at first but faster as she adjusted to the sway of the ship. Itch hoped she wouldn't look down; from where he lay it was one terrifying climb.

Once she had disappeared onto the *Strontian*, the two men who had been sitting on him hauled him to his feet.

'Your turn,' said the older man, who had a tattoo of a scorpion on the side of his neck.

His hands free, Itch pointed at his mouth, and the man nodded. Slowly Itch removed the length of nylon and spat out some loose threads, some strands of saliva landing in the man's hair. 'Oops,' said Itch and stepped onto the swinging rope ladder before the man tried to hit him. His hands gripped the thick, coarse rope and his feet found the thin metal slats. A fierce spotlight from high above picked him out, illuminating the route he had to take. He climbed out of reach of the men in the inflatable, and then stopped. He stared at the blistered painted hull just a few centimetres in front of him. The ship rose and fell as he clung to its side. Every step took him closer to Flowerdew, a man who had already tried to kill him and who had succeeded in killing Mr Watkins.

Better to jump into the sea and take my chances.

But every step also took him closer to Jack, Chloe and now Lucy.

And I could never abandon them . . .

Itch took a deep breath and started to climb again.

When he reached the top, four men appeared, their arms outstretched, straining to grab hold of him. Itch almost stopped again, but then felt himself being hauled over the side. He was sent sprawling onto the deck, crashing into the base of one of the cranes. After a few seconds the ringing in his ears was replaced by a woman's voice.

'Would you stand, please.' It was a quiet, accented voice, and Itch knew that he had heard it before. As he gingerly got to his feet, his heart still pounding from the climb, he saw the high heels, the pencil skirt, the white shirt under an immaculately cut jacket, and the smiling Asian face.

'Hello, Itch . . .' Her head tilted slightly and the smile broadened.

'Mary Bale,' said Itch breathlessly. 'Fake *International Herald Tribune* journalist. I remember.' He looked at the grim-faced group of men standing behind her. 'You came with thugs last time too. They beat up Dr Alexander at the mining school – remember? Well, of course you do – you ordered it.'

Her smile stayed in place, though it became cooler. She waited a few seconds. 'Finished?' She paused theatrically. 'I'm Roshanna Wing, the new CEO of Greencorps. I use the name Mary Bale when it suits me, and yes, I remember trying to obtain the 126. I took the measures I deemed necessary. As always. If I had been successful then

. . . we wouldn't be here now. Come this way.'

'But I need to be—' began Itch.

'You don't need to be anything other than very, very careful,' she hissed, the smile wiped away in an instant. Her face grew pinched, her eyes narrowed. 'You really must understand how much danger you are in. You and your buddies.'

'I think we've realized that,' murmured Itch.

Roshanna Wing turned, and he was pushed hard in the back. He stumbled after her, her men right behind. Wing wove her way past yellow and red painted hi-tech drilling equipment which was crammed into every available space. Pumps, pistons, cables, storage containers; Itch jumped over or was steered round all of them.

He tried to prepare himself for what he knew was coming. Somewhere on this ship was Dr Nathaniel Flowerdew, the man who had tried to ruin his life. The teacher who had stolen his 126 and assaulted him at school. The madman who had attempted to destroy his nervous system with neutron bombardment. The criminal who had sent him a parcel bomb and murdered Mr Watkins. Now he would face Flowerdew thousands of miles from home, with no rucksack of elements to help him out, and Jack, Chloe and Lucy expecting him to come up with something.

And he knew he had nothing.

Stepping under an enormous steel drilling rig arch, Itch looked around, increasingly desperate. He saw enormous tubes, banked and stacked high, ready to unfold into the sea like the seating in his school gym. He saw complex machinery labelled IRON ROUGHNECK, MUD PUMP and CATWALK SHUTTLE; he didn't understand any of it. It made perfect sense for Flowerdew to hide on what appeared to be a mining ship, but it was no use to him. *This is no good*, he thought. *No good at all.* They marched on, and every step took him nearer to Flowerdew.

Ahead, Wing had opened a door and was already inside. Itch noticed a sign for chemical dispersant, accompanied by a red WARNING! sign. *That's more like it . . .*

They had entered a lab area – two benches with computer screens and the paraphernalia of analysis; Itch recognized the spectrometers and had handled some of the solutions, but that was all. Stoppered bottles stood on shelves in a locked, temperature-controlled glass cupboard, but he couldn't make out the labels.

Another shove in the back, and Itch stumbled again. 'There's nothing here for you,' said Wing sharply. She had seen his desperate glances around the lab. 'You are so out of your depth.' She laughed at her own joke. 'And in so many ways.' Still laughing, she led the way below decks.

The steps were poorly lit, the corridor at the bottom almost dark. Emergency lighting gave the place a grimy, seedy feel, the flashing red lights of the smoke alarm and sprinklers glaring brightly in the gloom. Wing was now slowing down, and

Itch's stomach tightened further. *This must be it*. They passed a sick bay, then came to a cabin door that was slightly ajar. Itch caught the faint smell of whisky . . . he knew what was coming next.

Roshanna Wing stopped. She knocked softly on the door, and Itch held his breath. Hearing nothing from inside, Wing knocked louder.

Itch shut his eyes tightly. *Please don't be there . . . Please be nice . . . Please be dead . . . Please . . .*

'Yes. Come in.'

And Itch went cold.

He had known all along that Flowerdew would be inside, but hearing his mannered, sneering voice again left him numb with shock. His legs turned to lead, his stomach to water.

Wing pushed the door open. If anything, the room was gloomier than the corridor. Muttering, 'Wait here,' Wing disappeared inside.

As Itch's eyes adjusted, he saw a soft silvery light, diffused around the room. He heard muted conversation, then Wing appeared in the doorway. She dismissed her men with a wave of her hand, then pulled Itch inside. He stared wildly around the room, his heart racing, his throat dry. He thought he saw movement in the corner, and turned.

'Stand facing me, Lofte.' Flowerdew's voice was matter-of-fact, bordering on the casual.

'I would if I could see you,' said Itch, trying to match his offhand tone.

'I would if I could see you . . . sir,' said Flowerdew

softly. There was silence in the room, and Itch again sensed movement.

'Say it, boy!' Some of Flowerdew's nonchalance was slipping.

'No,' said Itch. 'I'm not playing your pathetic games.' More movement, this time accompanied by a strangled sound.

'Chloe? Is that you?' Itch called, his head darting first one way, then another, trying to peer into the shadows. He was answered by three muffled voices, each from a different corner of the room.

'Jack . . .? Lucy . . .?' More smothered voices, the nearest just a few metres away, and he stepped towards it.

'Stay where you are!' shouted Flowerdew, but Itch took no notice.

'I will hurt them if you do not stop.' The sudden venom in Flowerdew's voice stopped Itch in his tracks. He froze, but could now make out the shape of someone struggling to free themselves.

'Put the lights on!' shouted Itch. 'Show me what's happening!'

'I prefer things dark actually,' said Flowerdew, 'and that's your fault. As so many things are. But I will show you what you need to see.'

And around the edges of the room, soft lighting faded up. Itch stared in horror from corner to corner; from Chloe, to Jack, to Lucy. Each was gagged and held in place by a large black weighted belt strapped around the waist. They were all trying to pull themselves free, but the belts were holding them fast.

Chloe stared at Itch, her exhausted eyes wide with fear.

Jack stopped struggling when Itch looked at her; she saw how shocked he was by her sickly face and filthy clothes.

Lucy's eyes never moved from Flowerdew, her stare one of cold fury.

'I'm sorry,' Itch said quietly, and Flowerdew emerged from behind his computer screen that had kept him hidden from Itch's view. He moved slowly, as if in pain, and held onto a desk for support. Then he straightened, his head catching some of the light from the recessed lamps in the floor.

Itch stepped back, unable to suppress an involuntary gasp. At first he thought Flowerdew was wearing a leather mask – protection for the burns he had suffered in the fire at the Fitzherbert School. Then he realized that it wasn't a mask; it was his face. Maybe he'd had skin grafts, maybe they hadn't worked, maybe he was still receiving treatment . . . but the effect was terrifying. One side of his face was relatively normal, though the skin was red and blotchy and his chin unshaven. But the other appeared to be held together with stretched hide, patches of skin pulled tight over his features and stitched down. His right eye was half closed, the lid bloated and raw. And his ear – the one Itch had skewered with a steel tube in their fight at ISIS – was shrivelled. He had lost his curly white hair too; in its place was patchy grey stubble.

Itch couldn't help himself. 'Looking good, sir. A big improvement,' he said.

Flowerdew stopped, one hand on his desk for support. 'You may say what you wish, Lofte, it is of no matter to me. I shall kill you shortly and that will be the end of it.' Further muffled cries came from Chloe's corner; he ignored her. 'However, a brief chat might be fun. I have been wondering what to say for some time; I shall savour the moment.'

'I'm not interested in your speeches, Flowerdew. Not interested in your reasons, not interested in your justifications. Save your breath.' Itch hoped that the trembling of his legs wasn't visible, and fought to control them.

'Oh, I don't have to justify anything to anyone!' One half of Flowerdew's face smiled. '*I'm* in charge now. Greencorps is *my* company, this is *my* office. I run everything from this ship, and no one knows where I am or what I am doing. The capable Roshanna Wing is far more presentable than I, so she is the public face of the new, friendlier Green-corps. Telling all about the murky dealings of the oil industry, who now really, really regret how they treated me in the past. They can watch my success from their prison cells.'

Flowerdew made his way over to what Itch now realized was a porthole; tiny lights had appeared and were slowly sliding in and out of sight. A moment ago it had been pitch black; now, with the ship moving, Flowerdew watched the changing view.

'I realize you have no idea where you are, Lofte, so I shall tell you. We are leaving the island of El Hiero off the coast of Africa – the Western Sahara, to be precise. It was an old Greencorps watering hole. I still have friends here, and it has been the perfect place to hide while waiting for you.'

'You don't have friends,' said Itch. 'You have people who are scared of you.'

Flowerdew continued to stare out of the porthole. 'It amounts to the same thing,' he said. 'And when you actually run a company, you'd be surprised how many people are scared of you.'

'I don't think I would, actually,' said Itch quietly.

'Your destruction of the 126 was an act of extraordinary scientific vandalism,' said Flowerdew, 'though I admit that your knowledge of neutron bombardment was . . . surprising.'

Itch was on the verge of telling him that it was Lucy's knowledge, not his, but realized it would change nothing. It might put her in even more danger. He remained silent.

'But you left me with this face, Lofte. And every time I look in a mirror, I find myself thinking of you.' Itch wasn't sure whether Flowerdew was still looking out of the porthole or at his own reflection. The man turned to face him again. 'And every time I thought of you, I thought of this . . .' He waved his hands around the room. 'You see, I have had my revenge on Revere and Van Den Hauwe. I am in the process of having my revenge on the oil industry. And now I shall have my revenge on *you*.'

He looked at Lucy, Jack and Chloe in turn. 'All of you.' Chloe and Lucy tensed against their restraints, but the large black belts held them firm.

'Your face is your own fault, and you know it,' shouted Itch. 'You'd killed Shivvi and were about to kill Jack. The dust explosion and fire was the only way to stop you. You're greedy – you burned. It's that simple. Your revenge failed last time and it will fail again.'

Flowerdew nodded. 'Yes, I tried before, of course. My little parcel missed its mark in your case, though I got lucky with that idiot teacher of yours. A small triumph really.' Itch swore at Flowerdew, who smirked lopsidedly, the burned side of his face hardly moving. 'Watkins had it coming, the ludicrous academy had it coming – and the boss at ISIS too. Everyone who helped you paid the price.'

'Not everyone,' said Itch. 'Thomas Oakes helped us blast the 126 into oblivion . . . but you gave him a job.'

One of Flowerdew's eyebrows raised. 'You have worked out more than I expected. It was your demolition of the 126 that gave me the idea – I should thank you. After I acquired Greencorps, I realized that a new strategy was required. We needed more than oil if we were to keep our grip on the energy market. A South African contact – the one you fried in the fire at the school, in-cidentally – had told me how many mines were becoming available at the right price, and so we bought aggressively. To increase the price of the gold we now owned, destabilizing the euro was an obvious tactic. It has done a pretty good job of destabilizing itself, of course, but I thought we could just *help* a little. When everyone gets scared, they buy gold. And I'm quite good at making people scared. With my new rare earth mines in South Africa, I had access to the europium I needed to contaminate the bank notes. And with one of ISIS's top scientists working for me, everything was possible.'

Dad lost the mine to you? Itch thought. He glanced at Chloe, but her eyes were closed; she hadn't reacted. It was all making sense now . . . The riots were Greencorps riots, because every time the value of the euro dived, the value of their new gold mines rocketed.

'I knew the man who suggested using europium as a security feature in the euro,' continued Flowerdew, starting to pace around the room. 'He was very drunk by the time he told me. He thought it was hilarious. I didn't think much about it till recently.'

'Sorry to interrupt and all that,' said Itch, 'but why are you telling me this, Flowerdew? You must have people who you pay to listen to you—'

'I'm showing off, Lofte!' shouted Flowerdew. 'Why do you think? I'm a scientist, for God's sake. I'm proving to you that I have won, you have lost and why. If you hadn't been so arrogant, you might not be standing here, humiliated. So listen up.' He paused, then, as if finding his place again, continued. 'The europium in the euro is luminescent under ultraviolet light; if I could damage the europium in some way, the notes would show up as fake. My first thought was to blast the euros with neutrons, converting the europium to gadolinium – hence Oakes's usefulness.'

'But europium absorbs neutrons,' said Itch. 'I could have told you that. You always were a crap teacher.'

Flowerdew stopped a metre from Lucy and closed his eyes, then took a deep breath as though inhaling Itch's barb.

So Itch tried another. 'I've done some work on this – maybe you should have too. The 126 mostly turned into 63, so europium is, officially, the element that says to the world: *Flowerdew sucks*. It's therefore my new all-time favourite element in the Periodic Table and—'

Flowerdew whipped his stick into Lucy's ribs. Her eyes went wide with shock and pain. She would have howled if her gag hadn't been so tight, but the guttural sob told Itch everything he needed to know.

'Stop! Stop!' he cried. 'I'm sorry! Please don't!'

Across the room, Jack and Chloe were straining against their belts again; Jack stared at Itch and desperately shook her head.

Flowerdew walked over to her and raised his stick. Jack shrank away as much as she could. His stare followed her down. 'I'm happy to hit all of you in turn if your idiot cousin tries that again,' he hissed.

Jack stopped shaking her head and started nodding.

'I get it! OK!' shouted Itch. He took a few steps towards Lucy, but Flowerdew raised his cane again and he backed off. She was biting her lip and her eyes were full of tears, but she nodded reassurance to Itch.

'So . . .' he began, desperate to distract Flowerdew. 'Blasting the europium didn't work?' *Please just talk . . . Please don't hit.*

To his relief, Flowerdew began his pacing again. 'Yes,' he said, 'Oakes tried it on a sample and it didn't work; europium absorbed all the neutrons. We concluded that the neutron bombardment was not going to work. Then . . .' He smiled his crooked smile again. 'Then I had a brain wave.'

'Picric acid?' said Itch, interested in spite of everything.

'Precisely!' said Flowerdew, and for a second they were teacher and pupil again. 'And it gave us another way in. It gave us a note that would either burn, or register as a fake. Or both!' His walking had picked up speed, and Itch knew that Flowerdew was enjoying this. 'The inks that are used in the euros are made by causing a solution containing europium to react with an alkaline solution made from the molecules that wrap themselves round the metal and protect it − they also absorb the ultra-violet light and transfer the energy to the europium. This is crucial: it ensures that the europium will actually be able to glow as expected. We took one of these complexes and placed it in picric acid. And *bingo!* We got a naked europium, wrapped mostly in water. Which killed the fluorescence. The inks we provided looked the same as the original, but they turned a proper note into one that would register as a fake.'

'Then the paper dries,' said Itch quietly, 'the acid is unstable, and the note is ready to catch fire.'

'Exactly! Add this to the already miserable Spanish economy, bribe some of the low paid Royal Mint staff to look the other way, and we have action!' He bounced his cane off the ground and caught it again. 'By God it was good.'

'You whomped that sucker,' said Itch quietly, and Flowerdew stared at him.

'Of course . . . Thomas Oakes. His favourite phrase. Or it was. He served his purpose.'

'You got rid of him too?'

'He became unhappy. It is of no matter . . .' Flowerdew leaned on his cane as if exhausted. He bent over, breathing heavily; he seemed weaker, older, more tired, and Itch wondered if he should jump him.

When they had fought before, in the tunnel at the ISIS labs, he had badly hurt a weakened Flowerdew. *Maybe I could do it again?* he thought. *But if it goes wrong, Chloe, Jack or Lucy would pay the price.* Itch hesitated. Then, behind him, he heard the door open and knew he'd missed his chance.

'Yes, Roshanna, just in time,' said Flowerdew weakly. 'Is the radar fixed?'

'Not yet,' she said.

'No matter. It's about to get interesting . . .'

Itch turned to see Wing standing silently by the door, another large black belt hanging from her arm. *That one's for me*, he thought. It swung slightly as the ship swayed; it looked stiff and heavy.

What is in that thing? As far as Itch could see, there was a series of stitched panels, an adjustable strap and a brass lock. Were they weights? He noticed Wing's gaze alight on Lucy, Jack and Chloe, then settle on him. The brief thrill of the science talk had disappeared; the cold despair settled on him again.

At a nod from Flowerdew, Wing stepped forward and looped the belt around Itch's waist. She tightened the strap, and he heard the small metallic click as it locked. He was aware of the pressure of the belt as it sat above his hips. It was an uncomfortably tight fit, and he pushed the front panel away from him slightly. Glancing down at the stitched fabric, he saw *Nd* stamped in small letters. His heart beating faster, he felt around the panel. Underneath the fabric was a metal disc, about five centimetres in diameter, and as he pushed it down, he felt the top metal button of his jeans pulling up to meet it.

Itch's legs started to shake again, and his skin prickled.

Flowerdew was smiling his half-smile again. 'You know what it is, don't you?' he said.

Itch nodded.

'Well, come on, boy! You have an audience who want to know what they are wearing!'

Chloe, Jack and Lucy were all silent now; they watched Itch with a horrified intensity.

'It's neodymium,' he said, trying to push his jeans button back down. 'We are wearing neodymium magnets – the most powerful magnets in the world.'

He saw the recognition in Lucy and Jack's eyes – they remembered. Their terrified glances said: *You mean that butterfly earring Mr Hampton had? You mean the video of the fruit that got smashed to pieces? You mean* those *magnets?*

And Itch knew his face said, *Yes,* those *magnets.* He swallowed hard. 'I think we need to stay away from each other,' he said.

28

'I did mention revenge, I think,' said Flowerdew. 'And this is it.'

The door opened and four of the crew strode in, one for each of them. Itch felt strong arms take hold of him, then watched while the other men used long blades to prise Jack's, Lucy's, then Chloe's belts away from the poles he now saw behind them: he assumed their belts had smaller magnets at the back. If his arms hadn't been pinned to his side, he'd have checked.

'On deck!' ordered Flowerdew, his voice shrill. 'And keep them away from anything made of steel!'

Itch was spun round and frog-marched out of the cabin. He tried to see what was happening to Chloe, but a large hand twisted his head round to the front. He was marched back the way he had come, along the dark corridor, up the steps – tripping on two of them – and into the lab. Itch's eyes swivelled to the sealed cabinet he had seen on his way down. This time he had a better view of the labels. Some were still obscured or illegible; one said $AgNO_3$. He barely had time to register the large brown jar with a heavy-duty lid before he was propelled past the benches, his feet barely touching the ground. Occasionally he felt his belt tug, but he was moving too fast for the magnet to catch hold of anything.

As he was manhandled around the deck, he forced himself to focus, to think, to shake off the paralysing fear. He'd read about this at the museum in Madrid. *This is silver again! $AgNo_3$ – silver nitrate. Think it's poisonous. Was once used in photography.*

They were under the drilling rig now, and as he turned, Itch caught a glimpse of Chloe, her face white, her eyes staring. She hadn't noticed him, and he was glad. She would have seen her brother looking every bit as scared as she was.

Silver nitrate. Made by adding silver to nitric acid.

They were weaving their way through the drilling equipment; the *Strontian*'s stern was now only metres away. Beyond, the darkness of the ocean and the white churn of the ship's wake.

Think it's an antiseptic.

Itch was held beside a green barrier no more than half a metre high. He guessed it was iron – it was rusting and he could feel his belt being pulled again. It really was no barrier, though; more of a low, retractable rail marking the end of the ship. And the beginning, ten metres below, of the dark, rolling Atlantic ocean.

To his right, Chloe stole a quick glance at him,

then stared resolutely out to sea and the slowly dis-appearing lights of El Hiero. Next came Jack, her face white, her head bowed. Lucy was the last to arrive, struggling and kicking, her eyes blazing.

'Jack!' shouted Itch above the roar of the ship's engine. 'Jack! Look at me!' She half turned her head, but then seemed to lose interest. She closed her eyes and bowed her head again.

He's going to kill us. He's actually going to kill us.

Flowerdew appeared at Itch's shoulder. He smelled of hospitals and whisky. He was smiling his sloping smile.

And it is all my fault. All of it.

'It's a long way from the academy, isn't it, Lofte? And a long way from ISIS too. But here we are. And you are about to pay the price for humiliating me. And attacking me. And trying to kill me. And stealing my possessions. It's a long charge list.'

Itch found his voice. 'Is it worth pointing out that it's me you want revenge on, not the others? You keep telling me it's *my* fault. Well, you're right, it is. So let them go. Please.' He gulped and wiped his eyes. 'Please, sir.'

Flowerdew looked along the terrified line. 'You're right, it *is* your fault. So I will offer you one last chance to save your family.'

Itch stared at Flowerdew's stitched and stretched face, the sea-spray causing the skin grafts to redden further. 'What do you want me to do?'

Flowerdew stepped in front of him, and for a

moment Itch knew he could push him overboard. But also that Chloe, Jack and Lucy would follow soon after. The moment passed. Flowerdew licked his lips. 'I want you to tell me where the rest of the 126 is.' He ignored Itch's look of amazement. 'You destroyed the rocks at ISIS, but there will be more. If they arrived via a supernova, there will be more than eight small pieces. Supernovas are massive; their payloads are huge. You know that. Tell me where it is.'

Itch's heart sank. For a moment he thought there might be some serious bargaining to be done. He should have known better.

'There isn't any more. There really isn't. And how would I know anyway? Cake gave me the first and left me the others. I didn't find any more.'

'But there will be more, Lofte, of course there will. And it will have arrived thousands of years ago. I have my people searching Cornwall, looking for important sites where mysterious "magical" rocks might have been hidden or worshipped. But they have found nothing. If you want to save your girls, you'd better tell me what you know. Fast.'

'That was *you*? Well, I found two of your thugs with a Geiger counter by the church. I should have guessed. So that was Greencorps smashing up the ancient sites?'

Flowerdew looked pleased with himself. 'Who else?'

Itch couldn't keep the incredulity out of his voice.

'And that *Meyn Mamvro* stuff? The *MM*s that turned up everywhere? Really?'

Flowerdew nodded. 'A neat trick I thought up. I met a few crazed Cornish nationalists while I was at the academy. Dressing our search up in an ancient language made it all rather . . . dramatic, don't you think? Took off rather well. Every crazed hooligan with a grievance seemed to want to paint it on something. But, sadly, it didn't deliver any more 126.' He approached Itch and whispered into his ear. 'Tell me where it is or you die. You all die.'

He nodded to one of the crew, and the low rail started to fold into the deck. Itch, Chloe, Jack and Lucy were marched to the edge. With their gags still in place, there were no screams – but the ones in Itch's head were loud enough. He looked down. The floodlights picked out the heaving water below.

He spoke fast. 'All I know is that, hundreds of years ago, mysterious mine deaths were reported. No one knew what happened. Maybe there was 126 involved, but I—'

'Where were the mines?' Flowerdew shouted. 'Which ones?'

Itch tried to remember names from Watkins's book, but nothing came. 'I don't know! They were Cornish mines, that's all! And it was ages ago. I—'

'No good, Lofte! No good!' screamed Flowerdew. 'Your time is up!' He strode over to one of his men, who placed a gun in his open palm.

Itch had seen enough. He ran as close to Jack

and Lucy as he dared; he felt his neodymium magnet pull, and stopped dead.

He shouted into the wind, 'He's going to shoot! We have to jump!'

Jack and Lucy were paralysed with fear; then Flowerdew aimed his weapon.

'Stop it!' he shrieked. 'You can't help each other! That's why you've got the belts on! Get back, Lofte!'

But Itch turned and ran back towards Chloe, felt his belt tug, and this time carried on. He skidded, then propelled by an astonishing force, his belt crashed into Chloe's. Their bodies jarred, and Chloe's head smacked into Itch's chest, but she held on tight. As Itch straightened, Chloe was lifted off her feet, the magnets holding them together.

'We are going to jump,' he shouted into her ear. 'We're dead if we stay.'

'We're dead if we jump!' she yelled back.

They heard a metallic rattle behind them: Flowerdew was loaded and ready to go.

'Coming over!' shouted Lucy. She had turned to a terror-stricken Jack and run. A fierce metallic crack, a scream from Jack, and the pair were joined at the hip.

'No!' yelled Flowerdew.

Perched on the brink, with the roiling waves ten metres below their feet, Lucy and Jack turned to Itch.

They all saw Flowerdew raise the gun.

'We go now!' bellowed Itch.

As Chloe screamed, he walked them to the edge. And then over it.

Two seconds later, Itch and Chloe hit the sea. Amidst rapid gunfire, Jack and Lucy followed them, arms and legs flailing as they smacked into the water. On impact their heads cracked together; Lucy recoiled but Jack's head found Lucy's shoulder and stayed there.

Lucy recovered sufficient strength in her limbs to kick and thrash enough to slow the descent. Her held breath gave her some natural buoyancy, and for a few seconds she could see the lights of the dis-appearing ship, splintered and cracked as the light refracted in the water.

Sinking but forcing a fight, she screamed at her-self to keep going. But Jack was hardly moving and Lucy wasn't sure if she was even conscious. Jack's legs seemed stuck to hers, and Lucy tried to franti-cally frog-kick her way back to the surface. But the belts were killing them. Every surge upwards generated by the whipping of her arms and legs was cancelled out by the weight of the neodymium. Lucy wasted precious seconds struggling to force it off her hips but it was locked fast. And she felt her-self sink faster.

Itch and Chloe had entered the sea like torpedoes, forced deep underwater. They resurfaced quickly and took in great heaving lungfuls of air.

'Where are Jack and Lucy?' Chloe screamed, her

mouth in and out of the water as she turned her head from side to side. 'Did they jump?'

Itch's arms and legs were working furiously, his eyes darting around. But waves from the *Strontian's* wake were rolling over them, and he knew that they would have to look after themselves. The weakness in his muscles told him that. The look in his sister's eyes told him that. The enveloping darkness gave them no choice.

'Try to swim!' he gasped. 'Crawl!'

He leaned sideways into the waves and felt Chloe respond, but their arms and legs clashed repeatedly. As their rhythm stuttered, the weight of the belts started to tug them under. Chloe, eyes wide, mouth tight shut, started to panic; her breathing was shallow and rapid, her shoulders shook. Itch looked into her eyes; he could see that she was losing it. When her head dipped below the water, he twisted round, trying to pull her up.

'Chloe! Stay with me!'

For a fleeting moment it worked, and Chloe managed one more half-breath before her arms seemed to fold beneath her. And they sank beneath the waves again.

Itch hadn't finished fighting, but he feared that Chloe had. He kicked and clawed at the water, but still felt them dropping. He could feel Chloe, but in the enveloping blackness he couldn't see her; he was sure he was battling on his own. He felt bubbles on his face. She went limp. Somewhere in his head a voice told him that it was over; that this time he had lost.

Not yet. Not now. Not yet. Not now.

With a sudden burst of ferocious energy, he twisted and rolled to slow their descent. It seemed to work: they were coming back up. How long had they been in the water? A minute? Ten? If he could just keep this up . . . If he could just wake Chloe . . .

But a terrible pressure was building on his eardrums – an arc of pain shooting through his head – and with it the crashing, crushing realization that they weren't resurfacing. They weren't about to save Lucy and Jack. They were still sinking. In the ink-black sea, he no longer knew which way was up. Lights started to explode in front of his eyes. He tried to close them, then realized that they were already closed. The pain in his ears and chest was unbearable. He stopped kicking.

Itch blacked out at thirty-four metres.
   Chloe blacked out at thirty metres.
   Lucy blacked out at thirty-five metres.
   Jack's heart stopped beating at forty metres.

29

'They're falling fast!'
    'Too fast!'
    'No, we've got just enough . . .'
    'They're stuck together! What the . . . ?'
    'It's pulling me. Tugging my kit!'
    'Same here!'
    'Stuck fast!'
    'Must be magnets!'
    'Cut it!'
    'I'm there!'
    'Faster!'
    'Don't let them go past forty.'
    'Got that.'
    'These two gone. Got a pulse!'
    'Same here!'
    'Trachea shut, then!'
    'We'll need the BCDs.'
    'Control! Control!'
    'If we move too slowly, they're gone anyway!'
    'Get the RIB in place!'

The sea was alive with powerful lights, air bubbles and swirling, swooping divers. Fully masked, in identical black neoprene suits and split fins, they darted between Itch and Chloe, Jack and Lucy. They quickly found the belts holding them together, and Leila's knife was out first. Too close to the neodymium, it jerked out of her hand and stuck fast to the belt.

'Watch the belts!' she said. 'Find a section without metal! Chika, with me.'

They worked instinctively; Leila and Chika took Itch and Chloe, Aisha and Sade had Jack and Lucy. The wireless communication between the divers was loud in their earpieces; everything else was done with hand signals.

'These magnets will wreck all the kit,' said Tobi, swimming round Aisha and removing a small bag from a backpack. 'They have to go first.'

Leila found a stretch of Itch's belt that was free of metal. Chika produced her knife and immediately felt the pull of the magnet. Gripping the handle tightly, she guided it onto the fabric. It was just above Itch's hip, but she couldn't wait: she had to be quick. She slashed with the serrated blade, and the belt came apart. Blood pooled into the sea – Itch now had a five-centimetre cut that would need stitches. Assuming he lived.

'Cut the belt twenty centimetres from magnet. Space there,' called Chika, starting on Chloe's belt.

'Got it,' said Aisha who, twenty metres away, was dealing with Jack and Lucy's belts. She felt the magnetic pull on every single piece of metal in her kit: buckles, straps, oxygen tank.

'Arm's length should do it,' said Sade. With the belts held in her shaking fingertips, she let them go. They sank fast.

'They've gone,' said Aisha.

'Same here!' Chika called. 'Now stop the descent!'

Itch and Chloe were still falling, but now drifting apart. Jack and Lucy were falling, but their clothing had got tangled and they were still together. A diver grabbed each of them around the waist.

'BCDs now!'

Each diver inflated her buoyancy control device. Worn like a jacket, it was inflated from the tank of air on the back.

'Slowing!'

'More gas – this is too slow!'

'Stopping here!'

'Stopped!'

'Take them up a bit.'

The descent stopped, Sade, Chika and Leila reached for the next piece of equipment they needed. 'Lift bags to take them up!' called Leila. 'We have seconds – if that!'

Four small yellow packages with black straps were pulled from their packs, but Aisha, holding Jack, had a more pressing concern. She felt for her pulse. 'Tobi! Heart stop here! Defib now!'

Five powerful kicks, and Tobi was with Aisha and Jack. 'Wait for the surface?' said Tobi as she handed her the defibrillator, already powered up and with instructions flashing across its screen. Given that it restarted the heart with an electric charge, the machine was usually operated in the dry. But Aisha had experimented in the shallows of her local beach and believed it could work underwater. She had modified the unit to function at up to five atmospheres – around forty metres.

She shook her head. 'She hasn't time.'

Next to her, Sade was filling a lift bag with air from a canister. Meanwhile Aisha had ripped Jack's shirt apart and rammed two super-adhesive pads onto her chest. One stuck high on the left, the other low on the right; her heart in between. 'Tobi! Support Jack for me. Need something to push against.'

Tobi understood and swam round behind Jack, her tanks hard against Jack's spine. 'Ready!'

Aisha attached a breathing regulator to Jack's mouth and saw the EVALUATING PATIENT message scroll across the small screen. 'I've done that bit,' she said, let go of Jack and hit the power button.

Jack convulsed, her back arching. Sade pushed back against the spasm and held her in place. Aisha grabbed Jack again.

Leila's voice now, loud in everyone's earpiece: 'Bag's inflated. Tying to Itch now!'

Then Chika: 'Mine too. Small girl nearly ready. Seconds, people! We have seconds, that's all!'

Then a new voice. 'Right above you with the RIB now!'

'Coming your way, Dada,' said Leila. 'Bad down here. Gonna need everything we have.'

'Got that, Leila.'

'Ship gone?'

'Ship going.'

Above them, Dada was at the helm of the Ribcraft 12.0 offshore boat, its three outboard motors idling. Only the slightest adjustments were needed to maintain position above the rescue site. She wanted to use the searchlight mounted on its high, wave-swept bow, but the *Strontian* was still too close. The stars gave her only a limited visibility, and she strained her eyes across the surface. Seeing nothing, Dada shouted into her radio.

'Come on, guys! Let's see you!'

She got no response but wasn't expecting any. Everyone knew that they were working to tiny margins. When the brain is starved of oxygen, you move fast or your patient dies. You get the victim to the surface as safely and quickly as possible and work on them there. If you can get them to hospital, so much the better; given that this wasn't going to happen, Dada had laid out blankets, oxygen and medical supplies on the wide deck. She hoped they wouldn't be needed, she guessed they would be.

'Letting Itch go!'

'Chloe's on the way up.'

'Lucy too.'

As the three of them drifted to the surface on their hot-air-balloon-style lift bags, all the divers swam to where Aisha was treating Jack. She was watching the defib unit, its messages glowing brightly in the gloom. EVALUATING PATIENT, it said again.

'Leila, grab hold; Chika, take the box; Tobi, get to the RIB.' Aisha passed the defib unit to Chika as Tobi swam for the surface. Aisha placed the heel of one hand in the middle of Jack's chest, then her other hand on top. She was about to start the rhythmic compressions that were standard procedure for fighting cardiac arrest – 100 a minute – when Chika cried out.

'*Shock advised. Stay clear of patient!*' she read.

'OK, Leila, let go. I'm clear. Punch it!'

Chika hit the button, Jack spasmed again, and as Aisha started up the chest compressions, her limp, trailing arms swayed slightly with each push.

Aisha stared at the waxy, wasted face. 'Come on, damn it!' She pressed Jack's chest harder. 'Start – please start.'

At the surface, now circling the rescue zone with increasing anxiety, Dada was keeping radio silence. She knew what was happening below her; knew that three lift bags were bringing three people up to her, and that Tobi wouldn't be far behind – once she had taken the standard decompression precautions to avoid getting the 'bends'; if the gas expanded in their bloodstream, they could die too.

She knew that Aisha was performing an underwater defib. Maybe it was the first ever – she hadn't heard of anyone else trying it. She focused again on the circle of choppy water as her bow waves crossed and broke over each other.

And then one, two, three bright yellow balloons hit the surface.

'They're up!' she called. 'Counting three bags here!' and she brought the RIB in as close as she dared. Breaking the rules but seeing no other option, she dived off the boat. Three strokes, and she was among the unconscious, suspended bodies. Grabbing all three ropes, she kicked hard, towing the lift bags towards the boat. She secured Itch and Lucy's bags, then grasped Chloe around the waist. Kicking with all her might, she straightened her arms, and pushed Chloe over the side of the RIB. She unhooked Lucy and repeated the manoeuvre, heaving her onto the idling boat.

She looked around, hoping to see Tobi on the surface, but it was too soon. 'On your own, then,' she muttered, and pulled herself aboard. Stepping over Chloe and Lucy, she reached over and hauled Itch in. His hip was still bleeding, and she grabbed a towel, pressing it firmly over the cut. 'That'll have to wait,' she said.

Dada knew from the radio chatter that her friends below believed that Itch, Lucy and Chloe had blacked out but had not inhaled too much water. She knew that, underwater, the epiglottis behind the tongue folds backwards and closes off the trachea, preventing water from entering the windpipe and lungs. But the reflex doesn't last long. The rescue had been fast . . . she hoped it'd been fast enough.

Dada had done CPR – cardiopulmonary resuscitation – before, but never three at once. As the boat idled, swaying and drifting in the swell, she turned on her torch.

'OK, breathe!' she shouted. 'Breathe! Breathe!' Sometimes yelling commands brought a response, but all three patients were as lifeless as when she'd dragged them out. She threw blankets over all of them, but tended to Chloe first.

'Rescue breaths, then.'

She pulled Chloe's head back, opened her mouth, checked for an obstruction and put her mouth on hers. Chloe's lips were terrifyingly cold. Dada exhaled forcefully, feeling her breath make Chloe's chest rise. She turned her head sideways, inhaled, then tried again. Chloe coughed, rolled onto her side and vomited.

'You beauty!' yelled Dada. 'Welcome back, Chloe!' And before Chloe retched again, she was examining Lucy and Itch.

A cry from the water: 'I'm here! Coming in!'

Dada didn't look up, didn't reply – there wasn't time. Tobi would see what was happening soon enough. 'Breathe!' she yelled, first to Itch, then to Lucy. She knelt between them. Lucy first. Head back, mouth on mouth, exhale. Itch second. Head back, mouth on mouth, exhale.

'Breathe!'

Lucy again . . . Itch again . . .

'Breathe!'

The sound of Tobi hauling herself into the rig.

'On her!' Dada pointed at Lucy. She stayed with Itch as Tobi took over with Lucy. Chloe was still coughing and vomiting. Dada had left water and oxygen beside her; she took both, then tried to speak, but nothing came out. Propping herself up on one elbow, she watched, horrified, at the attempts to resuscitate her brother and her friend.

'Breathe!' shouted Tobi.

'Breathe,' whispered Chloe.

Thirty metres below the RIB, the defibrillator flashed again.

'Shock coming!' said Leila. 'Might be the last one. Let her go!' Aisha and Chika released Jack, Sade braced herself again, and Leila sent the electric charge through the cables, through the pads, through her chest, through her heart.

Which started beating.

Different lights flashed on the unit – all green.

'We got her!' said Aisha. 'We got her!'

Leila checked the breathing regulator and felt Jack's mouth tighten around it.

She inhaled.

She opened her eyes.

And panicked.

Eyes wide, legs kicking and arms windmilling, she spat out her mouthpiece.

'Need the slate!' said Aisha. 'Need it now!'

Jack's eyes were wild, her head tossing one way, then the other. Leila put the breathing regulator back in and held Jack's arms. She nodded and smiled, holding a torch to her mask. Jack nodded back.

Chika had found the slate and was writing furiously. She held it up a few centimetres in front of Jack. Leila shone her torch on it.

SAFE NOW. BREATHE.

Jack, with no mask on, squinted then nodded. Chika wiped the slate clean again.

SURFACE SLOWLY.

Jack nodded. Chika wiped.

OTHERS UP ALREADY.

Jack nodded, but looked up and started to panic again. Aisha held her hands.

THERE SOON.

Jack freed her hands. She looked around, then held up three fingers and stabbed them upwards.

Chika understood the reference to Itch, Jack and Chloe. She hesitated briefly, then wrote again:

DON'T KNOW.

Chloe was enveloped in a blanket and Tobi's arms, but she was still shivering uncontrollably. Sade occasionally made a slight adjustment to the RIB's steering, but always hurried back to where Chloe half sat, half kneeled in the middle of the deck.

Dada and Tobi worked on Itch and Lucy in perfect synchronization. Mouth on mouth, exhale. Head tilt, inhale. Mouth on mouth, exhale. Head tilt, inhale.

'OK, breathe!' shouted Dada.

'*BREATHE,*' roared Tobi, centimetres from Lucy's face.

'It's not working, is it?' said Chloe quietly. She turned and buried her face in the blanket, unable to watch any more.

She could hear the RIB's idling motor, the deck's sloshing water and the rhythmic breaths from Dada and Tobi. And then, suddenly, wonderfully, the rasp of two throats gasping for air.

Chloe spun round. Both Itch and Lucy were bent double, arms wrapped around their stomachs. But their chests were heaving, taking in lungfuls of air. Dada and Tobi high-fived, then picked up the oxygen and gave the masks to Itch and Lucy. Chloe saw that her brother barely had the strength to hold it, and she knelt down, holding first Itch's mask, then Lucy's. She looked from one set of glassy, unfocused eyes to another and beamed. 'Hi,' she said.

Itch managed a weary smile; Lucy gave a croak, but no words came out.

'Don't speak just yet,' called Tobi. 'It'll all come back in time. Rest up.'

But Itch wasn't listening. Sucking his oxygen in deeply, he hauled himself into a sitting position. He blinked, swallowed twice and coughed hard. 'Where's Jack?'

Chloe grabbed his hand. 'Not up yet,' she said. 'But the other divers are with her.'

'And she's going to be OK,' said Dada, who still had her wireless earpiece in place. 'She's coming up now. They're just talking her up the final few metres.'

Itch lay back on the deck and closed his eyes. There was so much to say, but for now silent gratitude would have to do. Chloe hurried to apply some steristrips to Itch's cut. She used six to close the wound, Itch only wincing once.

Tobi was back at the wheel of the RIB when Dada, pointing her torch twenty metres off the port side, called out, 'They're up! Patient incoming!'

Chloe followed Dada's beam into the gloom. Aisha was swimming strongly towards them, Chika and Leila behind, cradling Jack between them. An umbilical-like tube stretched from Leila to Jack's mouth, where she held an air hose and regulator tightly in place.

Aisha threw herself onto the boat, ignoring the helping hands, then leaned back out to receive her patient. She gently removed the breathing regulator and took her shoulders, while Dada took her feet. Together they lifted her aboard, then set her down on the deck with such gentleness, it was though they thought she might break at any minute.

Itch and Lucy half rolled, half crawled over to where she lay. Lucy reached for her hand, and Chloe threw a blanket over her shivering body.

'Hey, Jack!' she said, her voice breaking. 'Thought you'd gone. Thought we'd lost you.'

Jack opened her eyes and nodded. It looked as though it took all her strength.

'We *did* lose you,' said Aisha, bringing more blankets. 'You are officially a miracle. Your heart stopped beating down there, and we restarted it.

Always thought we could; never had the chance to prove it.' She laughed at the looks of astonishment she was getting. 'Hey, we experimented! But somehow a large pig was never quite realistic enough.'

'A pig!' croaked Lucy. 'You're kidding us, right?'

'No, she's not,' said Dada. 'It was weird, but it worked. Now you're alive because of a thirty-five-kilo swine.' Nobody had the energy to laugh, but there were a few smiles. 'I'm Dada, by the way.' She pointed around the deck as the figures took off their hoods. 'This is Leila, Chika, Aisha, Sade – and that's Tobi at the wheel, waiting to find out where we're going next.' In their wetsuits and hoods it had been difficult to tell them apart, but now the divers became recognizable as the crew from Shivvi's photo.

'Hi,' said Itch, Chloe and Lucy.

Leila came over with another oxygen canister. 'We need to get you to a hospital, Jack. All of you, really, but Jack especially. We're nearly out of air – this tank's empty – and that makes me nervous. You don't go through something like that and just walk away. She needs to be checked over. And Itch needs stitches.'

'Where's the nearest hospital?' asked Chloe.

'Back on the island.' She nodded into the darkness. 'Back on El Hiero. But it's hardly a hospital. Just a surgery really, open in the day, restricted hours.'

Itch managed to sit up. He was shivering under the blankets, his wet clothes clinging and sopping.

He had a question. 'How did you know where we were?' His voice was feeble and reedy, but all the divers heard and smiled.

It was Chika who stepped forward, shaking out her braided black hair. 'El Hiero is an old Greencorps haunt. We went there with Shivvi a few times. Flowerdew was always there, boasting with his oil friends. When we saw you at the TV press conference, we guessed where Jack and Chloe were being taken.'

Leila took over. 'And when you announced to all the world that it wasn't us who killed the Greencorps bosses, we knew we owed you. Big time. We came to El Hiero and waited. Sure enough, Flowerdew turned up in that mining ship – the *Strontian* – and we followed him.'

'Wow,' said Chloe.

'Debt paid in full, then,' said Itch. 'Thanks. Really. But we need to talk about Shivvi sometime—'

'Jack's not looking good,' interrupted Lucy. Under the blankets Jack was shaking un-controllably, her skin white, her eyes tight shut.

'Like I said – she needs proper care,' said Leila. 'Gran Canaria has a hospital, but that'll take us hours. This RIB isn't built for long haul.'

'What does she need exactly?' asked Itch, getting to his feet.

'Right now she needs body warmth,' said Leila. 'Chloe and Lucy, lie down beside her. Seriously – it'll help. But mainly she needs oxygen. And we are using our last supplies . . .' She glanced at Jack.

Itch looked around the deck . . .

At the divers who had saved him, and at his sister, his cousin and his friend.

At the darkness, the lapping waves and the empty sea around them.

'I know where she can find all those,' he said quietly.

'Really?' said Dada. 'Where? I can't think of—'

'On Flowerdew's ship,' said Itch, cutting her off. 'On the *Strontian*. I saw the sick bay. It has all that.'

There was silence, interrupted only by coughing from Jack.

'We're not going back,' said Lucy. 'Please tell me we're not going back to that ship . . .'

30

The RIB bounced along on the Atlantic waves, its crew deep in discussion. It was still dark, the only light coming from the stars and Leila's torch. The divers were crouched by Itch; Chloe and Lucy were still lying next to the sleeping Jack. Every few minutes, the torch beam swept over her. The oxygen mask magnified her deathly white, clammy face. The sight gave an extra urgency to their arguments.

'If we run out of oxygen – which we will in under an hour – and Jack is still like this, we might lose her.' Leila looked at the faces around her. 'That's the risk we take if we cut for home.'

'I'm not going back on that ship,' Lucy said firmly. 'I'll do anything else to help Jack, but please—'

'That's fair enough,' said Aisha. 'You won't need to. The issue is whether we can board the *Strontian*, collect the medical supplies she needs, and get off again.'

'Are there any ships nearby who could help . . . ?' Even as she said it, Chloe sounded unsure.

'Yes, there will be, but we don't have time, Chloe. We could catch the mining ship in thirty minutes if we hit top speed,' said Leila.

'They'll see us coming,' said Lucy. 'You've got radar, so they certainly will.'

'It won't be a problem. And if they *do* challenge us, we can say we need urgent medical supplies. Which we do.'

Aisha looked at her colleagues. 'Are we doing this?' One by one they all nodded. 'You'll be safe here,' she told Lucy. 'We can handle ourselves quite well, you know.' She smiled and Lucy nodded. 'You guys will watch Jack; Tobi will stay on the boat, Chika too. The rest of us will go and steal some oxygen.'

Chloe was aware that Itch hadn't said anything for a while. He was hugging his legs to his chest, staring off into the distance.

'I've seen that look before, Itch,' she said. 'What are you thinking?'

He turned to his sister. 'I'm going too.'

'No, Itch! No, you can't! Please—'

'Itch, you should stay here,' said Aisha. 'Seriously, you've been through enough.'

'I know where the sick bay is,' he said. 'It'll be faster with me.'

'Draw a map then!' said Lucy.

'I'm going,' said Itch. 'All this is my fault. All of it. And I've had enough.'

Aisha nodded to Tobi, who ran to the wheel. She corrected their heading, checked her radar and opened the RIB's three engines to full throttle.

As the boat speeded after the mining ship, Chloe looked at Itch. 'Those didn't sound like the words of someone who was just planning on liberating some oxygen.'

Itch didn't look at her. 'What did they sound like?'

'Like someone planning revenge.'

'Maybe.'

'Really? After all this?' Chloe was angry now. 'Itch, if we need the oxygen and drugs for Jack, then OK, but that is it. You come back here – you don't go and give Flowerdew a kicking.'

'What if—?'

She put her hand over his mouth. Tears in her eyes, she glared at her brother. 'You come back. You understand?'

He nodded and she took her hand away. 'OK,' he said.

The 900-horsepower engine sent the RIB crashing through the swell. At the bow, the divers were checking their equipment.

Leila called Itch over. 'We've downloaded the plans of the ship.' He saw that her phone displayed a map of each deck. 'This the medical room?' She pointed to a room with a red cross on it. Itch nodded. Leila looked at him. 'So we don't really need you to show us when we get there.'

'Guess not,' he said flatly.

'Unless you feel you might still have something to contribute . . .'

He stared back at her. 'Chloe has made me promise to just get the oxygen and come back.'

'Of course she has. And I'm sure we'll all try to keep to that. If we can . . .' Itch saw the beginnings of a smile on her face, and slowly realized what was going on.

'You want to go after Flowerdew too,' he said.

Leila's voice was barely audible above the roar of the engines. 'He's a few kilometres away, Itch. We might never get another chance.'

'Yes, but you'd be doing this for Shivvi, and she was as bad as him! Cruel, greedy, ruthless . . . She tried to kill me and Jack!'

Leila gazed out over the sea. She was silent for so long, Itch thought the conversation was over. Just as he was turning to check on Jack, she took his arm.

'I know what she became. And I know what she did . . . But she wasn't always like that. When we started diving together, she was just one of us. We made a great team. She was always the fiercest competitor, always had to be the best, and Flowerdew exploited that. The Greencorps machine turned her ambition into cruelty and recklessness. By the time she went to prison she was virtually unrecognizable, a different person, and we blame Flowerdew. But she was still our friend and we want to tell him to his face.'

'And then?' asked Itch.

'We'll see,' she said.

She didn't need to explain and he didn't need to ask. She turned away, but he caught her arm.

'What's up with the radar?'

Leila looked surprised.

'When Lucy asked about the radar, you said it wouldn't be a problem. Why not?'

Leila smiled again. 'Glad we're on the same team, Itch.' She took a breath. 'When we got to El Hiero, we knew the sort of ship to look out for. When the *Strontian* blew in, we knew that Flowerdew was on it. We thought this moment might come. Chika got on board and placed a small scrambler by the masts. We switched their radar off as soon as we got near.'

Itch's bloodshot eyes were wide with shock. 'You planned all this?'

'Too loud, Itch — keep it down. Don't make this trickier than it needs to be.'

'But your intention was always to board Flowerdew's ship?' Itch couldn't keep the astonishment out of his voice. 'It was lucky for us you were around — but you were following him, not us? Is that right?'

Now Leila held onto Itch's arm, her olive skin contrasting sharply with Itch's waxy paleness. 'What I said before was true. We decided to do this after seeing how you stood up for us at the press conference. Saving you guys was the first part; this is the second.'

'Five kilometres!' called Tobi.

Itch and Leila peered into the gloom and saw the *Strontian*'s lights.

'You coming?' asked Leila.

Itch looked at Chloe and Lucy, who were still trying to warm Jack up. 'Try and stop me,' he said.

She nodded. 'OK. We all need to talk.'

The mining ship's outline was becoming clearer by the minute. The divers and Itch gathered around Tobi at the wheel; Chloe came over to listen too.

'How many men on board?' Leila appeared to be directing operations now.

Brother and sister looked at each other. 'There's Flowerdew,' said Itch, 'his new puppet – Wing, or Bale, or whatever she's calling herself today – and about twelve others? Fifteen maybe.'

'There seemed to be loads,' said Chloe. 'We were always surrounded, right from when we arrived.'

'Presumably there are technicians and scientists somewhere,' said Itch, 'but we didn't see any – just Flowerdew's thugs.'

'With Greencorps,' said Leila, 'they're often one and the same. I think we've all learned that.' There were nods and murmurs of agreement. 'We'll have the element of surprise,' she continued. 'Just before dawn, they'll still have a skeleton crew on duty – if we're lucky, just two on the bridge. The sleeping quarters are clearly marked on the plans. If we can lock them in, we'll be able to reach the medical supplies without interference. Which is Flowerdew's room?'

Chloe replied, 'When you go down the main stairs, his room is on the right, after the sick bay.' She looked straight at Itch. 'But hopefully you won't see him, will you?'

'Obviously,' he said quietly.

'We've got a spare wetsuit,' said Aisha. 'We'll have our headwraps on too, so we should all look the same. That way, we talk to each other and they won't know who we are. Or that it's you, Itch – which might be helpful. Chika will show you.'

At the front of the RIB, sections of the deck lifted to reveal cavernous amounts of storage. From it, after flares and more backpacks, came a wetsuit of indeterminate shape and Chika threw it at Itch.

'Should fit,' she said.

Itch grabbed it and started to peel off his wet clothes. This was no time for modesty, but he was glad that it was still dark and the torch was at the other end of the boat. Every wetsuit is a struggle, and this one was no exception – especially with a nasty hip wound. After he'd got it on, Lucy came over and zipped him up.

'You sure about this?' she whispered.

'Jack needs the oxygen, Luce. She looks terrible. We don't have a choice.'

She hugged him briefly. 'Sure it's OK if I don't come with you? I can look—'

'Lucy, stop . . .' Itch pulled away, conscious of being watched. 'You keep Jack warm. When the O_2 arrives, get it to her quickly. She needs you here.' He bent down and felt in his trouser pocket, retrieving a small stone.

'Itch?' said Lucy.

'It's a surprise,' he said, zipping it into his wetsuit. He went over and knelt down beside Jack. Her chest was rising and falling in short, quick breaths.

'Doesn't look right, does it?' said Chloe.

'No. But she's alive and we're going to make sure she stays that way,' he said. 'We'll be as quick as possible.' He got up before he got another lecture, and joined the divers again. They gave him a small round of applause as he approached.

'Six inches taller than the rest of us, and clearly not a woman, but apart from that, you'll blend in perfectly,' said Aisha, and they all laughed.

The looming mining ship ensured the levity was brief. The churn of the mining ship's engines could be picked out, as could the letters of its name. There was the first hint of lightness in the sky off to their right; they could now distinguish between sea and sky for the first time.

'We need to get on with this,' said Leila. 'Itch, you're with Dada and Sade. Aisha's with me. You all know what you're doing. Let's make it look like it's just Tobi and some injured friends. Take us in.'

Following in the mining ship's wake, the RIB bounced hard as it closed on the *Strontian*. Ahead, the bright deck lights of the ship made Itch uneasy; the darkness had seemed safer. Raising his head, he could now see the place at the stern from where he and Chloe had jumped. How long ago was that? An hour? Two? Five? He had lost all sense of time. But he didn't care. As his strength had returned, so had his anger. He glanced back at Jack, oxygen mask clamped to her mouth, Chloe and Lucy lying beside her, trying to warm her.

'You're going to pay for this, Flowerdew,' he whispered. 'It ends here.'

The RIB adjusted course so that it avoided the propeller's turbulence and came in hard on the *Strontian*'s starboard corner. They were close enough to touch – Tobi was on tiptoe, making minute adjustments and corrections to the wheel to avoid any collision. The noise from the engines was deafening as Aisha ran onto the RIB's v-shaped platform. Under her arm was a slim extendable metal ladder with a curved hook at the top.

That's a grappling hook! thought Itch. *I thought they were just for pirates!*

Feet spread wide against the roll of the boat, Aisha held it up high, then let it fall onto the mining ship's railings. It hooked over first time, and she let go. The ladder swung against the ship's hull and Aisha waved Tobi in closer. When the gap between rig and ship was no more than a metre, she leaped across. Her feet found a rung, her hands the sides, and she climbed. Before she'd reached the top, Leila jumped too. As Aisha disappeared over the rail, Leila scurried after her.

'I'm last up,' said Dada to Itch. 'You wait here. We'll wave you up when we think it's safe. You'll hear what's happening in your earpiece: pull up your hood and it should just hook in. Copy me.' She forced the tight-fitting neoprene over her head, and a small bud swung on a cable. She tucked it under the hood and into her ear.

Itch grabbed his hood and struggled to wrench it over his wild hair. 'Must get short hair next time,' he muttered, then winced as he pulled it tightly over his face. It snapped around against his cheeks and fore-head. Dada caught his swinging earpiece and helped him push it into place. Instantly his head was filled with hushed, urgent conversation. Aisha and Leila were swapping observations about the ship and the location of its crew.

'Sade and Dada. Need you now.'

'Your mic is in the hood,' said Dada. 'From now on we all hear what you say. Wait here. Good luck.' She ran over to the platform from where Sade had just launched herself onto the ladder. Dada watched her climb. As soon as she was halfway up, Dada flew at the ladder. Her ascent was the fastest, nearly catching Sade at the top.

And then they were gone.

Chloe and Lucy had moved Jack over, near to the wheel. When Itch turned, Chloe and Chika both gave him a thumbs-up. He returned the gesture, then crouched again under the platform. On board the *Strontian*, the divers sounded busy:

'Bridge first.'

'On it.'

'How many?'

'Three. One's on the radar.'

'Wait.'

'Now!'

'Hands away from the controls!'

'Step back!'

'Lie on the floor!'

(Muffled shouting.)

'Lock – lock!'

'How many?'

'We need oxygen. We want Flowerdew. We don't want you or your ship.'

(Muffled shouting.)

Itch turned to Chika and Tobi, both with hoods up and the live feed in their ears. Tobi's attention was on the gap between the RIB and the mining ship, but Chika, pacing around the stern of the rig, caught his eye and nodded slightly.

'Doors locked. No one's moving.'

'Secure?'

'Secure. Got them all.'

'OK, Itch. Your turn. Come on up.'

He didn't stop to think, didn't look back. As soon as he heard his name, he ran to the platform. The cracked and peeling paint of the *Strontian*'s hull filled his vision, the rungs of the ladder a few centimetres in front of him. He waited until the bow of the rig was high and cresting a wave.

Then he jumped.

31

Itch hit the ladder hard. His hands grabbed at a rung; his bare feet scrabbled and kicked before they found a footing. Below him, the Atlantic Ocean – and the ship's propellers, which would surely turn him to mincemeat if he fell. He looked up. Ten metres above him, Sade beckoned, then disappeared.

He climbed fast. In seconds his hands found the *Strontian*'s rail and he was scrambling over. He allowed himself one look back down at the bobbing RIB – Lucy and Chloe giving him thumbs-up salutes – then ran across the deserted deck. Past the cranes, past the drilling equipment, he weaved his way towards where he guessed the divers would be. Then he stopped, realizing that he could join in the rapid, urgent conversation in his earpiece.

'I'm here. On deck,' he said. 'Should I get the oxygen?' He hesitated, not wanting to stray any-where he shouldn't.

'Sade with you now . . .' Aisha's voice crackled in his ear.

He looked around. The entrance to the lab and the living quarters was a few metres ahead, the steps to the bridge and the helipad just beyond that. He realized that the ship was stopping, the engines suddenly quiet. In the new silence, the rattle of feet on metal echoed loudly, and Sade appeared, jumping up the steps three at a time.

'Let's get the oxygen!' she said. 'It's you and me. Show me.'

'But it's down there,' said Itch, pointing below decks, 'where Flowerdew is.' He hoped he didn't sound too scared.

'He's not there any more,' said Sade matter-of-factly. 'Let's go.'

'No,' said Itch. 'Where is he? I'm not going down there . . .'

A brief smile flickered across her face. 'He's being dealt with. The crew and the captain are locked in their quarters, Leila and Aisha have the bridge. It's amazing what a dawn raid by a few divers can achieve. Now, the first-aid room – quickly.'

Itch had a feeling there was something he wasn't being told but thought better of asking. They needed the medical supplies and he'd seen the room. He led the way through the lab and down the dark steps, his heart racing. The medical room was the first on the right, but beyond it, Flowerdew's door swung open as the boat swayed. Itch hesitated, but Sade reassured him.

'It's fine. He's not there. You can look if you want to.'

'No thanks. Let's get the air and go.'

From the first-aid room they took four small oxygen tanks, packets of painkillers and a variety of plasters and bandages. Itch stuffed what he could into Sade's rucksack and they ran for the steps, with an oxygen tank under each arm. As they emerged on deck, they saw Dada waiting for them by the rail.

'My job to get the tanks to the RIB,' she said as they approached. Looking down, Itch saw that it had eased away from the *Strontian*, but on seeing Itch and Sade, Tobi brought it in close again.

'We'll take it from here,' said Dada. 'But I'll be straight back.'

'Itch, get to the bridge.' This was Aisha's voice again, and he looked at Sade, who waved him away.

He jogged back along the deck, weaving left at the lab door and up the steps. As he climbed, the lightening sky revealed other ships on the horizon. Would they realize that the *Strontian* had stopped? Would they come and rescue them? As he turned at the top of the steps to enter the bridge, he realized that he had no idea what the divers wanted to do next.

The door from the bridge opened and Aisha appeared. 'Follow me,' she said, and they carried on climbing.

The helipad? thought Itch. *Why are we going up here?* 'Aisha, I don't understand. What are we—?'

'Give yourself another ten seconds,' she said. The

huge circular platform above them was only metres away, and they climbed the tightly winding steps in silence. The small hole at the top was just wide enough for Aisha and her backpack to squeeze through. Itch followed her.

He barely noticed the sweeping panoramic view of an Atlantic dawn that greeted him from the helipad. Instead he stared at the large letter H painted in yellow on the black platform; at the figure of Nathaniel Flowerdew who knelt there; and at Leila, who was holding a gun to his head.

And he said nothing.

He felt nothing.

He did nothing.

Instead it was Flowerdew who reacted. His head pulled sideways by Leila, he peered at the boy who had climbed onto the platform. His mouth fell open. His whole body seemed to sag. And then he howled with rage.

'But you're dead! All of you are *dead*! I saw you . . . You couldn't have survived . . . Not unless . . .'

At that moment Chika climbed through onto the helipad and Flowerdew stared in horror from her face to Aisha's.

'Unless,' said Leila in his ear, 'unless someone killed your radar, followed your ship, then saved their lives. *Then* it would be possible.' She walked in front of Flowerdew, pistol aimed straight at his forehead. 'We came for medical supplies, but we all have unfinished business with you too.'

Chika walked to the edge of the H. 'You killed

our friend. You killed so many people back in Nigeria. You tried to kill these kids. You're a monster.'

Flowerdew's good eye narrowed and he spat at Chika. 'This is about *her*? Shivvi? Really? Oh, please. *She* was the monster. I did the world a favour there.'

Leila swung the gun and it cracked against Flowerdew's head. He slumped to the deck. 'You haven't worked it out yet, have you?' she shouted. 'You're not in control any more. You've lost. It's over. The crew are locked in their quarters — those steel doors are sealed pretty tight — and none of them actually seemed that keen to fight for you anyway. The ship is adrift. Someone will notice eventually, and when they arrive they can rescue them. But it will be too late for you. Now *kneel*!'

Flowerdew didn't move and received a kick in the ribs. Slowly he hauled himself up, his face bleeding where he had hit the deck.

Leila stepped back and raised the gun. 'It's decision time. Tobi and Sade?' she said into her hood mic.

'Agreed,' said two voices from the RIB.

'Chika?'

'Agreed.'

'Dada? You hearing this?'

'Yes,' said Dada from somewhere on the *Strontian*. 'Agreed.'

'Aisha?'

She nodded. 'Agreed.'

'The motion is carried,' said Leila.

'No!' shouted Flowerdew. 'Wait!'

Leila removed the safety catch and Itch suddenly woke up. 'Stop! No – not agreed!' He ran from the edge of the platform where he had stayed, paralysed. Like a computer that had frozen running a new program, seeing Flowerdew again – and with a gun at his head – had rooted Itch to the tarmac. He heard the roll call of divers calling for Flowerdew's death, but somehow he hadn't understood. The metallic snap of the safety being released broke the spell. 'I have a vote too! So does Jack. And Chloe. And Lucy. You can't just shoot him – that'll make us the same as him!'

Itch walked over to the man who, just a few months ago, had been marking his science homework. He waited till Flowerdew looked him in the eye. 'And being the same as you would be terrifying.'

Flowerdew sneered. 'You couldn't be the same as me . . .'

Itch dropped to the ground and shoved his hand hard against Flowerdew's jaw, shutting his mouth. 'I'm saving your stupid life, you imbecile. Why don't you just *shut – up.*'

Flowerdew glowered at Itch through his one open eye; he looked totally mad.

Itch turned to Leila. 'If you shoot him, then you'll probably get done for the Van Den Hauwe and Revere killings too. You'll have every police force out looking for you. For ever.'

'He deserves to die,' said Chika, still holding the gun to Flowerdew's head. 'If you'd been in Lagos when he was terrorizing the Delta . . . If you'd seen his victims . . .'

'Maybe,' said Itch, 'but Shivvi was in his team too. They worked it together.'

'He had got to her by then. We'd lost her.'

'I say prison,' said Itch, 'and maybe that Nigerian prison Shivvi escaped from.'

The effect was immediate. Flowerdew recoiled in horror, and Sade and Aisha smiled. From the RIB, Tobi's voice crackled, 'Neat idea.'

'The Ikoyi prison in Lagos?' said Sade. 'The worst in the world! They'd really enjoy having such a local celebrity in their midst. That even sounds like justice.'

'And Roshanna Wing should go there too,' said Itch, remembering that the Greencorps CEO was on board too. 'Where is she anyway?'

'She's here with me,' came Dada's voice over his headset. 'She's out cold. She had a collision with the wall. She's tied up but easy to transport. I'll bring her up.'

'No,' said Itch. 'Leave her there – I—'

'OK, people,' broke in Leila, 'I get the prison thing. But it's messy! We can't take him there; we can't even hand him over to anyone – we need to be off this ship soon. But if we shoot him, we leave and it's all neat and tidy.'

'And you're a murderer,' said Itch. 'We're all murderers. Listen, I've got an idea. I need to check the labs to see if I can do it, but if it works . . . well, I think you'll like it.'

'Does it involve Flowerdew dying?' asked Leila.

'It's a possibility,' said Itch. 'Depends.'

'What happens to the crew?' said Sade.

'They are secure behind locked cabin doors.' That was Aisha. 'Cabin doors made of steel. They'll be released once we're gone. We'll radio details to the nearest ships. But we tell the Moroccans that Flowerdew's here. I'm sure they'd like him.'

'Can we leave the ship in forty minutes?' Dada's voice again. 'I've got the radar unjammed. There's a ship heading towards us. Reckon we have forty minutes before they see who's here and what's going on. What about it, Itch?'

He considered his answer. 'Just about. Yes. And you'll have time to film a confession while you're waiting. Get him to confess to everything. Wing too. We could leave it for the Moroccans to find.'

'Do it,' she said. 'But if your plan isn't working and we have to leave, Flowerdew dies.'

Running from the platform, he jumped onto the steps. 'Don't let him move,' he shouted, and disappeared from view.

Leila called after him, 'If he moves, I'm pulling the trigger anyway!'

Itch took the steps two at a time, then sprinted for the lab. *When Sade said it was amazing what divers could do*, thought Itch, w*hat she really meant was, it's amazing what divers could do with a gun.*

'Tobi, how is Jack?' he shouted into his mic.

'She's got the new oxygen. Doing fine.'

'Can you spare Chloe or Lucy? Need more hands here. If they're up for it . . .' He headed for the sealed cupboard while Tobi shouted his request. He crouched down in front of the brown jars and read the label of the largest one out loud. '$AgNO_3$. Silver nitrate.'

'What's that, Itch? Missed that . . .'

'Oh, nothing, Tobi. Forgot everyone can hear what I'm saying.'

'No worries. Chloe's coming up . . . Chika, can you help her?'

'On it,' came Chika's voice.

Itch was back with the jars. He knew he needed to piece together his silver knowledge from Madrid and his explosive knowledge from *The Golden Book of Chemistry Experiments*. He was looking at three large vessels of silver nitrate, and rows of sulphates and oxides. A jar marked ALCOHOL ABSOLUTE caught his attention, and he gently eased it off its shelf.

'You'll do nicely,' he muttered. Small samples of europium oxide were piled neatly on top of each other. Next to them were jars of picric acid, filter papers, and piles of what Itch assumed were fake euros. 'Someone's been practising . . .'

The lab doors burst open and Chloe ran in. 'Itch! What are you doing? You said you'd come straight back!'

'I'll explain later. Now I need some nitric acid –

might say HNO_3 on the bottle. And something to mix it in. And heat. And matches. And gloves. And if we don't get this done in time, Leila kills Flowerdew.'

'Is that bad?'

'Probably.'

Chloe scanned the shelves and reached for a bottle with a handwritten label. 'Nitric acid. Got it.'

'Now the largest glass container you can find. I'll look for some heat.' Brother and sister ransacked the *Strontian*'s lab for what they needed; cupboards, drawers and shelves were pulled apart.

Matches and thick heatproof gloves appeared, then, from under a sink, Chloe called, 'Is this big enough?'

Itch saw that she was holding a ten-litre flat-bottomed flask. 'It's huge – doubt there's anything bigger. Let's try.'

'Itch, is this safe?' said Chloe.

'No, Chloe, it isn't. And do you think anything "safe" will actually help anyone? If we keep the windows and door open, I reckon it'll be safe enough.'

Chloe held her breath as she watched her brother work. From the acid and alcohol mix came wisps of steam and brown fumes, and a fierce, sharp, chlorine-like smell filled the lab. Itch's eyes watered and he looked away. 'Need safety glasses and a fume cupboard,' he said, and coughed as his throat started to burn. 'Pass the brown jar, Chlo.'

She handed him the silver nitrate. He unscrewed

the top and poured in another colourless liquid mixed with a sediment of silver crystals.

'Itch, what are we doing?' said Chloe, agitated now. 'You're not being fair!'

'Have you seen a thermometer?' he said.

'Yes – in that drawer next to you. What are we doing?'

Itch swirled the mixture round and placed the flask on a stand. He slid a burner under the mixture, turned on the gas and lit it. 'How long have we got, Chloe?'

It was Leila who answered. 'Thirty minutes max. That ship is getting closer.'

Itch grabbed another gas burner and lit that too. He placed it next to the first and the mixture started to react: bubbles formed, steam rose and the crystals started to dissolve. 'OK, this part takes a bit of time,' he said. 'Did you get the thermometer?'

'Like I told you, it's in that drawer. But if you won't tell me what we're doing, I'll go back to the RIB. I thought you needed help.'

'What?' said Itch, turning to look at his sister. 'Of course I need you. You should have said. We're making silver fulminate. We need to heat and cool; but it mustn't boil or it won't work.'

'*Itch!*' shouted Chloe. '*I don't understand!* What does silver fulminate do? Why are we making it? How is it an alternative to shooting Flowerdew?'

Itch stared at her, at last realizing his mistake. 'Sorry, Chlo. Silver fulminate . . . It's an explosive. When this mixture is ready, we can paint it on – it's safer while it's wet. As soon as it dries it becomes dangerous. Any movement can set it off. If I paint it on too thickly, it could detonate under its own weight. If I get it right, it's a paint-on prison for Flowerdew and Wing. They'll be trapped. If they keep still, they'll live; if they move, they'll set off the explosive.'

Before Chloe could respond, Itch's headset buzzed with reactions from the divers:

'That's cool!'

'Yeah, that's a plan!'

'Go, Itch!'

He smiled. 'That's the theory anyway.'

'Where do you do the painting?' It was Leila with the practicalities.

'Up there,' he said. 'That way it's well away from the crew. Can we get Wing up there?'

'I'll haul her sorry ass there now,' said Dada.

'But why don't we just lock Flowerdew up in a room or something?' said Chloe. 'Wouldn't that be easier?'

'Because this' – Itch waved at the flask – 'will be beating him with science. Beating him with chemistry. Beating him at his own game . . . and that will be the ultimate humiliation. He will hate it. That's why.'

'OK' – Chloe smiled – 'understood. Let's do it.'

Itch checked the thermometer and removed the heat.

'You said it mustn't boil . . . What would happen if it did?' Chloe saw the glance he gave her. 'OK,' she said. 'I get it. I'll watch the thermometer for you.'

'Sea lanes getting busy,' said Chika. 'Radar showing quite a few ships coming our way. Any way you can speed that magic potion along a bit, Itch?'

He stared at the contents of the flask. The silver crystals had dissolved, the temperature was steady, but the cooling process took time.

'No, sorry . . . Wait, yes,' he said. 'Ice would be good. Anyone seen any?'

'Sade here . . . I'll check the galley. They've got a freezer.'

'Leila here. We need to be gone in fifteen. I shoot Flowerdew if you're not done.'

Itch pulled a face and checked the flask again. 'OK, Leila, it's show time. Tie him up. Tie them both up. Tie them up together.'

'Is it ready?' asked Chloe. 'Just going above sixty.'

'And that is what we've been waiting for!' He pointed at the liquid: small white crystals were now suspended in it.

Chloe stared too. 'Silver fulminate?'

Itch nodded. 'Gas off,' he said. 'We need it at room temperature.'

Sade appeared with a bucket of ice. 'Where . . . ?'

'Here!' She set it down on the bench, and with gloved hands Itch put the flask in the bucket. They all stared at the changing mixture.

'More crystals appearing, Itch,' called Chloe, pointing to clumps of white in the solution.

'They're precipitating, not appearing,' said Itch absentmindedly, and missed her look of exasperation.

'Flowerdew and Wing strapped up and ready . . .' Leila again. 'You better get painting soon. We need to be gone! Your plan's artistic and everything, but it's not worth getting arrested for.' He heard the click as she removed the safety catch on her gun.

'We're coming, Leila!' he shouted. 'Just let me try this, OK?' He turned to Chloe and Sade. 'This next bit will need to be done quickly. The crystals are settling, and the solution will clear. We'll need to drain the acid, wash what's left, and then we can go. It gets more dangerous as it dries. Ready?' They both nodded.

Grabbing filter papers and another glass beaker, Itch stood next to the ice bucket and flask, pushed his hair out of his eyes and balanced himself. Taking a deep breath, he picked up the flask with both hands and with all the care he could muster, tipped most of the liquid into a sink.

'Itch, where are you?'

He mouthed, 'Shut up, Leila.' Then, nodding in Chloe's direction, said, 'Fold the filter paper and make a cone and shove it in that beaker. Quickly.'

When it was in place, Itch poured the wet sand-like sludge into the paper. It folded slowly into the improvised funnel.

'Need you here!'

'Leila, he's handling high explosive,' barked Sade.

'He's going as fast as he can.'

'It's getting busy. Someone is going to get very suspicious of a ship that isn't moving. If we're approached, I'm pulling the trigger.'

Tobi's voice next. 'I'm going off the starboard side. Less traffic. You'll all be jumping.' It wasn't a question, just a statement, but Chloe looked horrified.

'I'd thought I could climb back . . . Not sure I'm ready . . .'

Sade took her hand. 'We'll jump together. Of all the things you've done today, trust me, this'll be the easiest.'

'Can we just concentrate here!' Itch was rinsing the white mixture under the tap. 'Three more of these and we'll be done. I'll finish this one and you can take the first batch up to the helipad.'

'Me?' said Chloe. 'I thought you'd—'

'Both of you. I'll bring the second batch.' Itch poured and rinsed again, then offered the first beaker to Sade. 'This is a quarter of a kilo. It's stable at the moment. Don't drop it.'

Sade took the still warm container and shot them both a nervous glance.

'And hurry,' said Itch.

'Carefully,' added Chloe.

Sade picked up a large spatula, hooked it onto her belt and strode out of the lab cradling the silver fulminate.

'Sade's on the way with batch number one!' Itch called.

Someone whistled though the comms system.

'Go, Sade!' whispered Tobi.

Itch handed the next beaker to Chloe. 'Before you ask, I'm not going without you,' she said quietly. 'We do this last bit together.' Her tone brooked no argument.

'Of course,' he said, putting down the beaker. 'Last two.'

Between them they poured and folded the white slurry into the remaining beakers.

Nervously Chloe picked up one; Itch the other two.

'On our way,' said Itch.

'One minute . . . or less,' warned Leila.

Chloe led the way, arms outstretched. Itch followed a few paces behind, his exhausted arms straining under his half-kilo of explosive. The ship rolled, but they walked across the deck with the fierce concentration of tightrope walkers. Sweat streamed into Itch's eyes. He blinked, but dared not risk wiping them with his sleeve. His focus was on the wet crystals in each hand. He was sure the grains were becoming more defined by the second. The drying-out process – and the increased instability that followed – was happening right in front of his eyes.

'Where are you?'

In silence they climbed the steps to the bridge, where Sade was waiting for them. Itch handed over a beaker so that he could use the handrail for the last ascent.

'You first,' she said. 'This is your bit.'

The last few steps to the helipad were an agony of drying explosive and screaming muscles. Itch knew that he had only seconds to finish the job: the urge to hurry was overpowering. He tried to take two steps at once, but his foot caught the tread. He grabbed the handrail, his knee crashing into the step, and he gasped in pain. The flask tilted sharply, the explosive sliding up the glass. He righted it quickly but some white slurry slopped over and splashed onto his trousers. He swore loudly.

'Slow down, Itch!' cried Chloe behind him.

Alarm now from all the divers:

'What just happened?'

'Everyone OK?'

'Itch, talk to us!'

He steadied himself, blinked away the pain and continued climbing. 'I'm fine. I'm here.' He emerged slowly onto the helipad, both hands holding the flask in front of him. He paused, looking up at the scene in front of him. Flowerdew and Wing were handcuffed and tied together, back to back on the large yellow H. Aisha, Dada, Chika and now Sade stood around; Leila was still aiming her gun firmly at Flowerdew's head.

'The confessions went well,' she said. 'We only got a fraction of what they've been up to, but it'll do. Enough to send them away. We strapped the camera to the deck.' She indicated a small package covered in black masking tape a few metres away. Leila then pointed at the flask. 'Is it going to work?'

Itch knew there were ships around – he could see

them in the distance – but he only needed two minutes. Just two minutes to stop Flowerdew and say what he needed to say. Sade handed him the spatula and, ignoring the pain in his knee, he knelt in front of Roshanna Wing. She was now in jogging gear, her eyes closed against the rising sun and the faces of her accusers. Itch's shadow fell across her face and she opened her eyes and stared at him, then at the flask of white slurry in his hand.

'You hunted Flowerdew,' said Itch. 'You knew what he was like. And yet you still wanted to be a part of his future . . . Well, congratulations – you're tied to everything coming his way now.'

'I'm not the same as him!' Her voice was croaky and desperate. 'I could get you—'

'Not interested – it's too late!' shouted Itch.

He dipped the plastic spatula into the silver fulminate and started painting it onto the deck. He applied it in a broad stripe around Wing's feet, her legs, then followed the curve of her body. As he came to Flowerdew, he dipped the spatula in again.

'What are you doing, Lofte?' he whispered. 'You know this makes you a criminal, don't you? These girls are just crooks in wetsuits—'

'Shut up, Flowerdew,' said Itch, applying the paste around his legs. 'They wanted to kill you. Actually, they still do. And maybe they still will . . . But this' – he waved the dripping spatula in Flowerdew's face – 'is so much better. I am proving to you – how did you put it? – that I have won, you have lost, and why.' He painted around Flowerdew's stockinged feet. 'If you hadn't been such an arrogant cretin of a teacher and scientist, you might not be sitting here, humiliated. If you'd been a better oilman you wouldn't have killed those seventeen men in the oil spill. If you'd been a better teacher – any kind of a teacher – you'd have stayed at the Cornwall Academy. If you'd been a better scientist you wouldn't have tried to sell the 126 for millions.'

Chloe passed him another flask of the silver fulminate; Itch circled round Wing again, adding to the layer of explosive.

'But you're none of those things. So this silver fulminate is for Mr Watkins – a better, nobler man than you have ever been. It's for the hurt and misery that follow you everywhere. It's for my parents' marriage, for Jack lying in that boat, and for Chloe and Lucy.' Itch's hand had started to shake. He breathed deeply.

'And for Shivvi,' said Sade, handing him the final flask.

'OK – and maybe,' added Itch, 'even for the Greencorps bosses you killed. Look at this . . . Look at each crystal surrounding you now . . . See it drying? See it cracking? You and Wing had better not move, better not talk. The *slightest* movement . . . And I know you're not worried about the crew, but feel free to make the silver fulminate go bang. They'll be safe in their quarters, though the platform would probably fall into the sea. The divers here knew who to call. There's a ship on its way from Morocco. They have an extradition treaty with Nigeria. The Lagos police will look forward to renewing their acquaintance with you. A prison cell in Ikoyi is where you belong.'

There was no doubting the fear in Flowerdew's eyes now. He started to struggle against the handcuffs, but Wing hissed, 'Keep still, stupid,' and he stopped, slumping slightly against the ropes that held him.

Itch stood up to check his work. A white, crusty stripe followed precisely where Flowerdew and Wing's bodies touched the deck. He scraped out the last of the fulminate, painting it under Flowerdew's legs.

'If you are lucky enough to be rescued,' he said, 'there'll be information on how to neutralize the silver fulminate. But for now—'

'Out of time,' called Aisha. 'There's a nosy ship heading our way.'

'Well, that's the last of it.' Again, Itch waited for eye contact. Slowly Flowerdew looked up, his face twisted with hatred and defeat. Itch stooped till his face was centimetres away, and spoke; his voice firm and clear – it carried to everyone on the platform. 'So, the great scientist is beaten by science,' he said. 'Trapped by chemistry. AgCNO, isn't it, sir? This element hunter catches you with silver, carbon, nitrogen and oxygen.'

Applause from the divers; then a running hug from Chloe, who took the flask from him.

Itch reached into the zip pocket of his wetsuit. Retrieving the small stone, he placed it in front of

Flowerdew. 'And I'm sure you know what this is. It's monazite from your rare earth mine in South Africa. It contains a strand of europium. The element that for ever more will declare your *total* failure. It'll look pretty as the sun rises.'

Flowerdew howled and screamed his rage – but then Itch took the flask from Chloe and placed it on the deck. He dropped the spatula from head height, and as Flowerdew and Wing watched, it hit the drying silver fulminate. The glass exploded, small shards landing all over the helipad.

'RIB in position,' called Tobi in their headsets. 'Time to jump, everyone.'

The divers had already disappeared down the stairway. As Itch and Chloe reached the steps, he turned and called out, 'So long, sir. Don't forget to keep still.'

They made it to the deck in time to see Aisha and Chika jump from the starboard rail, swiftly followed by Dada and Leila.

Sade appeared at their side. 'You're next, guys.'

Itch looked at Chloe.

'I'm not even thinking about it,' she said, and led her brother towards the edge . . . Two steps and they were both balanced on the top bar.

Thirty metres below, Aisha and Chika were climbing on board the RIB; Dada and Leila were close behind.

'Well, *look at this*,' called Tobi, still at the RIB's steering wheel.

Itch and Chloe saw Lucy waving; next to her, one hand clearly raised, sat Jack.

'She's awake! She's OK!' called Chloe. 'And your wetsuit's on fire, Itch.' He looked at the flames emerging from the patch of spilled silver fulminate. 'Time to go,' she said.

She took Itch's hand and they jumped.

32

As reunions go, it was a memorable one. Back on El Hiero, Itch, Chloe, Jack and Lucy were taken to the surgery. Chika had explained that she and her team would disappear before they got arrested, and they had done just that. Itch was telling their story to a young nurse when, mouth falling open, she recognized him. In fact, she recognized all of them. Pointing to their photos in the local paper, she called the police, then, with increasing excitement, everyone in her phonebook. By the time the police launch arrived, it seemed that the whole island had turned out to see them.

Using the nurse's phone, they had all called home. They were brief, ecstatic conversations, with promises to call back as soon as possible. Then, on the police launch to Tenerife, the captain had let them use the satellite phone.

At the port of Santa Cruz, the huge crowd of onlookers forced the launch to delay its arrival. Police reinforcements, and then a van with blacked-out windows, helped them get safely out of the harbour. In spite of Jack's protests – 'They checked me out at El Heiro! I feel OK!' – the others insisted that she go straight to the hospital.

'Jack, you actually *died* out there,' said Lucy. 'Of course you're getting checked over.'

They were still in the Hospital Universitario Nuestra Señora de la Candelaria when their parents arrived. Itch, Chloe and Lucy were standing waiting in the corridor when Nicholas and Jude, then Zoe, Jon and Nicola came tumbling out of the lift. In the sprint that followed, a bellowing Nicholas reached his children first, followed by Jon and Zoe who ran straight into the room to find Jack. Then came Nicola and Jude, both with tears already coursing down their cheeks. After a series of word-less embraces with their children, they all traipsed into Jack's room.

It was a five-bed ward, but Jack was the only occupant; she was sitting up, beaming, and holding her parents' hands. Around the room were assorted doctors, police officers and a thin, perfumed man who introduced himself as a representative of the British ambassador.

'Callum Nave at your service. I can offer you the full support of Her Majesty's Government.' Itch and Chloe both suppressed a laugh, and Jack and Chloe were smirking. 'I know you want to get home as soon as possible, but maybe I can act as your trans-lator in the meantime . . .' he said. 'Once Miss Lofte here has been given the all clear, a local five-star hotel has offered to put you all up until your plane lands. And when you're strong enough, a press conference would be a good idea . . .' There were loud protests from everyone at that, and the embassy man held up his hands. 'They are outside already! Give them the story, and then ask them to leave you alone . . . It usually works . . .'

Lucy hooked her arm through Itch's and whispered in his ear, 'The adults are deferring to us, Itch. It's our call . . . But we have a few things to say about the divers, don't we? You say it worked before.'

Itch and Lucy sat opposite Jack and he waved Chloe closer.

'Lucy suggests we tell everyone the truth about the divers,' he said. 'If you're strong enough, Jack . . .'

There was a second's hesitation, then she nodded. 'Of course. If you guys do most of the talking . . .'

Callum Nave rubbed his hands together. 'Lovely! Super! I'll set it up . . . Erm, just one thing . . .' He looked around, then approached Itch, suddenly speaking quietly. 'Her Majesty's Government's position is that you discovered some plutonium, er . . .' He consulted an email on his phone. 'Some plutonium 238, but that no one knew how it came to be in Cornwall. How does that sound?'

'Honestly?' said Itch. 'It sounds ridiculous. Plutonium 238 is used as a thermoelectric generator on space missions. But the truth sounds ridiculous too – so why not, if it keeps everyone happy.'

Nave rubbed his hands together even more vigorously. 'It certainly will. Excellent!' He almost bowed before leaving.

'What a clown,' said Itch.

It turned out that there were two press conferences. At Itch's suggestion, the police and parents did one and they did another.

'No mayors, no officials. We learned that last time. Just us,' he said.

Waiting in the hotel lounge for their turn, the four of them watched as their parents talked about the ordeal of the last few days. Television got the pictures they wanted – there were tears from everyone – and radio got the quote they wanted: Nicholas's 'We think our kids are the most extraordinary and brave people we have ever met, never mind that they're family,' made it into all the news bulletins.

The police answers were all in Spanish, apart from one to a British reporter. 'Yes – thanks to these children, our currency is safe now. You British should be proud, you have saved the euro!' Everyone laughed at that. Two further answers from the chief policeman included the word *plutonio*, and Itch realized that they had all been fed the same story.

But it was Itch, Jack, Chloe and Lucy that everyone was waiting for, and when they climbed onto the makeshift platform, everyone applauded. They shuffled to their seats, embarrassed, stealing brief glances at the throng of journalists.

Jack did, after all, have to answer questions: 'Yes, apparently my heart stopped. I don't remember much, I'm afraid.'

Chloe had the hall captivated with her story of how they had left the element-based clue in the car after their kidnap. 'If anyone understood what it meant, I knew it would be my brother!'

Lucy was asked about the news that Flowerdew had been captured alive and was awaiting extradition in a Moroccan prison. 'I hope he rots in the darkest cell. Lock him up for a hundred years.'

A British journalist shouted, 'Are you Itch's girlfriend, then?' Lucy flushed a deep scarlet, smiled awkwardly but said nothing. A murmur of disappointment ran round the room.

Itch received the most questions, but he waited his moment and picked his man. When he saw a familiar well-coiffed figure raise his hand, he stood up. A volley of camera flashes hit him as he pointed at the journalist.

'You!' he said. 'You're the reporter I shouted at on the bridge!'

The man with the waxed hair nodded and smiled enthusiastically.

'Right then, this is for you . . .' Itch aimed all his comments straight down the man's camera lens. 'We wouldn't be here, and we wouldn't have stopped Flowerdew, if it hadn't been for the divers. Aisha, Leila, Chika, Tobi, Dada and Sade . . .' He laughed. 'I don't even know their surnames. I've said before that they didn't kill the Greencorps bosses, and now you know that they saved our lives. Flowerdew is in prison because of them. All charges against them should be dropped. As soon as that happens, they'll come and talk to you. But don't annoy them – they don't like that.' Itch smiled and shrugged to show he was joking. 'Oh well, that's it.'

He turned to leave the stage, the others rising to their feet, when one more question was shouted from the back.

'Might there be more of this *plutonio* somewhere?'

Itch heard the question well enough, but he just shrugged and followed the others off stage.

Jack took his arm. 'That's the question, isn't it? That's where we started, back in the library. Is there any more?'

'No idea,' said Itch. 'Hope not. Who knows?'

'Flowerdew was convinced there was.'

'Flowerdew was mad,' said Itch.

Back in Cornwall, there were more journalists, then more police visits. No detectives or sergeants this time – Itch lost track of which chief superintendent had apologized for which error; he just wanted them all to go away. The CA principal, Dr Dart, had visited and offered a week's extra recovery time before they were expected back. A handwritten letter from Colonel Fairnie had arrived, saying how relieved he was that they were all OK, and how it gave him no pleasure to have been right about Greencorps.

But the thought that stayed with Itch day and

night was: *Flowerdew was right*. He may well have been mad, but he was surely right about the 126. Somewhere, there would be more. With a start, Itch realized that this was clearly what Mr Watkins had been thinking too. If Flowerdew and Watkins had both come to the same conclusion, he had to take it seriously.

He recalled Flowerdew's admission that the whole *Meyn Mamvro* idea had been his (a source of some embarrassment now amongst those who had claimed it as a revolutionary motto). His theory – that if the rocks of 126 had been discovered before, they may well have been considered 'magic' and buried somewhere significant – seemed plausible to Itch.

On his laptop he returned to the photos of the Hurler stones, the damage at St Michael's Mount and the vandalized carns. *Nothing found there, then.* The next image was a still from the video they had taken in the churchyard, disturbing the Greencorps vandals. He shuddered, remembering how stupid he'd been, and Jack's anger. Taking a deep breath, he pressed PLAY.

What was I doing? he thought as he watched the surprised, then frightened, men drop the spray cans and run for their van. He was about to press STOP when he noticed the stone they had been digging around – an old 'magic' logan stone, according to the vicar. It had been turned over and was now propped up against a tree. Itch zoomed in on the damage, then peered at the inscription. He read it aloud twice, took a screenshot and emailed it to himself, then bolted for the door.

Itch ran for the library. He had pulled a cap low over his eyes in an attempt to avoid the stares and comments, but to no avail. Even though he was sprinting along the cliff path, he was still the most famous boy in the country, and he met with countless greetings and requests for photos.

He welcomed the peace of the library; he nodded breathlessly at Morgan the librarian as he walked past her desk and headed again for the local history section. He found *Mining Tales* and slumped at a table. He flicked through the pages at speed, finding the pages with Mr Watkins's annotations. The sight of the familiar handwriting brought sudden tears to his eyes; he blinked quickly and reached for his phone. He noticed he'd missed a few calls, but texted Jack, Chloe and Lucy:

Need you guys in library. URGENT.

Itch pulled a number of old books from the shelves. He checked indexes, opened maps. As he read, he became increasingly agitated. His phone buzzed.

This had better be good. C

There soon as. Luce x

He borrowed some paper from the librarian's desk and started scribbling notes, arranging them around the tables. Itch couldn't keep still; when he paced, it was frenetic, when he sat, his knee bounced vigorously.

Another buzz: *Heard from Dada! I'll be 5. J*

Itch read that again. He checked his phone – the missed calls included one from Jack and two from a blocked number. He went onto Facebook and immediately saw a news line that said: THE HEROES OF EL HEIRO ARE IN THE CLEAR.

'Yes!' he exclaimed loudly, punching the air. He glanced over at Morgan, who smiled but put her finger to her lips. Itch mouthed 'Sorry,' and carried on reading. Apparently neither the Nigerian authorities nor Interpol had any plans to charge the divers who had rescued the kidnapped British students. There was a brief recap of their story, concluding with the words, *The divers' current whereabouts are unknown.*

'I wonder . . .' murmured Itch.

Jack burst through the library doors and hurried over. 'Itch, they're coming!' She was out of breath and red in the face. Itch mouthed another 'Sorry,' to the librarian and cleared a space for Jack. 'Dada rang me!' said Jack excitedly. 'No one's going to charge them . . .'

'I know, I read—' Itch began, but Jack cut him off.

She leaned forward. 'They're here, Itch! In the UK! Took a lift from a trawler that dropped them at Bristol. But they don't want anyone to know. They want to keep it quiet.'

Itch smiled. 'You could have fooled me,' he said.

Jack looked sheepish and glanced around. 'Oh, yeah, sorry. I just called Lucy – she shouted too!'

Chloe arrived, and Jack anticipated her squeal of

excitement with a lightly placed hand over her mouth.

'Dada said they'd hire a van and be here tonight,' Jack went on. 'I've mentioned it to Mum and Dad, and we've got rooms ready for them.'

Chloe and Jack were starting to plan a tour for them while Itch, unnoticed, went back to his notes. It was only when Lucy arrived that they remembered why they had been summoned to the library in the first place. Chloe and Jack suddenly noticed the open books.

'What have you found, Itch?' asked Chloe. 'Your text sounded excited.'

He raked his fingers through his hair. 'Actually, mainly I'm scared. Here's the *Mining Tales* book we got out, and Mr Watkins's notes about checking with *Flow*. I looked for books by anyone called Flow, but couldn't find anything. I assumed that it was an obscure book of his – maybe it got destroyed in the fire. But look at this.' He held up his phone, showing the inverted stone in the graveyard. They all leaned in and stared at the image.

'It says *Florence of Worcester*. Fl of W. He's Flow.'

'It's a *he*?' said Lucy. 'Who is he anyway? Why would Mr Watkins mention him?'

Itch took a deep breath. 'Right, here goes. This is going to sound nuts . . . Anyone heard of inundation theory?' Blank faces. 'Me neither. Anyway, ten thousand years ago the sea was four miles away, the sea level thirty-seven metres lower than it is now. That's all fact. Slowly, the climate

422

warmed and the seas rose. That's fact too. Now for the weird bit. Florence was a twelfth-century monk and historian. He says that in 1099 there was a massive tide, like a tsunami, that hit Cornwall. It destroyed towns and villages, churches and farms and everything. He says the whole area that was lost was called Lethowsow.' He looked up from his book; Chloe, Jack and Lucy were riveted, all thoughts of the divers put on hold.

'Lethow what?' said Lucy.

'Lethowsow. Here's the quote: *We believe that Cornwall once extended further west may be inferred from hence, that about midway between the monastery and Scilly are rocks called in Cornish Lethowsow; by the English, Seven-stones.*'

'More stones, then,' said Jack.

'Apparently they were stones of great and terrifying power,' Itch continued.

'How did we guess . . . ?' muttered Chloe.

'But these are just myths,' said Lucy. 'There are so-called "magic" stones all over Cornwall. These will just be more of the same.'

'Yes, possibly,' agreed Itch. 'Even probably. But we know that a supernova delivered the 126. Even if it crashed into Cornwall thousands of years ago, it will have left its mark. The debris would have been terrifying.'

'Where was that guy's monastery?' asked Chloe.

'Up on the cliffs at Provincetown. Where the . . .'

'. . . mine was that dug up the 126,' Lucy finished his sentence. 'Wow.'

'What are you saying, Itch?' said Jack.

'I don't know what I'm saying.' Itch rubbed his hair vigorously again. 'Except that maybe, if it's anywhere, the remains of the supernova is out there, under the sea.'

They looked at each other, mouths open, unsure what to say next.

'Would it be as radioactive as the rocks we destroyed?' said Chloe eventually, feeling the need to lower her voice to a whisper.

Itch shrugged. 'Don't know. But probably, yes.'

'Wouldn't a whole bunch of radioactive stuff have been noticed before?'

Lucy answered that, also in a whisper: 'Not necessarily. If it's alpha radiation, it would only be detectable from a few centimetres away.'

Jack leaned in closer. 'So . . . it could have been lying underwater for thousands of years, and no one would know?'

'That's about it,' said Itch.

Chloe looked horrified. 'We nearly killed ourselves getting rid of eight rocks of 126 – now you're saying there's loads more!'

'There may be,' said Itch. 'I don't know. I hope not. But if it is there, *we need to get there first.*'

Jack nodded. 'Because if we've worked it out, someone else will. Maybe someone else has already. Let's not deal with this on our own this time, Itch. Nearly dying has made me more cautious. We need to tell someone before another Flowerdew comes along.'

'Agreed,' said Itch. 'When did you say the divers get here?'

The Atlantic Ocean, three kilometres out from Boscastle harbour, Cornwall

On the twenty-metre Blyth catamaran *Platina Fury*, the charts were pored over one last time. Aisha, Dada, Tobi, Sade, Leila and Chika were arguing over who should accompany Itch on the final dive of the day. They had chartered a boat normally used for shark cage diving, adapted for their needs. In place of the cage, wetsuits, air tanks and masks were scattered around the deck; while they talked, the divers fussed over their kit obsessively.

Taking their line from the ruins of the monastery on the cliff, they had been stopping every five hundred metres and diving to the sea bed. Each time, one of the divers accompanied Itch, their descent slow and deliberate. On the first dive, to ten metres, they'd had decent visibility, the sea floor consisting entirely of fine sand. Each successive dive had been deeper and darker; powerful torches were needed to show them the way up and down.

All week the weather had been warm and the winds light. The boat rose and fell, the engine idling. Now it was Tobi who came over to Itch, zipping up her wetsuit.

'My turn,' she said, smiling. 'You ready?'

Itch was exhausted but exhilarated. He had never

enjoyed anything in the water before, being comfortably the worst surfer in his year, but now he couldn't wait to get back in. The sensation of actually breathing underwater made his head spin; on his first dive he had actually forgotten for a few moments why he was there and started following a fish before Sade had waved him back down. Now he felt more confident; he'd actually tried a backward-roll entry and was at last enjoying the expensive wetsuit his father had bought him. He felt more than ready – he felt buzzed, almost intoxicated. He couldn't wait to get back in, even if there was virtually nothing to see. All they'd found at the bottom was acres of sand and some rotting wood.

'Course I'm ready,' said Itch. 'Just need the clickers.'

On cue, Chloe came over. In her hand swung the waterproof radiation detectors their father had given them in South Africa. She hung one over Tobi's head, the other over Itch's, each of them stooping as though they were receiving a medal.

'They're on the digital setting so it'll show me the number of clicks on the screen. Keep watching it. Remember, you can't take another dose of radiation,' said Chloe. 'Sure you want to try again?'

'Last go,' he said. 'And yes, I'm sure.' He glanced at Lucy, who was sitting in the sun with Jack. 'When Cake gave me the 126, he didn't know where it had come from, but maybe we do. If I'm on the sea floor and this meter goes crazy, I'm off. I'll keep watching. But if this stuff is out there, it has to be us who find it.'

'Fine,' said Chloe, 'but Tobi's in charge!' and she went to join the sunbathers.

Itch got dressed: weight belt, hood, left glove, tank, fins, right glove.

'She's very protective,' said Tobi, going through her safety checks.

'We've been through a lot,' said Itch.

Tobi nodded. 'Shall we go?'

As they were about to pull on their masks, Lucy ran over, kissed Itch on the cheek and whispered, 'Good luck.' She jogged back to the others, leaving him frozen to the spot.

'You'll need to close your mouth or the mask won't fit,' said Tobi, grinning.

'Oh, right,' said Itch. He glanced back at Lucy, but she was talking to Jack and didn't look up.

'Itch, let's check the air one last time,' said Tobi. 'If you're still diving . . .'

'Sure. Of course.'

'You up for this? You concentrating?'

He nodded. 'Let's go.'

'Give us a countdown, people!' called Tobi as they stood at the edge of the deck. Then, to whoops of encouragement from everyone on board, they jumped.

The Atlantic was never warm, and the impact of the sea made Itch gasp again. Below the surface they briefly trod water, made the O sign with thumb and forefinger, then Tobi dived. Itch followed, learning again to trust his equipment: when he needed air it was fed to him; when he breathed out it was directed into the sea. As he followed Tobi down, the only sounds he could hear were the bubbles from his own breathing regulator. And he loved it.

This is more like flying than swimming, he thought, *even if there's not much of a view.* There was just enough light from the surface to show them that there was little of interest in these waters. A few fish and the odd strand of seaweed were never going to attract any of the diving expeditions that were popular along the coast; they preferred to explore Cornwall's many wrecks.

Wonder if anyone has ever dived here . . . Why would they?

As they descended through the darkening sea, Tobi turned on her torch. The powerful beam pierced the gloom, and Itch caught sight of a patch of green at the edge of his vision – thirty, forty metres away. Tobi had seen it too, and together they swam further out, the sea bed dropping gently away beneath them. His depth gauge said twenty-nine metres. Itch knew that the continental shelf was many kilometres away – the sea bed fell away to 8,000 metres there – but he shivered.

The green turned out to be a particularly dense area of seaweed and vegetation. It started quite suddenly, the sand giving way to foliage as though it had been planted there. It stretched away as far as their torches would allow them to see. Tobi pulled out her camera from her pack; this was the first time there had been anything worth photographing on any of the dives. When she was done, Itch pointed further out. She nodded, and together they swam over about an acre of plant life, small fish darting around some of the fronds and leaves.

The green stopped as suddenly as it had begun; sand and a few rocks marked what looked like a border. Tobi swung her torch round, picking out two more areas of green – one to the left, the other further out. She pointed left and they kicked off again. This vegetation was more patchy. As they floated ten metres above it, more and more areas of dark colour came into view. Tobi held up one finger and Itch nodded.

One more.

The next one was more densely packed, with small, tightly woven strands of seaweed threaded through clumps of what looked like clover. Tobi had found the board and was writing on it. She held it up.

This is weird! it said.

Itch nodded and took the pen. *And goes on for ever,* he wrote.

She tapped her watch and pointed back up towards the boat. Nearly time to go.

Really? Itch was surprised; on the previous dives he had got cold and was soon ready to return to the surface, but this time he wanted to continue. *Presumably because there's something to see,* he thought.

Unless . . .

Itch swam deeper. His depth gauge said thirty-one metres when he pulled up sharply.

You're imagining it.

He swam lower. Thirty-two metres. He wasn't imagining it.

The sea was warmer.

In spite of his wetsuit, he felt the change in temperature. He beckoned Tobi over, and she glided towards him. Through her mask, Itch saw her widening eyes and knew she'd felt it too.

They drifted towards the bottom, his heart beating hard; he could actually hear the blood pumping around his head. Itch had one flipper on some slippery greenery, the other on a patch of dark rock. Tobi pulled out Chloe's radiation detector, but indicated that Itch should go first. He tugged at the string around his neck and pulled the device free. He checked his own meter.

No clicks, no radiation.

He knelt down on the sea bed and held the detector in front of his goggles. The reading was zero.

Slowly he lowered his hands, his eyes on the dial . . .

Zero.

Zero.

Zero.

Ten centimetres from the rock . . .

Zero.

Zero.

Five centimetres from the rock . . .

Zero.
One centimetre from the rock . . .
500,000 . . .
Itch dropped the detector.

Dr Jacob Alexander of the West Ridge Mining School was alone in his office, feeling tired and grumpy after a long day. The exam papers he was looking at were poor, the fracking research was not making the progress he'd expected, and Nicholas Lofte had missed his meeting. His subsequent text saying, *Stay there, coming over*, had seemed neither apologetic nor adequate. He was frowning over the 'Mineralogy of Cornish Tin' essays when there was an ear-splitting screech of tyres in the car park. Surprised – West Ridge wasn't usually a haunt for joy riders – Alexander looked up from his scripts into the dusky glow of the evening. Careering towards his office, then swerving to park horizontally across three spaces, Nicholas Lofte's Volvo came to a neck-jarring halt.

'What on earth . . . ?'

Out of the car came Nicholas, then Itch, Chloe, Jack and Lucy, all sprinting for the college entrance. Alexander realized that something was up, but when Jude Lofte climbed out of the passenger seat, he realized the news – whatever it was – must be big. She had never before visited the college.

He emerged from his office and opened up the reception for his late visitors. 'Well, welcome to you all—' he began, but Itch interrupted breathlessly.

'Back in your office! We need to be private!'

'Itch, everyone's gone,' said Alexander. It's seven thirty. You can talk freely. Even the cleaners have left.' Puzzled, the director looked at his visitors. Nicholas was smiling; all the others were serious, Itch almost frantic.

'I found it. I actually found it! You'll never—'

'Sorry, Itch,' Dr Alexander cut in. 'I realize this is important or you wouldn't all have come, but . . . found what?'

Itch just carried on as though he hadn't been interrupted. 'We've been out in a boat with the divers we met, and when we were out past Boscastle—'

Jack pulled Itch's arm. 'Itch! From the beginning!'

'OK, sorry, Dr Alexander,' he said. 'Of course. Right . . .' He took a deep breath. 'OK. You remember the 126 – you remember all that stuff about Earth's last chance and everything? You told me there were great things that could have been done with it. You said that the Earth has a regulatory mechanism, a thermostat that it uses when necessary, and that the 126 was going to be part of it; that it would get us through the new hot stage. I think I might have been sceptical.'

The director nodded. 'You were, Itch, you were.'

'And then you told me that one day I'd come and tell you that you were right.'

There was silence.

'I did say that, yes . . .'

'Well, here I am. You were right.'

Another silence. A long silence.

'I was?'

'Can you make a waterproof spectrometer?' asked Itch. 'It would need to operate at about thirty metres.'

Alexander laughed. 'I don't know. Maybe. Yes! Why?'

Itch ignored the question. 'You'd better get out there before everyone else does, Dr Alexander. You need to come element-hunting!'

'It's off Boscastle, Jacob, just three kilometres out—' Nicholas could barely contain himself, but Jude covered his mouth with her hand.

'Hush, Nicholas. Let the kids tell their story,' she said.

And over the next hour Dr Alexander listened as Itch, Jack, Chloe and Lucy told him about their extraordinary day and showed him Tobi's photos.

At the end he reprised his 'discovery dance', but Itch stopped him.

'No. Wrong,' he said. 'This is *so* dangerous. It could be a disaster, a catastrophe if this goes wrong . . . We've all seen what happens when energy of this power gets out there. It makes people do terrible things. Look what's happened to us – all over a tiny amount of 126. Now there might be tonnes of the stuff out there, just waiting to be picked up. There might even be people there now—'

'Itch, this has been a secret for years—'

'Nothing stays a secret. Not now. You need to tell your friends in high places to move fast.'

'Actually, I agree,' said Alexander.

'They must shut the beach . . .'

'I agree.'

'Maybe the navy will need to get involved . . .'

'Itch, I agree,' Alexander repeated.

'He agrees, Itch!' shouted Chloe and Lucy together.

'Oh, sorry – er, good, then.'

'So. It's late and I have some calls to make and an X-ray spectrometer to make waterproof. See you all at the beach tomorrow.'

They all turned to leave.

'Oh . . . and Itch?' called Dr Alexander. 'You and the find in Boscastle are big news. Trust me, the biggest news anywhere. If one supernova has been found, why shouldn't there be others? Everyone will go crazy for this story. You might not like it, but your life is about to change again. Cornwall will change . . . the UK will change. This is like a new industrial revolution! And who knows what the consequences will be?'

His words hung in the air. It seemed like a solemn moment. A historic moment.

'In which case,' said Itch, 'before it all goes crazy, could we please all go for pizza?'

Report from Dr Jacob Alexander, Future Energy Group Chair
CONFIDENTIAL

As requested, I enclose my full report on the discoveries off Boscastle, Tintagel and Crackington Haven, Cornwall. Alerted to their existence by the remarkable Itchingham Lofte, I have completed what is clearly just a preliminary study of the six acres in question. The site contains the debris of a supernova which struck the Earth at the end of the last ice age. What is left, in my opinion, has the potential to rival the Industrial Revolution in its impact on the region and the country. It can certainly make the UK energy-independent. Its existence will, of course, become general knowledge very shortly. At the time of writing the internet seems to be quiet on the matter, but we have little time.

Some of the deposits we have seen before; others are unique. In summary, the ocean bed contains various isotopes of plutonium, uranium, thorium, curium and californium. The element 126, which first emerged last year – provisionally called lofteium – is present in abundance. I would highlight the uranium particularly. It is present in a different form here; the balance of the isotopes 235 and 238 appears to be capable of creating a naturally occurring nuclear reactor in the geology of Cornwall. The potential can hardly be overstated.

We have taught for years about the probability of

an 'island of stability' where new, undiscovered superheavy elements might be stable. The lofteium discovery proved the theory right. What no one imagined was that there was a *real island* where these elements were waiting to be discovered. This island exists, and lies in British waters.

You must act swiftly to protect what is now our country's greatest asset. Until longer-term plans can be drawn up, MI5 and the Royal Navy must provide protection from those who will be jealous of our good fortune.

This energy revolution will transform our country for good if this bounteous gift is harnessed for us all. Itchingham Lofte, at great risk to himself and his friends, destroyed the first eight pieces of 126, believing them to pose a great threat. He may well have been correct, but the discovery of these vast deposits has changed the equation.

I have persuaded him that he can trust you – that he has to trust you – to use them in the best interests of the nation and of humanity.

I hope I was right to do so.

Jacob Alexander

Acknowledgements

Once again, the genius of Profs Andrea Sella and Paddy Regan at UCL and Surrey University respectively have been invaluable. Indispensable. Itch takes his science seriously, so I have to too. I have always wanted the 'magic' of the books to be real science that really works, and thanks to Andrea and Paddy I hope I have achieved that. And adding research scientist Dr Jon Speed to the triumvirate of wise men has given me all the wise council that a history graduate who plays records and watches films for a living could ever need. Professor Andrea's copy of *Nature's Building Blocks* by John Emsley is still on my desk, an element hunter's bible if ever there was one.

Geography and Cornwall adviser was once again Bob Digby, Senior Vice President of the Geographical Association. He can arrange a wet tour of the Hurlers on Bodmin Moor if you need one. I still have his copy of *Cornwall: A History* by Philip Payton, an invaluable guide to the stones, geography and culture of the county. If you want to learn how you can use the word 'granitic' and terms like 'the Variscan collision', this is for you. I shall return all books before the fines are too great.

The BBC's Hugh Pym (formerly Chief Economics Correspondent, now Health Editor) was the first to learn of my plan to set fire to the euro and gave me some great background on the importance (still) of banknotes in an electronic world.

With the six divers being such an important part of *Itchcraft*, I once again turned to Master Scuba Diver Laura Storm. The last section of the book would have been impossible without her. Who wouldn't want to dive with Tobi, Sade, Leila, Chika, Aisha and Dada? Could Itch have more female assistance in one story?

Thanks again to top agent Sam Copeland at RCW – the man to have fighting your corner; Chiggy and Emily Rees Jones at PBJ – always Itch believers; and Kelly Hurst – returned editor and speaker of wisdom.

And with thanks and love, Hilary, Ben, Natasha and Joe. Best family evs.

Author's Note

I have been researching topics for interview or to write about for many years now. None have proved as difficult as the whole business of printing money. This is, for the most part, reassuring! No one wants a currency's secrets to be known; no one wants forgers to know how to sabotage banknotes. But if making banknotes burn is at the heart of your story, you are going to find very few people available to help you out! I only found one insider who was prepared to explain some of the process, and he/she only helped out on condition of anonymity. So thank you, secret undercover agent.

I have taken a small liberty with the banknote production in Spain. In reality the euro production is split between two sites, one in Madrid and the other in Burgos, where the paper mill that prints the notes is located. I have brought them together here to speed Itch's adventure along.

Defibrillation plays an important part in the story and you might have been surprised by the circumstances under which the divers operate their equipment! Certainly what they attempt isn't something that you hear about but the theory is apparently possible. Usually, if a person's heart stops underwater, you would attempt CPR and rescue breaths at the surface. If you had the option, equipment and training, you would also use a defibrillator to shock the heart into beating again. But a report in 2006 from the National Center for Biotechnology Information in the USA concluded (after working with a 35kg pig!) that defibrillation can be performed effectively underwater.

There are a lot of 'magic' stones in *Itchcraft* and even more throughout Cornwall. All the sites that get vandalized in these pages really do exist and are well worth a visit. It isn't surprising that in earlier times elaborate stories were constructed giving the rocks 'special powers'. Some of the formations do look scary; it's not difficult to understand how our ancestors might have attributed their shape and position to giants or witches! According to the legend of the strange Cheesewring, the top stone revolves three times when a cock crows! The Carn Kenidjack (where Debbie Price goes for her project) can make extraordinary noises – from hoots to low mutterings – and these were often blamed on the devil. Modern thought would suggest the wind is the culprit here.

The logan stones mentioned in relation to Itch's churchyard adventure were believed to have the ability to turn you into a witch. Mr Watkins would add at this point that this is all about the mass of molten granite which welled up in a line from Dartmoor to what is now the Isles of Scilly. Over

300 million years (give or take a week or so) erosion has left this wonderful landscape which makes Cornwall such a special place. The words *Meyn Mamvro*, which appear all over the county, do mean 'Stones of the Motherland'. This is also the title of a magazine which promotes conservation of prehistoric sites, though Itch is unaware of this!

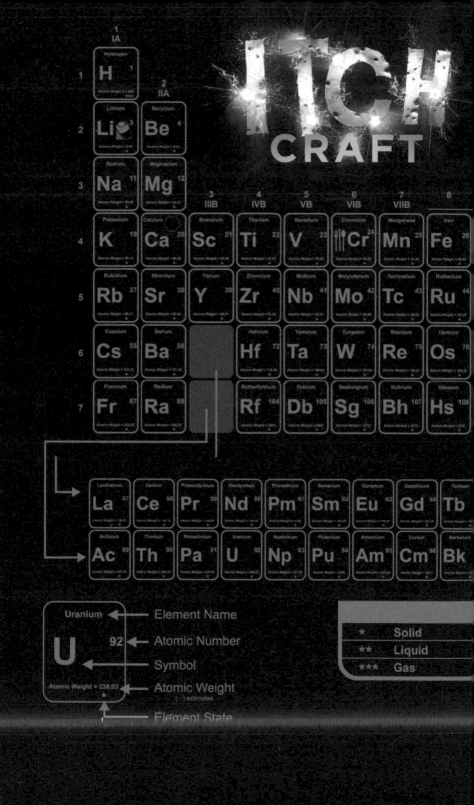